RED, WHITE, and You

Shari Cylinder

other books by Shari Cylinder

Making Waves
Kaleidoscope of Stars
Sands of Time
Watercolors

For my Luv-N-Bunns family –

you inspire me every day,
and it's an honor to work with you
as we speak for those who have no voice.

Thank you for the constant reminder
that home is indeed where the hop is.

Acknowledgements

To Mom, Dad, and Marissa, for all your unwavering and unconditional support. Thank you for being there and for always cheering me on, not only with my writing, but everything. From reading and editing early drafts of this book, to sharing jokes and laughter, to listening with understanding and empathy, you do it all. I am so glad I have you – to listen, and to lean on, and to love. Being part of "Team Cylinder" makes me the luckiest!

To Jasper Jellybean and Bandy, for sharing your special kind of sunshine and smiles. The rescue storyline in this book is a nod to the paw prints etched on my heart. I am such a fortunate bunny Ma to have you to light up my life. Jasp, having you at my side is the very best kind of "furapy," and Bandy, your antics make me laugh out loud. Thank you both for filling every day with nose boops and binkies!

To Stacy, for your steadfast dedication and kindness. The person I am today would have been unrecognizable to the one who first walked into your office, and so much of that is because of your guidance. You always go above and beyond, and I am so thankful. One step at a time, you've shown me that it's possible to go such a distance. How grateful I am to have you as an integral and inspiring part of this journey.

To Annette, for once again taking my vision for a novel and bringing it to life. Your talent turns my manuscripts into books, and I am ever so appreciative for your thoughtfulness, wisdom, and generosity all throughout this publishing adventure. Thank you, as always, for all your tireless effort on this "work of heart."

To Mr. Pezza, for sparking my interest in history and politics. From American Studies, to Involvement Day, to the media symposium – how lucky I am to have learned from someone so dedicated to making this world a better place. The lessons you taught inspired much of what these characters fight for and believe in – and what I believe in, too.

To the most fabulous family and friends, for being a support system that is incredible beyond words. Your enthusiasm means more than I can express, and your "cheerleading" is such a gift. Each one of you makes the world more special just by being in it, and I am blessed to have you in my life. Thank you for everything.

And to anyone who reads *Red, White, and You* and goes on a journey alongside Melina, Bradley, and all the characters, I hope you love reading about their adventures as much as I did writing them. May their story inspire you to blaze your own trail and act as a reminder that glass ceilings are meant to be broken – because that's how the light shines in.

Chapter 1 1
Chapter 2 9
Chapter 3 17
Chapter 4 25
Chapter 5 35
Chapter 6 45
Chapter 7 55
Chapter 8 65
Chapter 9 73
Chapter 10 81
Chapter 11 91
Chapter 12 99
Chapter 13 107
Chapter 14 117
Chapter 15 125
Chapter 16 133
Chapter 17 141
Chapter 18 149
Chapter 19 159
Chapter 20 169
Chapter 21 177
Chapter 22 187
Chapter 23 195
Chapter 24 203
Chapter 25 211
Chapter 26 221
Chapter 27 229
Chapter 28 237
Chapter 29 245
Chapter 30 255
Chapter 31 263
Chapter 32 271
Chapter 33 281
Chapter 34 293
Chapter 35 303

1

Melina

It is the hundredth time I've heard this song over the last year. There's the drumbeat that hums low at first, then gets increasingly louder, the lyrics that repeat themselves until they're ingrained in the thoughts of everyone listening, and the twang of a guitar that fills the air after the final chorus. I have every nuance memorized, and I smile now, as the opening chords begin to ping off the walls of the high school gymnasium, which is packed with supporters.

"He did it," my co-worker Kira says, as a cheer ripples around the room.

"Was there ever any doubt?"

From the back of the gym, we watch as our boss dances his way across the makeshift stage and takes his place at the podium. "Ninety-nine rallies," he told his campaign staff when we met for the first time last May. "I want to have ninety-nine rallies, all over the state, and the hundredth will be our victory celebration."

It seemed like such a far-off goal, but from day one, I believed the finish line was within reach. I believed that Nathan Ford could become the next governor of Pennsylvania, *should* become its next governor. Now that he's won the primary, I believe it even more. It was a tough field of candidates to beat, but Nathan worked tirelessly to stand out. I've lost count of how many times we traversed the commonwealth. There were rallies in Philadelphia, town hall meetings in Pittsburgh, visits to ski resorts in the Poconos and wineries in Erie. Nathan wanted to take his campaign right to the voters, and that's exactly what we did.

There's so much work ahead, and I know the next six months will prove the most challenging yet as Nathan goes head-to-head with his new opponent, Madelyn Morgan. Neither is an incumbent, so in theory, the playing field should be level. Madelyn won her primary by a landslide, though, and it's no secret that she's got a wealth of resources and funding at her fingertips. Between that and Perry Talmudge, an independent who actually has a small chance of earning enough traction and support to make it onto the ballot in November, we will have to double our efforts to win – but not tonight. This is a time to reward ourselves for the long days on the road, the fact-checking and speechwriting and meetings with everyone from school superintendents to board members of major corporations. It's Nathan's celebration, his moment in the spotlight before he sets the focus back to the people he hopes to serve.

"Family, friends, and supporters," he begins, voice booming over the microphone. "First, let me say thank you, from the bottom of my heart. I've given a lot of speeches this year, and every time, it is such a joy to see smiling faces in the crowd. I was lucky enough to have that right from the start." He gestures to the elderly couple standing next to him. "If you ask my parents, they will regale you with tales of the speeches I used to give to my stuffed animals and action figures." At this, a chuckle floats around the room and Nathan's eyes twinkle merrily. "That's true," he says. "I did. But I was also blessed to have parents who listened, even when I was too young to really understand what the political process was. I'd corral them into the living room and lay out my plans for making the world a better place. Not only did they listen, they encouraged me to take those plans and put them into action. Fifty years later, here I am. And here you are." A smile turns up the corners of his mouth as he looks at the sea of people. "You've shown up for me, time and again. You've made phone calls, knocked on doors, and passed out flyers. You've stood behind me, and I promise: as governor, I will stand behind you."

As Nathan continues, talking about the road ahead and everything he hopes to accomplish, I let my attention wander to the first time I heard a candidate speak. Sometimes it's tough to believe it's been nearly twenty years since that damp November day. If I close my eyes, or even if I don't, I can still feel the wind whipping my hair against my face and the chilly drops falling from a foggy sky and landing on my cheeks. It was a Monday after school, fifteen hours before the polls were set to open on Election Day, and I had accidentally stumbled upon a last minute rally as I walked home from the corner shop that sold groceries at a discounted price. No one saw me as I stood at the back, juggling three heavy brown paper bags, but I saw them.

I saw them, and I heard them, and I felt them.

And it changed my life.

That ten-year-old girl, balancing groceries as rain slid under the collar of her too-small coat? She is forever inside me. She's forever pushing me, driving me, inspiring me, and, most of all, reminding me.

I think of her now, as I glance at my picture on the ID badge clipped to my suit jacket. At thirty, I have long since outgrown the clumsy fifth-grade version of myself, with her legs that were too long, her arms that were too thin, and her face that was too freckled. I've grown into myself. I've grown up. *Melina Radcliffe, Policymaking.* That's what it says on my badge in bold black letters. I run my finger over them, and despite the soupy atmosphere of a gym packed with people, a chill unleashes and springs down my spine. Sometimes I still can't believe this is my life. The thought of this is what kept me going all those years ago. It's what kept me going when all I wanted was to give in and give up.

"Hey." Kira nudges me with her elbow. "Are you okay?"

I raise my head to look at her, and that's when I realize there are people starting to ease past us. Nathan's speech is finished and the crowd's beginning to disperse. A little girl hurries by, her pigtails swinging as she holds a doll and exclaims something about wanting to be President, and I catch the amused expression her parents share as they follow closely behind. I want to tell them not to dash her dreams or to put a limit on all she can achieve. The world's so big and bright at her age, bursting with possibilities, and the moment someone tells her she can't grab onto them all, that's when she'll start to believe it. The balloons of hope will slide out of her grasp, their ribbons getting further and further out of reach.

I shake my head to clear the thought.

"Yes," I tell Kira. "I'm fine. Come on, let's join the others."

"Are you sure? Because – "

"I'm sure," I say firmly. I straighten the bottom of my already-straight jacket, double-checking to be certain the camera Nathan gave me earlier is still inside its pocket, and start off toward the front of the room with Kira at my side. Nathan is chatting with a small cluster of people, and we wait until he's finished to congratulate him again. "I'm proud to be on your team," I tell him. "Today is proof of the amazing things you're going to do."

"The amazing things *we* are going to do," he amends. His campaign staff is small, only ten of us, and as we circle around him, it feels like a family of sorts. "Thank you so much for your great work," he tells us all. "I couldn't have done it without you. I know we have a long way to go, but I'm also a believer in celebrating how far we have come. To that end, I'd like you to take the rest of the week off. Go home. Watch TV. Read a book. Take a walk. Sleep late."

"Sleep late?" asks Cole, who works with Nathan on his speeches. "What does that even mean? I don't think that phrase is in my vocabulary."

Everyone laughs. It has been an endless cycle of early mornings and late nights for … honestly, I don't even know how long. Some of my coworkers are getting a little weary at this point, physically and mentally drained after the craziness that characterized the homestretch of this primary election. Not me, though. I'd rather stay here in Hershey, Nathan's hometown and the site of tonight's rally, than drive back to Philadelphia. The last thing I feel like doing is going home to an empty apartment right now. I ask the others if they would be interested in grabbing a drink first, before we all go our separate ways, but nobody takes me up on it.

"Sorry," Cole says, giving me a hug goodbye. "My eyes are

practically closing." He makes a huge show of yawning, then hugs the others and hurries off across the gymnasium. One by one, the rest of my colleagues follow suit. Even Kira, who's not only a co-worker, but also a friend, is eager to get home to her husband and their daughter.

I sigh, say my goodbyes, and start walking toward the small office attached to the gym. I tossed my purse in there prior to the rally and have to pick it up before I leave. The gym is hushed now, the *Nathan Ford for Governor* banner presiding over only a couple lingering people, mostly the janitorial staff, and my heel catches in a messy bundle of crepe paper that's fallen out of one of the oversized trashcans.

"Crap!" I shriek, as my arms fly out to my sides like helicopter propellers in a desperate attempt to regain the balance I can already tell I've lost. My foot slides out from underneath me, ensnared in the red, white, and blue streamers, and I brace myself the best I can as I hit the floor. Hard. A sharp ache shoots through my palm as it smacks onto the tile. Waves of pain travel up my arm, and I shift my weight off of it, trying to catch my breath. I'm still sprawled on the floor, inhaling and exhaling in rhythmic succession, when I hear a man's voice.

"Whoa. You hurt?" His words are soft, lilting, with an almost sing-songy Southern drawl. "I saw that spill from across the room. It was actually kind of graceful looking."

"It wasn't." Automatically, my mind flashes to all the tumbles I used to take as a kid. There was the time I tripped over my untied shoelaces and landed in a snow bank outside school, and the time I took my younger brother and sisters to the playground and didn't see the pinecone near the jungle gym, and the time my best friend Amie and I were running down the steps at her house and I missed the bottom one. It has been a long time since my feet betrayed me, but not long enough. "I've got no doubt," I say, taking the man's hand as he offers it to help me up, "that there was nothing even a bit graceful about that fall. Do me a favor? Pretend you never saw it."

"Saw what?" Behind his wire-rimmed glasses, a smile lights up his blue-gray eyes.

I can't help smiling back. "Thanks," I say gratefully.

He sticks out his hand again. "I'm Bradley, by the way."

"Melina." As his fingers close around mine, something warm softens my edges. "Do you know Nathan?" I ask. "Friend? Family member?"

"Not exactly." He holds my gaze for a moment, then steps back. "It's sort of a long story. Let's just say it was important for me to be here." He clears his throat. "Seriously, though, are you okay? The Incident That Shall Not Be Named … well, it looked like you went down pretty hard."

"Nothing I can't handle."

"Do you need some ice?" he persists. "I can try to round some up."

"I'm fine," I tell him. "Truly. Thanks for the assist, though. I appreciate it." I glance at the clock on the gymnasium wall. It's ten on the nose. "I'd better get going. I have a long drive ahead of me. But maybe I'll see you around? I work for Nathan, and he's planning to campaign here often. He'd really like a strong showing in his hometown."

Bradley's mouth twitches slightly, almost imperceptibly. "Yes," he says. "I imagine that we'll be seeing a lot of each other, then." He gives an awkward looking wave, or maybe it's more of a salute, I can't especially tell, and spins on his heel. I watch as he ambles toward the doors. They clang shut behind him, echoing throughout the cavernous space, and I stare at them for a second longer before heading in the opposite direction. It is time, finally, for me to get out of here, too.

* * *

There are people who are good at steering their thoughts. They can switch the track their minds are traveling on, compartmentalizing one area so they can concentrate on another. I am not one of those people, at least when it comes to work. It doesn't matter that Nathan's given us the week off. Even as I drive back to Philly on a turnpike that's basically devoid of traffic, it's impossible for me not to think about the election. By the time I'm trudging up the stairs to my third-floor apartment, I am already brainstorming productive ways to use the time. It will be a great opportunity to work on my proposal for opening ten new homeless shelters across the state. I ran the idea by Nathan a couple of months ago and he loved it. There's no guarantee – there never is in politics – but he told me he would be glad to take a look at whatever plans I drew up on the topic.

"You take the lead," he said. "There's a fire in your eyes when it comes to this."

Yes, there is. There always will be.

This week will give me the time to work on adding new embers to the flame.

I can't wait to strike that match.

I slip my key into the door, turning it swiftly to the right, and balance the overflowing pile of mail against my chest as I use my non-bruised arm to flip the light switch. A warm glow immediately fills the small entryway. I blink against it, looking around, reacquainting myself. It's the weirdest feeling, coming back to a place that, even after two years, doesn't really seem like mine. There's the potted plant in the hall, its leaves so green you'd think they were real, and the wall of built-in bookshelves, stuffed to the gills with colorful covers and creased spines. A family picture from when I was nine – just before the rug was yanked out from under us – sits, framed, on the desk, and in the kitchen, my Gram's old china dishes are stacked neatly in the cabinets, lonely from disuse. As I walk through the apartment, systematically turning on the lamps and watching as each room's darkness gives way to light, it's almost like I'm moving in again. It's always like that when I return from a long time on the road.

I circle back to the living room and toss the mail onto the desk, suddenly too tired to sift through it.

I'll do it tomorrow. Tonight is for a hot shower and sweet, sweet sleep.

I leave the lights on and head for the bedroom, pulling my jacket off as I go, so I can hang it up in the closet. But just as I reach for a hanger, something hits me: the jacket, it's not heavy enough. An instant panic seizes me, slamming into my heart and ratcheting up its steady beat tenfold. I push my hand into the jacket pocket and claw inside. It has to be there. Please, it has to be there. But even as I turn the pocket inside out, stretching the fabric like it will magically reveal some kind of hidden trapdoor, I know it's not there.

The camera that Nathan gave to me earlier tonight for safekeeping, the one that's supposed to play a key role in the race for governor and the one I swore I would keep safe ... it's gone.

2

BRADLEY

This is not how tonight was supposed to go.

My job was easy. Straightforward. Cut and dry. As my father would say, an ace in the hole. So why am I still sitting in my car and staring at the school building? I should turn the key in the ignition and crank up the old Frank Sinatra CD I like to listen to while driving. There's no reason for me to be here anymore. It's time to go home.

But I can't stop thinking about that woman. Melina.

I hate that I deceived her. Technically, everything I said was true, but that doesn't make me feel any better. Bradley Williams, master of manipulation. The notion turns my stomach upside-down. I know it shouldn't matter – after all, once the election's over, I'll likely never see Melina again – but it does. There's something about her I can't seem to shake. I think it's her eyes. They're mostly hazel, but I saw some other colors, too, when the light hit them a certain way. Green. Brown. Blue. Like a watercolor painting.

"Stop." I say the word out loud, testing it and maybe testing myself. "This isn't helping." I force myself to start my SUV and back out of the parking space. What's done is done. I can't change the way Melina and I met, nor can I give an alternate explanation for why I was at the victory rally for a candidate I don't support.

Not that it would've been wise to say anything else.

"Keep a low profile," my boss told me, when we went over my assignment earlier in the day. "It is imperative that you blend in with the crowd. That's the only way you'll be able to bring me what I

"

need." I nodded, but dropped my gaze at the same time, and I guess she noticed, because her next words were more gentle. "Thank you," she said. "I know you're not thrilled about this. I'm sorry to put you in an uncomfortable position, but it had to be you or Hannah, and since she's sick ... "

"It's up to me."

Hannah is my speechwriting partner. Of all the days for her to be trapped at home with a nasty bout of food poisoning, it just had to be today. This was supposed to be her job. Instead, I got stuck with it. My conscience won't let me forget it, either. It weighs heavy on my mind the whole drive to my house. By the time I pull into my driveway, I'm trying to decide whether it would be best to pour myself a scotch or to simply go right to bed. I think I'll opt for the latter. It has been such a long day, and things always seem clearer in the morning. I'll get a good night's sleep and wake up refreshed, with no lingering thoughts of Melina. Hurrying to help her when she fell was the complete opposite of keeping a low profile. My boss won't be too happy if she finds out what I did, so yes ... that's the end of it.

I get out of the car and head for my townhome. I'm about to open the door and go inside when I hear high-pitched crying coming from the house adjacent to mine. The window's open, inviting in the warm May air, and I see Cameron, my neighbor, inside. He's standing in the middle of the living room, holding his daughter Lissie and trying to calm her down. No dice. The tiny redhead seems to be inconsolable.

"Cam?" I bend down, speaking through the window. "What's wrong? Need some help?"

Relief passes across his face. "Hang on," he calls.

A second later, the door swings open and Lissie's sobs tumble out into the night. "Hey," I say, as I walk inside. "What's going on with my favorite girl?" I reach over to wipe away her tears.

"Bananas ... got ... broken," she blubbers.

I turn my gaze to Cameron questioningly. "Bananas?" I ask.

"Her stuffed monkey," he clarifies. "Let's just say there was an incident. Lissie's been hysterical ever since." He sighs. "I don't know what to do. Jill always handled situations like this. Would you believe I was so desperate before that I called her?" His eyes grow cloudy. "It was terrific timing on my part. She was on a date with her new boyfriend."

"Ouch. I'm sorry, man. That had to be rough."

I don't know how Cameron does it. Rebuilding your life after a divorce must be difficult enough if there aren't children involved. With three-and-a-half-year-old Lissie and her one-year-old brother Cooper in the equation, it's no surprise Cam seems tired all the time. Having a constant connection to Jill through their kids is a never-ending reminder that the family he thought would be forever has faded away. That's gotta hurt.

"Look," Lissie says, twisting around in her father's arms and pointing to a big brown blob on the armchair. "He's drowned. Daddy gave us chocolate ice cream after dinner and I spilled mine on the monkey. I wanted to clean him up." The corners of her mouth tip down again. "I gave him a bath. With bubbles. But he couldn't swim," she says woefully.

"We'll get a new one," Cameron promises, but this only makes Lissie burst into tears again.

"I want *this* one!" she cries.

Cameron and I both watch as she shimmies down out of his arms and bolts across the room. It's sad, seeing the way she kneels by the chair and lovingly cradles the stuffed monkey to her chest. Its fur is matted, the stitching coming out of one eye and an arm hanging, literally, by a thread. Any kid would probably be upset to see a favorite toy in ruins, but Lissie's taking it really hard.

"Jill bought that for her," Cameron explains to me. "She's been attached to it ever since she was a baby. That's why it's so tattered. I think the bubble bath was the final straw." He shakes his head. "Anyway, Lissie keeps it here as a reminder of her mom and keeps the doll I bought her at Jill's." He manages a half-smile. "That way she has Mommy and Daddy at both of her houses. I think Cooper's the lucky one. He'll grow up not knowing that things were ever any different."

"They're both lucky," I tell him. "I know this shared custody thing is hard on you, but you never stop trying. You always put the kids first. Do you know how many children never have that, even in homes with both parents?"

A brief image of my family comes to mind. Mom, with her pearl necklaces and pants suits. Dad, with his nose always buried in the newspaper. Jake and Eric, my older brothers, with their trophies and medals and scholarships. Grandfather, with his Purple Heart for his service in World War II, and Grandma, with her homemade biscuits and banana pudding. None of them live nearby. My parents and grandparents are still in Georgia, and my brothers are off doing their own thing in Washington, DC and Connecticut. I'm normally glad to have the distance. It's less stifling that way. But tonight, after the kids have fallen asleep and I've stuck around to have a beer with Cam, I find myself actually wishing I could talk to Dad. Or even my brothers. They'd tell me to snap out of it and stop letting a stranger influence my thoughts.

"You're a Williams, born and bred," Dad would say. "That means you're destined for greatness. Do me proud, son. Do our family proud." I can almost hear his gruff voice, half admonishing me and half praising, as I walk into my house and head right for the study. I sink into the leather chair that's behind my desk and let my elbows rest on its arms.

This used to be Grandfather's chair. I loved it as a child, climbing up to sit on his lap and listen to the stories he'd tell of his time overseas, and when I made the move up to Harrisburg after graduate school, he insisted I take it. I can still smell his cologne on it now. I close my eyes for a moment and breathe it in. I breathe in the memories. All of them, good and bad. Fishing with Grandfather at the lake and coming home to fresh bread, complete with raisins and cinnamon, as Grandma stood at the stove with a gingham apron tied around her waist. Competing in the middle school spelling bee, hot tears gathering behind my eyes as I misspelled a word and became the only Williams brother to lose the crown. Being named the editor-in-chief of my high school's newspaper, something Jake and Eric never took any interest in.

The memories blend together, swirling into each other until it's impossible to determine where one ends and the next starts. So much to remember and so much I'd rather forget. But I can't. Not really. And so I lean forward in the chair, open the laptop sitting on the desk, and click into my email account. I am wide awake now, somehow weary and wired at the same time, and I know that sleep will elude me until I take care of this.

Until I tell Madelyn that my mission has been accomplished.

It's done, I type. *I have what you requested.*

A minute later, her response zings back. I knew she'd be up late, waiting to hear from me. She asks if I can come by at ten o'clock the following day, and even though I don't want to, even though I didn't want to do any of this, I agree anyway.

Great, she answers. *Thank you. You've gone above and beyond to help out with this campaign, and I won't forget it if I'm elected. You have a very bright future in politics. You should be proud.*

Proud.

I should be proud.

Then why do I feel so lousy?

Something squeezes at my temples as I slap the laptop shut and push back my chair. I stride out of the room and head for the kitchen. It has been hours since I've eaten anything, so maybe that is why my head hurts. I tug at the refrigerator door and scan the nearly empty shelves. A value-sized box of cereal. A carton of milk. A package of shredded cheddar cheese. A head of romaine lettuce. A half-eaten pizza, still in its take-out box. When did I let things get this sparse? When was the last time I actually cooked a real meal?

I have no idea.

Tomorrow, I'll go to the grocery store. I'll stock up on everything and spend the whole evening experimenting in the kitchen. "Because this is disgusting," I mutter, cracking open the pizza box and looking at the greasy cheese. I toss it in the trash, opting for cereal instead. Oh, if Grandmom could see me now.

"Bless your heart, darlin'," she'd say. "Oy vey, does your meal choice need help."

People frequently do a double take when they hear her talk. I guess the combination of Yiddish and Southernisms, all spoken in a German accent, *is* pretty unexpected. I love it, though. I love that she isn't afraid to show her story – all of it, even the painful parts. There's something so refreshing about her candor. People could learn a lot from her.

I've learned a lot from her.

How to sauté okra and marinate chicken. How to grow a garden. How to read Hebrew. How to keep the faith, even when it seems like everything is going wrong. How to move on and go forward. She's taught me all those things and more.

How would she feel about what I did tonight?

Would the light dim in her blue eyes? Would the wrinkles in her cheeks flatten as she frowned? Or would she say that she understands what it's like to do what you have to do? That life isn't black and white, but shaded in a whole spectrum of grays?

I don't know.

I do know what Grandfather would say, though.

I just don't want to think about it.

I turn on the faucet, rinse out the remainder of my milk-soaked cereal, and leave the bowl in the sink. My headache's still there – in fact, it's getting worse – so I gulp down medicine before going up to bed. But I can't sleep. All I can do is lie there and stare at the ceiling through the darkness. A dog barks somewhere outside, and my ceiling fan whirs, casting a cool breeze down on me until I have to pull the blanket up to my chin. I toss, I turn. I roll over to my left side, I move back onto the right. I count backward from a thousand. I count forward the number of days until the election. It's no use. My prize from tonight – or, more accurately, my steal – is sitting atop the dresser and taunting me. I can feel its presence, big and bold and brazen, hanging all around me.

You're not good enough, it whispers.

You'll never make it on your own, it mocks.

You can't find the courage to stand on your own feet, it scoffs.

I throw back the covers, stride across the room, and thrust the blasted thing into a drawer.

There. That's better.

And it is better. It's enough to grant me a temporary reprieve, a break in the storm thundering in my brain. Finally, as I close my eyes again, I'm able to drift off. Even in sleep, though, rest doesn't come. I dream about my first internship at Georgetown, working in the Washington office of one of Georgia's congressmen. He was an incredible mentor, strong and supportive, and on my last day, he gave me an old book, its leather soft and cracked from use. "This," he told me, "has been my guide for decades. Politics can be tough. The stress to get it right, to deal with the underlying factors and always take your constituents' best interests into consideration, can wear you down. You've got to remember why you fell in love with this career. This has been my reminder."

When I flipped open the cover, the Declaration of Independence stared up at me in all its glory. That wasn't all, though. The Constitution, the Bill of Rights, all the most important documents from our country's history were reprinted inside. The congressman had written something in the front, in big block letters: SERVE THE PEOPLE. For him, that's what politics was all about.

I thought that's what it was about for me, too.

I mean, sure, I never really had any choice in the matter. My path stretched out ahead, waiting, before I even took the first step. But I believed in it. I believed in working to make this great nation even greater. I believed in defending it, celebrating it, and preserving it. Is that what I'm doing now, though? Or did I lose myself somewhere along that path?

As I ring Madelyn's doorbell the next day, I ponder the answer to that question. There's a twisty feeling deep in my stomach, a knot that refuses to unravel. It only clenches tighter when I walk into her home office. "Morning," I say, shuffling into one of the chairs in front of her glass-topped desk. "How are you?"

A smile stretches across her face. "Good morning," she says. "I'm fantastic. Take a look at this headline." She hands me a copy of the morning paper.

Madelyn Morgan Moves Mountains.

I skim the newsprint. No wonder she's so thrilled. The article is about her victory in last night's primary. It's the type of press most candidates only dream of getting. Not only does it outline how she trounced the rest of the field, but there are even a couple paragraphs that go into detail on her positions on key issues. It's truly a perfect set-up for the next portion of the race. "This is wonderful coverage," I tell her.

"Isn't it?" She beams. "If I didn't know better, I'd think you wrote it yourself."

"Sorry." I hold up my hands. "Can't take credit for this one."

I can only take credit for something much more underhanded.

Something that goes against that book from the congressman. Against his advice.

"Here you go," I say, sliding the object across the desk. Its silver case gleams in the light, and my hand lingers on it a beat too long, not wanting to let go. Wanting to take it back. Wanting to make things right.

But it's too late for that.

The path has now veered off into a dangerous direction.

3

Melina

I tell myself to stay calm, not to panic. There could very well be a reasonable explanation for the camera's disappearance. Maybe it just fell out of my pocket in the car. That's feasible. I dart out of my bedroom and run through the apartment, my heart still doing a two-step that's out of sync. The front door feels heavy as I yank it open. I let it slam shut behind me as I race down the steps and out into the breezy night, my mind whirling the entire time. There are a lot of places where the camera could have gotten wedged in my car. It has to be in one of them. I can't, *won't*, let myself consider the alternative.

I pull the car door open, crouch down, and start to search, shoving my hand below the front seat and feeling around. There's nothing, though, just like there's nothing under the passenger seat or in the back of the car. The camera isn't anywhere.

Anxiety prickles at my skin as I give my Prius another once-over. Forget the car. The camera must have slipped out of my pocket when I fell earlier. I don't remember it happening, but my focus was elsewhere, and it would have been easy to miss if the camera landed in the bunched-up pile of crepe paper.

I remind myself, again, to stay calm and not panic. That won't do any good. It's better to think clearly and figure out my next step. Part of me is tempted to turn around and drive back to Hershey, but there'd be no point. Surely no one is at the school anymore to let me in. I'll have to wait for the morning and give them a call. Perhaps one of the cleaning staff discovered it and took it to the lost and found bin.

Do they even have those anymore?

They'd better, or I'm sunk … and probably fired.

Nathan is a good guy, one of the nicest I've ever met, but I can't imagine he'll be able to forgive such a careless mistake. *Careless.* It's the antithesis of who I am, who I want to be, and yet how can I deny it? Nathan trusted me, and I messed up. I don't do that. I don't mess things up. I fix them. I find solutions.

"This is bad," I say, trudging back across the parking lot and up the stairs to my apartment. "So bad." I go directly to my bedroom. Forget the shower. Forget the peaceful night I'd hoped to have. As I sink down into bed, cocooning myself in the blankets, I can almost feel the nightmares creeping in. I've come to expect them at times like this.

They're like rapid-fire shots, all night long.

There's the dream about losing my job, my well-maintained dam crumbling to pieces and letting out the tears I've managed to hold back for so long. There's the one about my twelfth grade history class and the words my teacher uttered which have haunted me ever since: "history will repeat itself unless we do something to alter its course." There's the one about the breaking of glass, the crying behind closed doors, the endless days of cooking food and doing laundry and tucking my sisters and brother into bed. Some people have long, extended dreams. I have short ones, these brief glimpses into what once was and what soon could be. They linger, though. They linger even after I've broken out of them.

Even after I've broken myself out of that life.

When I wake up the next morning, I'm exhausted. I might as well have not slept at all. But still, I jump out of bed and am in the kitchen, stirring sugar into my coffee, before the alarm has a chance to go off. I take one sip, then another, letting it warm me from the inside out. Then I sit at the small breakfast counter, rest my feet on the rungs of the stool, and do a quick search on my cell phone for the school in Hershey where Nathan had his rally. I punch in its number, saying a silent prayer while I wait, and launch into a plea the moment somebody answers. "Good morning," I say. "My name's Melina Radcliffe. I work for Nathan Ford. He had his rally at the school last night? I'm really hoping you can help me with something."

"Of course," the woman says pleasantly. "What can I do for you?"

I explain what happened, then wait not-so-patiently as she puts me on hold to see if anyone has turned in the camera. It'll be there. It makes complete sense for it to have popped out of my jacket pocket when I fell. The woman will find it, and I'll drive back right away, and no one will be any the wiser. Except ... something is nagging at me, and I'm not certain what. All I know is that by the time the woman returns, I'm holding the phone so tightly that my knuckles are turning white.

"I'm sorry," she says, and just like that, all the color drains from my face. "I checked the lost and found," she continues, "and also the gym. I even asked the people who were working last night. No one has seen it, but we'll keep an eye out and let you know if it shows up. Is this the best number to reach you at, Ms. Radcliffe?"

"Yes," I answer, fighting to keep my voice steady. "Thank you so much for trying. I appreciate it. Would it be okay if I come over and look around the parking lot? Maybe I dropped it there." And if so, it might have been run over by a bus already. The thought of it smashed underneath a tire, all its images lost forever, makes a cold sweat inch over my neck. What am I going to do?

What in the *world* am I going to do?

My first move is to call Kira. I hate having to admit that I made such an awful mistake, but I hate the thought of not finding the camera even more. The woman I spoke to from the school said I am welcome to do my own search, so long as I check in at the office first, and I don't want to waste any time. Hopefully Kira can help.

"Hello?" she chirps perkily.

I take a deep breath, then force myself to bring her mood crashing down. "The camera's gone," I tell her. "When I went to hang up my jacket last night, I realized it wasn't there. I've already called the school, and they can't find it, but I'm driving over in a few minutes to look around and see if they missed it somehow. They *have* to have missed it."

"I'm sure they did," Kira says soothingly. "When was the last time you saw it?"

"After Nathan's speech. I checked on it as we were heading up to join him." I tell her about my fall. "That's the only explanation I can come up with," I say. "It landed in the streamers and nobody noticed." I curl up my nose as a thought occurs to me. "Oh God, I bet it was thrown out. I'll have to sift through the dumpster."

"You're kidding," she says, and I hear Gemma, her two-year-old, give a high-pitched giggle in the background. It sounds like she's laughing at me, and for a nanosecond, it makes me smile. Then I'm right back to fretting.

"What other choice do I have?" I ask. "There are only five days until we're back to work, and if I don't have the camera by then ... " I trail off, imagining all the repercussions. It makes me physically ill. "He'll fire me," I say sadly. "And he'll be entirely justified."

"Stop it," Kira says. "No one's getting fired. Give me a bit to find a babysitter, then I'll meet you at the school and help you look. I'm sure it's somewhere. Things are always where you least expect them."

"Or where you most expect them." My words come out on a sigh. "Thank you, though. You are a lifesaver. Oh, and Kira? Please, please, please can you keep this between us? I don't want Nathan to know unless he absolutely has to."

Fake it 'til you make it and take care of the problem on your own before it spirals out of control. That's what I've done since I was ten years old, and most of the time it serves me well. This can't be an exception, it just can't. It'll ruin everything I've worked so hard for, everything I've dedicated my life to, everything I've planned and hoped and dreamed. I'm not ready to give all that up yet. I will find the camera if it's the last thing I do.

Two and a half hours later, I'm not so certain. I'm standing on my tiptoes in the school's parking lot, gripping on to the top of a dark red dumpster as I peer over its edge. The smell is overwhelming, enough to make me take momentary breaks to gulp in fresh air, and my head spins as I rake my eyes back and forth across the enormous collection of trash. There are uncapped pens, plastic forks that are smeared with the remnants of yesterday's cafeteria food, a protractor that's cracked in half, and a glue bottle that's still full. A green nylon pinny takes me back to my own school days and the way my classmates would often pick me last for the team during gym. The memory flicks its way through my mind, unwanted and unsettling, but I shove it aside and continue my search. There are wads of gum, a Spanish test covered in red pen, a copy of *A Farewell to Arms*, and a flyer for a school dance. It's a treasure trove of teenage life.

But there's no camera.

"Please tell me you're not entertaining any ideas about actually going in that thing," Kira says as I move to the other end of the dumpster and hoist myself up a little to get a better look. "Not even Lucy Ricardo and Ethel Mertz would take it that far."

"I don't know," I say, scanning the mountain of garbage. My gaze falls on half of a heart-shaped best friend necklace, and I briefly wonder if it was thrown out by accident or discarded on purpose, tossed away like it meant nothing. "Lucy had some hair-brained schemes. I wouldn't put it past her to do something like that and drag Ethel along. Don't worry, though. You couldn't pay me to get in this thing." I would never set foot in a dumpster, not after the way those kids teased me when I was younger. Kira doesn't know about that, though. She never will. The only person in my life who can attest to what happened on the school playground all those years ago is Amie, who stood up for me and told our classmates to back off.

I should call her. It's been months since we've talked.

I'll probably have lots of opportunities for that soon, seeing as how my days of being busy all the time will likely come to a screeching halt. That camera is nowhere, which means I'm done for. "This is a disaster," I say, giving up on the dumpster and reaching for the hand sanitizer in my purse. "I've let Nathan down. Those pictures were supposed to play such a big part in his campaign. Now what are we going to do? Everything's ruined, and it's all my fault."

"No, it isn't," Kira says. "It's not like you deliberately sabotaged things. You lost the camera by accident. Nathan will understand. And what's to say he doesn't have a back-up of the pictures? I'm sure they're on a computer somewhere."

I brighten a little. I've been so upset, something as logical as that didn't even occur to me. I pull out my phone to call him, crossing my fingers as he picks up after only one ring.

"Melina?" he says. "Now, I'm certain you have more exciting things to do on your time off than chat with me." Mirth colors his words. "I know you're a workaholic, and I respect that because I'm one, too, but take it from me: everyone needs to recharge their batteries sometimes."

"Oh I am," I fib. Or at least I would be, if not for this debacle. "It's just hard to turn off my brain. I woke up early this morning – force of habit, I guess – and couldn't help thinking about the next part of the campaign. You know the pictures you're planning to release? I was thinking it would be cool to design a pamphlet around them, something we could hand out at events. If you'd like to send me the photo files, I can start working on a draft. I know painting is more my thing, but I'm pretty good with Photoshop, too."

I hold my breath.

"That's a great idea," he says. "Though I will repeat: you don't have to work this week. If you're so inclined, though, you can just use the memory stick from the camera. I know I told you to keep it tucked away, but I actually don't have another copy of the files." He sighs. "My wife is the best, but let's just say she and technology don't get along. She somehow deleted the entire picture folder on our computer the other day."

That breath comes rushing out of me, jagged and harsh.

"What?" Kira whispers. "What's wrong?"

All I can do is shake my head and listen as Nathan continues. "It's a good thing we still have the originals, huh?" he asks. "I'll make another copy next week, after we all reconvene in the office.

On second thought, perhaps you should hold off on working with the pictures, just in case there's some sort of glitch. Technology can be so temperamental. Better to play it safe than sorry, right?"

"Right," I manage. "I guess I'm forced into relaxing, then." I laugh, but it doesn't sound normal. It's squeaky, pinched, taut.

"Good," Nathan says. "Enjoy your vacation. You deserve it."

I don't. I *so* don't.

Nathan hangs up, and I drop my phone back into my purse. "I'm doomed," I say.

Kira is normally level-headed, as even-keeled as they come, but as she looks at me, I can tell that even she is beginning to worry. "Maybe there's something we can use to fish around in there," she says, her gaze traveling to the dumpster and appraising it warily. "A field hockey stick? Anything to move things around. I'd imagine the camera would have to be near the top, since last night's trash would've been the most recent to be dumped in." She slides off her engagement ring and wedding band, then tucks them into her purse for safekeeping.

"What are you doing?" I ask.

"What does it look like I'm doing? I'm playing Ethel to your Lucy."

I don't know whether to laugh or scream.

Maybe both.

"You don't have to – " I start.

"I know. I want to. Well, I don't *want* to," she amends, arching an eyebrow as the wind picks up and a crumpled potato chip bag flies out of the dumpster and lands near her feet. "But I will. That's what friends are for."

A bizarre blend of emotions skitters over me. There is gratitude, embarrassment, and guilt.

And then, as Kira begins fishing through the dumpster and says, "please pretend you never saw this," there is something else: realization.

Because I've heard that before.

I said it yesterday, to Bradley.

Bradley, who appeared out of nowhere after my fall. Bradley, who helped me up. Bradley, who would have had ample time to snatch the camera when I turned around to check the clock. Bradley, who seemed very anxious to leave after I assured him I was alright.

Oh my God.

How could I have missed this?

My eyes go wide, a furious flush spreads over my face, and a familiar mantra resounds inside my head. This time, though, I can't stay calm.

This time, I do panic.

4

BRADLEY

"We need to come out swinging," Madelyn says, gesturing with her hands as she addresses the group of us sitting around the room. It's just after noon, two hours after I presented her with what could be the ticket to pulling an early lead in the race against Nathan, and we've moved to her usual campaign headquarters across town. As she goes on and on about formulating the best strategy, it makes me antsy. Uneasy. Other than Hannah, I don't think any of my colleagues know about what went down last night, and since she's off today, still recovering from the food poisoning, I feel like a lone wolf.

I wish Madelyn hadn't put me in this position. I wish she'd played fair.

Mostly, I wish I'd had the courage to defy her request.

Why is it always so hard for me to fall out of line?

I listen as Madelyn dances around the truth. She talks in vague, general terms about broadening her campaign and addressing new issues. Everyone else is nodding along. I wonder whether they'd still agree with her if they knew everything I do.

Maybe they can. Maybe there's a way for me to salvage this, after all.

But I have to be careful about it.

"Are you sure this is the best idea?" I ask, and a sea of heads turn to look my way. "It's just that your supporters are in your corner for specific reasons," I explain. "I understand wanting to reach a wider demographic, but you also don't want to be perceived as going whatever way the wind blows. The press and public will question it if you suddenly begin declaring a passion for issues you've never mentioned before. People are observant. They won't be pleased if they think you're insulting their intelligence."

Madelyn walks over to the table we're sitting around and takes her place in the lone empty seat. "I don't want that, of course," she says. "So maybe we should proceed slowly, then, and tackle only one thing at a time. Like, perhaps ... hmm." She gazes into space for a minute, thinking, and I know it's coming.

Save this, my brain pleads with me. *Forget about being careful. Stop her before it's too late.*

This isn't fair to Nathan.

To Melina.

An image of her comes to mind. The caramel-colored hair. The eyes shiny with adrenaline. The smile playing on the corners of her mouth as she watched Nathan speak to everyone. Even before I knew who she was, Melina stood out in the crowd. She seems like a strong person – you have to be, working in politics – but last night, seeing the glow on her face, the way she leaned forward slightly and nodded at Nathan's comments, that's when something else shone through. I'm not fully sure of what it was, but something softer was there.

I don't want to be the one who sweeps that away.

I shift uncomfortably in my chair, sitting up ramrod-straight.

"Go on, my boy, do it. Speak for those who have no voice." This time, it's Grandfather's words I hear in my head. I glance at the pinky ring on my left hand. The one Grandfather gave me. The one Grandma gave to him back in the forties, after he saved her. It's my most prized possession, a family heirloom straight from Germany. Grandfather trusted me with it, and I can't let him down.

I can't let myself down.

I open my mouth to speak up.

"Homelessness," Madelyn says, before I get any words out. I'm a second too late. I can feel my shoulders deflate. Or maybe it's my conscience deflating, it's tough to tell. I'm so upset, I'm barely able to focus as she continues. "It's a real problem," she says. "One that I know Nathan Ford is very committed to fixing. He and his team feel strongly about this." Here, she shoots me the tiniest and most inconspicuous smile. "It'll be a priority for them. Let's make it one for us, too. Nathan is a top notch opponent. If we can beat him to the punch on this, we may be able to neutralize some of the momentum he has, coming out of the primary."

There's a flurry of activity in the room. Pens scrawling atop paper. Fingers gliding across tablet screens. Voices murmuring as everybody starts to discuss the idea. Not me, though. "Excuse me," I mutter. The legs of my chair screech against the floor as I push it backward. Nails on a chalkboard. That's what this entire day has become.

I hightail it out of the room and don't stop until I've left the building. The sun is warm, and I can smell lilacs blooming on a nearby bush. Lilacs. My grandma's favorite. They don't grow down south because it's too hot, but they were plentiful in her neighborhood in Germany. "My Aba liked to pick them for my Ima," she told me once, calling her parents by their Hebrew titles. "When they were in season, we'd have a vase in the kitchen all the time."

Maybe I should call Grandma now. See what advice she has to offer.

But before I get a chance, my phone rings.

It's Lucas.

He still lives in Georgia, too, and though I know this isn't exactly a good time for a conversation with my best friend, I answer anyway. Lucas is a pediatrician and hasn't ever understood why I'd let myself get swept into the craziness of politics, but he's the least judgmental person I've ever known and he's always a great sounding board.

"Hey," I say. "What's up? How are you doing?" I walk over to the low stone wall that surrounds the courtyard and plunk down onto it. The longer I stay out here, the more time Madelyn will have to reconsider her plan – and the more time I'll have to hide away from my role in it. I'm not ready to face what I've done yet.

"I can't complain," Lucas says. "The practice is doing well, and I went on a date with a fantastic woman last night. Her name's Caroline, and I think she just might be the one who ends my streak of hopelessness on all those dating websites." This makes me grin, despite the day's events. Lucas has signed up for basically every dating site out there. It never seems to work out, but that doesn't stop him from persisting. He wants so badly to find love. Nothing prevents him from trying, not even an endless string of terrible first dates. I really admire that about him. He knows what he wants and he goes after it.

"Glad to hear it," I say. "Tell me about her."

It is cowardly to deliberately steer the conversation away from me. I know this, but I can't help doing it anyway. Listening to the details of his date is so much easier than confessing my secret. So I do. I listen intently, guiding my attention – or perhaps tricking it – to a safer place.

"She sounds great," I tell Lucas, after he's finally stopped to take a breath.

"Want to know the best part? She hates sports." He chuckles. "Clearly we are a match made in heaven."

Lucas despises sports, too. That's actually how we became friends. We were on the same Little League baseball team in second grade, and I felt bad for him when he'd swing and miss each time he was at bat. His parents had meant well when they signed him up for the team – they thought it might bring him out of his shell, since he was quiet at school and didn't have too many friends – but it just ended up upsetting him. "Wanna come over to my house and practice?" I asked him one day. "It'll only be us. You don't have to worry about the other kids watching."

"I don't know," he said, looking at the ground and scuffing his sneaker over the dirt.

"Come on," I said. "It'll be awesome. My grandfather will play with us. He watches my brothers and me when our parents are at work. He taught us how to hit homeruns, and I bet he could teach you, too."

As it turned out, Grandfather was no match for Lucas's uncoordinated ways, but we had a lot of fun those afternoons, running around a makeshift baseball diamond in the backyard. It was only the three of us most of the time, but every now and then Jake and Eric would join in. I didn't like it, not when they'd hit the ball farther and run the bases faster, but there was nothing I could do about it. I just smiled and pretended it didn't bother me.

Some things never change.

I stare straight ahead at the building. Madelyn will probably come looking for me at any second.

I stand up. Cross the courtyard in three quick strides. Move purposefully toward my SUV.

Some things never change ... but others do. I'm out of here.

Lucas can't talk any longer – his next patient has arrived early – but instead of putting my phone back in my pocket, I send a text to Madelyn's travel assistant, Kristi. She's always got her cell phone nearby, so I ask her to tell our boss that I don't feel well and am going home. Technically, that's not entirely false. I *don't* feel well. There's a pressure in my chest, a brick of remorse that seems like it will knock me flat if I don't put some space between my colleagues and me. Usually I enjoy working with them, especially at this point, when we're starting to brainstorm and a surge of energy bounces around the room. But not today. It's like a storm cloud is hanging over the election now.

So I do the only thing I can: I drive directly toward the sun.

Cause For Paws Rabbit Rescue.

It's a foster-based rescue, and as I pull into the driveway of the woman who founded it, a wave of relief washes over me. Here, I'm not Bradley Williams, speechwriter and press coordinator. It doesn't matter who's polling ahead and by what margin, and I don't have to spend hours debating whether I used the right wording in one of Madelyn's addresses. Instead, I can spend my time with the most joy-filled animals I've ever seen. Stumbling upon this nonprofit was actually an accident. It's been about a year now since I was researching animal rights legislation to work into a speech for Madelyn and found a link to the group's website. I clicked on it, curious, and I suppose you could say I fell down the rabbit hole after that. I'm especially grateful for that today.

"Hi," Callie says as she opens the door.

"Hi." I smile hopefully. "Any chance you need some help today? Any pens to clean or vet visits scheduled?"

"No vet visits." She motions for me to come in. "I do have a bunch of pens that need cleaning, though. I was just finishing up a blueprint and then I was planning to get started." Callie works from home as an interior designer and dedicates much of her free time to helping the rabbits in her care. The rescue's goal is to one day open an adoption center, but until that dream becomes a reality, the bunnies are all with fosters, including Callie. "What are you doing here?" she asks me, as we walk through her house and into the rabbits' area. "Shouldn't you be at work?"

"Yeah. I needed a breather."

"Everything okay?"

"Not really." I sigh. "But I'd rather not talk about it. Just point me in the direction of the paper towels and trash bags. There's nothing like cleaning cages to get my mind off things, right?" I'm not even joking. My career in politics is fulfilling in many ways, and I love the idea of serving my country, but volunteering at Cause for Paws is rewarding in its own right. Looking into the soft, big eyes of a rabbit whose life could've ended if the rescue hadn't saved it ... it's inspiring. Touching. Humbling. Working in politics means I often see the bad in this world. Spending time with animals means I also get to see the good.

And it's not only the animals, but also the humans who help them. The rescue community is an amazing one, filled with people who let their hearts crack wide open time and time again. Rescue work can be difficult – I have seen and heard things that literally take my breath away – but it is also indescribably special. There's nothing like witnessing a "hoppily-ever-after," as Callie calls it, and seeing these bunnies find the forever homes they so deeply deserve. Getting to be even a small part of that is an honor. Over the past year, the Cause for Paws team has become more than just my colleagues. More than just my friends. They are family, and our mission to save as many rabbits as possible is one of the best things I've ever been a part of.

Speak for those who have no voice.

As I crouch down, lifting Ruby from her pen so I can swap out her blankets and change her litter box, I think again of Grandfather's words. They're his motto in life. "It's what I've always done," he told me once, "and what I'll always do. If there's one thing you learn from me, my boy, let it be that. Use your life to positively impact others. Leave a legacy you're proud of, a legacy your children will be proud of."

I'm trying.

Every day, I try to make myself and my family proud.

They'd be conflicted about the Madelyn situation, though. I know that for certain.

"What would you do?" I ask Ruby, and she twitches her nose at me in response. I chuckle. The bunny twitch will never get old. "It's a no-win situation," I tell her. "If I come clean, Madelyn might fire me. If I don't, Melina's job could be on the line. I know it isn't like we're friends or anything, but how could I live with knowing I robbed her of that?"

Another twitch. Ruby pushes her warm nose against my hand, asking me to pet her again, then decides she's had enough of being held. She squirms in my arms, wanting desperately to break free, and I kneel down to let her. For a minute I simply stand, watching as she hops around and stops by the other cages to peek in on her furry friends.

"I'm hoping to bond her soon," Callie says, walking up to join me. "I'm thinking she and Ernie would make a good duo."

That's another thing I love about bunnies. They find such joy in having a partner. Watching the bonded pairs together could make even the most stone-faced person smile. To see them grooming each other, or sharing a leaf of romaine, or racing through a room in a game of Follow the Leader, it shows you that there's happiness in the simple things. Life can be so complicated. So complex. But here, spending time with the rabbits who binky in the air, then flop down dramatically to snooze, it's different. Easier. Calmer.

It's a respite that I grab on to today.

Eventually, though, after all the litter boxes are changed and all the pens cleaned, it's time to go. I can't hide forever. "Thanks for letting me hang out," I tell Callie, slipping my jacket back on. My fingers brush against the small flag pin I keep attached to it, and it reminds me that I've got some important decisions to make. Not that I ever really forgot. "Whenever my schedule calms down, I'm definitely adopting," I say. I've wanted to bring a bunny home since the day I first started volunteering at the rescue, but with all the time I spend on the road, working the campaign trail, it's not feasible.

One day, though. Someday.

Sometimes I feel like my life is one giant 'someday.'

I say goodbye to Callie and head back to my car, pulling my phone out as I walk. Three missed calls from Madelyn. One from Cameron. One from my father, who saw an article about Madelyn's win online and wants to congratulate me on "choosing such a worthy person to align with."

"Yeah," I mutter. "Congratulations to me."

The phone rings again, still in my hand. Madelyn.

I stare at the screen, then press the red 'reject' button.

Not now.

Instead, I get into my car and drive to Wildwood Park, one of my favorite spots in Harrisburg. It is especially nice this time of year. I breathe in the freshness of spring. The smell of newly-cut grass. The sound of birds chirping high up in the trees. The sight of the lake in the distance, and the nature center, and the boardwalks. This is my other escape. I come here often to hike the trails, and even though I'm not dressed for it today, I still head for the Wildwood Way. That and Tall Timbers are my favorite trails. They're a little more challenging than the others.

Fast.

My feet pound the blacktop as I head up a hill. The birds' song gets louder as I go until it creates a soundtrack of sorts, and if I peer through the trees, I can just make out the lake. I keep moving.

Fast.

Faster.

By the time I cross over to Tall Timbers, sweat is dripping down my back and soaking my shirt. I still keep walking. I don't care that I'm not dressed properly for this. Hiking is my outlet. It's where I feel the most free, and God knows I need that right now. The path is steeper here, and I dig in. Dig deep.

Fast.

Faster.

Fastest.

I take advantage of the log steps as I lower myself down into the gorge, and then I climb up the adjacent ridge at a steady pace. It takes me awhile to circle back around to my starting point. When I finally get there, I decide to keep going. This time, though, I head for the lake. There's a handful of people peppering its banks, so I scout out a quiet area. My heart is beating quickly as I drop down to the grass, and I take a deep breath as I run my hands over the smooth blades. It is rejuvenating. An oasis. An answer.

I reach for my phone.

Time to make the call I've been dreading.

5

Melina

"It's him. It has to be him." I exhale heavily, sending my long bangs flying, and throw my hair up into a messy ponytail. Suddenly I'm hot, so hot, overheated to the point that I feel like I might faint.

"What are you talking about?" Kira asks. "It's whom?"

"Bradley." I spit out his name, and it leaves a bad taste in my mouth.

"Bradley?" she echoes. "Who's he?"

"He has the camera. He stole it."

"What? I thought you said it was in the dumpster? You were so sure about it."

"Now I'm sure it's somewhere else." Quickly, I fill her in on what happened. "You have to admit that it makes a lot of sense," I say. "It's like you were saying before: it's been, what, fourteen hours since the camera disappeared? Even if it got tossed into a trashcan and then the dumpster, it would be somewhere on the top. We'd have found it."

"I don't know." Kira shakes her head a little. "Who is this Bradley guy? Why would he steal it?"

"I have no idea."

"Something doesn't add up." She leads me over to the curb and we plop down onto it. "You're making it seem like a calculated maneuver, but no one knows about that camera except those of us working for Nathan. Whoever Bradley is, he wouldn't understand the significance of it. There'd be no reason for him to take it."

"I know it seems that way," I agree, "but it's – " I break off abruptly as another snippet from the previous night crashes into my head: the way Bradley took a step back from me after I asked how he knows Nathan. He tried to change the subject pretty quickly.

"What?" Kira's voice draws me out of the memory. "What are you thinking?"

"I'm thinking he's definitely behind it. He was nice at first," I say. "He had this whole Southern gentlemen vibe going on, and I fell for it." I lean down, pick up a stone from the gravel lot, and hurl it through the air. I'm so angry, I could scream. That isn't me, though. I never scream. I never cry. "I am so stupid," I groan. "How could I not have seen it? I asked Bradley if he was a friend or family member of Nathan's, and all he said was 'not exactly.' Then, after I told him that I work for Nathan, he said we'd be seeing a lot of each other."

She looks at me, and I can tell she's thinking the same thing I am, that Bradley's cover was hiding the book inside.

"Maybe he works for Madelyn Morgan," I suggest. "Or he could be a reporter, looking to scoop the competition. Or could Nathan have enemies of some sort? Someone who was at odds with him when he was a state senator?" My brain goes into overdrive. "I'd wager any amount of money that Bradley was at the rally for one reason only, to snatch the camera."

Kira runs a hand through her hair, and the sleek bob falls back into place immediately. "It surely seems like it," she says. "But here's where I'm getting stuck: he would've needed to know you were the one holding the camera. Nathan gave it to you before things got underway, so it's not as though Bradley could have seen."

"Unless he was spying on us all along."

Kira wrinkles her nose. "Someone would have noticed him."

"Not necessarily. It was such a long day. We visited so many polling places. He easily could've scouted out our locations and followed us back." I pick up another stone and send it flying after its predecessor. It hits the ground and skitters for a bit before slowing to a stop, and for some reason, this reminds me of my father and the evenings when he'd walk with me to the pond near our house to skip stones.

Even after things got bad, we still went. Not much stayed the same after he lost his job, but that did, and so did our Saturday mornings at the library. Every week, he and Mom would take us to pick out books. At first, it was because they wanted us to know and appreciate the unique kind of magic a library can awaken in someone. It was a choice. Then it became a necessity. We had to check out books from a library because we couldn't afford to buy any new ones. We couldn't afford anything, really.

There are people like that now, so many people, too many people.

They are the reason I'm so passionate about politics.

The ten-year-old girl who stopped being a child and grew up overnight, she's the reason.

I won't let her down.

I refuse.

"It was Bradley," I tell Kira. "I don't know how, and I don't know why, but I am positive he's the culprit. How can we track him down, though? I don't even know his last name."

Kira opens her purse, takes out a pen and a pad of paper, and hands them to me. "Write down everything you can remember," she says, "even if it seems trivial. Sometimes the smallest detail can be the biggest clue."

"Okay."

We sit in silence as I wrack my brain for something, anything, that will help.

Southern accent

Blue-gray eyes, glasses, medium height, copper-colored hair

Strong, with a comforting and firm grip

Black pants, green sweater over a shirt and tie

Seemingly empathetic and concerned

Quick – was by my side before I even realized it

Fidgety, anxious to leave after learning who I am

I stare at the paper, desperately trying to remember more, but there's nothing. Well ... nothing except the way he made me feel warm and fuzzy inside the moment our hands touched, but there's no way in hell I'm including that. I already feel like the biggest fool on the planet. There is no need to add to that.

"This is it," I say, handing the pad back to Kira. "Nothing that's of any use."

"You don't know that." She scans my list. "If he were a reporter, wouldn't he need something to take notes? A legal pad or a voice recorder, maybe?"

"The voice recorder could've been in his pocket," I point out. "They're small enough to fit easily. It doesn't matter, anyway. Even if we could pinpoint him as a journalist, it still wouldn't help. There could be dozens of reporters with that first name. What we need is his last name." For what seems like the umpteenth time today, I flash back to the previous night. Was Bradley wearing an ID badge? I command my mind to be a camera, to call up every freeze-frame. I come up empty, though, which isn't a surprise. If Bradley was there with subterfuge as his intention, he would've taken precautions to conceal his identity.

"Hey." Kira puts an arm around my shoulders and gives me a little hug. "Don't worry. It will be okay. We'll get to the bottom of this."

"I want to believe that," I say quietly. "I really do. But at this point, I think I owe it to Nathan to fill him in. It was one thing when I thought the camera was just lost. This is a hundred times worse. Bradley obviously took it for a reason, and Nathan needs to be prepared for whatever that reason is. I can't let him be blindsided."

"I guess I can't argue with that." Kira is quiet, too. "I'd do the same thing."

We dissolve into silence again, Kira staring up at the clouds and me down at the ground. Slowly, a ladybug makes its way across the blacktop. I almost have to laugh at the irony. So much for them bringing good luck. It feels like I'll never have any of that again, like my trail has led me straight off a cliff with no warning.

I've been there before and prayed I'd never have to experience it again.

Every prayer can't be answered, though.

That's not the way the world works.

We have to take charge of our own lives and create our own luck – or, at the very least, own up to our reality.

I take out my cell, hand trembling a little, but before I can call Nathan, the phone rings.

I don't recognize the number, only the area code. It's local, and for a second, hope spirals up in my chest. Maybe it's someone from the school, calling from a different extension. Maybe I got it all wrong with my conspiracy theory and the camera actually is inside the building.

Without hesitation, I answer. "Hello?"

"Hi. This is … ah … may I speak to Melina Radcliffe, please?"

The voice on the other end of the line is formal, but soft and almost melodic. It's also decidedly Southern.

Bradley.

"This is Melina," I say stiffly, as my heart rate begins its climb.

He clears his throat. "It's Bradley," he says uncomfortably. "We, ah, met last night. At Nathan's rally? In Hershey?"

"Oh yes, Bradley," I say, raising my voice in exaggerated naiveté. Kira's eyes go wide at his name and she scoots a little closer, trying to hear both ends of the conversation. "Yes, I remember you," I continue. "How could I forget? It was so nice of you to help me up. A real white knight, that's what you are." I lay it on thick. If he's going to wreck my life and destroy my dreams, the least I can do is put him in the hot seat for it. "How'd you get my number?" I ask. "Are you calling to check on me? How sweet."

"I remembered your name," Bradley says. "From your badge. I Googled it and – wait, does that sound strange? I'm not a stalker, I swear. I just … ah … " He must take a long breath, because I hear a puff of air as he exhales into the phone. "I *was* actually wondering how you're doing. Is your arm any better today?"

"It's fine."

"Good. That's good. Great, in fact."

"Yep. As it turns out, that wasn't even the worst part of my night." My brain is moving a million miles a minute. What's the best way to approach this? Throw out accusations? Try to guilt him into a confession? Get more information about who he is, then try to take the camera back without him knowing? It suddenly seems like there are too many fish in the sea of possibilities, and I don't know which one to reel in.

"What happened?" Bradley asks.

I guess I'm not the only one feigning oblivion.

I opt for a blunt approach. I've always tackled life head-on, so why should this be an exception? "Something very important was stolen from me," I say, and listen for any sign of a knee-jerk reaction from him. There's nothing, not a sound. "A camera," I push on, "with some irreplaceable photos on it. Nathan was planning to use them in the race. I had the camera since it would've been my job to incorporate the pictures into his campaign material, but after I got home last night, I realized it was gone."

"Oh man," Bradley says. "That's horrible. When was the last time you saw it?"

Is he kidding? He has to be. Except ... he seems rather sincere.

"After Nathan's speech. I absolutely had it then. It must have happened when I fell. There was that big pile of streamers. I assume it slipped out of my pocket and ended up there. You didn't see anything, did you?"

It's a dare, a challenge.

But he doesn't take the bait.

"I'm sorry, no." He sounds genuinely apologetic. "Though, honestly, I was only focused on you. I easily could have missed it. In case you don't know, you're pretty magnetic. You sort of command all the attention in a room."

Okay ... I was not expecting that.

I feel it again, that warm fuzziness, and kind of want to slap myself for it.

Stop, I think. *He's snowing you. Don't fall under his spell. That's what he wants.*

"Thanks," I say brusquely.

He clears his throat for a second time, and I can just make out the sound of birds chirping in the background. "There's another reason I called," he says. "I mean, I *did* want to see how you are, but there's more to it and I felt compelled to tell you personally."

I make a snap decision to plunge in further. "To tell me what?" I question. "That you're the one behind the camera's disappearance?"

"What?" His voice ratchets up into a much higher pitch. "No. I'm not. That's absurd."

"Is it?" I get up from the curb and start pacing alongside it. I've never been very good at staying still. "Do you take me for that big an idiot?" I ask. "You materialized at my side after my fall, gave a cagey answer about why you were there, and said we'd be seeing a lot of each other once I told you I work for Nathan. You already knew I work for him, though, right? You were hiding something the whole time."

His sigh sounds weary. "I was," he concedes.

Part of me feels vindicated.

The other part feels sad.

I didn't realize it until this moment, but I was actually hoping he would somehow turn out to be blameless.

"What was it?" I ask, spinning on my heel and heading in the opposite direction.

"Not what you think."

"Then what?"

"I wasn't there last night because I support Nathan," he says evenly, "which clearly you already figured out. I was there because I work for his opponent. Madelyn Morgan." I suck in my breath. I *knew* it. "But before you jump to conclusions," he continues, "let me assure you that I had nothing to do with that camera's disappearance." His tone slips back down to something more gentle. "You have no reason to believe me, and I understand why you'd single me out as a suspect, but I'm giving you my word that I never even saw the camera, let alone grabbed it. I did take something else from you, though, and for that, I'm so sorry."

What is he talking about?

"I'm not following," I say, sitting back down. "I didn't lose anything else."

"Not physically. But your words. Your ideas. I took those. Nathan's, too. Madelyn asked me to attend his rally for the sole purpose of getting the inside scoop on Nathan's campaign strategies. It caught me off guard at first. I mean, I write her speeches, I don't steal someone else's and amend it to fit her agenda. But she insisted. She knows Nathan will be a tough competitor and she wanted to get a leg up. She thought if she had insider information on what programs he was planning to push, it'd help her win over some of his voters. Battleground state and all."

I feel dizzy, unsteady, like the earth's tilting off its axis.

"I don't ... that speech was already out there in the public," I manage to say.

"Yes." He pauses for a moment before continuing. "But the meeting you all had before the rally wasn't. The one in the office. You left the door open, so I just hid behind it and recorded the entire thing. Please," he practically begs, "you have to believe that I didn't want to. I know a lot of people think anything goes when it comes to politics, but I'm not one of them. I'm a straight shooter."

"Yes," I say shortly. "It sounds like it."

"I deserved that."

"You think?"

"I want to make it right," he tells me. "I swear. Integrity is important to me."

"Mmhmm. That's why you eavesdropped and recorded a private conversation. Am I correct in assuming that you turned over the recording to Madelyn?"

"Yes. But it's been killing me. I hate myself for what I did. That's why I called," he explains. "To give you a heads-up. Madelyn is planning to make homelessness one of her focal points. We know Nathan is passionate about it ... I know *you* are passionate about it since you're the one who kept on discussing it at the meeting ... and I couldn't let her steal your idea for the initiative without warning you." There's something almost helpless in his words, and even as I open my mouth to question him again about the camera – which is a far bigger problem than the recordings – I feel in my gut that he is telling the truth: about his guilt, about his deceit in one area and innocence in the other, about it all.

Which begs the question ... where *is* the camera, then?

Is someone else out to take Nathan down?

6

BRADLEY

$\mathcal{A}$ camera. Huh.

I stare down at my phone after Melina's hung up, then slide my finger across the screen to check the call log. Eight minutes. We only talked for eight minutes, and certainly not about anything even remotely enjoyable. Telling her what I'd done was painful. So why, then, do I want to call her back? Why do I want to hear her voice again? Why do I want to help her find that camera?

I don't actually call.

Instead, I sit there on the grass and think about the way Melina accused me of doing something so underhanded. I'm strangely hurt that she'd assume I was capable of such a thing, but at the same time, I completely get it. In her mind, all the factors added up. Hopefully I managed to convince her otherwise.

"Do me a favor," she said, before disconnecting the call. "If you remember anything more about last night, keep me in the loop. Maybe you saw someone who seemed out of place at the rally? You know, someone other than you." Her tone was snarky, but she didn't sound angry anymore. Is that a good sign?

A good sign for what, exactly? I don't even know.

What I *do* know is that I have a second person to call. I can't avoid Madelyn for any longer. Not when I have a sneaking suspicion that she actually may be behind the camera's disappearance. Just because she didn't ask me to do the job doesn't mean she didn't call upon somebody else. I hate to consider it. For as long as I've known her, Madelyn has been an honorable person. She's played fair and never stooped to the attack tactics that frequently plague politics. It's one of the reasons I was excited to work for her. But now? That same principled woman is starting to test the waters on the other side, and I'm worried they will pull her under. Maybe, hopefully, I can toss her a life preserver before it's too late.

I stand up and head for my SUV. This is a conversation I would rather not have in public. I sit in my car instead, the sun streaming in through the windshield and warming my face. I love spring. It's my favorite season in Pennsylvania. I wasn't really prepared for northern winters, not after growing up in a suburb of Atlanta, and even though I've come to sometimes enjoy the snow, there is still no match for when it all disappears and the world comes alive again.

That's what I want, too. To come alive again. To feel the energy and enthusiasm that have been slipping away as of late.

Maybe this call will help. I hit Madelyn's number on my speed dial and drum my fingers against the steering wheel, waiting for her to answer. She picks up after the third ring. "Bradley," she says. "I'm glad to finally hear from you. Are you feeling any better?"

Right. I asked Kristi to tell her I was under the weather.

"A bit," I say. It's the truth. I do feel better now that Melina knows what happened.

"Good," Madelyn says. "All the same, why don't you take the remainder of the day off? You've been working so hard. You deserve a break."

"That's really nice of you, but ... ah ... " I drag a hand through my hair and bite my lip. How do I say this? How do I essentially accuse my boss – the woman I'm trying to get elected as the governor of Pennsylvania – of a crime? Quickly, I glance down at my pinky ring. Grandfather would do it, and he'd have no qualms. Neither should I. "Listen," I say, "this is probably out of line, but I have to ask. Did you send someone to steal a camera from Nathan Ford?"

"Excuse me?"

I fill her in on what I learned from Melina. "It occurred to me," I explain, "that if you told me to sneak in to the rally, you just as easily could've sent somebody else to grab – "

"Bradley." She cuts me off. "I most certainly didn't ask any of my staff to steal private property. How could you think that?"

Because I never would've thought you'd send your staff to spy on your opponent, either, is what I want to say.

"It's just that you're so intent on winning," is what I do say.

"Not that intent," she replies forcefully, then sighs. "But I suppose it was a natural conclusion to come to, after what I asked you to do. I want you to know I've put the kibosh on the homelessness initiative. When you walked out of our staff meeting earlier ... let's just say I knew why you left, and it got me thinking about the type of candidate I'd like to be. My whole campaign is supposed to be based around the fact that I've never been caught up in the political circles before. I can't do that if I resort to playing dirty." She sighs again. "I want to make this state the very best it can be, and that starts with its leadership. I can't in good conscience run a campaign that compromises my ethics."

Talk about a one-eighty.

I'm surprised, but also not. I knew Madelyn was a good person at heart.

"I'd rather focus on new proposals of my own," she says. "I'll need your help in drafting a killer speech to outline them."

"You've got it."

"Excellent. Thank you. Oh, but Bradley?" she asks. "I'm curious, how did you find out about the camera?"

Shoot.

For some reason I can't quite put my finger on, I don't want to tell her about Melina.

"I heard it through the grapevine," I say quickly. "You know how fast word travels, right?"

"I suppose so."

I don't think she really buys my answer, but her landline phone rings and it thankfully lets me off the hook. I'm beyond relieved. No more worrying. No more stomach tied in knots ... just one that's starved, because I've barely eaten all day. I'd already been planning to go to the grocery store, since my refrigerator's empty. But now, instead of being a way to cheer myself up, it can be a celebration. The market is my playground, my candy shop. The aisles are filled with such possibility. I like to take my time, wandering back and forth to find the ingredients I'm looking for – and also the ones I have no idea I'm looking for until they call out to me.

Cheese. Radicchio. Arugula. Tomatoes for fresh sauce. Oregano. Parsley. Butter. Pasta.

I place the items into my cart, one by one.

By the time I'm finished, it's a full hour later. I smile as I carry the bags out to the SUV and stack them neatly in the back. What to cook tonight? There are so many choices. It has been a long time, over a month, since I had a free night to experiment in the kitchen. I already can't wait to see what this cooking session has in store.

Sometimes they're a disaster. There was the frittata that looked like someone had rolled over it with a truck. The lasagna that was so spicy I needed two glasses of water to wash it down. The lime and parmesan crusted salmon that tasted great, but looked like a child's art project. And sometimes they're a success. Sometimes they come out well on the first try, and sometimes it takes a little bit of tweaking to get it right. I like those meals best. There's something rewarding about it. Knowing I figured out the exact combination of ingredients gives me a rush of satisfaction. It reminds me of all the times I used to help my grandma in the kitchen and see the smile on her face when she finished with a new recipe.

I miss her and Grandfather so much. I wish I still lived around the corner from them. I would've called them tonight. Asked them to come over for dinner and a game of cards. I used to love that as a kid, sitting on Grandfather's lap as he taught me first how to play rummy, then poker. There were so many days when my parents were at the statehouse for work, leaving Jake, Eric, and I to fend for ourselves. But my grandparents stepped in. They helped to raise us when Mom and Dad couldn't – or wouldn't.

I take out my phone to call them on the drive home, but then, as I look at the car full of grocery bags, I get another idea. A ridiculous one. A stupid one. I shouldn't do it. It would be a mistake.

But some mistakes are meant to be made.

Before I can second guess myself, I scroll through my recent call list and redial Melina's number. She answers immediately.

"Bradley? Did you remember something?" She sounds so desperate, I hate to dash her hopes.

"I'm sorry, no."

"Oh." Her voice deflates like a week-old balloon. "Then why are you calling me? I'm confused."

"Well, I was wondering ... "

I glance again at the overflowing grocery bags. Suddenly this feels so foolish.

"What?" she prompts. "You were wondering what?"

Just do it, Bradley. The worst she can say is no. "If you'd like to join me for dinner tonight." The words fall all over themselves as they drop from my mouth. "I've got a trunk full of fresh groceries, and I'm fairly decent in the kitchen, if I do say so myself. I can whip up some spaghetti carbonara, or maybe a homemade pizza, if that's more your taste. Do you like dessert?" A nervous laugh sneaks past my lips. "Who doesn't, right? I can make cream puffs. My grandma taught me how." Even as I speak, I will myself to shut up. I sound like the Energizer Bunny.

"You're inviting me to your house?" she asks. "So you can cook for me? That sounds like a date. Is it?"

"No." I reconsider. "Yes." I reconsider again. "No."

"Well, which one is it?" I can't be certain, but it sort of seems like she's amused.

"No," I clarify. "I'm asking you to dinner as ... as someone who knows what it's like to be on the road half the time and also knows how nice it can be to come back home afterward." I pause. "And maybe even as a friend?"

I know, though, that I already like her as much more than a friend. I did from the moment I first laid eyes on her. I haven't wanted to admit it, especially not to myself, but why bother denying it? I have spent so long, too long, doing what was expected of me. Maybe it's time to listen to myself for a change.

"We're not friends," Melina says. Her lighter side fades away. "We're opponents."

"Technically, that's Madelyn and Nathan. We're only – "

"Opponents," she reiterates. "We're working to achieve goals that totally contradict each other. And am I supposed to simply forget what you did? I value my job, and I'm already going to be in hot water over the camera. I'm certainly not going to add to that by hanging out with one of Madelyn's staffers."

Part of me wants to continue the conversation. To tell her we're much more than our politics.

The other part knows that's not my place.

"Okay," I say. "I respect that. The offer still stands, though. I'll be cooking anyway, and I'd even be glad to help you figure out who really took the camera."

"No, thank you," she says smoothly. Almost too smoothly. "My co-worker's already on the case with me."

"Alright. If you change your mind, here's my address." I rattle it off.

"I live in Philly," she tells me, "and am headed there shortly. Staying for dinner would mean I'd have to drive back late, and I already did that yesterday. I have no desire to do it again today."

"Who are you trying to convince? Me, or yourself?"

The questions are out of my mouth before I can stop them. It surprises me. I'm not typically so gutsy. All those times when I should've been, when everything inside me yearned to speak up, I did the opposite and stayed quiet. I never really felt like I was able to step out of the shadows everyone cast on me. But this is different somehow.

"You," Melina answers quickly. "I'd better get going. Thanks for the invite. Have a good dinner, and – "

"Wait!" I suddenly remember something important. "I forgot to tell you: Madelyn had a change of heart. She's not using Nathan's platform anymore. We had a long talk about it, and she told me she wants to win fairly."

"Since when?"

"Since always. She just had a moment of weakness, that's all."

"I don't know. I'm still not convinced she's not the mastermind behind the whole camera thing. Clearly she has a motive."

"I asked her," I say. "Flat-out. She denied any involvement."

"Well, of course she would," Melina says. "But thank you for asking. I appreciate it." Her voice is softer now.

Something about it strikes me, even after I've hung up and driven home. I carry the groceries to the kitchen and set them down on the granite countertop. What to make? The spaghetti dish I told Melina about sounds good. It's been awhile since I had Italian. I change out of my work clothes and into jeans and a t-shirt, then pull up a recipe on my phone and get to work. Pasta. Olive oil. Bacon. Garlic. Rosemary. Parsley. Eggs. Parmesan cheese. As I add the different ingredients, listening to a baseball game on the radio while I work, I can't help wishing that Melina had agreed to join me. I'd have enjoyed having some company for a change. Frustrating as it sometimes was to grow up as the youngest of the Williams brothers, I'll say this: our house was never quiet. Between Jake's drum set – he was a prodigy at them, of course – and Eric always practicing speeches for debate club, I could barely hear myself think.

Tonight, I can hear myself think all too well.

And I don't like it.

So, after the spaghetti is done and I've toasted garlic bread to accompany it, I pick up the phone and call my grandparents. They've always helped to fill the void.

"Grandma, hi," I say, when she answers.

"Bradley!" she exclaims. "How are you? I'm so happy to hear your voice."

"Same here. It's been a long day," I say, twirling a forkful of spaghetti.

"I thought you would be celebrating. I heard about Madelyn's victory. You must be thrilled."

"I am. It's just ... "

What? What is it? I'm not sure.

"It's just a lot," Grandma says. "All the running around,

meeting with the voters. I'll tell you the same thing I've told your parents and brothers: I don't know how you have the stamina for all that. It makes me so very proud to think of y'all out there, changing the world, but goodness, I don't think I could do it."

"You *do* do it, Grandma. Every day. Every time you tutor a kid in Hebrew. Every time you visit a school and talk about the Holocaust." A chill snakes down my spine, and I have to stop eating. Each time I say that word, it robs me of my breath. My grandparents have always been very open about how they met. Countless times, I have heard the story of how he liberated her from a concentration camp, how he took her under his wing afterward when she had no place to go and found her a safe place until the horror was over. It never ceases to stop me in my tracks. My grandma went through hell and she lived to tell about it, thanks to Grandfather.

"There is a reason for everything," he told me once. "A 'why.' I thought my life was over when I got drafted to fight in the war. It was the worst thing I've ever experienced, but it gave me my Adi. I found my soulmate, and that's when my life really started."

Their love story is a blessing. A miracle. A mitzvah. An inspiration.

I hope to have a love like that one day.

But for now? Now it's a plate of spaghetti, a piece of bread, and a glass of soda that I drink as I look out the window and listen to Grandma talk about how warm it's already getting in Georgia. "I was in the garden for only an hour today," she says, "before I had to go inside and make a pitcher of sweet tea to cool myself off."

"You take it easy, okay?" I say. "Be careful in the heat."

"Sweet Bradley." I can almost hear her smile. "Always looking out for his grandma."

"Like you've always looked out for me."

Just then, the doorbell rings.

It startles me. I'm not expecting anyone.

I toss my napkin onto the table, stand up, and head over to the door, the phone still in my hand. Maybe it's Cam, needing help with the kids? Or one of the guys from the intramural baseball team I play on once a week when I'm home?

No.

It's none of those people.

When I peer through the peephole, it's Melina I see.

7

Melina

The plan was to go home to Philly. After I finished talking with the janitorial staff who worked at Nathan's rally, I got into my car and starting heading east. I was weary and tired, and I couldn't wait to fall into my apartment and lose myself in a good book or a painting canvas. Before I got onto the turnpike, though, I had a change of heart and typed Bradley's address in my GPS. Now the question is ... why? It wasn't only because I thought he may remember something else about who could have Nathan's camera. No, there was more to it than that.

What, though?

Why?

"It's only three letters, but it's still the biggest word in the English language," my mom said once, a couple of months after my dad was let go from his job as an x-ray tech at a local hospital. He took it really hard, and not just because it meant our family had to live without his paychecks to support us. I still remember how he'd put on a brave face all day, reassuring everyone that it would be okay, even as he constantly applied for new jobs and rarely got so much as a call back. At night, though, it was a different story. I'd hear him sometimes, after all of us kids were supposed to be asleep. He'd talk to Mom in the kitchen, or he'd pace back and forth in the rec room, or he'd slip outside into the inky night and not come home for hours.

"Daddy's sad," I said to Mom at one of those times. I'd crept downstairs after hearing the front door shut and found her on the couch, a tissue clenched in her hand and tears pooled in her eyes. "I don't understand. He's a good worker. How come they took his job away?"

My mom dabbed her eyes, pulling herself together for my sake. She was constantly doing that, trying to stay strong for the rest of us. We all needed her – Gabrielle, Lara, Dylan, me, and Dad, too. "He *is* sad," she told me, winding an arm around my shoulders and pulling me close. "So am I. Bad things happen to good people sometimes. Life isn't always fair."

"Why?"

"Your father's been asking that a lot, too," she said. "I wish I could give you both an answer, but I can't. Sometimes there is no reason. Sometimes the world just gives us lemons, and do you know what we have to do?"

"Make lemonade?" I volunteered.

"Exactly."

She went on to talk about 'why' being a long word and about how it didn't do anybody any good to stress over things that were out of their control. Even while she said it, though, her voice cracked and she had to act as the gatekeeper to her tears, swatting them away before they got loose again. I felt bad for her. I felt bad for our whole family, and I vowed then to do everything in my power to make it better.

Twenty years later, I'm still doing that.

Or, at least, I was.

I'm not sure how standing on Bradley's front stoop helps the cause.

His face breaks into a grin as he opens the door, his cell phone in hand. "Melina," he says. "This is a surprise. I thought you couldn't make it?"

"So did I."

He gestures behind him. "Please, come in."

I hesitate. Driving here, ringing his bell, that was one thing. If I actually go inside, that's another entirely. A home is supposed to be a sanctuary, the place to go for comfort and security and peace.

It shows the heart and soul of the person, or people, living there. I don't know that I'm ready to see into Bradley's world like that. I glance past him into the entryway. There's a large photo hanging on the wall, a shot of a park at nighttime with what appears to be the Olympic rings all lit up in colored water, but that's it. Maybe he just moved in, or maybe he feels the same as I do, that the open road is home. It's freer there, less constricting and more inspiring. You don't have to worry about the so-called sanctuary fading before your eyes, nor do you have to be afraid of putting down roots, only to have them snatched up and out.

I wonder if Bradley agrees.

I should leave. I should march myself right back to my car. But I don't. Instead of taking a step backward, I take one forward. Then I take another, and another, until I am sitting at Bradley's dining room table. He sets his phone down – he'd been talking to his grandmother before I arrived, he says – and serves me a plate of steaming spaghetti. His is still sitting, partially eaten, on the cherry wood table.

"What can I get you to drink?" he asks, after he's refilled the bread basket. "I have soda, water, grapefruit juice … " He purses his lips, and it makes his eyebrows pinch together. "There's beer, but you don't seem like a beer person. I might have a bottle of wine … "

"Water is fine." I let myself smile. "I have to drive, after all."

His cheeks flush the color of a stop sign. "Right. Of course. I knew that. It's not like I expected you to stay the night. Obviously. We barely know each other. Not that I wouldn't love to know you better. I … " He shoves his hands into the pockets of his jeans and clears his throat. "Let me try this again," he says. "Without inserting my foot into my mouth this time." He rocks on his heels a little. "I'm glad you're here," he tells me. "And I'll be happy to get you water." He fills up a glass and joins me at the table.

I take a bite of spaghetti, and bursts of flavor instantly pop against my tongue. Bradley was right – he *is* decent in the kitchen. He is better than decent. "It's delicious," I say. "Where did you learn to cook like this?"

There it is again, the smile that puts a twinkle into his eyes. "My grandma," he says. "She spent hours teaching me when I was a kid. My brothers were never interested in cooking – they were too busy conquering the world – so it was just the two of us. Every now and then my grandfather would sneak in and sample what we were making."

"That sounds like fun."

"It was." He sips his soda. "I used to beg my grandma to open a restaurant. She'd have been so good at it. But I could never convince her."

"How about you? Did you ever consider going that route instead of politics?"

It's an innocent question, a curious one, but I guess he reads something more into it because his mouth flattens into a straight line. "No," he says. "I'm sure I would've loved that, but the plan was always politics." He shakes his head slightly, and the fog lifts. "How about you? What made you go down this road?"

I'm not telling him the answer to that. I don't tell *anyone* the answer to that.

"I think I've always been intrigued by politics," I say instead. "Even as a kid, I'd pretend to be the President. My family still teases me about that. If I had to pinpoint it ... " I trail off and do the best impression I can of having to think about the memories. "It was probably sixth grade," I tell Bradley. "We learned about the government in my social studies class, and I was hooked." That is technically true. We did have a whole unit on the government in Mr. Penza's class. My interest in politics had already blossomed by that point, though.

It was when my family lost everything that I became determined to protect other families from a similar fate. I wanted to save them, and I wanted to save the world. It was farsighted and naïve, the sort of picture only a child's eyes can paint, but I didn't care. I still don't. I'm not as idealistic these days, but I do genuinely believe in the power of making a difference.

I will *always* believe in that.

I look across the table at Bradley. I don't know what this pull is that I feel toward him, but it has to stop. This is too huge of a risk for my career and for my plans … and maybe even for my heart. I must put an end to this before it's too late. I push back my chair and jump up. "I'm sorry," I say. "I know I just got here, but I have to go."

"What?" He blinks, confused. "Already? Was it something I said?"

"No. This was just a mistake," I tell him. "You and I travel in different circles, and I think it's best that they don't converge. It's like I said before: we're on completely opposite sides of the spectrum. You stay on yours, I'll stay on mine, and we won't have a problem." I take off through his house and he follows behind. "Thank you for dinner," I say as I reach the door. "You really are a fabulous cook. It seems like you were born to do it." I pull open the door for myself before he can put his Southern charm to use.

But … there's something sad in his eyes when I turn to say goodbye. "Thank you," he says softly. "Are you sure I can't convince you to stay for dessert?"

"I don't think it would be a good idea." I step out into the evening air. There's a mist hanging in it, the promise of a sweet springtime rain. "Bye, Bradley."

"Bye, Melina."

I take one last look at him and am irritated at the way my pulse picks up accordingly. Why can't my heart get in line with my head? It's all the more reason to hightail it out of here. I hurry past the cherry tree, the birdfeeder, and Bradley's car, which is parked beside mine. I hurry past all of it, past this night … past what could have been the greatest choice of all, but what also could have been the worst.

* * *

Four days.

When I wake up the next morning, I make a decision and set a deadline. There are four days left until I'm due back at work. I'll use them to try to track down the camera on my own, to fix this mess like I've fixed so many others before, and if it doesn't pan out, then I will come clean to Nathan first thing Monday morning. I'll admit that the situation is out of my hands, much as it'll kill me to do so, and I'll offer to resign so he won't have to fire me. That feels reasonable. With Bradley insisting he had nothing to do with the disappearance, I can't even be positive now that the camera *was* stolen. Maybe there's some other explanation.

Four days.

Then three days. Then two.

Finally, one.

I spend hours on the phone with Kira on Sunday morning, dissecting every single possibility, but once again we come up empty. No one outside of our team was there when Nathan handed me the camera. No one went out of their way to interact with me that night except Bradley. No one acted suspiciously. But if the camera wasn't taken, then where is it? I have searched everywhere. By the time Kira and I hang up, I'm beginning to think I'll never know what happened.

"It's awful," I tell Gabrielle that evening. Of all my siblings, I'm the closest to her. I don't know if it's because she's nearest to me in age or because she was the only other one who was old enough to understand when everything fell apart all those years ago, but whatever it is, we have the kind of relationship where we can often read each other's mind. Even now, when she's living in Manhattan and working as a museum curator, our bond has stayed every bit as strong. Hearing her voice over the phone is just about the only thing that helps me feel better ... or, at least, helps me to not feel so damn lousy.

"It certainly sounds awful," she agrees. "But the sister I know would never admit defeat. She'd keep on fighting until there was no fight left in her."

"I am. It's just that I don't know who to trust." An image of Bradley comes to mind, not for the first time, since I left his house and didn't look back. "Take this Bradley guy, for example. He works for Madelyn, and told me she was adamant about getting inside information on Nathan's campaign. He admitted to being the one to secure that information, for God's sake. So how do I know whether he was telling the truth when he insisted he has nothing to do with this?" A light bulb suddenly goes off in my head, and its flash is both blinding and illuminating. "Oh my God."

"What?"

I ball my hand into a fist. "He invited me to his house the other night," I tell her, "and I thought it was weird. We'd only met once, briefly, and I spent a good portion of our phone call earlier in the day accusing him of theft. So what would compel him to open his home to me?"

Instantly, she knows where I'm going. "You think it was a set-up?"

"I think I'm an idiot," I groan. "He pulled the same act as after the rally, playing all innocent and sweet. How could I fall for it again? How could I walk into his house – into his trap – and not realize it?"

"But ... why?" Gabrielle asks. "What purpose would it serve him? If he really is the culprit, what does he have to gain by inviting you over? It seems like it'd be a risk to have you in his home, where you could find out he'd been lying."

"A clever risk," I say. "He's basically hiding in plain sight. Maybe it was a bunch of bullshit when he said Madelyn was getting back to the straight and narrow. He could've just wanted to pump me for more information."

"Or maybe he likes you," she offers. "Why does there have to be something deceitful about it?"

Because it'd be so much easier that way.

Then I wouldn't have to keep thinking about the peach-shaped magnet on his refrigerator door, or the Cause for Paws bumper sticker on his SUV, or the framed picture of him and his grandparents in his living room. I could be angry at him instead of intrigued by him.

"It just makes sense," I say. "It's the most logical explanation."

"I don't know. I think you *want* it to be him, but that doesn't necessarily mean it is."

I sigh. "Well, whatever. It's not like it matters anyway. After tomorrow, the ball won't be in my court anymore. I'm passing it to Nathan." I shift the phone to my other ear. "I was actually going to tell him days ago, but Bradley called and interrupted. It broke my momentum, I suppose, and made me lose the courage."

"That's not like you," she says. "Since when do you let anything stop you?"

She's right. Losing my courage has never been a problem.

But now … now I'm about to lose even more, I can feel it.

It weighs heavy on my mind all night long, a ticking time bomb in my brain and my heart.

Tick tock. You lost the camera.

Tick tock. You should've told Nathan immediately.

Tick tock. You let your own fear overshadow his right to know.

Tick tock. You won't accomplish everything you want to, not now.

Tick tock. You failed. You're a failure.

I curl up on the couch, sinking into its soft chenille and clutching one of the teal throw pillows to my chest. This sofa was my first purchase after signing the lease on my apartment. I was so excited. Having furniture that wasn't tattered, that wasn't pulling apart at its seams with its stuffing peeking out, was a big deal. I sat on the sofa for hours that first night, relishing it, then I rummaged through all of my unpacked boxes until I found my easel, and painted until the sun rose. I didn't have any curtains yet, and even now, two years later, I still remember how it looked to see the sky brighten into these breathtaking shades of orange and pink and yellow. It was a watercolor set on fire. I could feel its power, feel its strokes reaching out and caressing me. The sun's rays shone through the windows and warmed my skin. They warmed my soul and set it ablaze.

It was a new beginning.

Tonight, as I drag the same easel out of my closet, it's the opposite.

My brushstrokes are short instead of long, intuitive instead of deliberate.

Just like that first night, I paint until the stars dim and the blanket over the earth slowly lightens into pastels. My palette is filled with splatters in every shade of the rainbow. I don't bother to wash my brushes between colors. It's better to combine them. Life is messy and so is art. Sometimes we have to break the rules, go outside the lines, to create what's beautiful.

I step back to survey the canvas in front of me.

It's no longer blank.

It's certainly not beautiful.

But it *has* given me what I needed most: courage.

8

BRADLEY

It seems like you were born to do it.

Try as I might, I can't shake Melina's words. They follow me around for the rest of the week and straight into the weekend. Does she really think cooking is my calling? Or was it a clever attempt at getting in my head? Maybe she thought it'd take my attention away from the election and divert it elsewhere. She doesn't seem like a manipulative person, but I don't know her well enough to make that judgment. I wonder if that's the reason she had a change of heart and showed up at my house. Perhaps she was so annoyed about my undercover work for Madelyn that she decided to engage in some of her own. It'd explain her hasty retreat, if she had sudden misgivings.

Women are confusing.

Life is confusing.

Unless, of course, you're one of my brothers. Then life is a cakewalk.

"It took me months to pick a ring," Jake, my oldest brother, says on Monday morning. "It had to be perfect – big, but not huge, and elegant, but not flashy." Apparently he's about to propose to his girlfriend Gwyn. It's the first I've heard about it, and as I sit at the table, eating a stack of pancakes, I start to regret answering the phone.

"I'm sure you chose something great," I say.

"I hope she agrees. I want her to have the diamond she deserves." Cars honk in the background as he talks. Jake lives in Washington, DC and works for the State Department, so his world is always filled with hustle and bustle.

"Well, congratulations," I say. "I'm really happy for you guys."

I am.

My brothers often make me feel like a child playing dress-up in a life that doesn't quite fit, but I love them despite it. It's not their fault that it always feels like I'm chasing them, trying to keep up – or at least to catch up. I can't blame them for being smart. Driven. Successful. Perfect. I also can't blame them for the fact that I'm *not* perfect.

"So how are you planning to pop the question?" I ask.

"I'm taking her on a cruise around the Tidal Basin on Friday," he says. "My plan was to do it last month, when the cherry blossoms were at their peak, but the ring wasn't ready in time. I ended up having it custom-made."

Of course he did.

I wouldn't expect anything else.

"Do Mom and Dad know?" I ask. "They must be thrilled."

"They do, and they are. You should hear Mom, already going on about caterers and venues and bands. I keep telling her that Gwyn will want to be hands-on with the planning, but you know Mom. Once she gets rolling on something, it's hard to stop her."

It's more than hard. It's impossible.

I glance down at my pinstriped shirt and matching tie. All dressed for work.

I'm proof of Mom's persistence.

Of Dad's insistence.

Again, it makes me think of Melina's words.

Are we ever really born to do something, or do we discover our passions as we go along? Do we nurture them or do they nurture us? Maybe it's both. All I know for certain is that, for my brothers and me, what we were meant to do was decided even *before* we were born. Jake and Eric are okay with that. Sometimes I am. Sometimes I'm not.

As I sit in the conference room with Madelyn and Hannah an hour later, brainstorming ideas for Madelyn's first speech post-primary, it's the former. The political life might have chosen me instead of the other way around, but it's at times like this that I'm grateful for it. This is my favorite part of the process – standing at a white board, scrawling down ideas, figuring out how all the pieces come together to form a full puzzle.

"Hmm." I take a step back to survey the board. "I think we should nix the section on taxes."

"Really?" Hannah flips her dark hair over her shoulder as she looks at me.

"Really. Obviously it's an important issue, but this speech needs to be the kind that gets people cheering. Applauding. Believing. That was my biggest takeaway from Nathan's rally. He's such an enthusiastic speaker. The energy in the room was palpable. That's what we need. We need people to feel inspired."

"Especially since Perry's inching a bit closer to the ballot," Madelyn says. "Last I heard, he was a third of the way to the number of signatures he needs to be listed as a candidate. We can't let him split the vote. So ... what do you suggest to make me stand out?"

I cross my arms and let my gaze roam over the white board.

Job growth. Tax reform. Homeland security. Welfare. Environmental protection.

"You tell me," I say to Madelyn. "Pretend you're taking a speech class in college and you have to pick a topic for your first assignment. It's the one that'll set the tone for the entire semester, so it's important to choose wisely. What fires you up most? What earns you an A?"

She doesn't hesitate. "Environmental protection. Most people don't know this about me, but I actually grew up on a farm," she says, and my eyebrows skyrocket, because I'm one of those people. "My family still owns the land," she continues. "I don't get back to visit often, but I do love it. There is nothing like standing in the middle of a field and seeing acres of green stretch out around you. It's good for the soul. Of course I'd want to protect that."

Hannah is tapping feverishly at her tablet screen. "Do you think we can connect that to another issue or two?" she asks me. "Maybe even three? We'd be golden."

"Sure," I say. It takes awhile – lots of lines drawn and erased on the board – but we pull it off.

"We can write a great speech about this," Hannah says.

"And I bet we can get the press on board," I say. I turn to look at Madelyn. "What do you think about visiting the farm and letting them tag along? We could probably get a few feature stories out of it. If we stay on the property itself, Kristi won't even have to arrange travel accommodations for the reporters."

She smiles. "I think that's a fantastic idea," she tells me.

"Then I'll make it happen." I smile, too. Sometimes, in little pockets of time, I worry that politics will lead me to a dead end. But not now. Now I'm ready to forge a new trail.

Maybe Melina was wrong and my parents were right.

Maybe this really *is* what I was born to do.

* * *

After a day full of writing, editing, and writing some more, I'm wiped out by the time I get to the pet store down the street from my townhouse. Cause for Paws is hosting an outreach event where people can learn about proper rabbit care, fill out adoption applications, and even meet a bunny or two. Most of the time, we don't bring rabbits to events like this – as prey animals, many of them get spooked really easily – but this is a quaint mom-and-pop shop that doesn't allow people to bring in their animals when they come to browse the aisles, so we're comfortable having a few of our most outgoing bunnies join us.

I stifle a yawn as I walk through the door. As tired as I am, I volunteered a long time ago to do this with Callie and I don't want to bail on her. "Are things any better at work this week?" she asks, as I start transferring the clipboards from a cardboard box to our table.

"Yes. A lot better, thankfully. The speech for Madelyn's next rally is half finished, and we have a game plan for how to structure this portion of her campaign. It's gonna be pretty different. Instead of concentrating on Madelyn the politician, we'll highlight Madelyn the person."

"Smart move," she says, taking out our portfolio and opening it on the table. It has profiles for some of our adoptable bunnies splashed across its pages, so people can see the possibilities. "You know," Callie muses, "It's kind of like what we do here. Focus on what makes every rabbit unique." She bends down to pick up Sprinkle from her carrier, but before she can settle her into the exercise pen, the little black and white Dutch cuddles comfortably into in her arms.

"I know what makes you unique," I say, stroking the bunny's nose. "You like to pick up your hay twists and race around with them in your mouth, like a puppy holding a stick." I remember laughing out loud the first time I saw it. I had no clue bunnies did things like that. I never had a pet growing up – Jake, Eric, and I used to beg for one, but our parents would always veto it because they said we were too busy to give an animal the life it deserved – and so I really had nothing to go by. I wrongly assumed that rabbits were content to stay in a cage. That can't be further from the truth. They love to run free. To explore and discover and leap.

Some people could learn a lot from them, me included.

I can't quite seem to figure out what makes me leap. All weekend, I kept messing around in the kitchen. I tried three new recipes, I baked a batch of cherry chocolate brownies for Cameron's kids, and I whipped up a pot of Grandma's chicken soup. I did something else, too. Late last night, after I should have been asleep, I sank into Grandfather's leather chair and opened my laptop. I'd already bookmarked the page. The application. I clicked on it and stared at the words for a long time. I've read them so often that I probably have them memorized at this point. But I'd never taken the next step. I'd never let those words out from behind the screen. Until yesterday. All it took was a quick tap of the mouse, and it was done. The culinary school application was printed. I held it in my hand afterward and thought about what Melina had said. Then I tucked it safely inside my desk drawer.

It's a start. We'll see if there's a continuation.

Not tonight, though. Tonight is all about the rescue.

Over the next two hours, Callie and I talk to a bunch of people. A college student who tells us she saved her rabbit after someone dumped it on the side of the road, then asks if she can sign up to volunteer with us. A couple who falls in love with Violet, the other bunny Callie brought to the event, and fills out an application on the spot. We don't do same day adoptions – a team of people reviews the applications first – but they're so excited they say they want to "hop to it and get a jump start on things."

My favorite moment of the evening, though, is when a young girl, probably around eight or nine years old, sits down cross-legged in front of the exercise pen to greet Sprinkle. "She's so sweet," she whispers, then cranes her neck to look up at the woman standing next to her. "Please, Mom? Pretty please?"

The woman smiles first at her daughter, then at me. "I used to have bunnies when I was in high school," she says. "A pair named Ashley and Bandolino. I adored them. It'd be nice to have one again." She picks up a clipboard with an application. "What's your adoption fee?"

"Ninety for one. Ninety-five for a pair. And every rabbit we adopt out is fixed and vaccinated."

I explain the adoption process to them and promise Callie will be in touch as soon as the team has had a chance to review their application. The girl's excitement is priceless. The dimpled smile. The sparkling eyes. The voice that goes high-pitched as she says she knows that she and the bunny will become best friends.

I wonder how life would have been different if I'd had a furry best friend.

If only my parents had said yes when my brothers and I pleaded.

Maybe the three of us would have bonded over taking care of our pet.

Maybe it would have been something we did together, as equals.

Or maybe the responsibility would have fallen solely on me, because let's face it, Mom and Dad were right. We were busy. They spent their days working for the state legislature. My brothers and I spent ours in school and running around to a million extracurriculars. I'd gladly have stopped some of them, though. I'd have dropped playing the saxophone, or taking soccer lessons, or being part of my school's Star Readers club. I'd even have given up on my Little League team, despite how much I loved it. But the decision was made for me, just like so many others.

I think about that as I get home and shuffle through the door.

I also think about something else: Melina.

I'm sitting down at the table, dinner plate in one hand and crossword puzzle in the other, when she comes to mind. When she was here last week, she mentioned that today would be her first day back to work since the camera disappeared. I hope Nathan was understanding. I would hate for her to lose her job, even though that'd probably be best for Madelyn since Melina's such an asset.

I could call her. Ask if everything's okay. Tell her I've been thinking about her.

Not that she would answer. She made it clear that she wants nothing to do with me. But why? I don't buy that it's only because of work. I mean, obviously that plays a big role, but I saw the look she gave me before practically running down the front path. She seemed scared of something, and torn. Like she wanted to stay, but needed to go.

"Don't," I say out loud. "Don't do it."

I pick up my fork. Eat my chicken and mashed potatoes. Fill in the crossword puzzle.

27A: Troops landed here on D-Day.

Normandy.

I've heard Grandfather talk about it so much. He wasn't part of that invasion, but he had friends who lost their lives on that beach. All this time later, it still chokes him up to say their names. "But I must," he says. "We must. We must talk about what happened, and remember that freedom isn't free. Keeping their names alive means we'll never forget."

Maybe I should've told Melina about him. How he's a man of honor and courage. How I strive, every day, to follow in his footsteps and make him proud. Because those are shoes I want to fill. It's a legacy I'm proud to carry on, even in a different way. I might not be fighting battles overseas, but I can wage them here at home. I can help to make life better for people, just like my grandfather did. I can be what he calls an everyday hero.

I don't want to lose that part of myself, no matter what.

I think again of the culinary school application.

Then I pick up the phone. So what if it'll go to voicemail?

She'll probably never call me back, but that's okay. At least she'll know I care.

I care a whole lot.

9

Melina

There's a pit in my stomach as I walk into work on Monday morning and am greeted, first thing, by Nathan's wall of letters. Normally, it's my favorite part of our office. The whole thing began nine months ago, when a woman from Scranton wrote to tell him she'd been at a campaign stop and was inspired by his comments on education reform. She wanted to thank him for, as she phrased it, "the step forward in the right direction."

"See this?" Nathan asked, passing her letter around at our next staff meeting. "This is why I get up every morning with a fire inside me. This is why I hired all of you, because you have those flames inside you, too. This is why we do what we do." He tacked the note up on a whim and then started to add others. Piece by piece, the wall has grown to include all kinds of correspondence. There's an email from a city bus driver in Philadelphia, a letter from a seventh grader in Malvern, a card from a retired nurse in Pittsburgh. The wall is half full now, and Nathan's determined to have it all covered by the November election.

Knowing I might not be on staff anymore to see that makes the pit in my stomach deepen.

I don't want to leave before the wall is complete.

I don't want to leave at all.

I take a long breath, letting the air flood my lungs, and force myself over to Nathan's office door. It's open, and as I approach, he looks up from the newspaper clippings spread over his desk. "You're here early," he says. "No backup on the turnpike this morning?"

Everyone told me to move when I accepted the job offer from Nathan. Why keep my apartment in Philly when I could rent a place much closer? Commuting that distance was ridiculous, and I knew it, but the thought of having to start over again was incredibly unappealing. My apartment may not feel like home, but at least I can count on it being there. Life is bursting with so many uncertainties already. Why add another to the mix? Plus, I genuinely love being on the road. The world seems so much bigger, so much brighter, when I'm traveling from city to city, the windows down and the wind ruffling my hair. It feeds the hunger inside me.

So I stayed.

"Nope, no backup," I tell Nathan, settling into a chair in front of his desk. "I suppose miracles *do* happen." I aim for a light, airy tone, but it falls flat and he notices.

"Is everything okay?" he asks.

Tick tock. Tick tock, tick tock. Tick tock, tick tock, tick tock.

The clock runs out and the time bomb explodes.

I think of last night's painting, the splashes of color tossed across the canvas in bold, daring lines. I also think of my first painting from nineteen years ago, the hesitant strokes I made with a quivering hand while sitting in the corner of a homeless shelter. I was as close as possible to the intersection of the walls, wishing desperately that I could disappear into their folds. My parents were at a table nearby, Mom coloring with Dylan and Dad playing a board game with Gabrielle and Lara. No matter how many times they asked me to join them, I refused to move from my corner or relinquish all my paintbrushes. I was frozen in place, rainbow-colored splatters on my clothes and a black hole in my heart. Knowing that I hadn't been able to help my family, at least not enough, seemed paralyzing. A whole year of taking care of my younger siblings so Mom and Dad could try to pay the bills, of saying no to get-togethers with Amie and my other friends and dropping out of afterschool clubs so I could hurry home and do my part, felt like it'd been for nothing. Our money still ran out. Our house was still taken. I cried that day, sitting in the corner and holding onto the paintbrush like it was a lifeline. I cried until it made my eyes red and my cheeks chapped.

I still have that painting. It's framed now, and hangs in my bedroom as a reminder of where I've been and where I don't want to go ever again. There will be no more helplessness, no more inertia, no more tears.

Nineteen years, one month, and four days. That was the last time I cried.

Ticktockticktockticktockticktockticktock.

I take another deep breath and summon up every reserve of courage.

"No," I tell Nathan. "Everything isn't okay." Once the gate's open, the words pour out, fast and furious. I can hear how desperate I sound as I try to explain, but I can't seem to stop myself. It feels like the longer I keep talking, the more of a chance I'll have to convince him not to fire me. So much for the plan to resign. In the moment, I just can't do it.

When my waterfall of words finally runs dry, Nathan struggles to turn his on.

"I ... this is ... " he sputters.

"I'm sorry," I say again. "I am so, so sorry."

He rubs his temples with his thumb and forefinger. "Why did you wait nearly a week to tell me? If I'd have known from the start, maybe I could've done something."

I hang my head. "I know." My mouth is so dry, it feels like there's sawdust coating it. "At first, I just thought it was lost, and I didn't want to upset you unnecessarily, especially if there was another copy of the pictures. That's why I called to ask you about it. The whole pamphlet thing was a cover. But then I searched high and low, and the camera was nowhere. And I guess ... I was afraid." I force myself to look him in the eyes. "I was hoping that if I found the camera and returned it, then maybe you wouldn't have to fire me. Obviously that didn't happen." I begin to unclip my ID badge, but he holds up a hand.

"Nobody's getting fired."

What?

The springs around my heart uncoil ever-so-slightly.

"You're one of my best employees," he says, with a smile that's far too kind, given the situation. "I know there was no malicious intent on your part. Maybe you made some decisions that were too near-sighted, but I'm not going to punish you for somebody else's crime. I'd rather focus on finding the person who's actually behind it."

I am gobsmacked.

"For real?" I ask.

"For real."

"I ... I don't know what to say. Thank you. Thank you so, so much."

I'm sort of in a daze. The whole drive into work today, I was mentally preparing myself, trying to figure out what would come next and how I could pick myself up from such a sudden fall. So to hear this, to know that Nathan is standing by me when I've given him a damn good reason not to, is more than a bit overwhelming.

"Thank you," I say for a third time. Even three hundred times wouldn't be enough. "I promise, I won't let you down again. I'll make this second chance worth it."

"I'm counting on that."

Me, too. I'm counting on it, too.

* * *

It's dark outside by the time I get back to Philadelphia that night, the moon shrouded in a fog of hazy clouds and the temperature cool enough that I have to slip on a denim jacket before going for a walk to the pizza place down the street. I put in my order for a vegetable stromboli and huddle into the front corner table, gazing out the window as I take an eager first bite. The taste explodes in my mouth: cheese, spinach, tomato, and parsley. It's comfort food at its finest. I eat slowly and people-watch at the same time. Some people hurry along the sidewalk outside, in a rush to get somewhere or maybe to get nowhere. Others take their time, like the couple holding hands and the man with a bushy white mustache. All of these people, streaming forward like the sea.

Some are the big waves, the strong ones, that announce their presence without even trying.

Others are the ripples that pool around your legs, quiet and calm.

Most people who know me would say I fit into the first category. That's where I always try to fit, at least, because the quiet ones get lost in the shuffle and left behind. I refuse to let that happen to me. Sometimes it's nice to take a step back, though, to deliberately put myself on the outskirts and observe. It always makes me think: who are these people, and what are their stories? What do they want? What do they need?

Those are two very different things.

Philly is a diverse slice of life. Spend an hour in Center City and you'll stumble upon people with nothing and others with everything. Nathan often lets me take the lead on campaign events here in the city, and it's a unique kind of challenge, trying to cater to everyone. Sometimes it means visiting soup kitchens and food banks. Other times it means planning fancy fundraisers in Chestnut Hill and Rittenhouse Square. "Speaking of which," I say, slipping out a pen and pad of paper from my purse, "I have to get on that."

"Do you always talk to yourself?"

The voice comes from beside me and startles me to the point of dropping my pen. It clatters to the floor, and I bend to pick it up, but the man standing next to me beats me to it.

"Thanks," I say, as he hands it over.

"No problem." He grins broadly, showing a row of perfectly white teeth. "You didn't answer my question. Do you always talk to yourself?" Without asking, he slides into the seat across from me. I feel every hair on the back of my neck stand up, and not in a good way.

"No," I say tightly. "Only if I'm working." I'm hoping that'll get him to back off, but evidently he can't – or maybe he doesn't want to – take a hint. "That's what I'm doing right now," I add. "I have a lot to get done tonight, so if you don't mind – "

"Care to add me to the list?"

At first I think he's talking about the guest list for next month's fundraiser, which I had started to compile on the pad of paper earlier in the day. Then, as I allow myself a lightning-fast glance at him and see the way he's leering at me, I realize he's thinking about something else entirely. "No," I say. This time my voice is cold, curt. "In fact, if you could find another table, that would be great."

"Why would I wanna do that when I'm enjoying the view right here?"

My stomach lurches.

"Let me rephrase that. Leave. Immediately."

"I'm hurt." He gives an exaggerated frown, but still stays put.

"And I'm serious." I steal a sideways look at the front counter to see if anybody is watching, but the employees are busy with customers – and besides, it doesn't actually look like there's anything going on here. This man, whoever the hell he is, is talking quietly enough that no one would realize something is amiss. "I'm not interested," I say. "I already have a boyfriend."

Normally I'm not a liar, but right now, I just want this guy to go away.

"I don't think I believe you," he says.

"I don't care what you believe," I shoot back.

At that moment, like an answered prayer, my phone rings.

Bradley.

I grab it up, jab the green button with my thumb, and let my intuition win out over my common sense. "Hi honey!" I exclaim, in the most syrupy sweet tone I can muster. "Wow, your ears must be burning. I was just talking about you."

"Er ... what?"

"I figured I'd have a quick dinner out since you're stuck working late. Are you almost finished? I miss you."

I think the plan's working. The man's retreating, leaning away from me instead of ever closer.

"Melina?" Bradley sounds completely confused. "This is Bradley. I'm – "

"Oh, only another half an hour? Awesome." I plaster a smile

on my face. "I'll meet you at your place, then. Do you want me to bring you anything to eat? I got a stromboli that's out of this world. They're also having a deal on pizza: buy one, get one free."

"What's going on?" Bradley asks. "Is something wrong? You're acting kind of strange."

"I know," I say, side-eyeing the man. He's still at my table, eyes narrowed like he can't decide if I'm being honest or putting on some grand charade. "I'll fill you in later."

"Just tell me ... are you alright? Safe?"

"Yes."

He exhales into the phone. "Good. Your fake boyfriend is very relieved to hear that."

This makes me laugh. I can't help it.

"So pizza it is," I say. "Do you want the usual? Half black olives, half plain?"

"Actually," he answers, playing along now, "I prefer pineapple as a topping."

"What? You can't be serious."

"Scout's honor."

I can picture him holding up three fingers, and it makes me smile, in spite of myself. "Okay then, pineapple it is." I shake my head at the man, who is *finally* standing up from my table. "Six months of dating someone, and you still learn new things about each other all the time ... including bad taste in pizza toppings, apparently." He doesn't answer, just gives me one more long look and strides off. I keep up the facade until he leaves, gushing to Bradley about how I can't wait to see him tonight. It isn't until the door shuts behind Mr. Pushy that I stop.

"Melina?" Bradley says. "What was that?"

"That was you saving me from a jerk who wouldn't take no for an answer."

His voice dips down. "Are you sure you're okay?"

"Yes." I watch out the window as the man crosses the street and gets into a car. "He's gone. I'd have handled it myself, I *was* handling it myself, but then you called at the perfect time, so ... " I trail off. "Why *did* you call?"

"I wanted to see how things went with Nathan. I know today was the big day."

He remembered that?

And he still made a point of calling, even though I told him we couldn't see each other anymore?

Something flutters inside my chest, light, like a butterfly flapping its wings.

"He was upset," I tell Bradley. "But very understanding, thankfully. He didn't fire me."

"That's wonderful!" he says. "I'm happy for you."

"Thanks – and thanks for calling, too. I appreciate it, especially after the way I ended things last week. You didn't have to make another effort."

"I wanted to," he says. "That's the nice thing about some endings: they can always start again." He clears his throat. "Would you be up for that? Starting again and letting me take you out?" I can almost hear his smile. "I mean, if you think about it, we've already been dating for six months. You should probably know a bit more about me than just my preference in pizza toppings. Let me fill in the blanks."

I stare down at my half-empty plate.

Normally, I don't mind eating alone. Sometimes I even enjoy it.

But tonight, I'm lonely. Tonight, I'm not ready for that butterfly to fly away yet.

Plus, if there's still a chance that Bradley really *is* behind the camera's disappearance, then what better way to squeeze the truth out of him?

So, against my better judgment ... "Okay," I say. "Why not? Let's do it."

10

BRADLEY

$\mathcal{I}$'m shocked that she said yes.

Happy. Excited. Nervous. But mostly shocked.

We make plans to meet up in Philadelphia on Saturday, and all week long, the date dangles over my head. I want it to hurry up and get here, but I'm also worried Melina is right and our differences will be too big to surmount. Every time I edit one of Madelyn's speeches, or talk to a reporter who's planning to join the visit to her family's farm, or hear from one of her former opponents who's now throwing support her way, it just reminds me of the endgame. I'm working to get Madelyn elected. Melina is doing the same for Nathan. Maybe that's more than an obstacle in our path. Maybe it's a boulder we won't be able to push away.

"I don't know," I tell Cameron on Friday evening, taking out a bag of pretzels from his pantry and pouring them into a bowl. His ex-wife has the kids on weekends, so he hosts a bi-weekly poker night and I join in whenever I'm home. "What's the point of setting myself up for disappointment?" I ask. "She's made it pretty clear that work comes first."

"And yet, she still agreed to go out with you," he says. "That's gotta count for something, right? If she wasn't interested, she'd have said no." He takes a six-pack from his refrigerator, twists open a cap, and hands me a bottle. "Stop overthinking it," he advises. "C'mon, help me get things ready. It will take your mind off tomorrow."

He's right.

As a few of our friends arrive and we settle around the card

81

table, it does serve as a distraction. It also makes me glad I was able to find people to hang out with up here. That was one of the most difficult things about moving away from home. I had a lot of friends back in Georgia, but once we all went our separate ways, it got harder to keep in touch. Lucas is really the only one I talk to anymore these days, and even so, phone calls and emails are no substitute for actual face-to-face interaction. It was pretty easy to meet people in college and graduate school. Washington DC is a playground of patriotism, so my classes were filled with people who shared the same ambition. We all wanted to make a name for ourselves in politics. You'd think that would have set us up for rivalry, and it did, to a point, but it was also a great way to make friends. Here in Pennsylvania? I've had to work a whole lot harder at it. I had to put myself out there.

It's the same thing I'll have to do with Melina, if I stand a chance at winning her over.

The drive to Philadelphia the next day is long, which gives me a lot of time to think about what I am doing – or, rather, how other people would feel about what I'm doing. What would my brothers say? My parents? Madelyn and my coworkers? How would they react? I hate that I care about the answers to those questions.

"Listen to your own voice," my grandma told me once. I was a junior in high school, and I'd just been offered the position of editor-in-chief for the newspaper for the following year. I was ecstatic. But I was torn, too, because I'd also been told by the teacher in charge of the debate club that I had a good shot at being named its captain. Just like my brothers. That was the road I was supposed to follow. There wouldn't be enough room in my schedule to do both, not with all the honors classes I was taking. I didn't know what to do. "There's a Jewish proverb," Grandma said. "'Do not be wise in words. Be wise in deeds.' Don't ever say something just because you think it's what people want to hear. You speak up for your own heart. You figure out what your place is in this world, how you can use it to make your mark, and you trust in it. Trust in it like I trust in you."

I quit the debate team and threw myself into working on the school paper.

My parents were annoyed.

Jake and Eric were embarrassed.

But I was free.

I was happy.

When I knock on Melina's door and she opens it, her hair thrown into a messy bun and her shirt speckled with paint, I feel that same sense of unencumbered joy. "Hi," I say, holding out the tulips I stopped to buy at a flower shop near her apartment. "These are for you."

A smile blossoms across her face. "Thank you," she says, taking them from me. "They're lovely. Come in," she adds. "Sorry I'm not ready yet. I always lose track of time while I'm painting."

"No problem."

I walk into her apartment, lingering in the entryway while she goes to the kitchen and pulls out a vase. I sneak a quick glance around as she busies herself with the flowers. It's a nice place – a bit on the small side, but welcoming. Warm. The walls are painted a misty aqua color that reminds me of the ocean and the hardwoods are blonde. My favorite part, though, is the floor-to-ceiling bookcase along one of the living room walls.

"My dad built that," she says, catching me looking as she comes back to join me.

"He did? Wow. He must be pretty handy."

"He is. It was sort of out of necessity," she explains, setting the vase down and wiping her paint-spotted hands on her jeans. "We didn't have much money and couldn't afford to pay anybody to fix things that broke. He taught himself how to do it instead, and the hobby stuck. He lives alone now, so – " She breaks off and shakes her head, making the bun wobble a little. "Anyway. Let me change and then we can be on our way. Feel free to have a seat." She gestures to the sofa.

"Sounds good," I say.

She disappears down a hall, and I make my way to the couch.

Its cushions are ramrod straight, a perfectly angled throw pillow in each corner. The whole room is like something out of one of those HGTV shows my mother loves. Except for the drop cloth balled up in the corner and the cups sitting on the coffee table. One is filled with water, the other with paintbrushes.

I wonder what she was painting.

Does she paint often?

I sit down. Lean back against the cushions. Put my elbow on the arm of the couch, then move it away. Look around the room. There's an oversized conch shell on the end table and gauzy curtains ruffling by the open windows. I check my watch. Still no sign of Melina, so I stand up and walk over to read some of the titles of the books shelved neatly against the wall. Is that nosy? I don't want to be nosy.

I turn back around and am about to sit down again when I catch sight of the painting above the sofa. Immediately, it stops me in my tracks. The colors. The fluidity. The passion and emotion and power. Something about it commands my attention and captivates me. I can't exactly identify what it is, but maybe that's the point. Maybe art is about feeling, not reason. There isn't an artistic bone in my body – even my stick people look pathetic – but I do appreciate it. And so, when Melina walks back into the room ten minutes later, I feel compelled to share my thoughts.

"That painting is amazing," I tell her.

I can't be sure, but I think I see a blush creep into her cheeks.

"Thank you," she says, and the corners of her mouth turn up. "Usually it takes me a long time to get a piece to the point where I'm happy with it, but this one just kind of happened. I did the whole thing in a couple hours."

"Wait." I stare at her. "You painted that?"

"Guilty as charged." She holds up her hands, which are now paint free. There's something a bit off in her tone, almost like she's testing me, intentionally throwing the words out there. Maybe she hasn't forgiven me yet for recording Nathan's speech and their staff meeting. That's okay. I haven't forgiven myself yet, either.

"It's incredible," I say, choosing to keep things light. "I'm blown away by your talent."

"Flattery will get you nowhere."

Gone is the tension in her voice, replaced with a hint of laughter. I let myself relax.

"Shall we go?" she asks.

I briefly contemplate offering her my hand, but decide against it. Not yet. Too soon.

"Yes," I say. "We shall."

Melina leads me out the door and down the steps, and as I follow her outside, I can barely keep the grin from my face. It's been months since I was out on a first date. The last one was a disaster. Cameron had set me up with one of his CPA colleagues, and we had absolutely nothing in common. I don't know which one of us was more relieved when the date was over. I have a feeling that today will be different.

Our first stop is Penn's Landing, which Melina says is one of her favorite places in the city. "They have an ice cream festival every summer and an ice rink every winter," she tells me, as we get out of the car. "I used to come here a lot with my family to skate." She fishes around in her purse to find a pair of sunglasses and slips them onto her face. "I was terrible at it. My parents would have to hold my hands so I wouldn't fall. Even my younger sisters were better than me."

"You said you have a brother too, right? Why wasn't he there?"

I think it's an innocent question. At least, I intend it to be. But Melina stiffens a little and takes a step sideways, away from me. "He's eight years younger than I am," she says. "By the time Dylan was old enough to skate, our parents had already gotten divorced. Everything had changed." There is something so sad in her voice, and I instantly regret bringing up the topic. "I feel bad for him," she says. "Lara, too. Gabrielle and I know what it was like to grow up in a happy family. Lara has flashes of it, but she was only five when things started going south, so a lot of her memories are of the bad times." We round a corner onto the brick walkway that follows the riverbank, and Melina hooks her thumbs into the front pockets of her jeans. "Enough about me," she says. "Your turn. Tell me three things I don't know about you."

"Is this an official interrogation?" I joke.

She smiles slightly. "Of course not."

For a split second, I think I detect something in her tone again, but then it's gone before it even has a chance to settle. I choose to let it slide once more. "Okay," I say. "Well, I was born in Georgia, right outside of Atlanta."

"Ah, that explains the peach magnet on your refrigerator."

"Yep," I say. "My grandma made a care package for me before I left for college, and the magnet was part of it. She wanted me to have a piece of Georgia with me, wherever I went."

"She sounds sweet," Melina says. "My grandparents have all passed away. I miss them so much it hurts. You're lucky," she adds quietly, "to still have yours with you."

I touch her arm gently, and to my surprise, she doesn't pull away. "I'm grateful for it every day," I say. "I'm sorry your grandparents are gone. They're with you in spirit, though. I know that might sound corny, but I really do believe it's true."

She nods. "Me, too. I believe it a hundred percent."

"I guess we do have some common ground, after all," I say, and pull my hand back. I don't want to be too forward. We walk in silence for awhile, then Melina suggests we stop for a little and sit on one of the benches facing the river. It looks like a long blue ribbon, its water flowing calmly.

"Okay," Melina says. "Fact number two. Go on."

"My favorite color is green," I tell her. "It reminds me of a baseball diamond."

"Do you play?"

"Sure do. How about you? Any favorite sports?"

"Not so much," she says. "I love to swim and go on the occasional hike, but the athletic genes in my family mostly went to Lara. She's an insanely good volleyball player and a crazy fast runner. Not that I blame her. She had a lot to run from." Melina takes off her sunglasses, pushes them atop her head, and looks out at the water. I watch her for a moment. Rays of sunlight are angling down from the sky, and they reflect like prisms in her eyes. It's like she's got a rainbow inside.

What do I say? Do I pick up her train of thought or let it drop? Which would she prefer?

She's a tough person to read.

"Sometimes I feel like that, too," I finally say. "Like I'm running – not away from something, but more that I'm running to catch up. I'm the youngest in my family. My two brothers are the golden ones. Seriously. My oldest brother, Jake, just proposed to his girlfriend on a tidal basin cruise in DC. He and Eric can do no wrong. Ever since we were kids, it's seemed like I fall short in comparison."

"I'm sure that's not the case," she says. "You seem pretty successful yourself."

Just as she turns to face me, the breeze picks up, blowing her hair against my cheek. It sends an immediate shiver down my spine, and before I can think twice, I reach forward to tuck the loose lock behind her ear. My thumb accidentally brushes against her skin, whisper soft, and she stares at me, her gaze penetrating and on the edge of something wonderful. In that moment, all I want is to kiss her. I could lean forward, close the space between us. Taste her mouth on mine.

But I don't.

She doesn't give me the chance.

"Obviously I don't know your brothers," she says, breaking her gaze, leaning back on the bench to put distance between us. "I have a hard time believing you'd fall short of anyone, though. You're great at what you do. Madelyn clearly values you, if she's sending you on undercover assignments."

And there it is again. This time, I know I'm not imagining it.

"Assignment," I say firmly. "Singular. Like I said before, she's changed her mind about using the information, and even if she didn't, I would've pulled the plug on my involvement."

"Suppose she threatened to fire you?"

"Then I'd have been looking for a new job."

This is the truth. I know it with certainty now.

Melina narrows her eyes at me. Appraising. Considering. Evaluating.

I should probably be annoyed, but really, I'm just hurt. My feelings for Melina are genuine, and I see now that she doubts it. Is that all this date is to her, an opportunity to determine if I'm working an angle? The thought makes something tighten around my chest. "You know what?" I say, getting up. "Maybe this wasn't a good idea. Maybe you were right about us being better apart than we are together."

I take off walking, slowly at first and then faster. I dodge the kids gallivanting around. The birds gathered in a circle on the ground, devouring the French fries somebody dropped. The man jogging by and the woman holding on to the leash of a dog that looks more like a black bear. I hear Melina's voice, calling out to me, but I don't stop. I never should've tried again with her. Sometimes second chances are for fools.

But she's persistent. She leaps up, weaving her way through the crowd, and catches up with me a few minutes later.

"Don't," I tell her.

"Don't what?"

"Don't pretend anymore. I get it now. You just agreed to go out with me because you still have your suspicions. Keep your friends close and your enemies closer, right?" I whirl around to face her. She is red-faced, her cheeks the color of her cherry nail polish.

"Right," she agrees. "But also wrong." She steps closer and grazes my fingertips with hers. "I'll drive you back to get your car. Not until you tell me your third fact, though, and not until you let me give you three of my own."

Is she serious? She seems to be.

But why bother at this point?

"Fine," I say. Better to get it over with and move on. "A third thing you don't know about me is that I volunteer at a rabbit rescue." I glance down at our hands. Hers is still wrapped ever-so-lightly around mine.

"You're full of surprises, aren't you?" she murmurs. "Okay, now it's my turn. The Jersey shore is my happy place. I once lived in a homeless shelter for three months. And most importantly, I didn't agree to this date just for the reason you think. I said yes because I like you. I don't want to like you at all, because it complicates my life. It complicates everything. But I do. I like you, Bradley."

I guess she's full of surprises, too.

There's a stray spot of paint on her neck. Yellow.

This is what I notice as she pushes up on her toes, leans close, and kisses me.

11

Melina

What the hell are you doing?

Stop it. Stop it right now. You know better.

My brain issues a warning as I press my mouth to Bradley's, but for the first time in a long time, I don't listen. Instead, I lean in close as he winds his arm around my waist. I let him kiss me back, and I savor the moment rather than dissect it. The woodsy scent of his cologne swirls around me, and I feel the gentle pressure of his hand as it rests on my hip. His lips are sweet as they brush over mine, and though I can make out the sound of a tugboat as it chugs down the Delaware, it seems fuzzy and far off. The only thing my attention can land on is the kiss.

"Wow," I breathe, after we pull apart.

"Yeah," he whispers. "Wow. Definitely a wow."

We stand there for a few seconds, staring at each other, trying to figure out what just happened between us. I know I should offer him an explanation. I should tell him he was right, that I did have more than one motive when it came to the date. I should put it all out there and then I should end this, whatever it is. I can't bring myself to do that, though. "I haven't kissed someone like that in a long time," I say instead.

"I don't think I've *ever* kissed someone like that," Bradley says.

I raise an eyebrow at him.

"No, really, I mean it." He offers me a shy smile. "That was in a league of its own."

"Sweet talker."

Why am I flirting with him? Why didn't I just let him go when he walked away?

"Can I ask you something?" Bradley says. He takes my hand, threading his fingers through mine, and although it makes me sort of antsy, I don't back off ... because it also makes me happy. Damn it, why does it have to make me happy?

"Sure," I say, as we start to meander back along the river. "Go on."

"I hit the nail on the head before. You didn't just agree to this date because you're interested in me. There's more to it. I didn't want to see it at first, but ... " He sighs. "How far were you planning to take it?"

I steal a sideways glance at him. There's the faintest hint of a five o'clock shadow that's shading his jaw. "Do you remember what you said to me on the phone a couple of weeks ago?" I ask. "That I'm magnetic? Well, I feel the same way about you. I have since the day we met. I don't let myself get drawn in by people, but I can't seem to help it with you. I hate that, FYI." This makes him laugh, but really, I don't mean it as a joke.

I *do* hate it.

I hate that I'm letting someone put a crack in the walls I've so carefully constructed.

I've seen what happens when those walls come tumbling down, and it's not pretty.

"It's tricky, though," I continue. "You have to see it from my perspective. You purposely misled me before. How do I know you're not still doing it? Maybe I'm not the only one who had conflicting reasons for being here today." I stop walking, slip my hand from his, and turn to face him. "Tell me the truth. When you invited me to dinner, was it a ploy? And what about now? Is this entire thing a ruse to throw me off the scent?"

A pained look pinches his face. "No. I invited you to dinner on a whim. I wanted to get to know you better. I wanted to talk to you. I wanted to see your smile again. Same for today. I understand why you would think I was being manipulative, but you have my word that I wasn't. That I'm not. If that isn't enough," he says, "I'd rather you tell me now. I'd rather end things before I get even more invested."

Here's your chance. Take it, and cut him loose. It would be so easy.

My brain is taunting me again. It's testing me.

When I broke up with Cory, my boyfriend for two years after I transferred to Villanova during my junior year of college, it wasn't easy at all. We had different life goals – he wanted to marry me and start a family, and I wanted to marry my work and start changing the world – but it still killed me to turn down his proposal. It was our graduation day, a day that should've been full of happiness, but I ruined that for him when he took me aside and dropped to one knee. My heart just ... sank. Saying no, hurting him like that, was physically painful.

It was the same thing with Ian, my only other serious boyfriend. I met him while working for a local county commissioner. He's a lawyer and was at City Hall on business, and we literally ran into each other one day when neither of us was paying attention to where we were going. The coffee I'd been holding spilled, and I laughed out loud when he made this corny joke about having the hots for me. We dated for three years, and we were happy. We really were. When he asked me to move in, part of me wanted to say yes. Ian and I weren't my parents, after all. We weren't on a pre-destined course of failure. Then again, neither were Mom and Dad at the beginning. No one ever could have imagined what their happily-ever-after would become. And so, the day before I was set to move in, after all my things had been packed and all our plans had been made, I backed out.

"How can you do this to me?" Ian asked, as I kissed him goodbye and pressed the key he'd made for me back into his palm. "I thought you loved me." The hurt in his eyes broke my heart.

"I do," I said. "But sometimes love isn't enough. Always, love isn't enough."

This is precisely why I should walk away from Bradley.

There's a connection between us, this spool that keeps reeling me in even as I desperately try to snap the thread. I was able to do it before. Sure, I had my regrets with Cory and Ian, I had many of them, but I was able to put both men in the past. So why does that feel so difficult with Bradley? It doesn't make any sense. I haven't even known him for that long. There's no history there. There's no story of our own.

But there *is* that kiss, and also the fact that I really want to share another one ... in spite of it all, or maybe because of it all?

"I believe you," I say quietly to Bradley. "About everything."

I do.

I don't know who's messing with Nathan's campaign, but I truly don't think it's him. My mom is always saying you can tell a lot about people by their eyes. Bradley has honest eyes. They fix on me when he talks, windows to a soul I want to uncover. It's short-sighted and totally illogical, but I can't help it. I like how I feel when I'm around him. A light goes on inside me.

I take a step toward Bradley and rest my hands on his arms. They are toned, strong, sturdy.

Steady.

"You have my word, too," I tell him. "This isn't about the election. It's about you."

This time, he's the one who closes the distance between us.

He tips my chin up with his finger, brushing his mouth over mine, and immediately, goosebumps cover my arms. There is just something about this man. It's the way he smiles as he kisses me, the way he rubs a circle on my wrist with his thumb, and the way he makes me forget that we're right in the middle of Penn's Landing, where anybody can see us. Mostly, though, it's the way he makes me remember. He makes me remember that not everything has to be fraught with anxiety, trepidation, and memories.

Perhaps I was wrong. Cutting Bradley loose wouldn't be the easy part. Staying with him would be.

Over the next several weeks, I let myself give in to that ease. When Bradley and I get back to my apartment after our date, I invite him in for coffee instead of saying goodbye. When he asks me to go out with him again, I agree far too quickly. When we go hiking in Harrisburg, to the art museum in Philly, and to the amusement park in Hershey, I allow myself to enjoy our time together instead of questioning it. As the springtime breezes give way to the summer sun, I immerse myself in the heat of this new connection. I can't deny the fire it has lit inside me, and I'm not sure that I even want to. Is that really so bad?

If you ask my sister Lara, yes.

"I don't get it," she says flatly. It's a Saturday morning in early July, six weeks after my first date with Bradley, and Lara and I are at the bookshop. We meet our dad here sometimes to continue the tradition of a weekend morning spent among the shelves. Gabrielle lives too far away to join us, but Dylan does when his schedule allows. Today, though, it's only the two of us waiting for our father in the café, and evidently this morning's latte comes with a side of judgment. "It doesn't make sense," Lara says. "Are you actually *trying* to destroy your life?"

"Of course not. Why would you say that?"

"Um, the election? Hello?" She leans forward, arms resting on the table between us. "I mean, you thought the guy stole Nathan's camera, for God's sake. And correct me if I'm wrong, but isn't it true that you all *still* haven't found out who took it, despite working every angle possible?"

"It wasn't Bradley," I say firmly. "He swore he isn't involved, and I believe him."

"Exactly." She shakes her head. "I hope that doesn't come back to bite you. It's no secret that I don't believe in that whole one-person-can-change-the-world crap, but obviously you do. You have been talking about it for as long as I can remember. I can't believe you're gonna let some guy ruin it for you."

"I'm not."

"Oh, but you are." She fidgets with her long, low ponytail. "And then you'll end up right where you started – with nothing. I'd hate to see that happen. You deserve better. That's what you'd tell us, remember? All the nights in the shelter, when Gabrielle and I couldn't fall asleep? We piled into the same bed, you told us a story, and you promised things would improve someday because that's what we deserved. Now it's happened, at least for the most part, and you want to throw it all away for a man who's probably playing you?"

"He's not."

"You know that … how?" She stares at me with those big blue eyes of hers – she's the only one of us who inherited Dad's blue eyes instead of Mom's hazel – and for a moment, all I see is the little girl whose innocence was washed away far too soon. She's not that kindergartner with the pigtails anymore, though. She's twenty-five and full of sass. "He knows just how to push your buttons," she says, "and you're enjoying it so much that your reasoning has flown out the window. You're playing a dangerous game."

"Maybe." Even with my growing trust in Bradley, I have to admit this is a possibility. Sometimes playing with fire gets you burned. "But my eyes are wide open. I'm not going to let him – or anyone else, for that matter – pull one over on me. I know what I'm doing."

"That's what Mom and Dad thought, too."

I look at her.

And I see the tears, hear the slamming doors, smell the acrid smoke of a charred dinner.

It's like I told Bradley: Lara has too many memories of the bad times.

It makes me so sad that she can't move past them.

Can any of us, though?

It's why my life revolves around politics, why Gabrielle moved to Manhattan the first chance she got, and why Dylan is working as a waiter at three different restaurants to put himself through grad school. I remember something Nathan once said in one of his speeches: "The past is always with us, tucked into our back pockets. We can take it out sometimes, hold it, feel its weight. But we cannot, or at least we should not, let it anchor us in place. After all, we can't move forward if we're standing still."

It was from the early days of the campaign, when he and his wife were starting their grassroots efforts to get him on the ballot. I think there were twenty people listening to him speak, twenty-five tops, but he addressed the group like he was in front of thousands. That's when I knew I wanted to work for him.

Nothing will change that.

No one.

"Look," I tell Lara, "Bradley and I aren't even official yet. Maybe we will be or maybe not, but it won't change my priorities either way. I'm focused on the big picture."

"I hope so." She drains the rest of her coffee and stands up as Dad walks into the store and over to join us.

"How are my girls?" he asks.

I lean over to hug him. "Good," I say. "Glad to be here with you guys this week."

Last Saturday, I was in Pittsburgh with Nathan and the team. Next Saturday, I'll be in Reading. It always excites me to visit a different city, to meet the people and dive into the stories of their lives, but I'd have been sad to miss out on this time with Dad and Lara today. I always look forward to it. It's not exactly the same as those family excursions to the library, when Mom would remind us all to use our indoor voices and Dad would carry a growing pile of books as we made our way through the aisles, but it's close enough.

We fan out through the store – Dad heading for the biography section, Lara for the novels, and me for the current events – and a grin finds its way to my face. I told Bradley the Jersey shore is my happy place, and to be sure, it is. My family spent a few blissful weeks there each summer before it was no longer possible, and I make a point now of going back every year. The bookstore is another happy place, though. Painting was one of my escapes when life got too hard, when it all became too much, and reading was the other. Losing myself in the pages, living in the characters' worlds when it felt like the walls kept closing in on my own, was a refuge for me. The walls might have opened back up now, but their imprints remain. The love of reading remains.

"What's your favorite book?" Bradley asked me on one of our dates.

"Oh I could never pick just one," I told him. "I have a different favorite for each different season of my life."

"I like the way you think."

I like the way you think.

Does he really? Not when it comes to everything.

As I stand in front of the current events section, my gaze sweeping over titles like *America Today* and *Stars and Stripes: A Tale of Two Countries*, I'm reminded yet again of the fundamental ways that Bradley and I are different. If you ask Lara, that's a deal breaker. If you asked me a few months ago, I would've agreed. Now, I don't know.

Normally, I hate uncertainty. It makes me feel itchy, like there's energy pinging around my veins in a desperate attempt to break free. Maybe, though, I need to let that energy settle a little bit. I've always been so intent on directing my own sails, but I'm starting to realize that it's okay to see how and where the current flows on its own.

Here's hoping it doesn't leave me stranded in a dangerous sea.

12

BRADLEY

"Okay, so first we want to make the filling for the cream puff," I say, reaching for the ingredients lined up on the counter. It's a Sunday evening, just over six weeks since the day Melina and I shared our first kiss, and we're having a quiet date at my house before I leave tomorrow for the week-long work trip to Madelyn's farm. "Wanna do the honors?" I ask. "You have to mix the cream, pudding, and milk together."

"Sure." She follows my instructions, and I smile, watching her bite her lip in concentration. She doesn't even realize she's doing it.

"My grandma always put me in charge of this part," I tell her. "And I always snuck some of it to eat when I thought she wasn't looking. She'd pretend to scold me." I mimic Grandma's accent and inflection. "'Now, now, Schatzi, that cream, it is not for eating ahead of time.'"

Melina grins. "So your family is German, I take it?"

I rip off some wax paper to cover the mixing bowl, then pass it to her. "My grandmom's side is. She was born there. My grandfather is from a suburb of Atlanta called Marietta."

"Wow. So how did they meet?"

"World War II, believe it or not," I say. "My grandma's Jewish, and her family suffered so much during the Holocaust. It was an ... " Something thick clogs in my throat, just as it always does when I talk about this. "An unspeakable atrocity," I say. "But my grandfather saved her. He was part of the troops who liberated the concentration camp where she was being held. He even found her a

99

place to stay afterward, until she could determine if the rest of her family was safe."

"Were they?" Melina breathes the words instead of speaking them.

"Some, yes. Others … " I shake my head. "But my grandfather was able to find her mother and sister, and he personally reunited them." My eyes well up, just as my grandparents' always do when they get to this part of the story. "My grandma says it was a mitzvah beyond all mitzvahs. And then after the war was over and my grandfather was free to come home, he went to get them. I think it was the only thing that kept him going, you know? He'd seen so many horrors. But they were okay. They were alive."

"I … that's … wow." Melina just stands there, staring at me with those big, beautiful eyes.

"Pretty remarkable, huh?"

"Incredibly remarkable." She puts a hand to her heart. "So he brought her home with him after the war?"

"Not immediately. They stayed in Germany for a few months. I think they both needed time to heal. That's how they fell in love. They helped piece each other back together again." I pick up the mixing bowl, because I can see that Melina is too absorbed in the story to even remember that we'd been baking. "Their relationship is sort of my inspiration," I explain, opening the refrigerator to put the bowl inside. "I want a love like that."

My words are met with silence so loud it's deafening.

When I turn back around, Melina is no longer lost in my grandparents' world. She's studying the recipe card on the counter instead. "So what's next?" she asks, trying too hard to make her voice all casual and light.

Well, shoot. Now I've scared her off.

I don't know what to do. Try to explain myself, or just follow her lead and back off? Melina has been pretty tight-lipped about her own past. I never feel right prying. If she wanted to tell me, she would, and clearly she doesn't. Not yet, at least. I don't want to push her away. If she leaves again, I'm afraid she won't come back.

So I pick up where she left off. "Next we make the pastry shells," I say, pulling out a large pan. I place it on the stove. "First we add the butter and water. Then we'll bring it to a rolling boil before we stir in the salt and flour."

"Okay, got it." She nods. "This might be a good time to mention, though, that I'm not exactly a cooking connoisseur. I mean, I used to make meals for my siblings, but it was usually something like boxed macaroni and cheese. I'm not brilliant in the kitchen like you." She tosses me a playful smile. This is what she does. She throws out all these tidbits about her life – that line about spending three months in a homeless shelter, the one about her sister having a lot to run away from, and now this – but never elaborates. I wish she would. I feel like we could really have something great together, if only she'd let herself sink into it.

Maybe soon. Hopefully soon.

"Brilliant," I say, giving her a quick wink. "I like the sound of that."

"Then you'd better live up to it," she teases.

"I'll do my best." I motion for her to join me at the stove as I turn up the dial for the burner and add in the salt and flour. Then I hand Melina an oversized spoon and ask her to stir until the mixture forms a ball. "Voila," I say, when she's finished.

"You're really into this stuff, huh?" she asks, as I turn off the burner and transfer the dough back to another bowl.

"Yeah. It's fun. Cooking relaxes me. It excites me."

"So why didn't you give it a real shot, then?" she asks. "I know you said the plan was always to go into politics, but why?"

"Because that's what my parents do. That's what my brothers do. That's what I have to do."

She hoists herself up onto the counter and swings her legs a little. "Why?"

I reach into the egg carton and pull out two. "It was basically decided for me before I was born," I tell Melina. Maybe if I'm an open book, it'll get her to reveal some of her pages, too. "My father's set in his ways. He has strong beliefs and expects us all to agree with them. I think a lot of it comes from my grandparents. They raised him to love this country. To be proud of it. To fight for it. Dad grew up hearing about the sacrifices they made, and it inspired him. He wanted to serve in his own way."

"Hence the politics," she says.

"Yes." I beat the eggs into the mixture, then add another two. "That's how he met my mother. They were both interns at the statehouse. They think it's our civic duty to make the government the best it can be, and they're good at it. Really good. They wanted my brothers and me to follow their lead. You know how most parents tell their children they can be anything in the world? Well, mine didn't. They made it clear from the beginning that we were supposed to share the same passion for politics. Jake and Eric fell into it. Jake works for the State Department," I say. "And Eric is teaching political science at Yale."

"What about you?" she asks. "You didn't fall into it like they did?"

"No. Yes. Maybe. I don't know. It's hard to explain. I do like politics, and there's really nothing like hearing someone give a speech I've written. It's awesome to think that my words could inspire people. And I am passionate about this country. I want it to thrive."

"But?"

"But sometimes I wonder if there's more out there. If there's more in here." I tap my chest.

"Such as?"

I think of the application to culinary school. It's still sitting in my desk. Waiting for me to gather up the nerve. Waiting for me to fill out the pages. Waiting for me to stop dreaming and start taking action. Melina's comment is what encouraged me to print out the application in the first place, so it only makes sense that I should let her in on my secret. I've never told anyone about my desire to be a chef one day, perhaps even to own a restaurant. Not my friends. Not Rachel, the woman I dated for five years and almost proposed to. Certainly not my family.

But I want to tell Melina.

I want her to know.

I open my mouth to speak, and that's when the phone rings.

It cuts into the moment, and I'm irrationally annoyed at whoever's calling for interrupting. After the answering machine clicks on, my irritation ratchets up another notch. "Bradley? Are you there? If so, please pick up." There's just one person who always assumes I must be screening my calls, and her voice echoes through the room, crystal clear and full of authority. My mother. "Okay," she says, after a pause. "I suppose you aren't around. Call me back when you get a chance. I have to talk to you about the family reunion this September. I know, I know, it's still far off." She laughs, high and piercing. "Your father's always saying that I go overboard with the planning, but why do something if you're not willing to give it two hundred percent, right? Anyway, there are a couple changes that I'm hoping to make this year, and I'd like to get your thoughts."

"You can answer, if you want," Melina says, as my mom continues to ramble on. "No worries. I don't mind."

"Nah," I say, reaching for one of the baking sheets on the counter. "Phone calls with my mother are exhausting. I'll call her back later. Right now, I would much rather hang out with you. After all," I say, handing her a spoon so she can help me drop the dough onto the tray, "this is the last time I'll see you for a week." I lean over to kiss her and can't help smiling when she kisses me back. I seem to do that every time. I consider myself to be a pretty level-headed person – my brothers and I were taught to keep our feet on the ground and our daydreams out of the clouds – but when I'm around Melina, everything's different. Everything is better.

"I'm going to miss you." She looks almost startled after she says it, like the words have betrayed her. But me? My heart grows about three sizes.

"I'll miss you, too." I think of the long days ahead. The cross-state drive. The hobnobbing with reporters. The trailing after Madelyn around the farm and the speechwriting. "Usually I don't mind being on the road," I say, "but this time there's somewhere else I'd rather be instead. Someone else I'd rather be with. Even if she does have cream on her face."

"What? No, I don't." Melina reaches her hand up to check her cheek.

"Other side."

She swipes a hand across her cheekbone, then lets out an almost girlish giggle. I've never heard her do that before. This woman, she's always a surprise.

"Oops," she says. "It must have splattered when I was mixing everything before. Looks like I'm not the only one, though. You have some on your face, too."

Quick as a flash, she leans over and dabs the cream onto my nose. Then she jumps down from the counter and darts around the table as I grab the bag of flour, chasing after her. Around we go in circles, letting loose like we're a couple of kids. What is this? How is this my life? I don't know, but I don't want it to stop.

"Retaliation," I tease, holding up the flour. "It's waiting for you."

"In your dreams."

She zigs left, I zag right. But she's fast, this petite firecracker that has so much more power than you'd guess just from looking at her. Appearances are deceiving, though. I should know that better than anyone.

Why did I clam up after my mother called? Why did I let it derail my plan to tell Melina?

More words left unsaid.

I don't want to think about them. Not now.

Melina whirls around suddenly, trying to outmaneuver me, but I guess she doesn't realize quite how close behind I am, because she all but slams into me. "Crap," she says, laughing. She holds up her hands. "Okay, okay, I surrender. You've got me. Now the question is: what are you going to do about it?"

The bag of flour tumbles to the floor.

It hits with a thunk, spilling open and sending a sea of white everywhere. I glance down at it, then back at Melina. Her laughter quiets into something more serious, more intimate, and for a moment or two we simply stand there, wrapped up in one another's eyes. There's a story in hers. Hope, sadness, determination.

There's something else, too. A spark.

"Well?" she demands gently. "Are you going to kiss me already, or do I have to take the reins in this relationship?"

"Relationship?" I echo. My heart jumps around in my chest.

"That's what it's called when two people are dating, isn't it?"

"So are we officially together, then?"

"I guess it depends." She traces her fingers up my arm until they reach my shoulder. "There are a whole lot of reasons why we shouldn't be. Good reasons. Valid reasons. Reasons I remind myself of at every turn. But then, also, there's this." She brushes her mouth against mine, slow and sweet. So sweet.

"Yes," I murmur. "Yes, there is."

I kiss the corners of her lips. The freckle by her nose. The beauty mark on her neck.

"My dad stopped kissing my mom like that," Melina says quietly, after we've broken apart. She busies herself with dropping the remainder of the cream puff dough onto the baking sheet. "That's how I knew something was wrong. My entire life, I had always seen the love between them. It was palpable. Even after my dad lost his job, and they couldn't afford to pay the mortgage on our house … it was hard, living in a shelter." She bows her head, keeping her gaze on the baking sheet instead of me. I can see it's taking a lot for her to tell me this, so I don't interrupt. I just walk up beside her so she'll know I'm there. "Even in the shelter, though, we still had each other," she continues. "My parents had their love. Afterwards, when the shelter helped place us in a tiny apartment, something happened to my mom and dad. They just … broke."

I don't know what to say.

"I'm sorry." My words come out as a whisper. "I'm so sorry."

"Don't be." She clears her throat and takes a deep breath. "Just be different."

What I saw in her before, that power … I realize now that she has it in spades. That maybe this is what it's all about for her. Why she's been so slow to open up to me. Why she's letting me in on her own terms. She lost her power as a child. It was taken, despite all her attempts to hold on, so it has become the strongest weapon in her arsenal now.

"Okay," I say, putting my arm around her shoulders. I pull her close. Kiss the top of her head. "I promise. I'll be different."

13

Melina

It is a long, busy, hectic week.

On Monday, Kira and I spend the day combing through b-reel news footage and photos taken at Nathan's rally back in May, hoping to find some kind of clue about what happened to the camera. It isn't the first time we've done this, but as Nathan joins us, his face only inches from the screen as we pause the footage, then start it, then pause it again, it seems like it might be the last. "I think this is fruitless," he sighs, leaning back in his chair and crossing his arms. "Video from three news stations and all the pictures we took over the course of the night, and there's still nothing. If somebody stole that camera, he or she did a bang-up job at covering the tracks."

"What do you want us to do now?" Kira asks.

"I think it's time we focus our attention elsewhere," he says. "It's a shame not to have a chance to use the pictures, and we'll have to revamp the entire summer campaign, but at this point, it'd be counterproductive to devote any more time to this. Better to hope the whole thing was an accident and just move on."

I don't think it was an accident, not at all, but still, I do as Nathan asks.

I move on.

On Tuesday, I join the election team in Easton as Nathan meets with groups of senior citizens.

On Wednesday, we're off to Pittsburgh for a campaign stop with local steelworkers.

On Thursday, we're in State College to host volunteer sign-ups.

And on Friday, I'm in Philly to take the next step toward creating my homeless shelter initiative. First, though, is breakfast with my mom at a restaurant around the corner from her house. "Are you sure you're ready for today?" she asks.

"Of course. Why wouldn't I be?" As I look across the table at her, it's like staring into my future. Everybody's always told me that I resemble Mom. We have the same hazel eyes, the same crease of a dimple in our left cheek, and the same caramel-colored hair. I'm proud to look like her. She's the strongest person I know. She's a fighter.

She's also incredibly perceptive. She sees the part of me I don't let anyone else see. "Because it has been a long time," she says softly, "but once you walk through those doors, it'll feel like no time at all."

She's talking about the doors to Helping Hands, the homeless shelter we stayed in when the bills became too much, when everything became too much. It's been nearly two decades since I was last inside that building, and still, I remember all of its nuances – the water spot shaped like a cat on the bedroom ceiling, the sunny yellow paint in the kids' area, the green plastic tablecloths covering the scratched dining room tables, and the wall in the lobby where each resident signed his or her name before leaving. They called it the Wall of Success, and I was excited when we got to add our names to it. We toasted afterward, with boxes of apple juice from the shelter's kitchen.

"To us," Dad said. "To our new beginning."

"Things are going to be different now," Mom added.

Oh boy, were they ever, just not in the way she'd intended.

But that's not what I want to think about today. "I'll be fine," I tell Mom. "For all the hard times in that shelter, there were also a lot of good ones. Besides, I'll be concentrating on work today. If I want to draft an accurate proposal, I have to get the facts straight." I vow, right then and there, not to let my own feelings get in the way. There's a time and place for emotion in politics, and this isn't it.

As usual, though, Mom is right. The instant I step into the shelter, it all comes rushing back. The mornings when I'd have to wait for the shower, which always had cold water by the time it was my turn … the afternoons when Dad would pick me up at school, since the bus didn't stop at the shelter … the nights when I'd try to find a quiet place so I could do homework … the memories flash before me like an old flickering movie reel. "Whew," I say. "Okay, perhaps this *is* harder than I thought it'd be."

"I guess it's a good thing you're a tough cookie, then," Mom says.

I'd been planning to come to Helping Hands alone, but as I was paying for breakfast, she asked if she could join me. I contemplated telling her I'd be fine on my own, that I could handle it. Instead, I nodded. I suppose even thirty-year-olds still need their moms sometimes. Now, as we walk through the lobby, I'm so glad she's here.

"Nathan wanted to come with me," I say to Mom, as we stand in front of the Wall of Success. It has so many names on it now – so many people this place has helped, so many lives it has improved. "I told him it'd make more sense for him to wait until the fall, once it's closer to the election. He can visit the shelters then."

"He doesn't know, does he?"

Leave it to Mom to always hear the words I don't say.

I scan the wall until I find our names. They're about halfway down. "No," I say, gazing at mine. *Melina Grace Radcliffe*. It's written in an eleven-year-old's bubbly cursive, a smiley face drawn next to it. I was so optimistic then, and so naïve. "Actually, no one at work knows, and if I have my way, they never will."

"Why?"

"I don't need their sympathy," I say, "and I certainly don't want their pity."

"I don't think they'd pity you," Mom says. "They'd admire you, for taking a tough situation and finding inspiration in it." She reaches over and squeezes my hand. "You've worked so hard to make this life for yourself. A lot of people would've given up. They'd have made excuses. But not my girl. You didn't let the bad times defeat you. You defeated them instead. And look at you now, changing the world. I only wish I could have helped you more. It killed me not to – ”

"Mom, stop. You've always done everything you could for us."

"Right. That's why you had to work your way through college." She sighs heavily. "Why Dylan's first memories are of your dad and I fighting. Why Lara couldn't join the intramural volleyball team as a kid, because the registration fee was too high for us. Why Gabrielle couldn't get the prom gown she adored and had to settle for me making her one instead."

"Yours was prettier than anything she could've found in a store."

I'm not just saying that; I mean it. Mom's a seamstress and has an incredible talent for spinning thread into gold. She used to be a stay-at-home mom, but once Dad lost his job everything changed in a flash. There was no way we could afford to have Mom not work out of the house, so she took a job at a local bridal boutique. It didn't pay so well, but at least it was something.

Something was all we had in those days.

It was the best we could do.

I don't want it to be like that for other people.

The couple who lives in their car with their infant son, the single mother who goes door to door and begs restaurant owners for leftover scraps, the elderly man who has trouble affording his health insurance ... these are all people Nathan has heard from since he announced his candidacy. They're not facts and figures. They're not stories and anecdotes. The people I think of now, as I pull myself together, are very real. The homeless get lumped together often, defined by the one thing they lack instead of all they do possess. I want to change that. Because, for all the times I was so scared and sad during my stay at Helping Hands, there were also the times I felt safe and protected, thanks to a fantastic staff and group of volunteers. Now I want to be that helping force. I want to find a way to empower those in the shelters.

I slip my hand into my purse and pull out the camera inside.

It's not the one Nathan was supposed to use in this campaign, but it'll have to do.

I head across the lobby and knock on the office door of the shelter's director. Her name is Nora, and she's the daughter of the woman who ran Helping Hands when my family lived here. She smiles at me as I walk in and immediately extends her hand. "Ms. Radcliffe," she says. "It's so great of you to come by. Thank you."

"I should be the one thanking you," I say, shaking her hand. "Nathan and I really appreciate the kindness. We're excited about the prospect of building more shelters across the state, but we want to do it right. We want them to address the most important needs of the homeless."

"Of course." She nods. "That's what we always try to do here. Tell me how I can assist you."

I hold up the camera.

"Well," I say, "we have a very special assignment for some of your residents."

* * *

Some people hate crowds. They feel closed in and suffocated. I'm not one of those people. I actually love it when a room is full. The talking, the laughter, the vibrant pulse ... to me, those things give life to a place. It's the opposite that sets my nerves on edge. I don't like to be somewhere empty. It's why I crave the road so much and why I hang out at the hotel restaurant, or bar, or even its lobby, until the last possible minute before going back to my room. It's also why I always feel the need to be doing something when I'm in my apartment. To just sit and relax makes me too antsy, because that's when the memories flood in. That feels especially true tonight. Mom was right: visiting Helping Hands and spending the day there impacted me more than I predicted.

Of course it did. How could I have expected to not be affected? Everywhere I turned, there was another reminder. My past was hiding around every corner, just waiting to jump out and yell 'boo.' Sometimes I feel like that's what my whole life is like, a perpetual game of hide-and-seek where I'm working feverishly to keep my childhood behind a curtain. Everyone knows about my passion for all things political, but besides my family, there's only one person who really knows why: Amie, my best friend from all those years ago.

I pick up the phone to call her. I've been meaning to for ages, but life's been so busy lately. It's probably been calm for her, though, since she takes the summer off after teaching all year. She likes to have some time to relax, especially now that she's pregnant. It's just one of many ways that our personalities have diverged since our paths went in different directions. It hurts sometimes, to think of how close we used to be – and how close we no longer are. Neither of us can seem to figure out how to patch things up. I suppose that's why it's been so long between calls. But maybe, instead of trying to bridge the gap, we should be finding a way to cross it.

As I wait for Amie to pick up, I think of the morning we met. It was the first day of kindergarten, when I climbed up the steps of the bus, only to find that the seats were already occupied. I scanned the rows, then plopped down next to Amie, who was sitting alone. "I like your schoolbag," I said. It had the Care Bears printed on it.

"I like yours, too," she said shyly.

It was, truly, the beginning of a beautiful friendship.

For years, Amie was like another sister to me. We swapped Barbie dolls. We always chose each other as partners in gym class. We got our ears pierced together at the mall. We were a constant in one another's lives, during the good times and the challenging ones. When Amie's father needed a kidney transplant, I went with her to visit him in the hospital every day, and when my family lost our home, Amie came over to keep me company at Helping Hands. She's the only one I told about what happened then, and the only one I confided in when my parents' marriage fell apart. There's a bond between us that can't be broken. It doesn't matter how tautly the rope is stretched, how in danger it is of breaking. It will hold on, even if Amie and I are losing our grasp on it.

At least, I hope so.

She answers the phone after four rings. "Hello?" she says, in her soft-spoken voice.

"Hi." I settle into the sofa cushions. "It's me. How are you?"

"Melina!" She sounds sincerely happy to hear from me. "I was seriously just thinking about you a few minutes ago. The dishwasher broke, so I was washing everything by hand. It reminded me of the polishing parties." She chuckles. "Funny, the things we remember, huh?"

Polishing parties. They were Mom's brainchild. The apartment we moved into after the shelter didn't have a dishwasher, and we couldn't afford to get one put in, so she tried to make a game out of doing the dishes each night. She'd turn on the radio, hand everyone a towel, and promise a piece of candy to whoever ended up with the shiniest, most polished plates. When Amie was visiting, she would join in.

"Wow, I haven't thought about that in years," I tell her.

"Me either, until now." She clears her throat. "So, what's up? We haven't talked in forever."

"I know. I'm sorry." The words rush out. "I should've called sooner. I promise to do better."

"Me, too." Her voice dips down. "I've wanted to call you so many times lately, but I just ... your life is so busy and exciting. You're all over Pennsylvania, campaigning for Nathan, and I'm at home, ordering furniture so Tom and I can finally start designing the baby's nursery."

"Which is exciting, too," I say. "Tell me about it!"

It's an invitation she gladly takes. "Oh, it's beautiful," she gushes. "The crib is whitewashed, so I think we're going to do a beach theme."

The whole married-with-a-baby-on-the-way concept feels so foreign to me. I'm happy for Amie, but sometimes I struggle, trying to find the right thing to say when she mentions it. It's just different from my life, so very different. This time, though, she makes it easy. "That's perfect," I say. "Since you and Tom met at the shore."

"Thanks to you."

Instinctively, I smile. "Well, someone had to make a move and it wasn't going to be you."

After we graduated high school, Amie's parents surprised us with a week-long trip to Ocean City. It was the first time I'd been back to the beach since everything spiraled south for my family, and to say I was elated is an understatement. Smelling the sea air again, feeling the sand between my toes, hearing the familiar and comforting sound of my footsteps on the boardwalk, it was sunshine for the soul. I had the best time. Amie did, too, especially when we were at the amusements one night and Tom caught her eye.

"Hey," she whispered, as we stood in line for the Tilt-a-Whirl. "Don't look, but there's the cutest guy near the Scrambler. He's got all these blonde curls." Of course, I turned to see. "Melina!" she whispered, smacking my arm. "I told you not to!"

"Too late," I said in a sing-song voice. The guy was standing with three of his friends and they all seemed to be around our age. The one Amie had her eye on was looking our way, right at her. "Go over," I told her. "Say hi. Get his number."

"I can't do that." She sounded mortified.

"Sure you can. Watch." Then, before she could protest, I marched directly over to Tom. "Hi," I said. "My name's Melina. My friend Amie wants to know if you have a girlfriend."

I'd never seen her face so red. I think she wanted to throttle me ... until Tom answered.

"Nope." He winked at Amie as she joined us.

They've been together ever since.

I don't really believe in happily-ever-after, but they make me want to try.

As Amie tells me more about the nursery, and her Lamaze classes, and the lists she and Tom are making of baby names, I can't help wondering what it'd be like to have that kind of life. They're just so settled. So comfortable. What would have happened if I'd accepted Cory's proposal? If Ian and I had moved in together? Would I be settled now, too? Would there be a sweet little one flourishing below the curve of my heart? Or would I feel stuck? Confined? I'm not sure, but what I do know is that, when I try to picture the type of life Amie and Tom have, it isn't Cory or Ian who fills the place next to me.

It's Bradley.

The thought scares the daylights out of me.

All week long, Bradley's been flitting into my mind, but until this point I've been able to box him away, to separate our relationship in its own little section of my brain. But now my mind's going to him naturally, like that's where it's supposed to be. I don't like it.

"Question," I say to Amie. "When did you know Tom was the one for you? How did you know?"

"The first time he held my hand. We just fit together perfectly."

"You realize that sounds like something out of a Hallmark movie, right?"

She laughs. "I know, but it's true. When he held my hand, I never wanted him to let go. Why?" A note of curiosity creeps into her voice. "Is there somebody new in your life who you may actually want to keep around?"

Amie was angry at me when I broke up with Cory. We weren't as close anymore by the time Ian and I were dating – she'd already moved to New Jersey and we didn't see each other often – but she told me I should've taken a chance on him, too. That's Amie. She's a hopeless romantic and proud of it. That's exactly why I shouldn't tell her about Bradley.

And yet … "Yes," I say. "There might be."

14

BRADLEY

$\mathcal{I}$ used to love horseback riding when I was a kid. Jake decided he wanted to start taking lessons when he was thirteen, so our parents signed Eric and me up, too. I was only seven at the time, so it wasn't like I could do a whole lot, but it didn't matter. Going to the barn still became one of my very favorite things. It was such fun to ride the horses. I enjoyed all of it – tacking them, brushing them, feeding them. I didn't even mind mucking out the stalls.

But it has been a long time since my horseback riding days. I realize that within an hour of being on Madelyn's farm. It's a sprawling place, with rolling green fields, rustic gray fences, and red wood buildings. And animals. Lots and lots of animals. There are pigs. Chickens. Horses. Sheep. Geese. Cows.

All week long, Madelyn makes a point of taking care of them. It's odd to see her like this. Gone are the designer clothes, fancy jewelry, and perfectly applied makeup. Instead, she wears sneakers, t-shirts, and denim shorts. "Do you think it's an act?" I ask Hannah on Friday. She and I are tagging along while Madelyn takes the reporters on a tour of the property. They already have photos of her riding her favorite horse, cooking dinner in the high-ceilinged kitchen, and milking a cow. Seriously. Madelyn Morgan milked a cow. Hannah and I actually had to excuse ourselves before our laughter ruined the entire thing.

Now we're lingering outside the barn, watching Madelyn show the press how to properly ready a horse for riding. "I don't know," Hannah says. "I assumed it was at first, because painting herself as a nature lover is a clever move. So many candidates concentrate on the cities, but the rural vote counts too. This whole press series will be a fantastic way of connecting herself to that voting block. Except she genuinely seems to enjoy it, doesn't she?" She nods in Madelyn's direction as she puts a saddle on the horse's back. "You can't fake enthusiasm like that. She seems so much more relaxed here."

"More carefree," I add. "More free in general."

Madelyn peers over at us. "Come on," she calls, waving us into the barn. "Saddle up, you two. We're riding to the pond."

Hannah's eyes go wide. "We?" she echoes. She looks at me, a little panicked. "Do we have to? Like, is it included in our job description?"

"Not a horse fan, I take it?"

"They're pretty," she says. "From afar. The idea of actually riding one isn't the most appealing. Suppose it gets spooked and runs off? Or throws me to the ground?" She shakes her head. "Nope. Not a fan. Definitely not a fan."

"Why don't you go work on Madelyn's speech for tomorrow?" I suggest. She's holding an event while she's here, a meet-and-greet on the farm with whoever wants to come. It's a far cry from her usual campaigning, but we all think it'll be good to have something more informal. We still want her to give a speech, though, and I figure Hannah can fine-tune it while I jump onto a horse and join the others.

"I owe you one," she says gratefully, then takes off for the main house.

I head inside the barn.

Madelyn's surrounded by a small circle of reporters – two from different newspapers, one from a tv station, and two others from online news sites. This is going to be wonderful press. Sometimes the best publicity isn't a sound bite from a debate or a snapshot of a candidate meeting voters. It's this. It's seeing who a public official is in private. Getting a glimpse into Madelyn's life – this sort of secret life that she doesn't talk about often – will go a long way.

So do we. Literally.

I guess I expected it to be a short ride. The pond isn't too far from the barn, and out of the press folks joining us, only two have ever ridden horseback before. But, once Madelyn sees that the rest are okay, she extends the journey. By the pasture. Through the woods. Across the field. Along the trail. The horses' hooves clip-clop, that perfectly rhythmic sound that reminds me of all those hours I spent trotting and cantering as a kid. At first, I hold tightly to the reins in my hand. Then I let them relax a little. Riding a horse is sort of like riding a bike. Once you do it, you don't ever forget how. It feels natural to sit atop one again.

"You're a sweet girl, aren't you?" I ask, petting the horse's head as we all stop by the pond.

Madelyn navigates her horse beside me. "You're good with her."

"I used to ride when I was a kid," I say.

"I can tell." She hops off her horse and leads him to the water for a drink.

I do the same with mine. "This is nice," I say, squinting against the sunlight as it hits the pond. It is an almost majestic sight, the way the rays of light reflect on the surface of the water. "Do you ever wish you could live here full-time?" I ask.

"No." Her answer is immediate. "A visit or two each year is all I need. I think always being here would ruin it for me. It'd take away the magic, you know? If we experience something every day, it isn't special anymore. At least, that's how it was for me as a kid." She reaches up to stroke the side of her horse. "I took this place for granted. All I wanted was to live in a city. I craved the hustle and bustle, and it was just too quiet out here. But I was short-sighted. I was so busy looking toward the future that I missed out on seeing what was right in front of me. Don't do that." Her gaze travels to meet mine. "Everyone always says not to miss the forest for the trees, but I think it's the other way around."

"I agree," I say.

It's why, once we're back at the house, I find myself in the kitchen with Hannah. Her computer is in between us, its cursor blinking at the end of a paragraph we wrote days ago. It's a good speech. One I'm proud of writing. One I know would achieve its purpose. But I still hit the 'delete' key.

Hannah stares at me. "What the hell are you doing?" she hisses.

"I'm fixing things," I say calmly.

"I wasn't aware they were broken." She holds up her fist. "Your nose, though, I just may break *that*."

I laugh. She doesn't.

"No, seriously," she says. "We've been working on this all week. What is wrong with you? Did you fall off that horse and hit your head?"

"Nope. I did talk with Madelyn, though, and it gave me an idea for a new approach."

"Now? Less than twenty-four hours before this place is going to be filled with people?"

"Yes." I reach for a legal pad and start scribbling down thoughts.

"You're insane. The smell of horse manure must have gone to your head."

I glance at the clock. 4:14.

I want to call Melina tonight. We haven't talked since Sunday, and I miss her. I miss her a lot. I know she's been traveling all week and she'll be back on the road this weekend, so I'm hoping I can catch her in the small sliver of space when she's actually home. That means I don't have long to get this rewrite finished.

"Just trust me on this," I tell Hannah.

I roll up my sleeves, flex my wrists, and begin.

Two hours later, I type the final period and pump my fist in triumph. It's almost like the speech wrote itself. Now, as I sit back and read it, a smile plays on my mouth. There's nothing like this kind of writer's high. It's good for the mind. Good for the soul.

"Okay," Hannah says, after she's set aside her other work and read the speech, too. "I admit it. You were right. This is the way to go. Couldn't you have done me a favor and had your brainstorm *before* I spent forever revising the original version?"

"I could have," I deadpan. "But then you wouldn't have had an excuse not to go riding."

"That," she says, "is a very good point." She pushes her chair back and stands up. "I'm gonna go for a walk and stretch my legs. I've been sitting at this table for hours. Want me to give Madelyn a copy of the updated speech?"

"I think it'd be better to just email it. That way we don't have to worry about the press getting a hold of it ahead of time. If Madelyn leaves the papers lying around ... " I shake my head. "I think it will be good to have the element of surprise." I type a note to Madelyn explaining why we changed things, attach the file, and send it off. "Maybe just find her and give her a heads-up?"

"Sure thing. See you for dinner?"

Every night this week, Madelyn's been making the meal for everybody. I was shocked at first. I guess I expected her to have a staff to do that. But the farm is mostly quiet these days. Her brother lives here full-time and they have a few people who help out with the animals, but that's it. No cook or housekeeper or gardener for the main house, and the rest of the family, including Madelyn, only visits sporadically. She seems to like cooking, though, and the food's actually been pretty terrific. I was tempted to talk with her about it at first, to tell her I love being in the kitchen, too, but I came to my senses quickly. Probably best not to say anything, lest it slip out that I'm contemplating culinary school.

"Yep," I tell Hannah. "See you in ... " I check my watch. "Fifty-three minutes."

Every evening, dinner is on the table at seven-thirty sharp. Madelyn's a stickler for punctuality. Kristi was late one day, and Madelyn made a point of looking at her watch as she came hurrying in. I don't want to be in that position.

That doesn't give me long.

I shut Hannah's laptop and hurry through the farmhouse to the wing where the guestrooms are located. Mine is at the end of the hall. It's a big room. Open. Airy. The windows look out onto the pastures, and I stand by them for a minute, watching the horses graze. Behind them, the stretch of green seems to go on for miles. It's beautiful out here. Serene. Peaceful. Much as I wasn't looking forward to this trip, I'll actually be sad to leave on Sunday. The views at home don't compare to the ones here. "You should see it," I tell Melina, once I'm settled into the armchair and talking with her. "It's like living inside of a painting."

"Send me a picture."

"I will," I promise. "As soon as we hang up. I don't think a picture will do it justice, though. It's funny – when we first got here, I felt so out of place, but every day I like it more. How about you? I know you've always lived in Philly, but do you like the country?"

"I've never been ... well, unless you count driving through it on the way to campaign stops."

"Really?"

"Nope. I'd be willing to give it a try, but really, I'm more of a beach person. We used to go there every summer when I was a kid. My grandparents owned a condo in Ventnor," she explains. "They sold it when I was nine, and then my father lost his job the following year, so that was basically it for vacations." She sighs. "God, I adored that condo. I cried my eyes out when they sold it. One day, I would like to buy it back."

"I've got no doubt that you will," I say. "You're the most determined person I know."

"I visited the homeless shelter today." She changes the subject out of nowhere. Conversational whiplash. "The one where my family stayed. It was for work, and I'm glad I went, but ... it hit me so much harder than I thought it would. There was a girl," she says softly. "She must've been eleven or twelve. She was sitting in the community room, reading to a young boy, and it ... " She gets even quieter. "It took me back in time, I guess. That could've been me. It *was* me."

I wish we were having this talk in person instead of over the phone so I could take her hand and reassure her. Instead, I have to settle for just listening as she continues.

"I hate that this is still a problem," she says sadly, "that kids have to grow up in shelters. I mean, don't get me wrong, I think the shelters are a wonderful thing. They help a ton of people. But when children live there, they don't get to ... " She pushes out an exasperated sigh. "Sorry. I'm talking in circles."

"No. Not at all."

"I just want to help them," she says.

"You are," I tell her. "You're doing amazing work. Worthwhile work. Hey," I tease, "any chance I can convince you to switch sides? Join Madelyn's team and then we can spend more time together instead of going in opposite directions. What do you say?"

"Nice try." Her tone lightens. "I'm staying where I am. Unless *you* want to switch?"

I think of the speech I wrote earlier. Of the plans Madelyn outlined to the reporters for her goal of preserving the environment and helping it flourish. Of how proud I've been this week to be a part of her team. I needed this. It may not have settled the conflict in my head, but at least it quelled it for awhile. "Sorry," I say. "I'm not going anywhere, either."

"How did we get ourselves into this situation?" she asks.

I picture her curled up on her sofa, cradling the phone against her ear as she sips from a glass of wine and fidgets with the edge of the afghan. She does that a lot, I've noticed. Fidgets. It's like she has to be doing something rather than sitting still.

"You mean how did we turn into the Romeo and Juliet of Pennsylvania's political world?" I quip, and she laughs.

"You haven't told anyone, have you?" she asks. "At work, I mean."

"No." I try to imagine how Madelyn would take the news. "Did you?"

"No."

We're silent for a few moments. I glance at the clock. 7:27.

"I better get going," I tell Melina reluctantly. "Dinner's in a few minutes."

"Yeah, me too. I was on the phone with my friend Amie for awhile, and now you. I'm starving. Hey, what time do you get back on Sunday?" she asks. "I should be finished in Reading around six or so. Want to meet up afterward?"

"Definitely. I should be home by then, so do you want to come over after you're finished? Since you'll already be halfway there?"

"Sounds good. It's a date."

Her words make me grin even after we've hung up. I text her a photo of the view outside of my window, send a short message to Cameron to thank him again for grabbing my mail while I'm away, then shove my phone into my pocket and stride across the room. One minute to go. I will be late to dinner, but I don't care. Some things are worth breaking the rules for. Except ... it seems like I won't be the only one sliding into a chair after the others, because as I walk down the hallway I can hear a woman's voice from behind a mostly closed door.

Madelyn.

"No," she says. "I'm not sure it's a good idea, but what other choice do I have?"

Immediately, my curiosity is piqued.

What's she doing up here when it's time to serve dinner ? And what's she talking about?

I should keep moving. Pretend I didn't hear anything. Go downstairs and eat.

But I can't. I feel compelled to know what's going on.

I take a careful step closer, flatten myself against the wall, and listen.

"Look," she says, "obviously this isn't my preference. I think it's the smartest method, though. I have to do something. All is fair in love and politics, right?"

An instant chill slithers down my spine.

What does she mean by that? What is she planning?

Melina

My Saturday starts bright and early. I'm up with the sun, bustling around to pack the duffel bag that I should have filled the night before, but decided to leave until the morning so I could immerse myself in a canvas instead. Between visiting the shelter earlier in the day and confessing my feelings for Bradley to Amie – and hearing her tell me to go for it, like I knew she would – there was just too much on my mind. It kept bouncing around, a ball that'd lost its way, and I knew the only possibility of catching it would be to put some paint on my palette. Painting has always been all-encompassing for me. When a brush is in my hand and an easel is standing in front of me, waiting for my colors to swirl together, everything else fades away. The world is my canvas and the canvas is my world.

Last night's painting had a lot of gray and yellow.

I glance at it, my eyes resting on the strokes. I can't decide if I like it or not. Maybe I'll play with it more when I get back. Right now, though, I have to hit the road for Reading. Nathan has a full day of events ahead: a meet-and-greet at a local diner, a house party hosted by a volunteer who lives in the city, and a fundraiser at an area fire hall. It's going to be a long day, and tomorrow will be just as busy.

I need some coffee to fuel myself, some caffeine to wake me up after only getting a few hours of sleep. My Keurig has been acting up lately, but I haven't gotten around to replacing it yet, so I run in to WaWa before setting off on my drive. It starts drizzling as I walk back to the car, this sort of misty spritzing, and I find myself wondering if it's raining where Bradley is, too, and if they'll have to move Madelyn's event inside. That'd be a good thing for Nathan, since not as many people would be able to attend, then. But what about Bradley? It would be a shame if only a handful of voters heard the speech he wrote.

Ugh.

I should not care about that. I should be happy about it, actually.

Damn it.

Why did that man have to get under my skin?

I wish he didn't. I wish I hadn't felt all warm inside after talking to him last night. I wish I hadn't had that dream about him. It's been hours now since I woke up from it, my pulse pounding and my breath in an uneven rhythm, and I still can't wash it out of my mind. The smell of his cologne tickling my nose, the taste of his lips as they captured mine, the touch of his fingertips as they inched below my shirt ... it was both the best and worst dream I've had in ages. As I get back into my car, I make a concerted effort to forget about it and direct my attention to the day ahead instead.

Voter turnout.

Public opinion polls.

Direct mailing possibilities and costs.

One by one, I let these things pass through the sieve and filter into my thoughts. They are safer topics, and important ones, too. Madelyn is outspending Nathan by quite a lot, and we have to find a way to compensate for the deficit, especially if Perry files to be on the ballot before the deadline in August. Then we will be campaigning against two. Technically finances don't fall within the realm of my job – I'm really supposed to just focus on policy – but I'm determined to help out. The last thing I want is for Nathan to lose because he couldn't raise sufficient funding. It hurts to know that when money talks, it can drown out the other voices.

I should know. I've been there.

I won't let it happen again this time, and neither will Nathan.

I see that all day long, in the way he caters to each type of voter he meets. At the diner, as he's chatting with the breakfast patrons, he's more relaxed and casual. He joins people at their booths, speaking off the cuff and laughing a hearty laugh. At the house party, though, he's more formal. He gives a speech that Cole prepared and then opens up the floor for questions. He gets a lot of them, about everything from the cigarette tax to charter school reform to establishing a state budget, and answers them all like a pro. After the Q&A is finished, it segues into more of a mix and mingle. The cool thing about an event like this is that it gives Nathan a chance to talk with people one-on-one, to really get individual face time with the voters. That's also a bad thing, though, since it means there's downtime while people are waiting to speak with him. I try to use that to our advantage by passing around an iPad so the guests can sign up for Nathan's mailing list, and also to join his volunteer and fundraising teams.

"How much of a time commitment does that involve?" one woman asks me.

"As little as you want," I tell her. "Or as much as you want. We're glad to have anybody who is interested in helping."

She nods, using the on-screen keyboard to type in her contact information. "I'm a teacher," she says, "so I don't have a lot of free time when school is in session, but I'd love to help this summer. I can make phone calls, go door-to-door, whatever you want." She looks at me. "We need somebody in the governor's mansion who will really fight for us."

"Nathan is the perfect person," I assure her. "He'll make Pennsylvania the best it can be."

"I pay her to say that." Nathan pops over to join us, a twinkle in his eyes, and we all laugh. "It's Lauren, right?" he asks the woman. "You asked earlier about tuition rates at state-owned colleges?" She nods again, and I slip off as she and Nathan fall into conversation. Kira and Cole are working the room, too, along with a few of our other colleagues, and by the time the house party is over, we've managed to get another twenty-five names on Nathan's mailing list. A good percentage also sign up as volunteers, and some offer to contribute their cash, as well as their time. It is, by all counts, a big success for Nathan.

The fundraiser that night follows suit. It isn't a fancy gala like the sort of fundraiser Madelyn can host, but that doesn't make it any less enjoyable. The food is great, the fire hall is filled with people who are excited about Nathan's plans for the state, and the speech he gives is met with thunderous applause. I join in, clapping until my hands hurt. Sometimes I still can't believe this is my life, that I actually get to travel around and work for a man who is trying so hard to help so many. I hope that can be me one day. I would love to run for office. There is no greater honor than serving the public. I know many people are cynical when it comes to politics, that the stories of corruption make them critical of those in office, and I get that. Sometimes I feel weary, too, but then I'm part of something like this and it fills the well of energy up again. It feeds the hunger inside me.

When I get back to my hotel room that night, I'm on a total high. It's been such a fantastic day. I wonder how Bradley's has been. How did Madelyn's event go? How much press coverage did she receive? If today were a contest, who would come out on top? But these are not the only questions running through my mind. As I pad across the floor, push back the curtains, and look up at the foggy night sky, I want to know what Bradley's doing right now. Is he thinking of me like I am of him? Is it foggy there, too, or are there stars shining down on him? I touch my fingers to the window, its glass cool against my skin.

An image flashes through my head, from that beautiful disaster of a dream: the two of us in my apartment, a movie on TV as Bradley moves his hand to my knee and his lips to my neck. My heart beats a little faster just thinking about it.

Stop it, Melina, I tell myself. *Stop it, stop it, stop it right now.*

But I can't.

When I pull up in front of Bradley's house the next day, the memories of my subconscious desire still lurk around the corners of my mind. I sit in my car for a minute, drumming my nails against the steering wheel and trying to remember how long I waited before taking the next step in my previous relationships. Cory was my first real boyfriend. I'd been too busy to date anyone while I was in high school, and maybe a little embarrassed. The thought of a boy coming over and seeing where I lived, *how* I lived, made my cheeks go red. And then, once I started at college, I was determined to earn a terrific GPA so I could keep the scholarships I'd won. There was no time for a boyfriend, until Cory. I was feeling better about things by the time I transferred to Villanova. I had a great internship lined up, my classes were all poli-sci related, and it seemed like life was finally falling into place ... so when I met Cory at the library one day, I didn't shoot him down when he asked for my number. We took it steady, but slow, and it was the same with Ian.

With Bradley, I don't know if we have that luxury. It could be now or never. The closer it gets to the election, the more we'll have fighting against us. I don't want to think about that, but it's kind of hard not to, especially as we eat dinner outside on his patio and chat about how the weekend went. "I always used to enjoy the big events best," I tell him, taking the salad tongs and helping myself to a second serving. "The rallies, the debates, things like that. Now I'm beginning to love the small ones. Yesterday was Nathan's first house party, and it was awesome. You really can't beat the intimacy. I think people appreciate having the chance to tell their stories. Listening to candidates speak is one thing. Having a give-and-take with them is another."

"I agree." Bradley looks over my shoulder at something in the distance. "Everybody wants to be heard."

"Are you okay?" I ask, when his gaze doesn't falter from whatever's behind me. I turn around to see what it is, but nothing's there.

"Yes. Fine." He answers quickly, pulling his attention back to the plate in front of him. He made something called tomato orecchiette, which I had never heard of before, but liked from my first bite. It's pasta, topped with melted cheese, diced tomato, and chopped basil. It's like a party for my taste buds. Bradley, however, has barely touched his. "It was just a long week," he says.

"You sounded excited about it when we talked on Friday evening," I point out. "Did something happen with the event yesterday? Was turnout lower than expected? I know it couldn't have been an issue with your speech, because you're a marvelous writer." He truly is. I've admired Madelyn's orations since long before I knew the man behind them. I tell him as much, but his smile is only half-hearted.

"Thanks," he says. "You're the best. And turnout was good. The rain moved out in time and we must have had seventy-five people or so. The speech went over well. It's just that ... " He trails off, picking up his glass and swirling around the white wine inside. I watch him as he watches it. I don't know what kind of answers he finds in that moment, but suddenly his whole demeanor changes. His smile becomes dazzling, and he leans forward to rest his hand on mine. "I'm so glad you suggested this," he says. "I really did miss you this week."

"I missed you, too."

What was he going to say before? Why did he stop?

Part of me wants to push the issue, but I know it wouldn't be fair. After all, it's not like I've been entirely open with him. There are still so many pieces of my heart that I'm keeping safely under lock and key. So I let it go. I *am* working for Madelyn's opposition, so it's understandable that he would want to leave some things out of the conversation. Maybe it's foolish of me to think that way, but I don't care. With Bradley's hand blanketing mine and a splash of hazy evening sunshine warming us from above, I don't want anything to ruin this moment.

I decide a change of subject is in order. "So," I say, twirling a forkful of pasta, "tell me about the rescue you volunteer for. Is it a regular animal shelter, but for rabbits only?"

"Sort of." A light comes on in his eyes. "I guess the biggest difference is that it's all run through a network of fosters. There's no main building or anything like that. We have lots of people who'll take in the rabbits until they can find a forever home."

"A forever home," I echo. "Isn't that a lovely thought?"

We should all be so lucky as to find that, if such a thing even exists.

Sometimes I have my doubts.

I think Bradley must sense that my emotions are stirred up, because he squeezes my hand. "You should come volunteer with me one day," he says. "I guarantee you'll fall in love." A beat too late, he realizes how that sounds. "I mean, with the bunnies," he backpedals. "Not me. Not that I don't want you to fall in love with me. Obviously that'd be incredible. I just … I don't want you to get the idea that I'm rushing … " He withdraws his hand from mine and buries his face in both of his. "This is not coming out like I meant it to," he mumbles through his fingers. "Feel free to run for the hills. I wouldn't blame you."

I wouldn't blame me, either.

If this were any other man, the word 'love' being thrown around this soon would terrify me. It'd make me want to get in my car, drive away, and never look back. I won't lie, the thought does cross my mind. More than running off, though, Bradley's words make me want to stay. Maybe the dream I had was trying to tell me something: to take a chance, for once in my life, to leap even though I'm afraid of falling, and to be alright with not landing on my feet, because the flight itself is what's most important.

That's why, after we finish eating and the sun has sunk lower in the sky, coloring it with vibrant shades of pink and purple, I get up and walk around to Bradley's side of the table. "It's so pretty," I murmur, watching as the fireflies come out to do their dance. "The sky looks like it's on fire, doesn't it?"

"It reminds me of something you'd paint," he says.

I think of the canvas back at home, the grays of my Friday and the yellows of my phone call with him.

"I'm not good at relationships," I say, resting my hands on the back of his chair. "To be honest, I'm actually pretty bad at them. You are the one who should be running for the hills, but on the off-chance that you don't … " I let my hands settle on his shoulders and bend over to kiss him. He rises up in his seat, his mouth meeting mine, and then he's standing too. He's standing close, deliciously close, and all I can think of is how I can take that dream and make it a reality.

I trail my fingers up Bradley's arms and clasp them behind his neck. I can't even explain it. I just have an intense yearning to explore every inch of him. I want his skin on mine, his heartbeat in sync with mine, all of him on all of me. As I close my eyes, drinking in the moment as he rests his hand on my cheek and kisses me, I know I'm not the only one who feels this way.

"I ... I wasn't expecting this," he whispers, his breath hot against my mouth.

"Sometimes the best things in life are unexpected."

I drop a kiss on the corner of his lips. He tastes intoxicating, like wine and summertime.

"What do you say we take this indoors?" I whisper.

His fingers hook around the belt loops of my jeans, pulling me closer still. It's like the air around us is charged, like there are electrons crackling and sizzling and exploding. And then he's kissing me again. He's kissing me like no one's ever kissed me before, enough to make my knees buckle, and all I want is to get my hands under that shirt of his. I pull back slightly, eyes connecting with Bradley's, telling him all the things I can't find the words to say. He kisses me again, and then he sighs.

"I'm sorry," he says. "I can't."

BRADLEY

Instantly, Melina's shoulders sag. "You ... can't?" she repeats.

All at once, a hundred and one thoughts topple over each other in my mind.

Don't be an idiot. Melina's the best thing to happen to you in forever.

That's exactly why you have to turn her down.

What she doesn't know won't hurt her.

Yes, it will. It'll hurt you both.

Tell her the truth.

But what is the truth? You still don't know. Because you're a coward.

She could be the one. She could be the one, and you're destroying it.

"No," I finally say, voice heavy with regret. "I can't." Melina takes a step back, and although my first instinct is to reach for her hand and reel her back in, I don't let myself. "I want to," I tell her. "I want to more than you know. But I ... " I look into her eyes and make a silent appeal. "I don't think this is the right time."

"Why not?"

I wrack my brain for an appropriate reason, or at least one that isn't too absurd. "Because we're both exhausted," I blurt out. I regret it immediately. That *does* sound absurd – and stupid, too. But I have to go with it now. I have to make it believable. "We've both been traveling a lot lately," I say. "We've had long days. Long nights." I force myself to stay at arm's length for fear that if I get closer to her, my resolve will dissipate. "I think it's clear by now that you've become someone very special to me. I want our first time together to be special, too. Give me a chance to make that happen."

"I'm not buying this," she says. "You weren't exhausted five minutes ago."

I put on my best poker face, spinning the web of deceit further. Better be careful or I'll get stuck inside it. "You deserve the best," I say. "And I can't give you that right now. Did I tell you how big a hurry I was in on Monday morning before I left? My alarm didn't go off, and I woke up an hour late. I had to run around like crazy so I could leave on time. And then I only got home a few hours ago. I didn't have time to cook *and* clean, so I chose dinner. If you saw what my upstairs looks like, you'd think a tornado had blown through. So no," I say, letting myself take a step closer to her, "that's not the scene I want to set for something important. I'd rather wait until I can do it right."

She lets out a little puff of air that tickles my cheek. "Okay," she says. "Fine. I understand that. For the record, though, I wouldn't have cared." She leans forward and presses a barely-there kiss to my mouth. When I was a kid, maybe six or seven, a butterfly landed on my wrist while I was outside with Grandma, helping in her garden. That's what Melina's kiss feels like. Gentle. Soft. Hardly even noticeable.

But her absence when I slide into bed? That is very noticeable. Because there was no tornado.

The blanket is folded neatly, the sheets crisp and smooth, the pillows fluffed. My nightstand is a picture of preciseness – there's a spare pair of glasses, a memoir about World War II, and my alarm clock, which is fully functional. I look at it for a long time. The numbers glow an ethereal green. It's enough to make me tired, but not sleepy. Definitely not exhausted.

I hate that I lied to Melina.

I hate that I turned her down when I so badly wanted to do the opposite.

I hate that I stole what could've been a beautiful moment for us.

Most of all, I hate *why* I did those things.

Madelyn.

It's been two days since I heard her speaking behind what

she must have assumed was a closed door. The weekend was nightmarish. I was on edge the whole time, watching and waiting, trying to put two and two together to calculate what she was planning. Unfortunately, it didn't happen. She gave nothing away, not when she was addressing the people at the event and not when it was only her staff, gathered in the kitchen this morning for the breakfast she made us as a thank you for our hard work all week long. If I hadn't overheard her myself, I never would have guessed anything was going on.

Fragments of her conversation float through my mind.

I'm not sure it's a good idea, but what other choice do I have?

Obviously this isn't my preference.

All is fair in love and politics, right?

The problem is, it was a one-sided conversation to me. I never heard another voice, and by the time I got to the dinner table, everyone was already there except Hannah, who lost track of time on her walk. Madelyn was the only other person who was late. She came bustling into the kitchen ten minutes after we were all seated, apologizing as she carried the serving dishes over from the island counter and set them on the table.

I should have confronted her about it. I should have said something.

Instead, I said nothing.

I ate dinner with everybody on Friday night. Stood with Hannah at Madelyn's event on Saturday and let myself zero in on the words being spoken and not the person speaking them. Gave a quote to one of the newspaper guys to use in the feature he was putting together on Madelyn's campaign staff. Listened to Kristi on the phone, booking the next round of Madelyn's travel accommodations. And, finally, I went for another horseback ride today, before it was time to leave. It was a different horse than the first time, but we worked well together. "Your owner is up to something," I told her, as we trotted across the property. "Any idea what?"

She whinnied and flicked her tail.

I smiled a little. "Yeah," I said. "Me neither."

I wondered, not for the first time since overhearing Madelyn's conversation, just how much was going on beyond what I saw every day. She was so fast to deny any involvement in the incident with Nathan's camera. I believed her. But the camera still hasn't shown up. Melina said Nathan's made a point of letting it go and concentrating instead on moving his campaign forward. I know, though, that it still bothers her. Maybe it should be bothering me, too.

Ugh.

I flip over so I can't see the clock. I don't need to watch the time ticking away.

But it doesn't help. I still can't sleep.

I could have been with Melina tonight. She could have been wrapped in my arms right now, her back pressed against my chest as she drifted off. I would have cooked her breakfast in the morning. Waffles, eggs, fruit, and maybe some hash browns. I could have had that. *We* could have had that. But I pushed her away.

I know she was disappointed. Maybe even hurt.

I wonder if she's lying in bed now, thinking of me. Wishing we were together.

"Damn it," I groan. Grandma always told me not to curse, that swear words were off limits for a 'respectful family like ours,' and for the most part, that's stuck. But now I can't help it. Suppose I've ruined things with Melina? What if I'm ruining them at this very moment by keeping quiet about all I overheard?

Maybe I should tell her, even though there's nothing concrete or specific.

It's just ... how can I do that to Madelyn until I get some clarification? If there's any chance at all that I could have misunderstood, or jumped to the wrong conclusion, well, don't I owe it to her to at least give her the opportunity to explain? I've worked for her for over a year now. I like her both as a person and a politician, and I genuinely think she'll do wonderful things for our state if she wins in November.

Where does my loyalty lie?

It's a tug of war.

The rope jerks back and forth.

I sit up in bed. Grab my pillow. Chuck it across the room.

"Damn it," I say again, this time louder. "Just … damn it."

* * *

The first thing I notice when I hop out of the backseat of our family's station wagon is the sky. It is the same shade of blue as my favorite crayon in my Crayola box. There are no clouds this morning, just a lot of birds flying in a perfect 'V' shape. "Mom, Dad, look!" I point up with both index fingers. "It's a V for victory!"

Dad tousles my hair. "I like the way you think," he says. "You're a smart boy."

"So am I!" Eric clamors, climbing out of the car after me. Jake follows, and we trail after Mom as she leads us across the park. I look around at it, but don't see a playground. I had been hoping for a little time to play on the swings after Mom and Dad finished talking to the people gathered near the stage. That's all they do anymore. Talk, talk, talk. There's a name for it – campaigning, I think they said – but I don't understand. The other kids in my kindergarten class have parents with normal jobs. But not my mom and dad. They just keep right on talking.

"How'd you like to come up on stage with us?" Mom asks, when we reach the front of the crowd.

"Do we get to give a speech, too?" Jake asks eagerly.

"And make promises?" Eric adds. "Can I promise to have more ice cream choices in the school's cafeteria? And to make every Friday pizza day? I think that would be a great idea." He beelines for the podium, and I watch as Mom hooks an arm around his to pull him back.

"Sorry," she says. "The only ones who get to make promises today are your father and I."

They make lots of them.

They use a bunch of grown-up words that I don't really understand, but I guess the other people do, because they keep clapping after my parents are finished. "This is so cool," Jake whispers to Eric and me.

"Super duper cool," I agree.

It seems like one big party. Everyone's excited, even more excited than I get when my favorite tv show is on, and I feel proud that it's because of my parents. Maybe it's okay that they don't have too much time to play with my brothers and me anymore. It's kinda neat that we get to share them with all these people. They keep saying they'll make the world a better place. I want to do that someday, too. I want to be just like them.

Just like them.

The words rocket through my brain, yanking me out of the dream and into the quiet stillness of my room. What time is it? How long was I asleep? I squint at the clock. Three-thirty. I should close my eyes again. Get some more rest. Fill up my reserves for the week ahead. But that dream. I sigh. I've had that dream so many times. Except it's more of a memory, really. That's how all my dreams are. They're not a peek into the future. They're a flashback to the past. This one leads the charge. I get it. That moment was pivotal in my life. It's when I decided – or, maybe, when it was decided for me – that politics was in my blood.

It was so bright and shiny then. So invigorating. Now?

I roll over and look at the empty side of my bed.

Now I don't know what it is.

When I wake up again four hours later, I have an urge to call the one person who can help me to figure it out. Grandfather. He's always up early – a habit still ingrained in him from his military days – so I don't hesitate before punching in his phone number. Grandma's an early bird, too, so I know they'll be awake.

He answers on the second ring. "Hello?"

His voice is warm. Deep. Rich.

"Grandfather, hi, it's me."

"Bradley! Hi, my boy. Can you hang on for just a minute?" I hear some shuffling and creaking in the background. "Okay," he says, when he gets back on. "Sorry about that. I was just getting all my fishing supplies ready. Did you know Eric's in town? He's visiting in between those summer classes he's teaching. We're going out to the lake this morning. I wish you and Jake could be here to join us for it."

I smile at the idea. I used to love our fishing trips. It was just the four of us, before my brothers became golden boys and left me trying not to tarnish, and we had such a nice time. None of us ever kept the fish we caught, but it was fun to simply sit on the docks and feel the lake water pool around our ankles. We had a lot of good talks. Grandfather would tell us all the stories of his life and ask us questions about ours.

I miss those times.

Things were easier then.

"I wish we could be, too," I say to Grandfather, and I'm surprised to realize that I actually mean it. "I've been swamped at work lately. One of our fishing trips sounds like the perfect way to relax. Rain check?"

"Of course," he says. "Tell me about work. How's it going?"

"Funny you should ask. That's actually why I called." I pour myself a mug of coffee and carry it to the table. "I've kind of gotten myself into a tough spot."

"What's wrong?" he asks, his concern so strong it's nearly tangible.

I tell him the whole story. The sneaking in to record Nathan's meeting and speech. The denial Madelyn hurled my way when I questioned her about the camera. The trip to the farm, the words I overheard, the knot in my stomach that's been growing ever since. "It's a mess," I say. "And I don't know how to clean it up."

And then I tell him about Melina, too.

"You really like this woman, don't you?" he asks.

Of all the things I shared, that's what he chooses to zero in on.

"Yes," I say. "I do."

"Does she return your feelings?"

A grin tugs at my mouth as I think of Melina's kiss yesterday. "Yes," I say. "It's tricky, obviously, with the election hanging over us, but I'm pretty sure she feels the same way."

"Then I'll tell you what my dad told me when I called from Germany to explain that I wanted to bring your grandma home with me. 'Son,' he said, 'there are three things I've learned in life. First, it is important to always wear a pair of matching socks. Don't be caught with one gray and one blue.'" This makes Grandfather chuckle, and me, too. "'Second,'" he continues, "'Never underestimate the power of a helping hand. Third, love conquers all. Love matters most. We're nothing without it.'"

"Even if it means risking everything?"

"Especially when it means risking everything."

"I don't think Mom and Dad would be happy about it."

"And I think that doesn't matter," my grandfather says. "This is your life, my boy, and you only get one. You owe it to yourself to follow your heart."

As I listen to him, I reach for the newspaper on the table. I know that most people get the news online, but I still like to read the old-fashioned hard copy. It's delivered each morning. I just haven't gotten a chance to look at today's yet.

Grandfather is still talking, something about challenges making us stronger, but I don't hear the rest of what he says. Not a single word.

I'm too busy gaping at the newspaper in horror.

Oh God. It's right there in black and white, splashed across the front page.

The answer to my question.

Now I know *exactly* what Madelyn was talking about on Friday.

17

Melina

I've always been a morning person. There's something special in the air at that time of day, this sense of possibility that shines through the first rays of sun and brightens the world below. When I was younger, I'd often sneak out of bed and watch the sky go from an inky blanket to one painted in pastels. It was like somebody had turned a light on. That was my alone time back then, something I didn't get very often, living with five other people in an apartment the size of a postage stamp. As a kid and even as a teenager, I craved that serenity.

Now, not so much.

It's why I don't sit and watch the sunrise anymore, at least not without doing something else at the same time. Sometimes I'll flip on the television and listen to the morning news. Other times I'll take out my paintbrushes and play on a fresh canvas, or skim a few chapters in the book I'm reading, or jot notes for a proposal at work. Today, though, by the time I open my eyes, the sun is already in place. It pours into my room, glaringly announcing its presence, and I blink, trying to orient myself. What time is it? Or, perhaps, a better question would be – how *late* is it?

I reach for my phone on the nightstand, but my fingers come up empty.

Oh. Right.

That's why I overslept, because I never set an alarm. I dropped my phone as I was getting out of the car last night, and it smacked against the asphalt, etching little glass cobwebs across the screen. It was a total loss. The phone wouldn't turn on, and after a night that had already been frustrating, I couldn't find it in me to care. I was still too thrown by Bradley's behavior. One minute, he had been kissing me with reckless abandon, and the next, he was offering some lame excuse about his house being a mess. I know there was more to it than that. I'm just not sure what.

I glance at the clock hanging on the wall. Eight-thirty. Okay, that's not too bad. It's later than I normally start my day, but I can just stay after hours at work to make up for it. Honestly, I probably would've ended up staying late anyway. Nathan needs my draft of the homeless shelter initiative by next Monday, which means I've only got a week to piece it all together into a kickass presentation.

It's time to shift things into high gear.

I wolf down a fast breakfast, throw on a pair of linen dress pants and my favorite summery top, and then I'm off. My first stop is the phone store, to see about getting a replacement. Next, I go to Helping Hands to pick up the camera I left for the weekend. It's easier to walk inside this time. The memories of my months there will never fade, but now there are new memories, too, like when the little boy took me by the hand on Friday and asked if I'd play checkers with him. He didn't care that the board was ripped and the pieces were faded. To him, the game was just as it should be. I don't know whether that makes me happy or sad. The same goes for all the people I met last week, all the stories they told me.

There is struggle inside these doors. Heartache. Heartbreak.

But there is relief, too, that feeling of finally being able to breathe a little. There is hope, there is faith, and there is tenacity. I saw it in so many of the faces who looked my way on Friday, and I see it again today, as I sit in Nora's office and scroll through the pictures on the camera she hands me. It is amazing. *They* are amazing. "This is more than I ever imagined," I tell Nora, smiling. "Some of the shots are breathtaking."

"I thought so, too. And eye-opening," she adds. "It's true what people say: sometimes a picture *is* worth a thousand words."

"That's why I paint," I tell her. "I started here, actually. It was my outlet."

It's clear that the camera was the same thing for the current residents at Helping Hands. That's what I'd hoped for when I came up with the idea. I wanted them to capture the ins and outs of life at a shelter, to put their own lens on what homelessness meant. What's developed gives me chills. I can't wait to use these images in my proposal. I can't wait for Nathan's reaction, and more so, the reaction from people across the state when we begin incorporating the pictures into his campaign in a couple weeks.

I'm so excited about it, I go right to print the pictures after leaving the shelter. Seeing them on a screen is one thing, but as they spit out from the machine, it's another. It feels like I am holding the whole world in my hands. These people have entrusted me with their fears and worries, their hopes and dreams, and I feel so very grateful for their faith in me.

I wish I could tell someone about it, that I could share this moment. Bradley would've been my first choice, though it probably wouldn't have been a smart idea to discuss this with him. I know he said that Madelyn backed off of using Nathan's platforms, but still, some things are better kept close to the vest. Not that it matters anyway, since I have no phone. I hate to admit it, but I feel a bit lost without it. So much of my life is in that small device: my work contacts, my videos and pictures from the campaign trail, my voice messages to myself, because I always get my sparks of inspiration while I'm driving and record them so I don't forget. It's bizarre to be without all of that.

I remember when I got my first cell phone, right before college. My dad was worried about me driving back and forth from school each day. "What happens if you get a flat tire?" he asked. "Or if there's a detour and you get lost?" He'd been working at the post office for six years by that point – it was the only place to take a chance on him after he'd been let go – and although he didn't have a lot of money, he was determined to get me a phone anyway. It was a novelty then. Now, it's all but another appendage. Maybe it's good to take a brief break from it. It frees me up to concentrate on other things, like the sun's brilliant rays reflecting on the roof of the minivan ahead of me as I drive to work.

Today is going to be a great day, I can just feel it.

"Good morning," I say to Kira, a little sing-songy, when I get to the office.

She doesn't answer.

"Kira?"

She's staring intently at her laptop screen, too intently, and when she finally spins around, I see that her face is pale. "Good morning?" she repeats, gazing at me strangely. "I wouldn't say there's anything good about it."

Huh?

What does she mean?

That's when I notice it, glaring at me from her computer.

Oh my God.

Immediately, a pain slams into my stomach. It is literally like somebody has punched me in the gut. I can feel my heart rate start to speed up, but not in a good way. No, this is the worst possible way. Without thinking, I reach my hand out to Kira's desk, gripping tightly onto it for support as the room goes all topsy-turvy around me. Down is up, left is right, and everything is wrong.

"You have to be kidding me," I sputter. "How? Why? Who?"

"I don't know," she says. "Photoshop? That was my first thought, but – "

"But it seems so real." I lean forward and examine the photo splashed across the laptop screen. Bits and pieces are recognizable: the toddler girl with pigtails, her fist clenched around a lollipop like it's her most prized possession, her older brother with holes in his jeans and a shiny new toy truck in his arms, and their father behind them, shaking Nathan's hand. I remember these people. We met them in April, on Nathan's *Let's Get It Right* tour across the state. It was his last big push before the primary. For a month straight, we zig-zagged all around Pennsylvania until no ground had been left uncovered, and we took a camera with us. The idea had been to create a sort of photo-journal that we could use in Nathan's campaign ads if he won in May. That camera was the one I had been given for safe-keeping.

Now I know why it disappeared.

Someone definitely took it – someone who is undoubtedly out to destroy Nathan.

Because for all the things that *are* recognizable in the picture, there are many more that aren't: the white Mercedes parked by the side of the road, the sly grin on Nathan's face, and the trash bag at his feet, with a bundle of wrapped presents spilling out onto the grass. None of that is real. None of it was there when we visited this family on their tiny plot of land near the Appalachian mountains. Looking at this photo, though, nobody would ever know that. It seems authentic. It also seems like Nathan is trying to bribe these people with gifts to buy their vote – and that he is rather proud of it. He comes off as smarmy and crooked.

My eyes skim over the headline, and it makes my stomach lurch all over again.

Nathan Ford: the man behind the mask?

This is bad. This is so, so bad.

"There's more," Kira says scrolling down to show me two more pictures that are nestled among the blocks of text. One is from our visit to a nursing home in Bethlehem. Nathan joined in with the residents when we were there, playing bingo and talking with them as they ate lunch. In this photo, though, he's standing off to the side, alone, with his arms crossed. Then there's a picture of him by a café in Philadelphia, handing a stuffed envelope to a woman. I remember that, too. The envelope had workbook pages inside, left over from his wife's days as a second grade teacher. He was giving them to another teacher, since her district couldn't afford to buy enough materials for its students. But in this warped version? You can see the outline of rubber-banded money inside.

Something pinches my temples almost violently.

"Does he know?" I breathe.

"Yes." Kira's shoulders slump. "He's in his office. Won't talk to anyone. He's too upset."

"I just ... this is ... how do we ... "

There are no words.

"Hey, where were you?" Kira asks, as I drag a chair over and sit down. Suddenly I don't have the energy to walk to my own desk. "I kept trying to call you, but it went straight to voicemail."

"Oh, sorry. My phone is dead. I dropped it when I was getting out of the car last night and – " I break off as an image zooms into my head: Bradley, looking at me almost pleadingly as he told me it wasn't the right time to sleep together. Could this be why? I knew there was more to the story, and now, as a sickeningly hollow hole opens up somewhere inside my chest, I wonder if this is it. Maybe Madelyn is behind this. Maybe he knew. Maybe he's known all along and he really has been playing me from the start.

"Melina?" Kira asks. She peers at me. "Are you okay? You look like you're going to – "

Be sick.

That's what I look like. That's what I feel like.

If I thought the room was spinning before, now it's taking me on a dizzying roller-coaster. I think of all those moments Bradley and I have shared. The kiss by Penn's Landing. The hike at his favorite park and the way his fingers threaded through mine to help me climb the steep parts. The late night talks on the days when we weren't traveling and the text messages on the days we were. The cream puffs. The way he opened up so sincerely, or at least what I thought was sincerely, about his family. How much of that was real? Was *any* of it real?

"Whoa." Cole walks by, a stack of file folders in hand, and does a double take. "No offense," he says, "but you are one horrible shade of yellow, Melina. Kinda puke-colored. I guess you just found out about the article?"

All I can manage is a nod.

"I don't get it," he says. "Nathan's such a good guy. Why would somebody do this?"

"Because of what you said," Kira tells him. "Because he *is* a good guy. His track record is great. That makes him a threat." She exits out of the Internet browser. "I can't look at this anymore. We know what's out there and now we need to figure out what to do about it." She tilts her head up to meet his gaze. "Are you in charge of writing the denial speech?"

He shakes his head. "He won't even let me in to talk with him about it. I tried to explain that it's crucial to come back with an immediate response, but it's like he's in some kind of fog." Something shifts in his eyes for a second, from exasperation to something almost bordering on smugness, but it disappears as quickly as it comes and I have to wonder if I imagined it, since my head's not exactly in a good place. "Nathan needs to stop burying his head in the sand," Cole says, and now he's back to seeming worried. "The longer this goes on without any denial, the worse it is. Seeing is believing for a lot of people. We can threaten a lawsuit for libel, but that will take too long to prove. Plus, it's not like the pictures are printed in some tabloid. This is a pretty credible source. Whoever did this must be awfully smart, professional, and connected."

Connected. Like Madelyn, with her money.

My chest is burning now. It's on fire.

"Excuse me," I choke out, and jump up, making a mad dash for the door. I need some fresh air. It doesn't help, though. I actually think it makes things worse, because the humidity outside feels as though it's a clamp on my body. I am so nauseous. My eyes can't seem to focus, my legs can't seem to hold still, and my breathing can't seem to slow down. This is so much worse than I ever imagined when the camera first disappeared. And what about that new camera? All those pictures from the shelter, the ones I was so excited about only a couple hours ago ... they're basically pointless now. It breaks my heart: for Nathan, for myself, and mostly for the people at Helping Hands.

I wanted to make their lives better.

I wanted to be a part of something great.

Thud. Thud, thud, thud.

My heart drums inside me.

I have to call Bradley. Maybe Nathan is going to take this lying down, but I won't. I can't. I have been a fighter my whole life, and now is no time to stop. I take a deep breath, then another. Inhale. Exhale. Repeat. I can do this. I can put aside the memories that scrolled through my mind before. I can call Bradley, detach myself, and treat him like a contentious colleague instead of the man who's worked his way into my heart.

Except I can't.

I can't do any of those things, at least not right now, because my damn phone doesn't work.

"Duh," I chastise myself. "Dead cell and no replacement yet, remember?"

Not that it matters ... because, just then, I see a familiar car turn into the parking lot.

18

BRADLEY

I wasn't expecting her to be right there. But she is. As I pull into a parking spot, Melina's staring straight at me, hands on her hips, watching my every move. She knows. I'd been holding out hope that she hadn't seen the article, but it takes all of two seconds to see that the opposite is true. And why wouldn't it be? She works for the man being raked over the coals.

I hate confrontation. I have always hated confrontation. It's why I was so nervous about telling my family that I'd quit the debate club back in high school. Why I never called Rachel, who had been my girlfriend for five years, after she broke up with me through a letter she left in my mailbox. She had met someone else, she wrote. There were so many things I wanted to say to her, but it was just easier to let her go. Not with Melina. It wouldn't be easy at all to let her go. It'd hurt deeply to say goodbye to this woman who blew into my life and turned it inside out.

So I don't. I don't shy away from the confrontation I can tell is coming. Instead, I get out of the car and walk straight toward the path of most resistance. Melina's gaze is still unwavering. As I get closer, she folds her arms over her chest, like she's trying to protect what's inside. "Well," she says briskly, once I'm close enough to hear, "you're the last person I expected to see. I thought you'd be celebrating with Madelyn."

Her words are an arrow to the heart.

"Is there somewhere we can go to talk?" I ask softly.

She bites her bottom lip, and for a second, I think she's going to

149

say no. Then she lets out a slow breath. "There's a courtyard in the middle of the office complex," she says, and spins on her heel. I trail after her as she leads the way, shutting out the frenzy of emotion clanging in my brain. It's best to focus on logic instead. Reason. Rationality. I'll tell Melina everything, and apologize, and she'll ... what? As we sit at one of the tables in the courtyard, I realize I have no clue what she'll do.

"Okay," she says, leaning back in her chair and re-crossing her arms. "Go on. Talk."

"First, I want to say how sorry I am."

Her eyes flicker downward. It's the slightest movement, almost imperceptible, but I catch it just the same. "So you knew," she says. Actually, it's more of a whisper. "You knew, and you didn't tell me. How could you?"

"I didn't know," I say, but the words sound feeble even to my own ears. "At least, not any of the details." I briefly contemplate reaching out to her, but her arms are still firmly crossed and her back is rigid against the chair. "I did overhear something I was never meant to, though, and ... " I inhale a sharp breath. This is harder than I thought it would be. I spent the whole drive here practicing what I wanted to say, and it seemed half decent then, but now the words are stuck in my throat.

"And what?" Melina asks.

She's waiting. Watching. Maybe even hoping? I think she wants me to give her a reason not to hate me. God, how I wish I could. "And I kept quiet," I say. "I didn't have specifics, and I was afraid to say anything in case I had totally misinterpreted. It wasn't like I heard Madelyn talking about the actual camera." I lay everything out, piece by piece, and explain what happened at the farm. "I was going to ask her about it today," I tell Melina. "But obviously, it was too late for that."

"Obviously," she echoes coolly.

"I just ... " I rest an elbow on the table and rub my forehead wearily. "I never thought Madelyn would do something like this. It's not how she operates."

"Or it's not how she wants everybody to think she operates," Melina points out. "Come on, this isn't the first time she's done something underhanded." Her eyes zero in on me like lasers. "Tell me the truth: has this been the plan all along? Did she ask you to infiltrate Nathan's inner circle? Is that why you're dating me?"

The accusation is a slap in the face. It makes me flinch. "No," I say. "It most certainly is not. Is that really what you think, that all the time we've spent with each other has been about Madelyn?" I feel a tightness in my chest. "I like you because of who you are, not who you work for. Because of how your nose crinkles up when you laugh and how your eyes get squinty when you are really deep in thought. Because you're interesting. Kindhearted. Passionate. And especially because you make me happy."

She casts a glance up toward the sky, like she is looking for something in the clouds. "You make me happy, too," she says. "Or you did, anyway. It seemed too good to be true, and you know what they say about situations like that." She twists her bracelet around her wrist, staring at it instead of at me. "I let you wake something up inside me that had been asleep for a long time. That was a big mistake."

"It wasn't." This time, I do reach out to her, and to my surprise, she doesn't pull away. She lets me rest my hand atop hers. "I swear, I've never lied about my feelings for you. Maybe I was wrong not to tell you about that conversation right away. But I did the best I could with what I had, and if I mean anything to you, if I've ever meant anything to you, you have to believe that. Why else would I be here? I called out of work so I could come see you."

"I don't know. I just don't know."

"Can I ask you something?" I say, and she nods. "Is there a chance those pictures could be real? I know you think Nathan is amazing and that he wouldn't do something like that, but nothing about those photos seems doctored."

It is exactly the wrong thing to say.

Melina's sadness morphs into a fiery fury. "No." She practically spits the word at me. "There is no chance they're real. I was with him on that trip across the state, the whole staff was, and I know what happened. Someone deliberately altered those images to make Nathan look bad." She laughs caustically. "Not someone. *Madelyn*. She did this." She pulls her hand out from beneath mine and leaps up.

"Wait," I plead. "Don't leave, not like this."

"Like what?" Her voice cracks and she takes a moment to steady it. "Knowing that I've been so disrespected by someone I cared about?" She points a finger at me. "You're the one who pursued a relationship with me. You're the one who wouldn't give up. You're the one who started to knock all my walls down. And for what? So you could have a better view of my heart crumbling? This is why you turned me away last night, isn't it?" She barely stops to take a breath. Her face is getting more and more red. "It had nothing to do with your house being a mess. You couldn't in good conscience take that next step with me, not when you felt so guilty."

"No, I couldn't," I confess. "Part of what I said is true. I did want our first time to be special." I inch closer to her and she instantly backs up. "You mean a lot to me. Intimacy is ... well, it should be intimate." Good job, Bradley. So eloquent. "What I'm trying to say is that I didn't want there to be anything hanging over us. I think you and I can really be something great. We shouldn't ever settle for anything less."

"Past tense."

"Excuse me?"

"Past tense," she repeats. "We could've been something great, but not now. I can't date a man who's dishonest with me. I was right from the beginning. This was never going to work. There's too much standing in our way."

"Maybe it's us," I say. "Maybe we're the ones standing in our own way."

She looks at me sadly. "I think I could have loved you," she says. "I think perhaps, in the scariest and furthest corners of my heart, I already did. It doesn't matter, though. I've come to my senses. You can tell Madelyn that she officially has a fight on her hands. She might have won this battle, but we refuse to let her win the war."

"Melina." My voice pitches up into something desperate.

She loved me?

This is ... it's ... I feel light-headed.

"Goodbye, Bradley," she says, and all I can do is watch helplessly as she walks away.

* * *

It hurts. It hurts a lot.

I remember how upset I was when Rachel left. I read her letter over and over, searching for the meaning behind her words. I'd had a couple serious girlfriends before her – there was Ivy in college and Julia in graduate school – but nobody I could really picture an everlasting future with. Until her. She was the first person I met up here in Pennsylvania. It was the morning after I'd moved in to my townhouse, and when she turned around to smile at me in the grocery store's checkout line, I knew I wanted to see that smile again. We had a fantastic five years together. I even started to research engagement rings. And then whoosh, she pulled the rug out from under me. It took me a long time to get over her, but as I drive back to Harrisburg now, with Melina's words replaying in my mind like a broken record, I'm struck by the reaction I had to Rachel calling it quits. Honestly, it was more of a non-reaction. I spent half a decade with Rachel and just let her slip away. So why is it impossible to do the same with Melina?

With every mile I drive farther away from her, I want to turn around and drive closer.

She loved me?

I lose count of how many times I hear her voice in my head, confessing her feelings. She was so dejected when she said it. It's not exactly how you picture a declaration of love, but in a weird way, that made it even more meaningful. There were no sunshine and roses. No grand gesture. No big, impassioned pronouncement in the heat of the moment. She was so sure we'd reached the end of the line, and yet she still let me see the most vulnerable part of her.

Now all I want is to see more of it. But I can't, and I have no one to blame other than myself.

Actually, that's not entirely true.

"I am so furious at Madelyn," I tell Lucas, readjusting the Bluetooth piece in my ear as I wait at a traffic light. I felt bad at first, calling and interrupting his day, but I really needed someone to talk to and we've always had the kind of friendship where we can count on each other. "I'm at such a loss. How could she do this?"

"I don't know," he says. "I mean, yeah, you hear about all these corrupt politicians on the news, but it doesn't really hit home until it's someone close to you. That doesn't make it easier, though. I get it, man. You must feel like she stabbed you in the back."

"Not that I'm innocent here," I say. "I could've told Melina at any time, and I didn't. No wonder she hates me."

"I doubt she does."

"That's because you didn't see the look on her face." The memory of it makes my eyes feel like they're on fire, hot with the pressure of burning tears. "I really think she could have been the one. I could have seen myself marrying her. Now that's gone."

He sighs. "I wish I knew what to say. I think all my failed attempts at relationships have taught me this: if you find someone you click with, if you make each other happy and it feels right, then you don't give up on it. So don't. Don't give up on Melina. I know it isn't the same, but look at my track record. I had all those first dates without any second ones, and now I'm with Caroline. She's worth all those dating fiascos. If Melina's worth it to you, and it sounds like she is, then you have to refuse to throw in the towel."

Maybe he's right.

Or maybe the towel has already been shredded into pieces.

By the time I walk into Madelyn's campaign headquarters, my anger and devastation have both grown. We've been working our tails off for her, and this is how she repays us, with deceit? I'm not going to let her get away with it. Maybe there's nothing I can do now about the pictures, not when her plan has already set off such a dangerous ripple effect, but I can at least let her know I refuse to work for a person who will stoop so low.

"Bradley?" Hannah glances up as I storm by. "I thought you called out today?"

"I did."

"Then what are you doing here?"

"Quitting," I call over my shoulder. I don't care who hears. In fact, I *want* them all to hear. It's a normal workday around here. Hannah's sitting at her computer, fingers flying over the keys. Kristi's on the phone with what sounds like a credit card company, talking about Madelyn's account. Darci, Madelyn's chief policy director, and Phillip, who's in charge of research, are sitting with their heads together as they murmur about something. Probably about Nathan and his rapid fall from grace. If only they knew that our esteemed boss is the reason for it.

I find Madelyn in her office. "Bradley?" she asks, looking at me quiziccally. "Why are you here? I thought you said you were sick?"

"I am. Heartsick."

She tilts her head to the side. "I don't understand."

"Maybe this will clear it up for you." I brought the newspaper with me, the hard copy version of what Melina saw online, and I fling it at Madelyn. The pages drop onto her desk, fluttering open like oversized butterflies yanked down by the weight of the world. As Madelyn straightens them, I see a flash of recognition dart through her eyes.

"Ah," she murmurs. "Yes, this is rather unfortunate for him."

"You would know."

She folds the newspaper in half and gestures for me to sit. I keep standing. "I don't know what you think is going on here," she says evenly, "but I assure you, I had nothing to do with this."

"Please don't lie to me." The irony of my words hits me at full force. "I heard the whole thing at the farm. You were talking about having to do something you didn't want to, something that wasn't a good choice." Her mouth starts to open, but I don't give her a chance to offer an explanation. Not yet. "Who were you talking to?" I press on. "Were you on the phone, or was it someone else at the farm?"

I think of all those reporters.

It would have been easy for her to slip the fake pictures to them. The whole week long, she was busy playing up her down-to-earth side. But what was bubbling below the surface? What was really going on?

"Well?" I ask, when she doesn't answer.

"That conversation," she says finally, "is none of your business."

"Then perhaps you should have made sure the door was closed before having it."

The steel in my voice surprises even me. That is not who I am.

I don't push people. I don't speak out of turn. I don't cross the line. I don't stand up for myself.

I sound like my father now.

That's who *he* is.

The realization rushes at me. It's disorienting. Shocking.

"Look," I say, letting myself deflate a bit, "I have loved working for you. You're obviously smart, and dedicated, and in it for the long haul. I have sincerely enjoyed being part of your team. Writing your speeches reminded me of why I got into politics in the first place. Maybe it's naïve, but I really believe that words can change the world. But not words like that." I gesture at the newspaper still on her desk.

"I didn't do that," she says quietly. More quiet than I've ever heard her, in fact. "I don't know if those photographs are real or if they're manufactured, and I have no idea how they ended up in the paper. I know you don't believe me. That's your prerogative. I just would have thought all our time working together might have counted for something."

"I would've thought so, too." I hand over my ID badge. "But I can't trust you now, which means I can't work here. I wanted to be wrong," I tell her. "I so badly wanted to be wrong about this."

"You are."

"No," I say dejectedly. "I don't think I am."

"That phone call ... " She eyes my badge, which I'm still holding in my outstretched arm. "It was about an entirely different matter. I promise, it isn't what you think. None of this is what you think, Bradley. " She looks up at me beseechingly. "Please reconsider the resignation. You're an excellent writer. I don't want to lose you."

I didn't want to lose Melina, either.

This is what I want to say. I want to tell her all about it. About the way it physically hurts when I imagine a life without Melina in it. About the way I'll always regret not making love to her last night, because it turned out to be our only chance. About the way I have been questioning my path in life for awhile now, and the way this has made up my mind.

But I don't, of course. I simply drop the badge on her desk when she refuses to take it.

"I'm sorry," I say. "I'm already lost."

Then I turn to walk out.

I make it to the door, my hand on the knob, before Madelyn speaks again.

"Wait," she says. "Please, wait."

19

Melina

$\mathcal{I}$ want my mom.

As I stand in the bathroom at work and splash some cool water on my face, all I can think about is how Mom's always been there when we needed her. She worked really insane hours at the bridal boutique after Dad lost his job, but that never once stopped her from listening to stories about our day, or dispensing advice, or, if any of us was down in the dumps, spooning out some ice cream for us and topping it with mini marshmallows. Mom's always known how to make us feel better. Being with her is like a breath of fresh air.

In here, the air is sterile.

The bathroom smells like antibacterial hand soap, like broken hearts and tattered dreams. I sigh heavily, letting the curtain of misery fall over me. Bradley betrayed me. I, in turn, betrayed Nathan. Maybe it wasn't intentional, but how else can I look at it? I made a promise on the day I interviewed with him: to do everything in my power to help him get elected as the next governor. Instead I have done the opposite. I've spent the past several months letting Bradley worm his way into my life and now Nathan is paying the price. Maybe Bradley was telling the truth when he said he hadn't been in on the plan, or maybe he was lying. I don't know.

I don't know anything anymore.

I stare at my reflection in the mirror. Normally I have no time or inclination for self-pity, so why am I letting it control me now?

Why am I standing here, feeling sorry for myself? Yes, I made a bad call with Bradley. I fell prey to his accent, his smile, his candor. It happens. Mistakes happen. Life's not about what we do wrong; it's about what we do to make things right again.

I have never been a quitter before. Now isn't the time to start.

"There's one thing all successful people have in common," Mom told me once. "They never give up." I was in fifth grade at the time, and I'd had a particularly bad day at school. One of the popular kids had overheard me tell Amie that my parents couldn't afford to pay for me to go on the field trip that was coming up. She spread the news throughout the whole class, and I was humiliated beyond belief.

"What's the matter?" one of the other girls asked that afternoon at recess, as I bent down to tie my straggly shoelace. "Your parents can't afford to buy you new shoes, either?"

"That's what happens when you're poor," another said, in this disdainful voice that made a red blanket blaze across my cheeks. "You have to wear old clothes and bring your lunch in a brown bag instead of a cool lunchbox." As she looked me up and down, I deliberately kept my eyes trained on the ground. I could deal with dropping out of the art club and hurrying home after school to watch my siblings. I could deal with not getting the American Girl doll I wanted so badly for my birthday. I could deal with no longer going to the Phillies home opener game, which had been a family tradition each spring. Being teased about it, though, felt like more than I could take.

"That's okay," I said in an unsteady voice. "The food still tastes the same."

"Unless your parents run out of money to buy it," she said. "Maybe you should stock up now. I know where you can start." Every logical part of my brain warned me not to engage her, but when you're ten, logic doesn't always win out. I stood up and followed her gaze over to the dumpster by the school building. "There are probably scraps left over from lunch," she said. "If you find enough, it could be dinner for your family."

Kids can be so mean.

But, also, they can be so awesome.

"You know what?" Amie said, leaping to my defense. "Even if Melina's mom only had the scraps to work with, she could still cook a better meal than your mom. Mrs. Radcliffe is talented and super special. Does your mom put a note in your lunch bag every day? Does she play checkers with you? Does she cut flowers from the garden and stick one in your hair?" Amie went on and on.

I wanted to chime in. I wanted to tell the other kids to back off.

I just didn't have the words for it on that day.

I didn't have the words for it six months later, when we moved into the shelter.

Today, I do.

Today, I can.

Today, I will.

I take a long, stabilizing breath, tear off a paper towel from the dispenser, and dry my face from the water I splashed onto it. Then I appraise myself in the mirror again, deciding that I seem almost normal. That's the good thing about never crying when you're upset. Once you have calmed down and pulled yourself together, nobody is any the wiser. There are no telltale puffy eyes or red nose. I can go back to work now and pretend the last hour didn't happen.

I can pretend Bradley never happened.

I pull open the door, march down the hall, and head straight for Nathan's office. He needs to do what Cole said and issue a statement refuting the credibility of those pictures. It's probably too late to reach some of the people – once you see something like that article, you can't un-see it – but he's got to at least try. Ignoring this situation will only make it worse.

I rap on his door. "Nathan." No answer. "It's Melina. Can I come in, please?"

Again, not a sound.

I think of the way Amie stood up for me all those years ago. When I thanked her afterward, she said it was nothing. It was, though. It was something. It was everything. Sometimes we can't be an advocate for ourselves. Sometimes we need someone else to do it for us. Amie was that person for me. I want to be that person for others, and it starts with Nathan. I give another knock on the door, then open it. Nathan's chair is turned around, facing the window, and he makes no move to change that.

"Okay," I say, "let's figure out where we go from here."

"Home." Nathan sounds so defeated.

"Home?" I repeat.

Slowly, his chair circles around. "I've given everything to this election," he says quietly. "Do you have any idea how many times I had to miss my grandson's soccer games? I only made it to two of them this season. And my granddaughter? She's eight months old. That means I've been absorbed with campaigning for literally her entire life. For what?"

"For them." I take a seat in one of the chairs by his desk. "So they can grow up with the chance to do anything and be anything." I pick up one of the framed pictures on his desktop, a photo of him and the kids, and as I look at it, I realize what I have to do. "I don't tell most people about the day I became interested in politics," I say. "But I think you should know. I was ten, and I was on my way home from the corner grocery store. My dad had lost his job, and we were short on money, so I was doing everything I could to help out. Anyway, I was on my way back from the store after school one day, and I happened upon a crowd at the park. It was a rally. I didn't know who the candidate was or what he was running for, but I still stopped to listen. I heard him say that everybody deserved an equal opportunity, and maybe it was absurd, considering how bad off my family was, but I believed him. That day changed my life." I flip around the photo to face Nathan. "Tell me about the day that changed yours."

"Melina, I – " He shakes his head. "It doesn't matter."

"Yes, it does. It matters very much."

"Obviously you've seen the paper today," he says. "You should understand why I'm tempted to call it quits."

"Not at all," I say. "I can understand why you're upset. I can understand why this is a low blow. That should make you want to fight even harder, though. Do you want Madelyn to get away with it? Do you want her to taint everything you've done, or do you want to remind her and everybody else of who Nathan Ford really is?"

I hold my breath as I wait for his response.

It feels like an eternity.

Finally, he smiles. "It was the day Nixon was impeached," he says. "Maybe that sounds strange, since it wasn't exactly a bright day for our country, but that's when I knew. I knew I wanted to be on the ethical side of politics and to use the government as a way to help people. You're right," he tells me. "My grandkids do deserve that. Everyone does." He nods a little in my direction, a silent thank you, and stands up. "Come on," he says, "let's do what you said. Let's fight harder."

I smile, too. "Yes," I say. "Let's do that."

I follow him out into the main workspace and join the others as he gathers them around. "Okay, everyone," he says. "It's been a tough time of it today, but we're a resilient bunch and we're in it for the long haul. So ... we have a whole lot of work to do." He swivels around to Cole. "Ready to write an amazing denial speech?"

And so it goes.

We buckle down and get to work. Cole and Nathan craft a rebuttal and send it off to the media outlets, while Kira and I sift through the photos I printed earlier and start designing a new campaign around them. I'd planned to debut the pictures in my proposal, but I know it's important now to get them out into the public as quickly as possible. Cole was right when he said that seeing is believing for a lot of people. Now it's up to us to change the direction of their vision.

"How about this one?" Kira asks, holding out a picture. It's one of the most chilling of the group, a snapshot of a woman who has clearly been the victim of abuse. Her eyes have indigo half-moons below them, a long red cut glares up from her cheek, and there are fingerprint-shaped marks on the side of her neck. She's sitting with a baby on her lap and holding a piece of paper that says *I ran and didn't look back*. Unlike the majority of the photos, this one is posed. How will people react to it? I think of those commercials on TV, the ones for UNICEF and the SPCA. I wonder how often they're a success and actually convince the viewers to reach out – and how many times they become too hard to watch, so people change the channel. It's a tricky balance. Just because we don't want to see the difficult things, though, doesn't mean they're not there. Turning a blind eye simply leaves us in the darkness.

"I think we should include it," I say.

"I can't decide," she answers. "I know things like this are painful for people to see."

"Which is precisely why they *should* see it," I point out. "Raising awareness is good."

"Or maybe we should only be focusing on positivity right now?" she muses. "Nathan's just been put through the wringer. Anybody who read that article about him is going to be watching carefully to see what his next move is. Don't we want it to be the kind of thing that'll pump people up?" She rifles through the stack of pictures. "Like this one," she says, holding up one of my favorite photos, an overhead view of a girl, probably six or seven, reading a worn copy of *Where the Sidewalk Ends* to a man who's blind. There's a picture of him teaching her to read Braille in return, and Kira puts the two of them side by side.

"We could use all three," I suggest. "I think it would be good to have a diverse selection to really capture the – hey!" I look at her excitedly as an idea explodes inside my head. "What do you think about broadening this?" I ask. "We could drop off cameras in different communities and ask people to take photos. They could be of what makes them proud to live in Pennsylvania, or what they think needs more work, or what describes themselves. We could even ask people to email the pictures to us through Nathan's website. Then we'll piece them all together. It'll kind of be like a patchwork of Pennsylvania."

"Patchwork of Pennsylvania," she echoes. "I like that."

"It should go a long way in helping Nathan, too," I say. "I think we really need to portray him as the people's candidate right now, as the type of person who's willing to fight for everyone. I hate to say it, but that newspaper article is damning. Nathan can issue all the denials he wants to, but with no concrete evidence that the photos were doctored, some people won't believe him. By putting a real human face on his campaign, I think we stand a shot at reminding them of the great things he's done."

"And the great things he *will* do," Kira adds.

She sounds confident, and so do I, but it's tough to match that bravado on the inside.

Suppose it's not enough?

Suppose the voters think the Nathan in that sham of an exposé is the real one?

Suppose all these months of tireless work have been for nothing?

As I'm driving back to Philadelphia that evening, half listening to the radio, it's impossible not to let the worries and fears invade. The one thing I don't like about politics is the uncertainty. You can be here today and gone tomorrow. If Nathan doesn't win in November, that means I'm out of a job, just like my father was. The thought is enough to make my breath a little shallow, but then the song on the radio crescendos into its chorus and instantly yanks control of my attention.

Blues and pinks, reds and greens
Sometimes a world of difference, it seems
But like the whimsy of a watercolor, so we blend as one
When we reach out a hand
Who knows what we'll become?

Immediately, I love it. The lyrics just speak to me.

This song, what is it? I've never heard it before. It's mid-tempo, sort of a cross between a ballad and something upbeat, and it turns out that the DJ's equally taken by it. "That was Serena Spencer's debut single," she says, after the song is over. "It's called 'Watercolors,' and I'm making a prediction that it's headed for greatness."

Watercolors. Like artwork.

Now the song speaks to me even further. I love its imagery. I love its melody. Most of all, I love its message. The first thing I do after getting back to my apartment is turn on my computer and look up the song title and singer's name. A bunch of websites pop up, links to lyrics and a performance, but the one that stands out is an interview. In it, Serena speaks about how the song was born. "My best friend Eden wrote it," she says. "We met in a homeless shelter, and this song is the story of our time there. It's also the story of everyone else who finds themselves in a similar situation. There's a lot of bad in the world," she adds, "but also a lot of good. Eden wrote this with an important idea in mind, that all of us are connected. Life is about reaching out. Joining together. Choosing to change the world."

Goosebumps dot my arms.

I think of Nathan's campaign song, with its contagious melody and energy-sparking drumbeats. I wonder if he'd want to switch things up a little. This song encapsulates his message so well. I buy it from iTunes and listen again. I hadn't been looking forward to coming home tonight, not to a quiet, empty apartment that would only serve to remind me of how alone I feel. Now the music can be my company.

Every person has a story
Every person has a song
Appearances can be deceiving
And judgment's often wrong

I don't want to think about Bradley, but when I get to this point in the song, it's unavoidable. I realize that isn't the idea the songwriter was going for, but it's still where my mind travels. Bradley's appearance *was* deceiving, and I totally misjudged him. So why do I miss him already? I miss him a lot, and I'm disgusted with myself for it.

I stand up and walk over to the wall, where the painting I worked on last Friday is propped up.

How quickly things can change.

I trace my fingers over it, remembering how it felt to paint those shades of yellow and gray.

Then, with a hurting heart, I let it fall to the trashcan.

Keeping it will only bring back too many memories.

So much for pretending that Bradley never happened.

20

BRADLEY

I turn around silently, fixing my gaze on Madelyn. I'm so frustrated with her, and so angry, but I feel like I need to hear what she has to say. It's one of those things that'll always make me wonder otherwise. "What?" I ask. "What is it?"

She opens the top drawer of her desk, removes a manila folder, and shuffles through it. "Here," she says, holding out a sheet of paper. I step forward and take it.

It's the draft of a newspaper article, but not the one that ran today. The story in my hands isn't about Nathan at all. It's about Madelyn and her ... children? What? I jerk my attention over to her, dumbfounded. "You have daughters?" I ask. I am *floored*. All this time working for her and she has never once mentioned being a mother.

"Two," she says. She gestures to the paper in my hand. "Read it all and you'll understand." She rests her elbows on her desk and folds her fingers together. I can feel her eyes on me as I start, like she's trying to gauge my nonverbal cues, so I keep my face steady despite the natural inclination to let my mouth fall open. I kind of feel like I'm in the twilight zone. Because, according to the article, Madelyn was only in the eleventh grade when she gave birth to twin girls. As I continue to read, the reason for her keeping quiet on the subject becomes clear. She's never talked about her daughters because they aren't part of her life. She turned them over for adoption when they were only a few hours old. It strikes me, as I finish the article, how tough that must've been. It takes a strong person to be able to do that.

I can't imagine being in that position. Personally, I can't wait for the day when I get to cradle a newborn in my arms. I want to be the type of dad my own father wasn't. The type who coaches his kids' Little League teams, the type who plays board games with them, the type who they can look up to as their hero. Madelyn relinquished those kinds of opportunities. She did what she thought was best for her babies, even though it must have hurt terribly.

"Why now?" I ask quietly, giving her back the paper as I sit down again. "I assume you gave the go-ahead for this article. You've kept the secret for decades. Why are you opening up about it after such a long time?"

Her smile is half wry, half sad. "Because of the election. This is what you overheard me talking about on the phone. It was my high school boyfriend on the other end. Warren and I have been out of touch for years, but I thought it was only fair to give him a heads-up about the article. As you can imagine, he had reservations. He accused me of exploiting the girls' adoption for political gain." She sighs wearily. "Tell me, do you agree?"

"I ... " My mind whirls. "It's not really my place to comment."

"Please," she says. "I'm interested to know what you think."

What do I think?

I think this has been a very strange, very difficult, very tiring day.

"Do your daughters know they were adopted?" I ask.

Madelyn shrugs her shoulders. "Honestly, I don't know. It was a closed adoption," she explains. "All I *do* know is that the adoptive family was from Pennsylvania. Warren and I weren't ready to be parents. We had all these plans, all these dreams, and beginning a family while we were still in high school ... it wouldn't have been right for us. The girls deserved a lot more than we could give them, so we knew adoption was the best choice. But to keep those lines of communication open ... " She looks off in the distance somewhere behind me. "I think that might have broken my heart. Warren agreed, and that was that."

"Until now," I say.

She sighs again. "I thought I was doing a smart thing by telling my story to a reporter. Nathan's such a family man," she says. "Everyone knows he adores his kids and grandkids. It makes him real. Relatable. Then you've got me, who's basically the poster child for independent women. I've never been married and have spent my time being a board member for all these charities and foundations. Don't get me wrong," she says, "I'm proud of all the things I have accomplished. I just worried that I needed to soften my image a bit. One of the reporters on the trip with us asked about the future of the farm, who'd take care of it once my brother retired. I was telling him about my nephews and ... I don't know, something came over me, I suppose. Before I could stop myself, I was going on and on about my girls. Clearly, I gave him permission to run with the story." She gestures at the draft. "He faxed me a copy this morning, even though that's probably against policy. I'm afraid now that it was an enormous mistake."

"Because of how the public will perceive it?"

She's got a point. There will be people who praise Madelyn for her decision all those years ago and others who judge her for it. She has to realize by now that her life is under a microscope. Most of the time, she's okay with that, but as she raises a hand to the locket around her neck, I can tell it isn't the same with this.

"Warren surprised me with this necklace in the hospital," she says. "Right before the girls were born." She flicks it open and shows me the small photos inside. Two babies. "We didn't feed them or change their diapers," she says. "We left that to the nurses so we wouldn't get too attached. We did take these pictures, though, and one of all four of us." She snaps the locket closed. "So they can still be with me, even when the truth is that they were never really mine to love." Her voice grows a bit thick. "It isn't the public's reaction I'm concerned about. Whether my daughters know about the adoption or not, I just ... I don't want them to hate me. No election is worth hurting them." She falls silent, and I do, too. I honestly have no idea what to say.

I was so sure she was the mastermind behind the fake story on

Nathan, and who knows, maybe she is. Just because her fingerprints are all over this article doesn't mean they don't cover the other one, too. But now I have doubts. Now I don't know what to do. I could still quit. I could walk away from this campaign, and maybe from politics in general. Or I could stay a part of the team and see it through until November. Or ... wait. What if there's a way to combine both options? What if I can help Madelyn and Melina at the same time?

Melina would tell me not to. She'd say she doesn't need, or want, my assistance, and that's the absolute truth. I know she can handle things on her own. She can do better than handle them. She can be a total rock star. But even rock stars have people to support them. And maybe if I do this for her, she'll give our relationship a second chance. She'll see what my intentions are, where my heart is, and take me back.

It's certainly worth a shot.

"Why don't you give me the reporter's phone number?" I ask Madelyn. "I'll see if I can convince him not to run the story."

"You'd do that?" she says. "But I thought ... "

I reach over and pick up my ID badge. "Change of plans," I tell her. "You're still stuck with me."

Her relief is palpable, and it makes me feel guilty, but only a bit. If she has nothing to hide, then it won't matter that I'll be sleuthing around and doing some undercover work. And if she does? I'll be the one to find out and tell Melina so that she, in turn, can alert Nathan. I am going to get to the bottom of this mystery ... and Madelyn won't be any the wiser.

* * *

By the time I get home that evening, I'm exhausted. All I want is to zone out on the couch with a beer and the ballgame on TV. I can't think about the election anymore. I can't think about Madelyn, or Melina, or the fact that I've basically turned myself into a double agent. But I also can't *not* think about those things. That's always how it goes for me. The harder I try to banish what weighs on my mind, the more I fail. When I flip on the TV, the news is doing a story on Nathan and his response to the article. When I go into the kitchen to throw together dinner, I see the bowl of orecchiette in the refrigerator, left over from last night's meal with Melina. And when the phone rings, it's my father. He'd loathe what I'm doing. He'd call me a traitor, and maybe he'd be right. Maybe I am betraying Madelyn. But if I did nothing, then wouldn't it be a betrayal of all I share with Melina?

All I shared with Melina.

I don't answer the phone when I hear Dad's voice boom from the answering machine.

I just don't have the energy for it now.

Instead, I leave my plate of leftovers on the counter and meander down the small hallway to my study. It's neat as ever, with its framed photos of Georgia hanging up on the wall and its shelves of baseball memorabilia lining the bookcase. I sink into Grandfather's chair. Pull open the desk drawer and take out the culinary school application. It feels hefty in my hands, the papers so much heavier than their actual weight. Why not do it right now? I could grab a pen and write myself a new path. I could put this election behind me.

I flip through the pages. Read the words. Ponder what recipes I'd use if there was some kind of demo or presentation involved.

But what about Melina? If I give up on the election, and on uncovering the truth, where would that leave my efforts to win her back?

I sigh, then replace the application and shut the drawer tightly. I'm just heading back to reheat my dinner yet again when the doorbell rings. I do an about face and walk to the door. When I pull it open, Cameron and his kids all smile at me, almost in unison. "Bradley!" Lissie squeals, bouncing on the balls of her feet. "Hi, hi, hi, hi!"

"Hello to you, too, pretty girl," I say. This makes her flush with delight, and it's sunshine for my wilted soul. "Come in," I tell Cameron. "What's up? I thought the kids were with Jill this week."

"Change of plans," he says. "She had a last minute business dinner tonight. That's actually why I'm here." He looks at me almost pleadingly. "I was hoping you could watch the kids for a little bit. I have to run to the hardware store to pick up some things for a job this weekend. I've got meetings scheduled at work every other evening this week, so it's the only chance I have." Cameron's pulling double duty, keeping his regular hours at the accounting firm while also starting his own contracting business. Right now he's taking on smaller projects that can be done on the weekends, when Jill has the kids, but he's hoping to transition it into full-time within the next couple months. I really admire that about him. He's not happy with his work situation, so he's changing it. There's no dawdling, no second-guessing, he's simply going for it. I wish I had that kind of self-assurance.

"Sure," I tell him. "No problem."

"Thanks, man." He flashes me a grin. "You're a lifesaver."

"Glad to help."

Cameron passes Cooper to me. "They've already eaten dinner. Sometimes they still get hungry, though, so there's a snack in here." He sets down a gray checkered tote bag on the floor. "I'll try to be fast, promise."

"Take your time," I say. "I'm happy to watch them for however long you need."

I really am.

What better way to distract myself from the firestorm raging in my head than to chase after two kids? It's nice, getting to direct my attention to something positive. Something full of hope and joy and optimism.

And, I quickly learn, something full of rambunctiousness.

In the span of half an hour, Cooper and Lissie manage to turn my house upside-down. I literally can't comprehend how such tiny people can make such a big mess. The tote bag Cam brought? It is a bottomless pit. There are blocks and crayons, stuffed animals and books, toys that play music and toys that light up. But even with all those choices, the kids seem more interested in my belongings. Cooper tries to grab at just about everything, and Lissie wanders around, pointing at different things and asking to hear their stories. "That's what Daddy says," she tells me. "Everything's got a story." She motions to the framed picture of my grandparents.

"That's my grandma and grandfather," I tell her. "They live far away from here."

"You miss them lots?"

"I do."

She nods, then moves on to the lamp, and the poster-size print of Centennial Park hanging up in the entryway, and the entire collection of DVDs stacked neatly in the stand by the television. Well, they used to be stacked neatly, anyway. By the time Lissie is finished with them, they're fanned out over the whole room. "How 'bout this one?" she asks, holding up the last one. It takes me a second to figure out what it is, because I don't recognize the case at first.

Then I do.

It's *You've Got Mail*, which is Melina's favorite movie. It's funny, I'd never have pegged her for a romantic comedy type, but apparently she adores them. "They make me believe," she said, by way of an explanation. "In love, in destiny, in happy endings." Then she scrunched up her nose. "Even if only for an hour or two at a time." I couldn't exactly tell if she was kidding or not, but either way, it made me sad. I wanted her to believe in all that.

I guess I got my wish. Without even realizing it, I did make her believe in those things.

And then I took them away.

I think, again, of her confession earlier. It caught me so off guard. If only I had known. If only I had been prepared. If only she had given me the chance to answer instead of walking away. Then I could've told her that I love her, too. That it's the kind of love that snuck up on me when I was least expecting it, the kind that's worth fighting for, even when it's fighting against us. But I didn't say any of those things. The words stayed trapped inside, and now I might not ever get a chance to unearth them.

"Bradley?" Lissie taps my arm, jolting me from my thoughts.

"Yes. Sorry, sweetie." I try to pull myself together. "The story of that movie ... it belongs to the woman who used to be my girlfriend. She must have left it here after we watched it.”

Lissie tilts her head. “How come she’s not your girlfriend anymore?”

Cooper chooses that moment to toss one of his blocks across the room. I watch him toddle over to get it, his feet unsteady. He’s only recently learned to walk and he still tumbles down sometimes. But it never stops him, though. All he knows is to pick himself up and move forward. It occurs to me that adults could really learn a lot from children.

“Melina thought I did something unfair,” I tell Lissie. “And she’s angry with me because of it.”

“You should ‘pologize. Daddy says that saying you are sorry makes the other person feel better. That’s what I have to do if I get a time-out. I’ve got to tell Daddy I’m sorry and give him a hug.” She hands me the DVD case. “You can do it, too!”

Oh, to be a child again. It must be so nice to see the world through their eyes.

“Maybe,” I say, tousling Lissie’s hair. Then I pull her onto one knee and Cooper onto the other. I pick up one of the books strewn across the floor, a hardback called *The Rainbow Fish*, and open it up to the first page. “Story time,” I announce, and the kids settle in. It feels good, being with them, like I have a purpose in life that goes beyond penning speeches and tracking poll numbers and zeroing in on Election Day.

I wonder if Melina wants kids someday. We never talked about it.

I wish I could call and ask her.

I wish I could apologize again, like Lissie said.

I wish a hug was the answer.

I wish for a lot of things.

Melina

I wake up the next morning to the bright white smile of Perry Talmudge. His face beams out at me the moment I switch on the television, his teeth gleaming like a perfect row of Tic Tacs. He's the last person I expected to see on the local news today, but there he is, talking to a group of reporters. I half listen while I make breakfast, pouring a tall glass of pineapple-orange juice and tossing a frozen waffle into the toaster.

"The traditional two-party system needs some amending," he says. "Our founding fathers did a wonderful job, but let's be honest, a lot has changed since then. The country's a very different place now, and our government should reflect that." It's nothing he hasn't said before, so I chalk it up to a normal interview and reach for my waffle as the toaster dings. Then Perry continues, "that's why, as of today, I am officially throwing my hat into the race for governor."

I drop the waffle and whirl around to face the TV.

"I'm sure you have all heard the recent revelations about Nathan Ford," Perry says. "It knocked the wind out of me when I read that article yesterday and saw those pictures. I couldn't believe my eyes. I have always considered Nathan to be a stand-up guy. We may not agree on a lot, but I had a great deal of respect for him, just as I do for Madelyn Morgan. Now ... " He sighs, and I stare at his face, watching carefully. "I knew I had to do something," he says. "It is my hope for Pennsylvania to have a governor who thinks highly of its citizens. If the voters pick me on Election Day, I promise to be that governor. As of a few days ago, I secured enough signatures to petition to be on the ballot, and today, I'm so proud to formally announce my candidacy. Let's do this, Pennsylvania. Let's make certain you've got a governor who cares about the right things, who cares about *you*."

I turn the TV off and sink onto one of the stools at the counter.

I knew there was a chance of Perry joining the race, but I never really thought it would come to fruition. Now it has, and at the worst possible time. If people believe that article about Nathan and see Perry as defending their honor against a corrupt politician ... this could be bad. Nathan is going to need all the help he can get.

All week long, I try my hardest to give it to him. I work my tail off, ironing out the details of the Patchwork of Pennsylvania campaign, compiling information Nathan can use when he talks to all the reporters who are clamoring for interviews, and hitting the road to push his actual agenda instead of someone's version of a malicious one. The whole team is more determined than ever now to prove his innocence. Couple that with the after-hours work I am doing on my homeless shelter proposal, and it's basically the longest week ever. I go through a dozen mugs of coffee, three glasses of wine, two red pens, one yellow highlighter, and six drafts before I finally come up with a finished proposal. It's a labor of love, but still, by the time I type the final word on Sunday night, I'm both mentally and physically exhausted. I feel like I could sleep for a month.

And yet, even after I've fallen into bed, rest alludes me. My mind simply won't shut off. It races around in a frenzy instead. What if Nathan doesn't give a stamp of approval to the proposal? What if he does, but the public doesn't? What if they're still too fixated on what he supposedly did wrong to see everything he's actually done right?

One o'clock.

Two o'clock.

Three o'clock.

I watch as the hours tick by.

Eventually I can't stand it anymore. I throw back the covers and walk to the living room, where I plop down at my desk again and look at the framed family photo that's sitting on the shelf. I clearly remember the day we took that picture. It was Gabrielle's sixth birthday, and our parents surprised us with a visit to Sesame Place to celebrate. We had the best time. I can still hear Gabrielle's squeal of delight as we walked into the theme park. I can see Dylan pointing to the different Sesame Street characters as we watched their stage show, I can feel Lara's hand in mine as she dragged me toward the water maze, and I can smell the pizza we ate in the cafeteria. It has been such a long time since that wonderful day, and yet I can still feel the memories as though they're actually beside me.

Maybe they are. Maybe they always will be.

The happy family in that picture, though, is gone.

It makes me so deeply sad. Usually I'm a forward-looking person, but sitting here with the past literally staring me in the face, I wish I could travel back in time to relive that day. What would I tell my nine-year-old self? Would I warn her of the difficulty that'd soon rear its ugly head? Or would I simply tell her to soak in every moment of the day at Sesame, to steer her float under the waterfall on the Rambling River ride and to relish that scent of sunscreen and cotton candy and chlorine?

I'm not sure.

I sigh, tearing my attention away from the picture.

There's no point dwelling on it. I can't go back. I can't change what's already been written.

But I can pick up a pen and begin a new chapter.

Slowly, methodically, I page through my printed proposal. There are glossy photos, columns of text, tables and charts to illustrate the statistics. What I'm most proud of, though, is the conclusion I wrote. I put a lot into it and it took a lot out of me, but as my eyes drift over the words, some much more personal than I'd ever intended, I know it was the right choice.

Homelessness is everywhere – across the world, across the country, and across our state. Every day, there are parents who must beg for money to feed their children, and every night, there are men and women who must huddle in alleyways to sleep. Sometimes these people have traveled down the wrong path, but just as often, they've been taking steps along the right one, until it suddenly veered off in an unexpected direction.

I know this, because I am one of those people.

I was ten years old when my father lost his job. I was eleven when my family was forced to move into a homeless shelter. The bills had piled up, the mortgage couldn't be paid, and the utilities all got turned off. It was the scariest time of my life, and also the saddest. It felt like the past year had been a big waste. Everything we'd sacrificed no longer mattered, because here's the thing: homelessness doesn't discriminate. There are the veterans who fight so valiantly, then come home with scars that are way more than skin deep. There are the victims of abuse who find the strength to set themselves free. There are the people who lose it all in a fire, or when their company downsizes. So frequently, we see images of homelessness on television and we hear the stereotypes. There are other faces to it, though. You've seen many of them in this proposal, and now you'll see another when you look at me.

I stayed at Helping Hands for three months, eight days, and five hours.

I have that figure memorized.

Because homelessness stays with a person. It changes a person.

I want it to change people for the better. I want shelters to be a safe haven. I want everybody to have a soft bed and a hot meal if they need it. I want them to understand that it's possible to find a passion inside and keep going. I want them to create a new life for themselves like I did. In order for that to happen, we must open more doors and hold out more hands. Mine is outstretched. Will you please join me?

Goosebumps pop out over my arms as I come to the end, and I rub my hands against them in an attempt to shoo them away. When that doesn't work, I head into the kitchen to make myself some hot cocoa, then curl up on the couch with my mug and think about my Gram. She used to make me hot chocolate when I was a kid. She would add a sprinkling of caramel and peppermint, then top it off with whipped cream. I miss her. I miss all my grandparents. Bradley's so lucky to still have his in his life.

Bradley.

I shake my head as he floats into my thoughts.

I've desperately been trying to erase him from my life. I deleted our pictures from my camera, I gave the stuffed animal he won for me at HersheyPark to the girl who lives in the apartment below mine, and once I received my replacement phone, I got rid of all the texts from him that transferred over. But I couldn't bring myself to remove his phone number from my contacts. I haven't called it again, but knowing I *can* call if I want to is enough.

I wonder if he misses me.

I wonder what he'd think of me opening up to Nathan about my past.

It's funny, and also kind of strange: with Bradley, I had no trouble admitting the truth. I told him about the shelter on our first date. It felt right. Maybe I knew, even then, that he'd never judge me. It isn't that I think Nathan and my coworkers would, and it isn't that I thought Cory or Ian would. It's just that they met me in another season of my life. They saw the Melina I've worked hard to be, and I didn't want anything to change it. With Bradley, though, it was different. I just needed him to see all of me.

A dry laugh escapes my lips.

For what? I let him in and he trampled my heart.

You can wish on a penny

Send a prayer to the sky

Or you can take a step forward, offer your heart

For every journey relies on its start

For the umpteenth time, lyrics from "Watercolors" run through my head. I included the song in my proposal in the hope that Nathan will connect with it as much as I have. Now, though, as I finish the rest of my hot chocolate and lay my head against the sofa, letting my eyes flutter closed, I have to admit that I'm not too certain about the "offering your heart" line. Yes, every journey relies on its start, but sometimes those journeys lead you nowhere. Sometimes they dangle you off a cliff or fall into a dead end. As a hazy sleep finally creeps up on me about five hours too late, I grasp at the last moment of conscious thought to push Bradley out of my mind. I really don't want him to end up in my dreams.

Thankfully, unlike a couple other nights recently, he doesn't. It's a relief to wake up without an image of him lingering in the recesses of my mind. Maybe this means I'm beginning to get over him. It'd be nice if that were the case. I don't want to remember the way the corners of his eyes crinkle when he smiles, or the way his pinky ring catches the light in his kitchen when he's cooking. I don't want to remember how he'd rub my back when he was hugging me, or how, after he'd wind an arm around my shoulders, he'd let his fingertips tap dance gently on my arm. I want to forget. I *need* to forget.

There are so many other things to concentrate on right now, like my proposal.

I hand it in to Nathan first thing after getting to work. "Here's my baby," I say.

He smiles. "It's in safe hands, I promise."

I know it is. I know he'll read the whole thing, and that there's a good chance he'll like it enough to let me take the lead on the initiative if he gets elected. That said, it's still tough to let go. Letting my heart bleed onto the page was difficult. It feels like I have stripped away my outer layers and am standing with my most vulnerable self on display.

What was it my mom said about my coworkers the day we went back to Helping Hands?

"They'd admire you, for taking a tough situation and finding inspiration in it."

Dear God, please let her be right. I worry about it all morning. I'm supposed to be working with Kira, but my thoughts are scattered everywhere.

"What's going on?" she asks. "You're a million miles away."

"Oh, it's nothing," I say hastily.

"I don't believe you." She gestures to the notepad in front of me on the desk. "You're going all Picasso on that thing. Obviously, you're distracted."

I glance down to see what she's talking about and realize that the margin is covered in doodles. "Oops," I say sheepishly.

"Is it Bradley?" she asks. "Have you heard from him since you broke it off?"

I never planned to tell anyone about my relationship with Bradley, but Kira was so worried when I ran out of the office that I had to confess. I'm relieved she knows, though. It's really nice to have a friend to talk to about it. "No," I tell her. "Thank goodness."

"It's alright, you know," she says. "If you still have feelings for him. There's nothing wrong with wanting to work things out."

"No." I cap my pen and slam it down a little harder than I'd intended. "That ship has sailed and sunk. Bradley and I are over. Nathan could lose the election because of him, and that's something I can't forgive."

"If you say so."

"I do. Now come on, let's get back to work. I promise not to get distracted anymore. It was just the proposal," I explain. "Nathan said he'd read it after his conference call this morning. The wait is driving me crazy."

It continues to do so, all day long.

Each time Nathan comes out of his office, I jerk my head up to see if he's coming in my direction. He never does, though. He goes to talk with Cole about the speech he's scheduled to give Thursday. He goes to talk to Bill, his campaign manager, about last week's polling numbers, the first since that article appeared in the newspaper. He goes to talk with the reporter who shows up unexpectedly to ask for an interview. He never once looks my way, though, and I can't help but worry that Mom was wrong. Maybe Nathan isn't sure how to look me in the eye now that he knows where I came from, so he's avoiding me instead. I am legitimately afraid I have ruined everything. If he starts regarding me with that sympathetic expression – the one my sixth grade teacher had when Mom talked to him about the shelter, the one Amie's mom had when she offered to buy me a dress for the Valentine's dance that year, the one even my parents had when we moved into the apartment and they peeked in on us each night before we fell asleep – I don't think

I'd be able to take it.

Maybe it was a mistake to let my worlds collide. Sometimes a collision only results in shattering everything to pieces.

By the time the clock hits four-thirty and I still haven't heard anything, I need a breather. I step away from my desk, go outside, and call Gabrielle. She always seems to get where I'm coming from, no matter what.

"Mel!" she exclaims, picking up after the first ring. "This is so weird. I swear, I was just thinking about you. We're setting up for a new gemstone exhibit and it reminded me of you. Remember the time we went to Washington DC and Mom basically had to drag you out of the mineral room at the Museum of Natural History?"

The memory makes me smile. "Very well," I say.

It was the last vacation we took as a family, only a few months before the curtain fell on our joy. Mom still has the photo album with all the pictures from our trip sitting on her coffee table. I'll have to flip through it next time I'm there. It was too painful for a long time, seeing her and Dad so happy – seeing us all so happy, really – but enough years have passed since their divorce that it's no longer upsetting. Sometimes a 'what if' will run through my head and I'll ponder how life would have been different if they'd stayed together, but mostly I've grown to accept the split. It's just the way things were and the way things are.

Life happens. It's up to us to find a way to deal with it.

To that end, after asking Gabrielle about what's new in her world, I fill her in on mine, even the part about my breakup. Other than Kira, she's the only person I'm sharing it with at all. I just feel so foolish about the whole thing, so completely used and so completely sad.

"I loved him," I confess to Gabrielle. "I don't know how it happened, or when, but despite all my defenses, I fell head over heels. It's weird, right?" I press on. "It took so much longer with Cory and Ian. With Bradley, it felt right from the beginning."

"I don't think that's weird," she says. "I think it's sweet."

"Except for the part where he stabbed me in the back," I sigh.

"I should hate him. I *do* hate him. But I also can't stop thinking about him."

"Maybe there's a reason for it. Just because your head is ready to give up on him doesn't mean your heart is."

"Well, then, my heart needs to shape up and get with the program."

This makes her laugh a little. "I hate to break it you, big sis, but it doesn't really work that way."

"It should, don't you think?"

Before she can answer, the front door to the building opens and Kira comes rushing out. "Sorry to interrupt," she says, a bit breathless, "but I have news I think you'll want to hear. Guess who just called Nathan?"

"Hang on a second," I tell Gabrielle. Then, to Kira: "Who?"

"Madelyn." Her eyes narrow. "And you'll never believe what she wanted."

22

BRADLEY

I'm in the middle of editing a speech when Madelyn breezes into the room and gathers the team around for a meeting. Her smile's bright and her eyes have an energetic sort of glint. What's she up to? We weren't scheduled for a meeting this afternoon. Usually she likes to plan that type of thing in advance.

"I have excellent news," she tells us. "I just got off the phone with Nathan. I wanted to express my support as he attempts to battle back from that journalistic blow. If he's innocent, as he claims he is, then what's being done to him is a true disservice." Here, she makes eye contact with me, but doesn't say anything. I don't, either. No one else knows that I accused her of being the one behind the article, and I don't want them to, because then they may question why I'm sticking around here. I can't have that. So I stay silent, putting on my best poker face as Madelyn continues. "It was also a good opportunity to discuss our upcoming debates," she says. "We have agreed on the venues and should have all the dates worked out shortly. I'm hoping to schedule the first one sooner rather than later."

That'd be a smart move.

The public is pretty wary of Nathan at the moment. It's a perfect time for Madelyn to go head-to-head with him. She can juxtapose her sincerity and integrity against his alleged lack of it. I've got to hand it to her, it's clever. But it's also tacky. Nathan hasn't stooped to such behavior. As it turns out, I wasn't able to stop that reporter from printing the story about Madelyn's daughters. It would have been easy for Nathan to capitalize on that and have his team put together an ad depicting him as the ultimate family man. He didn't, though. He didn't address the subject at all.

I wonder what Melina thinks about this.

I could call her later. Ask her about it. Tell her how much I miss her and how my life feels empty without her in it. But something tells me she wouldn't even answer the phone.

I shake my head. Push her out of my mind. Consciously divert my attention.

" ... so I'm not sure what to do about that," Madelyn is saying. "Any ideas?"

I have no clue what she's talking about.

"I think you have to invite Perry to join the debate," Kristi says, tucking a strand of her dark hair behind her ear as the overhead fan blows it out of place. "Otherwise, it'll seem like you don't even consider him a contender, let alone a worthy opponent. You'll come off as too overconfident, which is never a good thing."

"But on the other hand," Hannah says, "it isn't like an independent or third party candidate has ever won the gubernatorial race in Pennsylvania before. Including Perry would basically just detract from the time Madelyn and Nathan have to state their positions."

"I don't know," I say. "He might not be a frontrunner, but he was able to get enough signatures to qualify for the ballot. That's a big deal. I think he should be part of the debates."

"Me too," Darci chimes in.

"Me three," Phillip says.

"Okay, then," Madelyn says. "I'll make the call."

She strides over to her office and everyone else scatters back to their desks, except for Hannah. "How soon do you think she wants to schedule the first debate?" she asks. "She wouldn't challenge them to be ready by next week, right? We need time, if we're going to come up with killer opening and closing statements."

"Your guess is as good as mine," I say. "I don't know what she'd do anymore."

"What's that supposed to mean?"

It means that I spent all of last week sneaking around.

That I tried to listen in on conversations and steal peeks at files when Madelyn didn't know I was looking. That I researched her colleagues from all the charities and foundations whose boards she's served on over the years. That, when I phoned the reporter to ask him about the adoption story he wrote, I also tried to find out what else Madelyn told him on that farm visit. I can't share any of this with Hannah, of course. She doesn't even know I was dating Melina, and I'm guessing she wouldn't react well to the idea of me going undercover to get information for her. No, it's best to keep quiet about the sleuthing.

"Nothing," I say, waving my hand like it was an off-the-cuff remark. "Just that Madelyn is really coming into her own as we get closer to the election. If you compare the candidate she is now with the one she was at the beginning of the year, there's an immense difference."

"Kind of like a flower," she muses. "Her petals have opened."

I nod.

It's a fitting analogy. It reminds me of Lucas, actually, and a long ago championship game from Little League. It was the ninth inning, the bases were loaded, and Lucas was at bat. He had gotten a lot better over the two years since we'd started playing, but still, the chance of him bringing it home was pretty low. I think the whole crowd was shocked when we heard the crack of his bat. In a way, that is what Madelyn is doing now. She's going for a grand slam. She's trying to knock it out of the park. Trying to knock Nathan out of the race.

Or someone is, anyway. I wish I could figure out for sure who's to blame.

Later in the evening, after everyone else has packed up and called it a day, I renew my efforts to uncover the truth. It's eerie, being at work in the silence. Normally it's full of hustle and bustle. But now the phones are quiet and the desks stand at attention, their surfaces stacked with tomorrow's projects. The clock on the wall ticks evenly, as though it's counting down, and when I drop the pen I'm holding, it falls to the floor and makes a much louder sound than it should.

Am I really doing this?

Poking into Madelyn's business was one thing. Snooping through her office is another.

But there isn't any other choice. If I'm going to find something incriminating, chances are that's where it would be. It's why I told everyone I was working late tonight, trying to finalize press details for Madelyn's visit to a local elementary school tomorrow. Nobody questioned me. There would be no reason for them to, because I've certainly stayed until all hours of the night before. Politics was a way of life for me for a long time. It *was* my life. I'd think nothing of working until nine or ten every night, stopping only to eat some take-out at my desk. So when my co-workers filed out, one by one, they just waved goodnight and thought nothing of it. Their mouths would probably drop if they saw me now.

Slowly, carefully, I inch open the door to Madelyn's office. Creep over to her desk. Slide out the top drawer. Shuffle neatly through the papers inside. There are letters from voters, clippings from a newspaper in Philadelphia and another in Pittsburgh, photocopied pages from the speech she gave after winning the primary. There's a photo of the farm, Madelyn and her brother sitting atop horses with the pond behind them, and another of her as a teenager with a guy I assume must be Warren. I stop for a minute to look at it. She's pregnant in the picture, but only slightly, and Warren's arm is draped loosely around her shoulders. They look so happy. It makes something twinge inside me. It doesn't seem fair, that she lost all she had then. What was it she called herself? The poster child for independent women? Even people like that need somebody sometimes.

That's not why I'm here, though.

I replace the photo, making sure it's in the right spot so she won't know anything was disturbed. Then I move on to the next drawer, and the one after that. Nothing. It has to be here. I don't know what I'm looking for, exactly – perhaps the stolen camera, or a record of her correspondence with a person from the newspaper that published the article about Nathan. Wait. I stare at her computer as something occurs to me. It'd make a lot more sense to keep the communication there, where it's safe from prying eyes.

Okay, now I'm getting somewhere. The computer springs to life as soon as I touch the mouse. I try to log in and hit an immediate roadblock when I realize I have no idea what Madelyn's password is. I wrack my brain. Could it be the name of her farm? Nope. The title of her campaign song? Not a match. Then I remember the photo in her desk drawer. First, I try Warren's name. No dice. Then I type 'twins.'

Bingo. I'm in.

My first move is to check her files. I navigate into the C drive, double click her documents icon, and start browsing the contents. There are dozens of subfolders, most pertaining to the campaign, and I go through them systematically, scanning for any and all file names that might give something away.

Budget Reform.

Environmental Protection Plan.

Jobs & Unemployment.

No Child Left Behind.

Proposed Tax Plan.

The list goes on and on. On the surface, there's nothing to implicate her, but I know that's not a declaration of her innocence, either. She easily could've hidden information under a false file name. I open a couple of them, careful not to hit any keys on the computer, for fear of altering the file and leaving a record of my detective work. But then, when I'm exiting out of a document which contains Madelyn's notes on labor unions, something occurs to me: suppose I am creating a footprint simply by opening the files? Can Madelyn access the timestamps for that?

Shoot.

Beads of sweat break out along my temples and I have a temporary bout of panic, worrying that Madelyn will uncover what

I'm doing before I can expose her. Then she'll fire me. I'll be out of a job I do truly like at times, and I won't be able to help Melina clear Nathan's name. She won't ever take me back then. This is my one and only chance at sealing up the cracks I chiseled in her heart. I can't blow it.

I take a deep breath and command myself to think logically.

First of all, it isn't like Madelyn suspects me. She wouldn't have any reason to think I was spying on her. As far as she – and everybody else – knows, I had a sincere change of heart about quitting. I have been putting on a front at work, pretending I believe her denial and that everything is fine, so if I leave her office as it was, there isn't much likelihood of her realizing my true intentions. Still, to be on the safe side, I decide not to check any more of her files. It isn't like there have been red flags so far, and I don't have a lot of confidence there would be if I kept going.

But her email ... that's another story. I hold my breath as I open her inbox, then let it out slowly once I see she's still logged in and I won't have to guess at passwords again. The last thing I need is to get her mailbox locked in response to multiple failed log-in attempts. "Alright," I whisper. "Here goes nothing." Except it's more like everything. Here goes everything.

Or not.

No more than two minutes later, as I'm scrolling through the week's messages, I hear footsteps. They are fast. Precise. Rhythmic. And getting increasingly louder, which means someone is heading in my direction. This is bad. This is really bad. In a flash, I exit out of Madelyn's email inbox and put the computer back to sleep, just the way I found it. Then I leap up from her chair, push it under the desk, and look around feverishly. A hiding place. I need a hiding place. There's no time to get away unseen. My heart rate begins to pick up, galloping ahead of me, and my hands go clammy. I *cannot* get caught in Madelyn's office.

The footsteps are echoing now, or maybe it just sounds that way in my head as I vault across the room, turn off the light, and slip into the closet. I shut the door right as the one to her office opens.

Safe, for the time being. Unless it's Madelyn out there and she came back for something she left in the closet. What's inside here? It's dark, so I stay perfectly still until my eyes have adjusted. Then I look around, trying to make out the fuzzy outlines of what's surrounding me. I think there are some clothes to one side – I vaguely remember her saying that she keeps an extra suit at the office, along with a dress, in case there's a last minute event to attend. What else? It's hard to see. Perhaps an umbrella? And I think there might be a pile of campaign materials, too. Buttons, pins, posters, and bumper stickers. I remember how excited Madelyn was when all that stuff came in. It was April of this year, after she'd had a new logo designed, and her face broke into a huge smile when it arrived. It was a little like looking at a child on Christmas morning. Could that same person really be capable of this?

Maybe.

Maybe not.

Something crashes outside, thunderous and sudden, and I jump. Because I'm so close to them, my foot hits the posters. Immediately, I try to steady myself. I can't fall. I can't bang into anything. I can't make noise. Not now, with everything on the line. If only I can get out of here unscathed and undiscovered, I'll quit my attempts at espionage ... or at least I will be way smarter about it the next time.

It's quieter out there now. A drawer – or at least what I assume is a drawer – is closed, and then I hear the footsteps resume. Click, click, click, across the floor and over to the door. It's definitely a woman. That's the sound of high heels. It must be Madelyn. But when I crack open the closet door a second too soon – I thought she had already left, but not quite – it's not her blond hair and slender frame I see disappearing out of the office. It's a tall woman with dark brown hair. Or maybe black? The glimpse I get is too fast to be able to tell. The only thing I get a good look at is her legs. There's a tattoo on one of them. I can't see it clearly, but I can tell that it winds around her ankle.

What is it of?

Who is she?

Part of me is tempted to go after her and ask what she was doing in Madelyn's office, but I can't, not without revealing myself. This woman, could she be helping Madelyn with a plan to take Nathan down? Maybe she's the one who doctored the pictures. Or a reporter from the newspaper? If only I had seen her face.

I step out into the office and do a fast survey of the room. Nothing seems out of place. But she must've taken something, right? I heard the desk drawer open and close. And what was that crash? Much as I want to take the time to look around and see if I can figure it out, I know I need to get out of here.

I tiptoe across the office and poke my head out to make sure the coast is clear. It is. Thank God. As surreptitiously as possible, I sneak back into the main area and sit down at my desk, where I was supposed to be this evening. I better stay for awhile. That way, if anyone comes back, my story will check out. No one will ever know what I was actually doing.

I pick up a pen from the holder on my desk and start jotting some notes about Madelyn's visit to the elementary school tomorrow. It's kind of a rote action at this point. I've been on her team long enough to know how things work. That's good, because I can't manage to concentrate for the life of me. I'm too distracted by that woman.

Who *is* she?

Again, the question bounces around my brain.

I have no idea how to answer it.

But that's not going to stop me from trying.

23

Melina

I feel sort of deflated as I leave work for the day. It's been nearly nine hours since I handed my proposal to Nathan and I still don't know what he thinks of it. Why hasn't he said anything? I nearly asked him about it. On my way out, when I passed by his office and the door was open, I paused for a minute. It would've been easy. I could have gone in, asked what he thought about Perry joining in on the debates, then segued into a discussion on the proposal. It just about killed me, not knowing what he thought. It would have hurt more, though, to question him about it and have my initiative shot down.

That's why I decided not to go in.

If I don't hear anything tomorrow, then I'll speak up. Tonight, I'd rather sit with the hope that it could be a success than live with the knowledge that it'll be nothing but a failure. I think sometimes we can trick our brains into focusing on the positive in life, even when the negative is smacking us in the face. That's what I did when Dad sat us down and told us he'd been let go. It's what I did when I woke up in the middle of the night at the shelter, thanks to a baby crying or the floor creaking when someone walked across it. It's what I did when the fights started.

They were minor at first, usually over something that wasn't even important. My parents were both working such long hours, trying to rebuild the world that had been snatched away from us, and they were tired by the time they got home. I guess that took their usually even-keeled, level-headed personalities and lit a short fuse beneath them. Sometimes they could extinguish the flame before it got to the end of its rope. Other times it quickly brought them to the end of *their* ropes. Then the fights grew more intense. Instead of Mom complaining that Dad forgot to take out the trash or Dad complaining that Mom hadn't cleaned up the toys Lara and Dylan had left on the floor, they argued about serious things. These fights were louder. Even holed up in the room I shared with my sisters, I could hear the slamming doors and the accusations flung around with reckless abandon.

It broke my heart.

I always tried to distract Gabrielle, Lara, and Dylan from it. We didn't have much in those days, but we did own a few board games. I'd pull one down from the closet shelf and set up the pieces for everyone, talking in a loud and cheerful voice to drown out the arguments that filtered through the closed bedroom door. Dylan was really too young to understand what was going on, but my sisters weren't as lucky.

"Melina?" Lara asked once. "Why are Mommy and Daddy shouting?" We were playing Mouse Trap, and she picked up her blue mouse playing piece, waving it in the air. "Maybe they should play with us instead. Then they can be happy."

"Listen to them," Gabrielle said. "Does it sound like *anything* could make them happy?"

They were fighting about us that time.

"I can't choose between my kids," Mom screeched at Dad, "and I can't be in two places at once. That's why you were supposed to take a half day at work. We had a plan. I'd go to the open house at Gabrielle's dance school and you'd go to Melina's art show. Now what?" Her voice rose. "Now I have to tell one of them we won't be there. Who should that be, Paul? Which of our kids should we disappoint? Melina, who's been sacrificing so much to help us out? Or Gabrielle, who already feels like an outsider at dance since I know the owner and she's going for free?" Her voice pitched higher still, a volcano reaching its eruption. "Go on," she demanded. "Tell me. Which one?"

Silence.

Gabrielle looked at me and I looked at her.

"We're making them mad at each other," she whispered, and her eyes filled with tears.

"Mommy sad," Dylan piped in. "Daddy sad."

"They're fine," I assured, but even he knew better, especially when Dad answered. It was quiet at first, so none of us could hear, but then it got progressively louder until we couldn't *not* hear.

"Do you think this is easy for me?" he barked. "I hate hurting their feelings. I can't just snap my fingers, though, and expect to get whatever I want at work. The other mail carriers have been there for years. I just started three months ago. That makes me the low man on the totem pole. It's not my fault there was nobody to cover. What do you want from me?"

"I want you to be there for our family!"

"You don't think that's what I'm doing by working all these hours?"

"Are you?" she challenged. "Are you *really* working all those hours, or are you sneaking around again? Because that's what you told me before, when I was trying so desperately to save our house. You said you were trying, too."

"I was. I am. Why can't you believe that?"

Gabrielle's tears had spilled over by that point, streaming down the curves of her rosy cheeks in two steady rivers. She reached up and grabbed her pink teddy bear from her bed, clutching it to her chest. "I'll tell them it's alright," she hiccupped. "I don't need them at my open house. It's a stupid thing anyway."

"You don't mean that."

"I do." She nodded, and a couple tears dropped onto her teddy bear's fur.

"You don't," I repeated. "You've been talking about it for weeks. What about the special dance you all put together for the parents? You couldn't wait to show it off." She couldn't argue with that, because she knew I was right. She'd been so excited about that routine. I didn't want her to be the only one in the class without a parent there to see it.

I knew what I had to do. "You guys stay here," I told the others. "I'll be back."

What happened next is seared into my brain.

The way Mom and Dad stopped yelling when I came into the room, as suddenly as if they were on a television show and someone watching had pushed the pause button on the remote ... the way Dad's eyes grew glossy and wet when I explained that it was okay if nobody could go to my school's art show ... the way Mom's whole face fell when she realized we'd heard the entire fight ... these are things that'll stay with me always. They're in my dreams sometimes, in my nightmares. Even all this time later, I remember the arguments so vividly. The voices might have faded, but their echoes still resound.

Sometimes I still wonder what would have happened if Dad didn't lose his job. If we'd been able to keep the house, if Mom and Dad hadn't needed to work around the clock to provide for us, if the money hadn't been so hard to come by, would things still have fallen apart between them? Did the situation shake them, break them, or were the fault lines already there? Maybe they'd have gotten divorced anyway, or maybe they'd have been happily married, two decades later. It's impossible to know.

Or is it?

I've never actually asked them.

Perhaps I should. They're in a place now where the animosity has dissipated. It probably won't ever be all sunshine and roses between them, but they manage to be civil to each other. Maybe this is finally the time to talk with them about it. It'd be nice to get answers, and I could use something else to concentrate on tonight so I don't dwell on my proposal nonstop.

I glance at my watch. Five-thirty.

If I hurry, I can make it to Mom's house just in time for dinner.

* * *

I love Mom's street. It's lined with modest-sized houses, many of them built decades ago, and if you follow the winding sidewalk you'll pass by flowering trees and bright green lawns. Mom bought a house here ten years ago, after she was promoted to an associate manager at the bridal shop, and I liked it immediately. After the apartment and then the duplex we moved to after the divorce, this place felt like a fresh start. It makes me happy, coming back to it now. There are terrific memories tucked inside. They fill each room and hide around every corner, just waiting to greet me whenever I walk through the door.

Tonight, though, it's Dylan who does the greeting. He still lives with Mom and he must've been looking out the window when I pulled up, because he has the door open before I can even reach for my key. "Hey," he says, flashing me his signature half-smile. "I wasn't expecting to see you tonight. You okay?"

"Fine," I say, leaning over to hug him. "How about you? How's my favorite brother?"

He chuckles. "I'm your only brother. And good. Enjoying a rare night off from work."

"It sounds like I picked a great time to visit, then." I set my purse down and head up to the living room. It's the same as always: cream-colored drapes framing the expanse of windows, Mom's plant collection proudly displayed on the wicker table, and the cherry wood piano holding court along the wall by the stairs. The piano belonged to the previous owners, and even though my mom can't play, she kept it when we moved in. Pictures are lined up on top of it, a book of sheet music closed on its little ledge.

"So what brings you here?" Dylan asks me. "Shouldn't you be working around the clock to save Nathan's bid for governor?" He shakes his head, making his shaggy blond hair flop. "That was some sucker punch somebody hit him with, huh?"

"It was awful," I agree. "And devastating on several levels."

"Several?" He shoots me a puzzled glance. "For the campaign, obviously. What else?"

For my heart.

The words sneak through my brain.

They are balloons, their strings dangling in front of me. I could reach out and grab them. I could own my pain. I could tell Dylan all about Bradley and how, although I'm mostly doing an okay job of pushing him from my life, there are still moments, too many of them, when I want so badly to forget about the betrayal and forgive him. I want to go back to the way things were, when our relationship was fun and dreamy and the one thing in my life to ever set me delightfully off-balance. I can't do it, though, I won't, so what's the point in talking about it? Dylan would tell me to give Bradley another chance. He's always been about second chances, ever since he was a kid. Even after the divorce, he used to talk about our parents getting back together.

No.

It's best not to tell him.

I let the strings go. I let them float away.

"For the other people in those doctored photos," I say. "I hate that their images are being used this way. They invited us into their lives, told us their stories, and this is how they're repaid?" I feel an angry flush start to heat the tips of my ears. "It's inexcusable."

Mom pokes her head around the corner then. "I thought I heard voices in here," she says. "Hi, dear. I didn't know you were stopping by."

"It was a last minute decision. Any chance you have room for one more at the table?"

"If that one more is you, then absolutely."

It's nice to have dinner with her and Dylan. It's been nearly two months since the last time I was here. I don't think I ever quite realize how much I miss it until I'm back again. For all the freedom of the open road, of driving with the windows down and letting the breeze ripple through my hair, of a day spent with voters and a night spent people-watching in the lobby or bar of whatever hotel we're staying at, I suppose there's something to be said for this, too. I don't crave it, not like I do the road stretching out before me and the sky sprinkling its stars above, but it does anchor me. I'm beginning to understand that staying in one place doesn't always have to be a bad thing, not like it was when I was a kid.

I think of the last nights we shared around the dinner table as a family of six. The conversations were often strained, riddled with pauses that were too long and chatter that was too rambling. My siblings and I may not have known that a split was coming, but we could tell something was off. My sisters and I used to compensate by going on and on about our days at school. If our parents figured out what we were doing, they gave no indication of it. Their poker faces were perfect, and I know it was their way of trying to shield and protect us, but I really wish they hadn't. It made the final blow even more crushing.

Tonight, there's none of that. Instead, there's talk of the brides Mom met today, the grad class Dylan just finished, and the proposal I handed in to Nathan. "I'm going crazy, not knowing what his thoughts are," I say. "He promised to make it a priority, but he hasn't said a word about it since. Do you think that's a bad sign?"

"I think you worry too much," Mom says. "You've always been that way. You care so deeply, it makes you – "

"Neurotic?" Dylan teases.

"Har di har har," I say, pulling a roll from the bread basket and chucking it at him.

He catches it with one hand. "Batter out!" he cries.

Immediately, the baseball reference makes me think of Bradley. I know it's his favorite sport.

Damn it.

It's time to trick my brain again.

"Forget about the proposal," I say. "I shouldn't have brought it up. I'm trying not to think about it until I know one way or the other." I take a sip from my water glass. "Can I ask you something?" I say to Mom.

"Of course. Anything."

The words tumble out in a rush.

"What if Dad hadn't lost his job?" I ask. "If we'd gone on living in that house? If everything had stayed the same? Do you think you'd still have gotten divorced? I don't ever remember you fighting before that. You were happy, *we* were happy, and I guess I've always wondered if things might have been different."

Mom's eyes soften. "Oh, hon." She sets down her fork and folds one hand on top of the other. "I ... I honestly don't know. Your father and I were so in love. We got married very young, when we still had some growing up to do, and I think we learned a great deal about each other after the fact. Most of it was good. Some made us realize we weren't entirely compatible. But we still loved each other, and we adored all of you. Maybe we'd have stayed strong if life hadn't gotten in the way and maybe we wouldn't have."

"Does it bother you?" Dylan asks. "Not to know? Not to have closure?"

"It used to." She nods a bit, more to herself than to us. "But 'what if' can be dangerous words, if we spend too much time on them." She clears her throat. "Let's talk about something else."

That's it.

The subject is closed, just like that.

24

BRADLEY

There's nothing like three hundred elementary school students bright and early in the morning. "Good Lord," Hannah says under her breath as we stand at the back of the multi-purpose room and listen to the kids cheering and clapping. "What did they have for breakfast, sugar?" She motions to the teachers. "They deserve gold medals."

"My brother teaches," I tell her. "College, not elementary school, but he's always saying that it's so rewarding." I grin wryly. "Do you think Madelyn would feel the same way?" We both watch her cross the stage, take her place at the podium, and wave to the children.

"Good morning, boys and girls," she says, and by some kind of miracle, they actually quiet down. "I want to thank you for having me here today. I know you'd rather be learning about math or social studies." This gets a boisterous laugh from the students, as I hoped it would when I wrote the line. "Well, guess what?" Madelyn continues. "In a way, we actually *will* be talking about these subjects, and also about science and English. Did you know that every subject you study in school plays a role in politics?"

"No!" some of the kids call out.

Others shake their heads.

"That's why it's so important for you to listen to your teachers," she says. "Politics isn't the only job that uses a variety of subjects. Who can tell me another one? Raise your hands, please." Within seconds, dozens of hands shoot up. I give Hannah a thumbs-up. It was her idea to make the speech interactive from the get-go, and she was right. It's the perfect way to capture – and hold – the kids' attention. As Madelyn points to them and asks for all their answers, they're totally absorbed in her presentation. Even after she segues into the part of the speech where she tells them why she loves politics and what she would do to help schools if she's elected, most of the students are still hanging on her every word.

"This was a smart idea," I say, as Madelyn finishes her speech and asks the kids if anybody has a question. "Not only does she get the students excited about the election, but she also gets a chance to indirectly talk to their teachers. Plus, who knows how many kids will tell their parents about the assembly?"

"It's a unique way of getting votes," Hannah says. "But I agree, a wise one."

Madelyn *is* wise.

That was one of the first things that struck me about her when I interviewed for the position on her team. She was, and is, very astute and articulate. She knows what to say and when to say it. In the hands of the wrong person, a visit like this to an elementary school could have been a total flop. Instead, it's been a wonderful boost. Madelyn even offers to stick around after the assembly so she can visit some individual classrooms and meet the kids one-on-one. Of course, this disrupts the rest of the morning – the plan was to spend it working on key points to address during her debates with Nathan and Perry – but she knows, just as I do, that the time is better spent here at the school. She can read the situation instinctively.

But what about when she uses her perceptiveness for bad instead of good?

I think again of the woman who was in Madelyn's office last night. Here's what I don't get: if she and Madelyn are working together, then what was she doing sneaking around after hours? It makes no sense. Unless she wasn't actually being secretive at all. Maybe it only seemed that way because I was. As Hannah and I go to sit outside while Madelyn visits the classrooms, I replay the incident in my head, searching for details.

The tattoo. That's the key to solving this, I bet.

"Hey," I say casually, as we drop onto a pair of swings on the playground. "Do you know anyone with a tattoo, by chance?"

She looks at me strangely. "That was random," she says.

I grasp for a story that sounds feasible. The only way I can ever pull off a lie is to tell one which revolves around a kernel of truth. "Remember Callie?" I ask. "The woman I work with at the bunny rescue?" Hannah nods. "She's thinking about getting one. The rescue just saved its five hundredth rabbit, and she wants to commemorate that." This is partially true. We did just hit the five hundred mark when we saved an English Spot bunny that was on the euthanasia list at a local shelter. Callie's never said anything about a tattoo, but Hannah doesn't need to know that. "She's afraid it'll hurt," I explain. "Obviously I have no clue. I thought I would ask around to see if there's anybody who can answer her questions."

Hannah shrugs. "Don't look at me," she says. "My pain threshold is way too low to consider it." She shifts a little on the swing, crossing her legs at the ankles. "But I think it's a cool idea. You all do an amazing job with the rescue. Why not celebrate that?"

"You should volunteer with us sometime," I tell her. "I guarantee it'll make your heart grow two sizes."

The second the words are out of my mouth, they remind me of Melina. I said something similar to her that night at my house, when she came over for dinner and we ate outside on the patio. That was the night everything changed. The night it all began to fall apart. God, how stupid I was. If only I could take it back.

My grandfather said something to me once, when I was trying to decide where I wanted to go to college. Jake and Eric had both chosen Harvard, but I was thinking about Georgetown instead. "My boy," Grandfather said, "it's always better to regret the things you have done, rather than the ones you haven't."

Just like that, I made up my mind. Georgetown it was.

I took a chance and actually never regretted it, not once.

When did I stop living my life like that? Did I ever really start?

Maybe that one time was more of an exception than a rule.

I think of my plan to double major in political science and journalism. The latter got tossed aside when my parents said it would be too difficult to juggle both things. Then there's the application to culinary school. It's still sitting, locked away in my desk. I've already missed the deadline for the fall semester. I let it slide right on by, just like I let Melina do the same. Well ... she didn't really slide, it was more like she ripped herself from my grasp and took a part of me with her. I was so hopeful at first that spying on Madelyn was the way to win Melina back. But where has that gotten me? I can't exactly call her and say there's an additional suspect, but I have no idea who it is. I need something concrete.

I turn to look at Hannah, who's talking now about her own charity work at a local food bank. "It really is a marvelous organization," she says. "We feed about five thousand people per year. We're hoping to double that eventually."

"That's great." I push my feet against the ground, propelling the swing, but stop when Hannah doesn't do the same. It feels silly to be swinging alone, especially as an adult. "How would you feel about getting Madelyn involved there?" I ask. "It'd be great PR for her." Not that I necessarily want her to have great PR, not if she's the puppeteer pulling the strings of the election, but Hannah can't know that yet.

"I like it," she says. "She could give a speech about volunteering, and we could bring in a bunch of people who receive regular donations from the food bank. It'd be a win-win situation. Madelyn would get positive press *and* she'd also make a name for herself with voters from that demographic. You, my friend, are a genius. My hat is off to you."

"Thanks. I – "

Right then, the wind blows. It's light, more of a breeze, but it's enough to lift up the bottom of Hannah's long skirt and ruffle it around her ankles. That's when I see it. The flash of midnight blue. I only get a fast glimpse before she smoothes her skirt back down, but that's all I need. That blue ... it looks like a tattoo. Like *the* tattoo. Even after she said she doesn't have one. Was she lying? Has she been lying all along? A queasiness crawls into my stomach. Never in a billion years would I have thought she was the accomplice. I was just asking her about the tattoo in case she had seen anyone who might fit the bill.

"Bradley?" I hear her voice, but it sounds like it's coming from the end of a tunnel.

"Hmm?" I murmur distractedly.

"You okay?" she asks. "You stopped talking in the middle of a sentence."

Of course I did.

The pieces are all falling into place now.

Hannah has brown hair. She's a couple inches taller than I am, and at five-eight, I'm not exactly short. She was at Madelyn's farm that week. She told me she was going for a walk on the evening I heard Madelyn on the phone, but then she was late for dinner. They both were. Maybe that whole story Madelyn gave me about Warren was fabricated. Maybe she was really holed up in that room with Hannah.

"Yo." Hannah's voice penetrates my thoughts again, louder this time. "What on earth is wrong with you?"

"Nothing," I spit out hastily. I can't accuse her yet. Not until I have proof.

Hannah and I have worked together for over a year. I consider her a friend. I don't want it to be her.

But what I want doesn't matter, does it?

Sometimes allegiance means everything and sometimes it means nothing.

For the rest of the day, I question that allegiance time and again.

Hannah's.

Madelyn's.

Mine.

It's confusing. Messy. Frustrating. All I want is to get to the bottom of this mystery, but instead the mystery seems to be getting to me. No matter how hard I try to find answers, they remain right beyond my reach. When I mention the previous night, joking with Hannah that she owes me since I stayed late to take care of the preparation for today's speech, she smiles and says she had a doctor's appointment and would much rather have been toiling away with me at work. When, later on, I ask if she'd mind bringing a folder to Madelyn's office, she simply takes it and strolls off, like everything is fine and she hadn't been snooping around there on her own. And when we begin to work on the opening remarks for the first debate, I deliberately bring up the controversy with Nathan to see how she reacts, but only get a shrug, like she can't imagine who'd do such a thing. Either she's a talented liar or my suspicions are totally off-base.

"Do you think Madelyn should acknowledge that article during the debate?" I ask, hoping to pry more information from her. "It's tricky. If she says something, it may make her seem like a bully. If she doesn't, it'll appear like she's out of touch."

"Or like she's above it all," Hannah muses. "That could be a good thing. The public will see her as someone who wades right through all the BS and gets to the heart of the matter." She shuffles a stack of papers that's sitting between us, searching for something, and finally pulls a sheet from the center. "Like this," she says, holding it out to me. It's a section we wrote for an earlier speech, but ended up not using. I remember it well. It's about a family Madelyn met on the campaign trail in York. There were three children, being raised by their dad since the mother was in treatment for an alcohol addiction. The kids were full of life. Madelyn met them on a playground, where she'd been chatting with all the parents, and I don't think I'll ever forget the way she jumped in and played with them. "This is the sort of thing we should highlight," Hannah says. "They'll cover all the main issues during the actual debate. But the opening and closing statements should really be about the people of Pennsylvania, like Nathan's been doing all along."

Like Nathan's been doing all along.

What does she mean by that?

Maybe it's just a comparison. Those are inevitable in political campaigns.

But maybe it's more.

"Alright," I say, making a note on the legal pad in front of me and then typing the same thing on my laptop. I learned long ago that it's good to have a double record of everything when it comes to politics. The one thing you can trust when technology is involved is that it'll always break when you need it most. "So we include this family, and maybe also the story about the ad exec whose job was done away with during the company layoffs?"

"The one who went back to school for nursing?" Hannah knits her eyebrows together, like she's trying to remember the details. "She works at a non-profit now, right? Or am I confusing her with a different person? We've met so many people that I can't keep them straight anymore."

Is that because you also have to remember all the people Nathan's met so that you can feed into Madelyn's supposed plan and twist their stories into something unrecognizable?

I want to say it so badly. I want to catch her off-guard and see how she responds.

But then I'd be playing all the cards in my hand.

That could give me everything, or it could leave me with nothing.

So I stay quiet. I opt, for now, to chug along the same path. Hopefully slow and steady will win the race. "Yes," I say evenly. "She started the free clinic in Philly. She'd be a great one to feature at the debate. Maybe we can get her a ticket to be there in person? We can do that for all the people we work into the speech, actually. It's always really effective when the camera pans to people after the politicians mention them."

A voice comes from behind me. "Kind of like the President's State of the Union address?" Kristi asks. She smiles. "Sorry. I was heading to Madelyn's office to discuss next month's travel budget. I couldn't help overhearing."

"No problem. And yes," I add, "exactly like that."

"Be careful," she cautions. "You don't want the invited guests to overshadow Madelyn. All the attention should be on her, not who she's brought to sit in the audience. At least, that's my opinion. You guys are the experts, of course."

"What do you think?" Hannah asks, after Kristi's gone on her way.

"Honestly? I think it'd be fine. If anything, it'll paint Madelyn as compassionate."

Hannah nods. "I agree. Maybe we should even add a third person, just for good measure. Any ideas?"

Immediately, a thought flashes through my mind. "Yes," I say. "I know the perfect person."

25

Melina

How are things going with that guy you told me about?

Amie's text pops up on my phone as I'm walking into work the next morning and it immediately makes my stomach drop. I should have let her know about the break-up. It's what I would've done before. It's what I *should* be doing now, if I'm trying to rekindle our friendship. Friends share things with one another. Amie was there when my previous relationships ended. Even if she didn't agree with my decision to call things off, she was at my side within hours, armed with a pint of Rocky Road ice cream and a stack of movies. This time ... I guess it was cowardly, leaving her out of the loop, but the idea of having to go through the story again, of having to explain how Bradley had betrayed me, felt too painful. I owe her an explanation, though, so I stop walking and type a text.

It didn't work out, unfortunately. Bradley wasn't who I thought he was.

A minute later, her reply arrives. *Oh, Mel, I'm sorry. It's his loss.*

Is it? I'm not sure about that. The loss feels pretty brutal for me, too.

Thanks, I write. *How are you? How's the little one?*

Kicking up a storm. It's crazy how strong she is! Hey, I'm getting ready to send out baby shower invitations. I hope you can make it.

Me too, I type. *I'll do my best to clear my schedule that day. Would love to be there!*

Baby showers aren't my thing, but I meant what I said: I miss Amie and truly do want to be there for her special day. Now, though,

I have to concentrate on work. I slip my phone into my purse and open the door to the building. Nathan's waiting by my desk when I get inside, coffee cup in hand as he talks with Kira.

"It was a huge mess," she laughs, as I join them. "My husband was covered in paint. I should've brought him some paper towels, but I ran for the camera instead." She smiles at me. "Hi. I was just telling Nathan about Gemma's not-so-little accident with her paints yesterday."

"Something similar happened to me once," he says, "but it was with melted chocolate. My kids were six and seven at the time, and they wanted to bake a cake for Mother's Day. Lesson learned." He chuckles. "Twenty-five years later, I can still picture the disaster area in the kitchen." He takes a final sip from his disposable cup, then tosses it in the recycling bin. "Do you have a minute?" he asks me. "I'd like to chat."

Instantly, I'm on alert. Is this, finally, about the proposal?

My heart rate speeds up to double time, and I nod. "Of course," I say.

When we get to his office, he shuts the door and motions for me to sit. "So," he begins, clasping his hands together lightly as he rests them on his desk. "I read your proposal."

And?

The question echoes in my brain.

Why isn't he saying something more?

Is he about to give me that puppy dog look, the one with the round eyes full of pity? I sure hope not. That's exactly why I've kept my colleagues in the dark about my past. I can't stand the thought of them seeing me as less adept, less capable, less professional ... just plain *less*. It'd leave a gaping hole that I wouldn't know how to stitch up. As I appraise Nathan, though, I realize he isn't looking at me with sympathy. He's looking at me with respect.

"I really apologize for not getting back to you yesterday," he says. "It was a crazy, busy day and time got away from me. But your work, it is wonderfully done. It would be an honor to implement your ideas."

My hopes rise up until they're floating somewhere above my head. Does that mean what I think it means?

Nathan grins. "I'd already been planning to hire you for my cabinet if I'm elected, but let's make it official," he says. "Melina Radcliffe, will you accept a position in my policy department? You'll be working in several areas, but with a concentration on homelessness in Pennsylvania. I truly believe we can make a difference here."

It's the best gift anybody's ever given me – not the job, but the opportunity. I've never been the kind of person who thinks that everything happens for a reason. There's too much bad in the world, these hardships and tragedies that, in my mind, happen for no reason at all. There's no purpose to people getting sick, or losing their homes, or being forced to throw out the dreams they'd held onto for so long. Sometimes life is just unfair, and there's nothing we can do about it.

Now, though, maybe I *can* do something.

Maybe I can do better.

Maybe I can do good.

"Yes," I say, and I feel a smile start to tug at the corners of my mouth. "I absolutely accept your offer. It'd be a pleasure. Thank you so much."

"Thank *you*," he says. He pauses for a second and looks me right in the eye. "You could've told me before, you know, about your past. I wouldn't have judged you. One thing I want my employees to always know is that I'm a safe place."

"I know. It's just … it's hard. My past will always be a part of me, it always *should* be part of me, but I've worked like crazy to get where I am today. I took out loans to pay for college and graduate school. I studied incessantly so I could keep my scholarships. At one point, I juggled two internships at the same time, just so I could try to graduate a semester early and not have to worry about extra tuition. My parents were in no position to help financially," I explain. "I had to do it by myself, aside from the fifty dollars a month my grandparents gave me." A wave of nostalgia floods over me at the memory. "They told me to use it to buy lunch on the days I was on campus for hours, but I brought food from home instead and deposited their money in the bank. Eventually, I put it toward the rent for my apartment."

Gram and Granddaddy were already gone by the time I moved back to Philly after grad school in DC, but I think they would have been happy with my decision. This way, it's like they helped give me a place to call my own. That was one of their biggest regrets, I know, not being able to do that when my parents lost the house. They were living in Florida then, where my granddad's job had relocated him a few years prior, and though they said, time and again, that we were welcome to fly down and stay with them, it wasn't feasible. Their apartment was much too small for eight people. It wouldn't have worked, and they didn't have enough money to afford their rent and to also contribute toward our bills. We used to talk to them on the phone instead, and they'd usually get choked up. I think they felt kind of helpless.

I hope they were looking down on me when I signed the lease on my apartment.

I hope that time, they were crying happy tears.

I hope they are today, too.

"I never wanted someone to look at me and only see the homelessness," I explain to Nathan. "I preferred to hide from it instead. The kids at school used to make fun of me, and I guess their words left more of a scar than I wanted to admit. I'm not proud of it, but now it's always in the back of my mind, the worry about people not being able to see who I am today if they know who I was all those years ago."

"That's not what you wrote in your proposal."

"I know." I stare down at my hands. "I meant what I wrote, I swear. Sometimes it just feels like there's more to the story. Does that make me a hypocrite?"

"It makes you human," he says. "You're allowed to feel conflicting emotions. But Melina, I wish you'd look at yourself the way you do at others. The descriptions of the people in your proposal are beautiful. Yes, those people are homeless, but to read your words, that's just one tiny part of them. They are parents. Teachers. Soldiers. Singers. Artists. Families. Fighters. They're individuals." He picks up my proposal and gives it to me. "Being homeless will change them. Clearly it has changed you. Maybe that isn't something to hide."

I look down at the proposal. There's a post-it note stuck to the cover with three words scrawled across it: *you inspire me.*

"Thank you," I tell him. "You have no idea what this means to me." But he does. I can see it in his eyes and hear it in his voice.

"Two more things," he says. "I just want you to know that I didn't tell anyone about your secret. I think it's something you should own, but that's your decision, not mine. Also, those song lyrics you included in the proposal … they're wonderful. I agree with you; 'Watercolors' speaks perfectly to my campaign. I'm going to start playing it at my events. Great call."

"I'm glad you like it," I tell him. Then, suddenly, an idea pops into my head. "Hey, wouldn't it be cool if we could get the singer to perform it at one of your rallies? She's fairly new on the scene, so she may be willing to do it as a way to get her name and music out there."

"I like that idea," he says. "I like it a lot."

"Then I'm on it."

It's the first thing I do when I get back to my desk. All it takes is a few minutes of research to get the contact information for Serena's representation at the record label. I type a short email, read it over twice, and send it off. I know it might be a long shot, but it can't hurt to give it a whirl, right? I have learned over the years that you'll never get anywhere if you don't try. That's why I applied for college when my parents couldn't afford to send me, why I set my sights on all the best grad schools in DC, and why I cast such a wide net when it was time to apply for internships. I sent my resumé to the State Department, the Supreme Court, even the White House and Congress. That expression, go big or go home, it's been a little different for me. It's more like: go big and maybe you won't have to go home.

I'm reminded of that when I visit my dad after getting off work for the day. Nathan and the rest of us are heading to the northern half of the state for the remainder of the week, and I want to talk to Dad before I leave. I'm hoping he'll shed more light on the divorce, because Mom's answers last night only left me with even more questions. Why did she change the subject so quickly? What did she and Dad learn about each other after they got married? And why are "what if" such dangerous words when it comes to their marriage?

"You always have been inquisitive," Dad says, as we sit on the small balcony of his condo. It has a view of the parking lot below, so not exactly the prettiest landscape, but it's such an improvement over the low-rent apartment he moved to after the divorce. He seems happy here, and that makes me happy for him. "Sometimes you'd ask ten questions in a row when you were younger," he says. He pours me a cup of lemonade from the pitcher he brought out and offers up a plate of microwave pizza bagels. That's his idea of cooking. Mine, too. "But they were easier questions when you were a kid," he continues. "I could explain why butterflies have wings and why a tricycle has three wheels instead of two. Now it isn't quite so simple."

"The big things in life never are."

"No," he says. "No, I guess they aren't."

We sit in silence for awhile.

An airplane flies overhead, a lawn mower hums from the front of the condo complex, and a bird hops onto the railing, cocking its head and chirping at us before flying away. But still, no words pass between us. Dad is looking into the distance – at the woods beyond the parking lot, and maybe into a further distance, too, into a memory from years ago.

"Never mind," I finally say. "I shouldn't have asked. What happened between you and Mom is your business."

"What happened between us affects you, too."

He stands up, sits down, then stands up again.

Suddenly, I'm nervous. I feel a little like Pandora, and I'm

that's exactly what I was doing. I got in too deep and lost it all. I lost more than what I made."

Again, we drift into silence as I try to wrap my head around this revelation.

Dad was a gambler.

He squandered the little money we did have.

No wonder Mom was furious.

No wonder she didn't want any of us kids to know.

No wonder she was so evasive last night.

I turn my head to look at Dad and to tell him I understand, because I do, sort of, but something catches my eye first. Behind him, inside the condo, the television is on. He must have forgotten to shut it off when we came out here. A news anchor is on the screen, her face serious, and I recognize the person in the graphic square next to her.

Madelyn.

And the word below her picture, written in big red block letters?

Thief.

26

BRADLEY

I have always felt a particular connection to people in the military. I suppose it's mainly because of Grandfather's service and all the stories he's told me about his time in the infantry, but it extends beyond that, too. I look at these brave people who are willing to put their lives on the line in order to fight for others' freedoms, and I'm in awe. They are courageous. They deserve to be recognized, and that's why I choose one of them, a marine who was injured overseas, to round out the group of people Madelyn will highlight at the debate.

Writing his story is the best part of my day.

It makes me hope I am wrong about Hannah, and Madelyn, too. I don't want to expose them. I don't want there to be anything *to* expose. Still, after Hannah leaves for the day, I feel compelled to keep searching for answers. I take a quick look around. There are a couple people still here, but no one is paying any attention to me. Even if they were, it'd be natural for me to need something from Hannah's desk. We work as a team, after all. She's always paging through my papers or borrowing file folders.

Quickly, before I can talk myself out of it, I roll my chair over to her desk.

There's a framed photo of her and her husband, taken on their wedding day last winter. I was at the ceremony. Just looking at the picture makes me feel guilty. If I accuse her and she's innocent, it will ruin our friendship. Maybe this isn't worth the risk. It's not like there's a guarantee Melina will forgive me. I could go to all this trouble and have nothing to show for it. No, that isn't right. Even if Melina never speaks to me again, I will still have the reassurance of knowing I followed my morals. I simply can't look the other way while Madelyn may be duping the people whose trust she claims to value. So I move past the photo. What else is on the desk? A calendar, with some dates underlined in red and others in blue. A legal pad covered with notes from our earlier brainstorming session. A post-it stuck to her phone, three different numbers written on it.

I should copy them down. Research them.

I steal another furtive look around the room. No one's so much as glancing in my direction, so I take a pen and jot down the first number on a piece of scrap paper. Then I write the second one. As I begin to copy the third, the phone rings.

I just about jump out of my skin.

The phone continues to blare, a siren that broadcasts my actions to everyone. I drop the pen. It clatters to the floor, and I take a deep breath when I bend down to retrieve it. I have to act normal. I'll just say that I was getting the notes Hannah and I came up with before. No harm, no foul. If I'm smart about it, I think I can get away with this. Except ... when I straighten back up, I realize that I'm the only one fazed by the phone. Nobody else is heeding its warning. Maybe it wasn't as close a call as I feared.

Still, that's it for my snooping today. I power off my computer, straighten up my own desk, and head out. It's been a long day and I want to go home. Once I get there, though, I'm antsy. I turn on the ballgame. Send an email to Lucas. Putter around in the kitchen. Normally that works wonders in cheering me up, but not even a successful adaptation of my favorite baked ziti recipe – I add in a sprinkling of lemon and some caramelized onions – does the trick. I sit down, eating my dinner as I simultaneously scroll through the pictures on Cause for Paws' website. Man, that English Spot is so cute. He's dove gray and white, with warm brown eyes and the longest eyelashes I've ever seen on a rabbit. If only there weren't another three months of campaigning ahead of me, I would call Callie and ask her to take him off the list of adoptable bunnies. He's such a cool-looking little guy. I'd love to give him his forever home.

But that's not how life works on the campaign trail. There's no such thing as being settled.

I exit out of the rescue's website and drop my phone onto the couch. I think I'll take a shower. I am beyond ready to wash this day off me. It feels good, letting a steady stream of water rain down. I stay there for a long time, trying to forget about the world that's waiting outside the shower door. But the world doesn't forget about me. After I have toweled off, thrown on an old t-shirt and track pants, and gone back downstairs, I hear my phone buzzing. I'm not in the mood to talk with anyone, especially my mom, who's now taken to calling my cell with updates on next month's family reunion in Georgia, but the buzzing is insistent. When I grab the phone, just missing the call, it immediately makes my eyes go wide.

It wasn't Mom.

It was Melina.

I just stand there for a minute, staring at the phone. I feel like I'm dreaming. Like this can't even be real. After Melina and I first broke up, I used to think about what a relief it'd be to see her name pop up on my phone screen again. I missed hearing her voice at the end of a long workday. Missed reading her texts, which were sometimes sweet and other times sassy. And now she's reached out. But why? Is she extending an olive branch or yanking it further away?

I'm half afraid to call her back.

My thumb hovers an inch over the phone screen as I try to figure out what to do.

Then Melina makes the decision for me.

She calls again, and I can't resist. I have to talk to her. "Hi," I say, a little breathlessly. "Melina. I can't tell you how good it is to hear from you. I've missed you."

"I've missed you, too," she says softly.

She has?

My heart stands at full attention.

"Have you watched the news tonight?" Melina asks.

What? That was not what I was expecting her to say.

"No," I answer. "Why? What's going on?"

"Are you sitting down?" she says. "If you're not, you should be." Her cautionary tone piques my curiosity and also my concern.

I do as she suggests. "Okay," I say. "I'm sitting."

She exhales a breath into the phone. "There was a report," she says, "on the six o'clock news in Philadelphia. I don't know if the Harrisburg stations aired something similar, but if they haven't yet, they will soon. It's too huge a story not to cover. Did you know Madelyn's been funneling campaign donations into a private account and using them to make expensive purchases that have nothing to do with the election?"

"What?" I shake my head a little. I must have misheard her.

But she repeats it. "Apparently she's been skimming off money from her fundraisers. You know that house she bought in the Poconos? And the new car? And the two horse trailers for her family's farm?" I do. I do know about these things, but I assumed Madelyn had paid for them with her own savings. It isn't exactly like she's lacking in that area. But I'm too shocked to express that to Melina. All I can do is listen as she continues. "I only caught the tail-end of the tv report," she says, "but the whole story is up on the station's website. You should read it." She relays the URL and, half in a fog, I reach for my laptop.

She must be wrong, or maybe the reporter didn't get all the facts before running with the story. Something I have learned since getting involved with politics: the media isn't going to shy away from breaking news. It doesn't matter if the details are scarce. They'll still rush to share the update with their audience. I get it. Journalism is different from how it used to be. Social media has taken away the divide. It has, quite literally, made the news available right at the public's fingertips. In the race to keep up, it's understandable how something like this could happen. But when I type in the link to read the story, I don't find a vague article. I find one that has clearly been well-researched and well-written. There are specifics, lots of them, and quotes from an employee at the car dealership where Madelyn purchased her new Lexus. He claims to have overheard a phone call Madelyn made, asking someone to transfer the appropriate amount of money into her personal account.

I can't believe it.

I don't *want* to believe it.

Messing with Nathan's campaign was bad enough. Stealing from the voters is a whole new level of awful. It sickens me to even think about it. "This is ... I can't understand why ... how could it ... " I stammer.

The room is spinning wildly.

"I'm sorry," Melina says, and she does sound sincerely apologetic. I don't know why. If I were in her position, I'd be jumping up and down with glee. Maybe this doesn't clear Nathan's name, but it will go a long way in painting him as the better candidate. It'll also bring his rebuttals into the news again, because if Madelyn is capable of stealing from her would-be constituents, then surely they'll realize she'd have no problem playing dirty with her opposition. Her loss is Nathan's gain. Melina's got to be thrilled about that.

"It's alright," I tell her. "You don't have to be sorry."

"Oh, don't get me wrong. I'm not sorry for Madelyn at all. If she did something that disgraceful, she deserves to be outed. I do feel horrible for the rest of you, though. To dedicate all that time to helping someone get elected, only to discover she's doing this behind your back, has to be such a big blow."

"Huge," I say dazedly.

I wish Melina were here with me. I am so upset, so furious and shocked, and it doesn't feel like there's anywhere to put all those emotions. If she were here, I could hold her hand and talk my way through it. If only I'd been forthcoming with her from the start. If only I hadn't messed it all up. But she did contact me. That has to count for something, right?

"Thank you," I tell her. "You made it clear you want nothing to do with me anymore, so it really means a lot that you called anyway."

"I had to." She pauses. "I wanted you to hear about it from

me. Sometimes it softens that blow when the news is coming from someone you ... " Another pause, this one longer. "Someone whose opinion you care about," she finally settles on, even though we both know our bond was once much deeper than that.

For me, it still is. I wonder if she feels the same way.

Has she moved on, or did hearing my voice again make her breath catch in her throat? Hearing hers certainly did that to mine. I remember something my grandma once said: "You can always tell if people are in love by watching their reactions when they talk to each other on the phone. They're free to be themselves, without any mask on their emotions."

I raise a hand to my face. Feel the curve at the corners of my mouth.

How could I *not* smile when talking to Melina?

Even now.

Even when everything else feels so hard, so wrong, she feels so right.

"I do care about your opinion," I say. "And I still care about you." Silence. I don't know how to interpret it, and maybe I don't want to, so I opt to keep going. As long as I'm talking, she won't hang up, and I'm not nearly ready for this conversation to end. "Have you had any luck proving Nathan's innocence?" I ask.

"Nope." She sighs. "We contacted the reporter who wrote the article, but he won't budge. He says it's his right to protect his sources. I can't decide if he's in on the plan, or if he honestly believes the story's true. Whatever the case, Nathan asked us to stop concentrating on that and to put all of our energy into the actual campaign instead."

"Understandable."

"That doesn't make it any less frustrating."

"Well, if it helps, I've been following up on it on my end." It could be a mistake to tell her this. It might push her even further away. But I want her to know. I want her to know I'm trying, that I will continue to try. So I do tell her. I go over the whole thing, starting at my decision to quit and ending with this morning's revelation that it may be Hannah who is working with Madelyn. I lay it all on the line.

"I ... I don't know what to say." Melina sounds flustered. "You did all that for me?"

"Of course."

"Why?"

How can she not know why?

Then I realize ... she doesn't know because I've never told her. She didn't give me a chance.

I think of what Lissie said when I was babysitting, about apologizing to Melina. I think of the way that sweet girl lives her life with arms wide open and the way Cameron is doing the same, teaching his kids by example. I should live that way, too.

And so I lay even more on the line. I put my heart out there. Melina can take it or leave it, that choice will be hers, but I know I'll never forgive myself if I let her go again without saying those three little words. They aren't little, though, not really. They are everything. "Because," I tell her, "I love you."

She inhales, sharp and strong. "Bradley, you – "

"Let me finish," I say. "Please."

"Okay." Her whisper is so quiet, I barely hear it.

"I've been falling in love with you since the day we met," I say. "I didn't even realize it at first. I think that's the best kind of love, though. The kind that takes you by surprise. The kind that comes into your life when you least expect it and just sort of fills in the empty spaces you didn't know were there. The day you broke things off, when you said you loved me ... " The words catch in my throat. "I wish you wouldn't have left, because I'd have told you that I felt the same way. I still do. I know it might not change anything for us, and it won't undo the mistakes I made, but I want you to know. I need you to know. I love you."

At first, Melina says nothing.

She's silent for so long, in fact, that I start to wonder if she's hung up.

When she finally speaks, her voice sounds almost musical. "I love you, too," she says. "I've tried to stop. I've tried so hard. But you – " Here, she laughs a bit. "You seem to have a permanent spot in my heart. Do you have any idea how inconvenient that is?"

Now I'm laughing, too.

"So what do we do about it?" I ask.

"I don't know," she says. "Because this *does* change everything. Even so, we can't be together. I wish love was enough, I wish we could just hang on to each other and say to hell with the rest of it all – "

"We can."

"No. We can't – or, at least, I can't. I've seen what happens when relationships fall apart. It can destroy people. I think we're lucky," she says carefully. "We got out before it was too late. It's best to love each other from a distance. That way nobody gets hurt, and nobody has to cover it up when things spiral out of control."

Okay, now I'm lost.

"What are you talking about?" I ask her. "Because somewhere along the line, this stopped being about you and me."

But she doesn't answer my question.

"I'm sorry, Bradley," she says, and then she hangs up.

27

Melina

My favorite spot in my dad's condo has always been the kitchen. With its swinging doors, white countertops, and blue floral wallpaper selected by the elderly woman who lived here before him, it has a retro vibe that is somehow comforting. When I would spend weekends here as a teenager, it was the first place I'd go after dropping my bag in the small guestroom. Dad would set out a plate of Oreos and pour us glasses of milk, and we'd talk about anything and everything, filling each other in on the past week. Now, though, as I sit in one of the white chairs, it doesn't feel like the safe place it once did.

I rest my hand atop my phone, which is sitting on the table, and listen in silence as the TV filters in from the living room. I know Dad's giving me space to deal with what I told him was a "situation," but I wish he wouldn't. I'd rather him join me. My gaze travels over to the open pantry and the bag of Oreos on the second shelf. Then I stand up and poke my head into the living room. "Hey, Dad?" I ask. "Feel like some cookies and milk?"

A smile lights up his face. "Always." He turns off the television, crosses the room, and squeezes by me into the kitchen. As he does, I catch a whiff of his cologne. The past is riding on its coattails, memories of a time that sometimes feels so long ago and other times seems as though it painted its pictures only yesterday. Normally I raise my hand to the past and attempt to shut it out. Today, I do the opposite. I simply plunk myself back in the chair, watching as Dad shakes out a column of Oreos and splashes a white waterfall into two Phillies tumblers. "Is everything okay?" he asks, sliding into the chair across from me.

"Not really." I take a cookie, twist off the top half, and dunk it into my tumbler. "It's all become such a mess. We assumed Madelyn was behind the false accusations against Nathan, but we could never find proof. Now there are allegations against her, too. It turns out she's been stealing money from her own campaign." I bring him up to speed, and his eyes grow wide.

"Well, this is good, right?" he asks. "Because now everyone will forget about Nathan's supposed wrongdoings and focus on Madelyn's. The pendulum will swing back in his favor. If he can ride that momentum into the election, he should be golden." Dad sounds pleased with himself. He's not too big on politics and even stopped voting for awhile after life fell apart all those years ago, but he has tried to take more of an interest in it since I got involved.

"I hope so," I tell him. "Nathan will probably issue another statement in the next day or so, just so he can reiterate his innocence while the story's in the headlines. Depending on Madelyn's reply and whatever Perry says, it could go a long way in winning him the election. But he has to be smart about it. It's a balance – " I break off, right in the middle of the sentence, as my own words echo in my ears.

He has to be smart about it.

Holy crap.

What if he was more than smart about it? What if he was cunning?

My mind takes off at a sprint, staying several paces ahead of me. Nathan said he was too busy to get to my proposal yesterday. It was a crazy day. Time got away from him. What did he mean by that? How exactly were things crazy? I think back, trying to pull up the details. He talked with Cole about a speech, with Bill about the latest poll, and with a reporter about ... what? Normally we get a briefing on his interviews, but no one told us anything yesterday. Is this why? Maybe that interview wasn't about Nathan's agenda. Maybe he'd been investigating Madelyn all along, even after asking us to take a step back. Could he have been the one to uncover her crime, and instead of confronting her about it, he released the information straight to the media?

Then it hits me, hard and fast and horrifying.

Could he have fabricated the whole thing, like she did with him?

No.

Nathan is a good man, an honest man, a worthy and upstanding man.

He'd never do such a thing.

Right?

Something is nagging at me, but I don't know what.

"Melina?" Dad taps my wrist and I jump, dropping my cookie. Crumbs scatter all over the table. "Sweetheart, what's wrong?" he asks.

"Nothing."

Maybe everything.

Nathan was set to drop out of the election, to give up, until I convinced him to fight. What if this is his way of staying in the ring? I don't think he would do something so underhanded, but ... damn, why can't I get a hold on what's bothering me? It's playing hide-and-seek, creeping out from behind the corners of my mind and then disappearing again. There was something Nathan said. I can recall standing with Kira by the printer, waiting for the mock-up of our new Patchwork of Pennsylvania ad. Nathan was nearby, chatting with Bill, and he said something that briefly registered in my brain. If I could only remember what the heck it was.

I look across the table at Dad. He's staring at me, worry clouding his sky blue eyes. I was going to tell him about Bradley. I was going to confess that I love him, that he loves me, that I'm scared to act on those feelings because I don't want history to repeat itself. I could still spill everything to Dad like I always used to, or I can twist the key and lock my heart back up again.

"Please talk to me," Dad says. "Is it the gambling? I didn't mean to blindside you."

"No," I tell him. "It's not that. But ... do you ever regret it? The gambling?"

His eyebrows knit together and he reaches for his glass, cupping his hands around it. "Yes, I do," he answers. "I always knew it was a poor idea. I wish I'd listened to my own doubts. Instinct should always win out."

"What about love? Do you think *that* can ever win out, or are we destined to fail at it?"

He sighs, and I instantly feel bad. I shouldn't be asking him about this. We're sitting here in this same kitchen, all these years later, and I'm basically a different person than I was before, but Dad is still cut from the same cloth. He still wears those button down shirts with the little alligator logo, he still shops at the same stores, and he still carries the scars of the divorce and has never had another long-term relationship, despite Mom moving on many years ago. "I think love can win with the right people," he says carefully. "And I think some of us are just better off alone. Some people work well that way."

"In your opinion, am I one of those people?"

His eyes soften. "Oh, Melina, no. Not at all. You have one of the biggest and most giving hearts I've ever known. You're just waiting for the right person to fill it. You'll find him."

I think I already have.

So why can't I admit it?

Maybe I've got to force myself. Maybe taking a leap forward is really just about taking the first step.

I open my mouth ... and that's when the lightning bolt hits me.

"She'll get what she deserves." That's what Nathan said.

Kira and I were chatting at the time, tossing out ideas for which communities we'd feature in the next Patchwork ad, when Nathan's words floated by and skimmed our conversation. I heard them, and it was enough to temporarily grab my attention, but I didn't think much of it. He could've been talking about anybody, and for all I knew, he meant it in a good way. Maybe he was referring to the young woman who came up to talk to him after a rally, telling him she was the first one in her family to apply to college, or to the grandmother who wrote a letter about her pension plan and her desire to enjoy her retirement by traveling to see her grandchildren.

Maybe, though, it was Madelyn he'd set his sights on. Maybe the connotation wasn't positive at all.

What tone did Nathan have? I try very hard to focus my brain on what happened that day. The printer was whirring, rain was slapping against a nearby window, and Kira was talking about taking a few cameras to Lancaster. She mentioned Dutch Wonderland, the American Music Theater, and the hotel that looks like an old-fashioned steamboat. These details come to mind easily, but the rest is a mystery.

"I'm sorry, Dad," I say, pushing back my chair. "I have to go."

"Already?" He sounds disappointed.

"I'm afraid so. You were right before: something *is* wrong, or, at least, it might be." I reach over to give him a hug. "I've got to get to the bottom of it before everything blows up and the election is turned upside-down. I'm really sorry."

"No worries," he says. I retrieve my purse and he walks me to the door. "Melina?" he adds, as I'm stepping out into the hall. "I am sorry, too – for the gambling, for making a bad situation worse, and especially for keeping it secret all this time. It was just, well ..." He grips the door tightly, until his fingertips turn red. "A father is supposed to be his children's hero. I don't think I could take it if you all hated me."

"Oh, Dad. We could never hate you. Yes, I'd rather have known long ago, but what's important is that you told me now. I'm sure everybody else will agree."

"Don't tell them, okay?" he asks. "Let me do it. They deserve to hear it from me."

"Okay. I promise."

Something settles in his face. "Thanks. Now go on." He makes a little shooing motion with his hand. "Go save the day."

That's so much easier said than done.

I call Kira the minute I get back to my apartment, hoping she'll remember something I can't, but we go over that day from each angle and she's just as stumped as I am. "I don't know," she says. "It really doesn't seem like something Nathan would do, but I suppose elections can bring out the worst in people."

"But Nathan? Do we honestly think he has a dark side like that? Can't some politicians truly be in it for the right reasons?"

"I certainly hope so," she says. "So what do we do? What's the answer here?"

I think of Bradley and how he's been sneaking around, trying to uncover Madelyn's deception. I could do that, too. I could be a fly on the wall. "Maybe we just keep our eyes and ears open," I say. "I don't feel right accusing Nathan when there's basically nothing to go on. He's always been such a good guy. I'm going to choose to believe that he still is, unless we find something concrete to prove otherwise."

"Alright. Same here. Chances are, he had nothing to do with it. If Madelyn can launch a smear campaign against her opponent, she probably has no qualms about stealing money from her donors. Those poor people. I wonder how many will stand by her and how many will jump ship."

"Who knows? Loyalty can be a strange thing sometimes."

For a moment, I contemplate telling her about Bradley. I never got the chance to talk about him with my dad, or maybe it's that I jumped at the excuse not to, but either way, my conversation with him is still following me around. Bradley's loyalty lies with me.

He's risked so much because he loves me. He *loves* me.

I don't know what to do with that. It's scary and magical and intimidating and wonderful.

Kira would be a logical person to confide in. She's been there through the whole thing, plus she is more than just a co-worker. She's a friend. With that in mind, I take a deep breath and toss aside the safety net. "Bradley loves me," I say. "He told me tonight."

"Wait, what?" She sounds confused and surprised, but mostly excited. "I thought you two were broken up?"

"We were. We *are.*" I correct myself quickly. "But I called him earlier, after I saw the report on Madelyn. God, it was so good to hear his voice again. I don't think I realized how much I missed it. It was like ... something opened up inside me. Something got bigger, fuller." I groan. "That sounds ridiculous, I know."

"Not at all. What it sounds like is that you love him, too."

Her words are gentle, but they drop on me with an intense force.

Is it that obvious?

"I do," I admit. "I love him, and I hate myself for it."

"Why?"

"Because he lied to me. He did all the right things, and he made me believe that we could work, and then he turned around and stabbed me in the back. I can't be with somebody who thinks it isn't a big deal to keep secrets." An image of my parents flashes before my eyes. "Secrets are powerful. They ruin relationships. That's basically why my parents got divorced." I think of what Nathan said earlier, about owning my past, then squeeze my eyes shut and blurt out the words. "It's why we lost our house and had to move to a homeless shelter ... why the bottom pretty much dropped out from my childhood when I was ten."

I open my eyes and hold my breath as I wait for a response. Please, don't let this be a mistake.

"Oh, Melina," she says. "I had no idea. Why didn't you ever tell me?"

"I hardly tell anybody. I just ... I don't want people to see who I was instead of who I am."

"I don't," she says. "I couldn't. But I *do* understand now why you're so passionate about certain things. I think it's awesome, by the way," she adds. "A lot of people use their past as an excuse, not a motivation. Your story is inspiring."

I should've known I could count on her.

"Thank you," I say. "You're such a great friend."

"Right back at you – which is why I want you to be happy. So going back to Bradley, I want you to tell me why you love him."

Why do I love him?

"I love him because he's warm," I say. "He's funny, and kind, and he has the sort of soul you can see straight into, if you look closely enough. I love him because he takes care of rescued rabbits and knows how to make the best cream puffs on the planet. Because, when we went to HersheyPark, it began to rain and instead of suggesting we wait it out in a store, he grabbed my hand and asked me to dance. Mostly, though, I love him because he makes me happy. He makes me feel like … " I stop, trying to find the right words, or any words, really, to explain it. "He makes me feel like the world is safe," I say. "Like I'm safe. He makes me feel different than everybody else does. He takes me to a different place."

Something cool and wet splatters onto my cheek.

A tear.

The first one I've shed in nearly twenty years.

I reach up to touch it.

I close my eyes, but a second tear slips through the lashes anyway, and then a third.

I make no move to wipe them away. I simply sit there, letting them drop. It is a sweet release, a sweet *relief*, and something occurs to me: maybe there's a reason I haven't cried in so long, a reason that goes beyond not wanting to feel that overwhelming sense of vulnerability. Maybe, all this time, my head's been strong enough to win out over my heart, but now, finally, my heart is fighting back. Maybe, without even knowing it, I've been saving all my tears for a moment like this.

28

BRADLEY

*I*t's almost eleven o'clock when my phone buzzes with a text. I'm in bed already, waiting for the news to come on, and my first instinct is to ignore the message. It's been an incredibly long day and I don't feel like dealing with anything more. I just want to know whether Madelyn's made the top of the newscast, and then I'm calling it quits and going to sleep. But curiosity gets the best of me, and I reach over to pick up the phone from my nightstand. It fits neatly into my palm, like that's where it belongs. Such is a life in politics. I readjust my glasses – I must've dozed off for a minute before and they've slid down my nose – and peer at my cell.

Melina. Again?

I called her back earlier, after she hung up, but she didn't answer and she also didn't respond to the message I left. Not until now, anyway. I skim her text, then sit up against the pillows and read it again, just in case I've misinterpreted it in my hazy, half-asleep state.

Are you on the road tomorrow or in the office? If you're around, do you want to grab lunch? I'll come to you. It's my last day in town before we hit the campaign trail ahead of the first debate, and there's something I'd like to talk to you about before I leave. Let me know what you think.

Within seconds, I am wide awake.

What do I think?

I think I would love nothing more than to meet up with her. To see the light reflect in her eyes. To hear her laugh. To smell her sweet perfume and to feel her fingers graze mine as we both reach for the check simultaneously – because, in all the time we dated, she never once let me pay for her without putting up a fight. She wears her independence like a badge of honor. I respect that. I just wish she'd realize that it's also okay to lean on someone. It's not necessary to do everything solo in this life.

I think that sounds great, I type. *But I'm picking up the check.*

Fifteen seconds later, her reply zings back. *You wish.*

I chuckle.

Is one o'clock good? I write. *Want to meet me outside my office and we'll go from there?*

Sounds good. See you tomorrow.

See you tomorrow. I'm looking forward to it.

It takes longer for her to answer this time, but eventually her text arrives. *Me too.*

I can't stop the smile from spreading across my face. I know it's foolish to get my hopes up, and yet the anticipation still takes hold of me, a hundred light bulbs turning on one by one. Nothing can put a damper on my happiness.

Not the eleven o'clock news, which does indeed feature Madelyn as its lead story.

Not the corresponding headline in the paper the next morning.

Not the sense of defeat circling through the air when I get to work.

Not even Hannah. "Did she seriously think we wouldn't find out?" she says. "She's supposed to be making the laws, for God's sake, not breaking them."

I study her for a moment. She seems sincerely distraught. Maybe I was wrong to assume she's helping Madelyn. Suddenly, the thought of investigating it behind her back feels pointless. Why not just ask? "So this is a surprise to you?" I say.

She looks at me like I'm speaking a foreign language. "Yes," she says. "Clearly. Why? It's not a surprise to you?"

"The new allegations, yes. But I've known for a long time that something else might be going on under the surface." Hannah stares at me blankly, so I continue. "That article about Nathan was a lie and the accompanying pictures were doctored."

"They were? Are you sure?"

"Yes."

"How do you know?"

I pause. If I'm expecting her to be honest with me, doesn't she deserve the same courtesy? And it's not like Melina and I are together any longer, so there really isn't anything to lose. "I was dating one of Nathan's staff members," I say, and it feels good to put it out there and to talk about Melina freely. "She was with him on that tour of the state. She saw everything firsthand and said the paper got it all wrong. I've been trying to figure out whether it was intentional or the reporter was duped. Either way, I think Madelyn was behind it."

The color visibly drains from Hannah's face. "Wait," she says. "You're telling me she's been up to her neck in this for months? Are you positive, or could it be that your girlfriend was skewing the facts to her advantage? Speaking of which ... you're dating someone who works for the opposition? You know that's not your brightest move, right? If Madelyn finds out ... "

"If Madelyn finds out, it doesn't matter," I interrupt. "Because first of all, I *was* dating someone in Nathan's camp. Not anymore, unfortunately. And second of all, even if I were, I don't give a darn what Madelyn thinks. If she really was stealing, she's going to end up getting prosecuted and having to drop out of the race anyway. That's fine by me. I was going to quit months ago, after I found out about the Nathan thing, but I stayed to see what I could uncover."

"And?"

She doesn't sound even remotely nervous.

"And I know now that she's working with someone," I say. "A woman with a tattoo on her ankle and dark hair. Remember how I was asking you about that? This is the actual reason why. It didn't have anything to do with my friend." I stop for a second to see what Hannah does next. It isn't that I think she'll outright incriminate herself, but maybe she'll trip up since the walls are closing in now on Madelyn's plan.

Nope.

"Crap," she says. "God, you think you know a person. How could we have been so wrong about her? I genuinely believed she was running for the greater good. All those speeches we wrote about wanting Pennsylvania to be the best it can be, about wanting to help people turn their dreams into realities ... she snowed them all. She snowed *us* all." She plunks herself down in my desk chair, and as she does, the bottom of her long skirt gets caught underneath its leg. She bends over to yank the fabric free, and that's when the blue mark comes into view again. But this time, I can see it for what it really is.

A long, jagged, painful-looking bruise.

My shoulders sag with immediate relief. It's not a tattoo. It wasn't her.

"Ouch," I say. "I just noticed that bruise. That must've hurt."

"Yep." She nods. "That's why I was at the doctor the other day. Would you believe I managed to fall over a suitcase? I hadn't put it away after our last work trip, and I accidentally crashed into it one night. It was dark, and I was tired, and I forgot it was there. I was still in pain a week afterward, so my husband kept bugging me to see a doctor."

Every ounce of tension drains out of me. I'm so glad it wasn't her.

But if Hannah isn't helping Madelyn, then who is?

Suddenly, a door opens behind us. Everybody goes silent, watching the person striding into the room. Her head's held high. Her shoes click smartly. I feel the tension, only gone for a few seconds, build back. It's standing right there with all of us.

Waiting for her to say something.

Madelyn has arrived.

For what seems like an eternity, she stays quiet. We look at her, and she looks at us, doing what she always does – commanding the attention in a room with an effortless ease. The energy is drawn to her, tiny metallic shavings being pulled in by the magnet. She has thrived off of that for as long as I've known her. Even now, with what I can only assume is potential jail time hanging over her head, she is calm and composed. I don't get it. How can she not be thrown by this?

"I'm sure you've seen the news reports," she says, her voice clear and deliberate. "I want you all to know I'm innocent. I have no idea where these trumped-up charges have come from, but I assure you: I don't steal, I don't embezzle, and I don't lie to the people I want to represent. The news has it all wrong, and I'm going to fight with everything I am to prove it." She looks at us steadily. "I hope you'll fight, too. I really believe we can do wonderful things for Pennsylvania, and that's why I have no intention of dropping out of this race."

I watch, slack-jawed, as she slips her fingers beneath her locket. The one with the photos of her daughters inside. Is she going to tell everyone the truth about them?

"We all have something that inspires us," she says, "*someone* who inspires us. A long time ago, I made a promise to two beautiful babies, that I'd take an incredibly hard decision and make it worth it. That was a difficult time in my life. Now this will be, too, but I think the mark of a politician who cares is that she doesn't back down. She keeps on standing. Please," she says, and her voice drops a notch, "I'd love for you to stand with me."

The room is eerily silent after she finishes.

Nobody speaks. Nobody moves.

Then, across from me, Darci begins to clap. One by one, most of the others join her. Only Kristi and Hannah look like they still have reservations. "What do you think?" Hannah whispers to me. "Is she telling the truth, or is it just more lies? I can't decide."

Neither can I.

It weighs on me all morning and into the afternoon. Even as I leave work to meet Melina, I can't shake Madelyn's words. I was so sure she was guilty. I didn't even give her the benefit of the doubt. Maybe I was right. Her speech could've been a cleverly crafted ruse to fool us. Or it could've been a passionate plea, in which case I was wrong. Who knows? This has turned into a bigger mess than I ever thought possible.

But where there is confusion, there is also clarity. Where there is darkness, there is also light.

Melina.

She's waiting in the front courtyard, sitting on the stone wall with her legs crossed at the ankles. I see her before she sees me, and I stop for a few moments just to take in the sight. She's wearing a blue suit, and as she leans forward a little, her long necklace sways slightly. Even from the distance, I can tell that her hair is lighter than the last time I saw her, highlighted by the summer sun in all the right places. Everything about her is right. I want to run to her, to take her by the hand and pull her into a kiss, but I don't let myself.

Instead, I walk slowly, footsteps echoing on the ground. I'm a few feet away from Melina when she hears them. She glances over her shoulder, and my heart basically melts as I see a smile sweep across her face. How I've missed that smile. How I've missed her.

"Hi," I say, shuffling my feet a bit as I come to a stop in front of her.

She stands up. "Hi," she says.

A bird chirps from one of the nearby trees. A butterfly glides by and perches on a bush. A car drives through the parking lot, music filtering out of its open windows. Melina's attention flits over to it temporarily, then she returns her gaze to me. She doesn't say anything more, though, and neither do I. There's so much to tell her, but I don't know where to start. Honestly, I'd rather stay in this moment. It's like something was askew the entire time we were apart and now it's straightened out. I know we'll just knock it off balance again once we talk. Sometimes it's nice to let things be for awhile.

If only it could stay that way.

Eventually, though, someone has to break the moment. I let it be Melina.

"Crazy day?" she asks.

"Insane." I shake my head. "Madelyn denied the whole thing. Come on," I say, nodding toward my car. "I'll fill you in at lunch." Instinctively, I reach out for her, to put my hand on the small of her back. I manage to catch myself in the nick of time, and we walk side-by-side instead, our feet falling into an alternating rhythm.

"Thanks," she says, as I open the car door for her.

It's so easy to fall back into place with her. I thought it might be awkward or tense, but really, it feels like no time has passed at all. We don't talk about the election on the drive, not a single word. She asks me about Cause for Paws instead, and I ask her how her painting is going. But once we are seated at a table at the little outdoor café down the street, we can't avoid it any longer. We have to jump in.

I tell her all about Madelyn's impromptu speech. "I don't know what to think," I say. "If you had asked me this morning, I would've said she was a hundred-percent guilty. Now I'm not so sure. Do you think someone could be framing her?"

"Yes."

Melina's response is much quicker than I expected.

She sighs and looks down at her menu. "I think Nathan could be, actually."

"What?" I say. "You've gotta be kidding me."

"I wish." Slowly, she lifts her gaze until it's locked with mine. "I might be off base. I hope I am. I thought I owed it to you to be upfront, though." She raises her eyebrows, and it's what she leaves unsaid that gets to me the most.

She owed it to me to be upfront. Like I wasn't with her.

"I'm really sorry," I tell her. "I wanted to be fair to you, but also to Madelyn. I didn't know then what she was capable of. I thought it was right to give her a chance to explain. If she couldn't, or if she wouldn't – even if she did, and I didn't like what I heard – I was going to tell you. Please believe me."

"I do."

"You do?"

"Yes." She takes the paper wrapper from her straw and curls it around her finger. "I get it now. I understand how unnerving it is to suspect that someone might be wearing a mask. You want to be absolutely certain before you send everything into an upheaval."

"Exactly."

"I debated for a long time last night whether I should tell you about Nathan," she says. "I don't have any proof that he did anything. He could be totally innocent, and I hope he is. When I thought about not telling you, though … " She trails off, and, against my better judgment, I reach across the table and rest my hand on hers.

She doesn't pull away.

"Thank you," I say. "For telling me, for setting up lunch … for not hating me."

"I tried." She smiles a little. "I tried really hard to hate you. I just couldn't." She takes a breath. "Anyhow, I have a plan. I think I know how we can get to the bottom of this, but we would have to join forces. Are you willing?"

I don't even have to hear what the plan is.

As long as it involves the two of us working together, I'll do it.

"Sure," I say. "I'm in."

Melina

I wish he would quit looking at me this way.

His hand is still on mine, a hotspot of warmth that I'm enjoying a little too much, and his gaze is so steady that I'm almost tempted to look away. I could get lost in a gaze like that. It is sunshine on my skin, making me hazy and happy and drunk on the love I would so desperately like to extinguish. I should move. I should break the hold, break the connection, break the thread that's clearly chosen not to break itself in all the time we were apart. Why is that? I saw Cory a couple of months after I turned down his proposal, and there was no urge to jump back into the relationship. Ian walked out of my life the day I walked out of his apartment, but even so, I know I would have stayed strong and not changed my mind. It's different with Bradley, though. Everything is different with him, even if I don't want it to be.

That's annoying, really damn annoying.

It's also kind of fantastic.

"Well?" His voice snaps me out of my thoughts. "Are you going to tell me what the plan is, or is it a mystery?"

Right, the plan. That's what I'm supposed to be thinking about now.

"No mystery," I say quickly. "I guess I got distracted for a minute. Sorry about that." I slide my hand out from below his. "So, I think I came up with a way to put both Madelyn *and* Nathan to the test simultaneously." I pull out my phone and swipe to open the calendar app. "The debates will be a perfect opportunity, especially the second one, since the format will be a town hall meeting. If we play our cards right, that can be our ace."

Cards. Ace. Gambling. Dad.

An image pops into my head, of him sitting around a table with a bunch of other men and trying to look confident as he risked more money than he had. I still can't believe he did that. Usually he's so level-headed. I suppose, though, when your back's against the wall, you have to take some kind of action.

"Melina." Bradley taps my hand, and for the second time, I disengage myself from the firestorm circling my brain. "I'm starting to get insulted," he teases. "Am I really so boring that you can't help but tune me out?"

"No, no, not at all. I was just thinking about my dad," I say. "I found out yesterday that he lost a load of money gambling." I don't mean to tell him this, but it's like my mouth has a mind of its own around him. My phone fades to black, Madelyn and Nathan and the election swallowed up inside it, as the whole story comes tumbling out. "I think that's what caused my parents' divorce," I confide. "The financial problems, the homelessness, the struggle to keep it all together … that started it. My dad's addiction finished it."

"I'm sorry," he says. "That's horrible. All this time, your parents kept it a secret?"

"Yep. My mom was trying to protect us, and I think maybe she was trying to protect him, too."

"Do you wish you would've known?"

"Back then? No." I take a sip of my lemonade. "Things were awful enough. Knowing what my dad was doing would have made it worse. I do wish they'd have been honest with us when we were older, though. We could've handled it."

"I don't think it was a matter of them thinking you couldn't," Bradley muses. "It was more that they didn't want you to be in a position where you needed to." He swirls his straw around his soda. "I'm not saying I agree with them. If my parents kept a secret like that, my brothers and I would've been upset, too. But I can sort of understand why they'd do it."

"So can I. I have all these questions, though. How did they come up with enough money to pay his debts? What finally made him quit? Has he ever relapsed? I wanted to ask," I say, "but it didn't feel right to pry, and then the news story about Madelyn came on … " As the waitress arrives to get our order, I let my voice trail off. Bradley motions for me to continue once she's finished, but I feel something cool settle over me. I am exposed again, the layers peeled off, and it's time to pile them back on. "So anyhow," I say, "I really think we can use the second debate to our advantage. All we have to do is plant someone in the audience who can ask a key question."

It is verbal whiplash.

To his credit, Bradley goes with it. "A question that'll either get them to incriminate themselves or prove their innocence," he says, and I'm so grateful to him for letting it drop about my father that I could kiss him.

I *want* to kiss him.

I want to kiss him so badly, and that's precisely why I can't. I can never be with Bradley because I love him too much. I don't want us to hurt each other any more than we already have. Setting him free is the best and only gift I have to offer him. Business over pleasure and life over love, that's the surest way to guarantee happiness.

Or is it?

Because, after lunch, when Bradley and I say our goodbyes, I let him take my hand for a second time today. I even let him brush his lips to my cheek. "This was nice," he says. "Maybe we can do it again after you get back from your trip?"

"I … I don't think so."

His eyelids droop a bit behind his glasses. "I'm not normally a fighter," he says. "But I'll fight for you, Melina. I'll fight for us." He raises his hand and grazes my cheek with the outside of his fingers. "We're good together. We have something special. Just think about it, okay? Think about what we could be, if we let ourselves." A grin blooms across his face. "You're stuck with me now anyway, at least until that second debate. We may as well enjoy our time together, right?"

"Wrong."

He gives a little wink. "I'm confident you'll change your mind. But I won't push. It's your choice to make."

It's my choice to make.

Over the next few weeks, I make plenty of them. I choose to continue campaigning for Nathan at full strength, crisscrossing the state in advance of the upcoming debates in Harrisburg, Pittsburgh, and Philadelphia. I choose to take it as a positive sign when Madelyn's poll numbers fall, despite her prompt and firm denial of any wrongdoing. I choose to track Nathan's actions very carefully, to see if he's up to anything that could be remotely categorized as devious. I choose to ask for the day off to attend Amie's baby shower, even though we're hosting a big Get Out the Vote rally on that same afternoon. Mostly, I choose not to do what Bradley asked. I don't think about us, or what we could be.

I do a good job of it, too … until the first debate in Harrisburg.

It's being hosted by the League of Women Voters, and as I hurry through the backstage area an hour before it's set to begin, a surge of adrenaline pulses through me. The air, it's electric. I can feel the excitement, the urgency, the parade of patriotism that sweeps up the candidates and convinces them, without a shadow of a doubt, that they truly are the best person for the job. How cool it is, to live in a country where discussion is encouraged – where it's celebrated, even. As a teenager, I used to love watching the presidential debates. I'd sit in front of the tiny television, entirely captivated. I wanted to be there, to be an integral part of the democracy playing out before my eyes.

Now I am. It is humbling in the best way.

My ID badge flaps against my suit jacket as I navigate my way through the crowd, trying to find a clear path to Nathan. I want to give him my folder of information on the homeless shelter initiative, so he can brush up on the statistics and mention them during the debate. After all, there's no better stage for it than a statewide one. It's hard to get to him, though. People are packed in like sardines, campaign staffers and press and representatives who were invited to be here. There's an American flag tacked up on the wall, watching over the proceedings, giving its blessing, and I stop for a second to look at it.

That's when someone crashes into me.

The folder I'm holding slips out of my grasp and falls to the floor, and I can only watch in horror as its contents fan out everywhere. Some papers fly under a nearby table and others skitter across the floor, immediately being trampled. I drop to my knees and start snatching as many as possible, pulling them from beneath people's shoes and wrenching them from below table legs. I'm reaching for one that's wedged underneath a speaker when I see a flash of black out of the corner of my eye. It's a freshly pressed pair of pants, and I glance up to check who they belong to.

Cole.

"I'm sorry," he apologizes, kneeling beside me and putting down his binder, which is presumably filled with copies of Nathan's speeches for tonight. "I was answering a text while walking. Guess I'm not so good at multi-tasking ... or coordination, evidently." He gives a self-deprecating grin and frees the paper I've been fighting to loosen. Then he picks up a handful of others. "I hope these weren't for tonight," he says, passing me the pages, some of which are torn and others of which are covered in dirty, dusty footprints.

"It's everything I compiled for my homeless shelter program," I explain. "I thought Nathan could look over it before going out on stage. So much for that."

"I'm sorry," he repeats, shaking his head slightly. "I'll make it up to you. Drinks on me after the debate?"

I look up for a moment and survey the crowd. Bradley's standing about ten feet away, in a deep conversation with his speechwriting partner. She's pretty. Her hair is long, she's dressed in a purple pantsuit that looks like it's straight out of the pages of a magazine, and she exudes chicness. They'd actually make a nice couple. Maybe he should be with her and maybe I should go with Cole. Maybe we should both do whatever it takes to get over one another.

"Sure," I tell Cole. "Why not?"

"Great." He flashes his dimples at me. "It's a date."

Something flops in my stomach, but I ignore it. "Great," I echo, standing up and shoving all the papers back into the folder. "I'll see you later, then." I give him a wave and head off, refocusing my thoughts on the debate.

I settle into my seat up front a few minutes before it's set to start, and watch intently as Nathan, Madelyn, and Perry are introduced by the moderator, a news anchor from one of the local stations. The three of them shake hands and take their places behind their podiums. For the next hour, it is a virtual ping-pong game on stage: taxes, education, job growth, pension reform, equal work for equal pay. Sometimes they hit the ball back and forth and other times they slam it. Nathan contends that Madelyn would cut education funding, she fires back by accusing him of being deliberately vague on his tax plan, and Perry takes them both to task over their shared position on appointing, rather than electing, judges. I have to hand it to them, they're good at this game – especially Perry, who brings up the allegations against Madelyn more than once. He, along with everyone else, has to know that there are some viewers tuning in solely for that. Nathan, though, stays mum on it.

"Kudos to him," Kira whispers from her seat beside me. "He's a bigger person than most."

It's that integrity which wins him the night.

As soon as the debate is over, I take out my phone and open the Twitter app. It's become such a useful way of gauging public opinion. "Good news," I say. "Nathan's getting positive feedback."

"How about Madelyn?" Kira asks.

I scan the commentary. "It seems to be about fifty-fifty. Some people think she did a terrific job of distancing herself from the charges and others think it was a transparent attempt to shift focus. I don't know," I say, scrolling through the feed. "It was kind of both. I mean, yeah, she stayed on the topics at hand and didn't bring up anything else, but it was almost worse that way, because then she had this undercurrent running through everything she said. I wonder if it would have been wiser to acknowledge it briefly and get it out of the way."

A voice comes from behind me. "We did consider that, but decided not to bring it up on the off chance that voters had already let it go." Instantly, a flutter lets loose in my chest. It's Bradley. Kira and I stand up to greet him, and I see that he's alone this time. "Hi," he says, extending his hand to Kira. "I'm Bradley."

"Kira." They shake. "It's lovely to meet you," she says. "I've heard a lot – " Quickly, I nudge her with my elbow. "A lot about your speechwriting talents," she improvises, shooting a sideways look at me. "Cole's always saying you make him work twice as hard to keep up."

He laughs. "Ditto."

"So what brings you to our part of the auditorium?" Kira asks.

He smiles at me. "I was hoping to borrow this lady for a bit."

"I think that's a fabulous idea," Kira says. "Normally, we'd have a team meeting after a debate, but Nathan's whole family is here and it's his grandson's birthday, so they're going out for ice cream to celebrate. That means Melina's free."

Part of me wants to throttle her. Kira is not a pushy person by nature and so I never would have expected her to shove me at Bradley. Part of me wants to hug her, though, because I know why she is doing it. After listening to me ramble on about him, listing all of those reasons why my heart can't seem to wriggle its way out of his grasp, she wants me to act on them.

Bradley takes a step closer, brushing his hand against mine ever so slightly, and that prior flutter unleashes fully. It flies sky-high. "I … I have to work," I stammer. "I need to reprint documents that got ruined earlier, and I have to monitor reaction to the debate – "

"She's free," Kira repeats. Then she makes a grand show of taking out her phone. "I better call and say goodnight to my daughter. Don't want to miss her bedtime." She lifts her hand and wiggles her fingers. "Ta-ta." Then she's off.

"I like her," Bradley says.

"Why am I not surprised?"

"Come on," he says. "We should really talk things over anyway, right? Compare notes on how it went tonight and whether or not we're any closer to figuring things out. If you think about it, that'd be in everyone's best interest. The faster you and I find out what's going on, the sooner the election will go back to being fair. The people of Pennsylvania deserve that. You wouldn't want to let them down, would you?"

"Now you're just playing dirty."

"Is it working?"

He's only a few inches away. I could reach out and touch him, press my mouth to his. It's been such a long time since our lips met. Except ... what am I thinking? I can't do that, not with all of our colleagues around. "No," I say. I take a step back and bang into the chair behind me. Crap. "I ... it's not a good idea. Besides, I already have plans tonight."

His brow furrows. "You do?"

"I do." I look around the auditorium almost wildly, until my eyes land on Cole. He's talking with a small group of people by the stage. "Cole invited me for a drink," I tell Bradley.

"He did? Like, a date?"

"Yes," I confirm. "We'll meet up soon, though. You're right – we have a lot to discuss." I force myself not to meet his eyes. "Hey, maybe you should ask your speechwriting partner out."

"Hannah?" He sounds perplexed.

"Yes. You'd make a gorgeous couple."

"Melina." He reaches out a hand and lays it on my arm, effectively stopping me as I start to inch away. "First of all, Hannah's married, but even if she wasn't I'd have no desire to date her. The only woman I want is you, and the only man you want is me. I know it, and you know it. You can go out with Cole, but it won't accomplish what you're hoping. It's not going to erase your feelings for me."

Damn it.

Why does he know me so well?

When did that happen, and how do I make it stop?

And why can't he understand that I'm trying, really trying, to do right by him?

Maybe I need to try harder.

"I guess we'll just see about that," I say. Then I turn on my heel and march over to Cole.

30

BRADLEY

$\mathcal{I}$ watch for a minute as Melina joins Cole up front. She puts a hand on his arm, light and casual, and something yanks at my heartstrings. This is wrong. It's all wrong. Cole isn't right for her. He's smooth, and confident, and charming, the sort of person who attracts attention without even trying. He's been a worthy opponent in the speechwriting field – I will be the first to admit he has a way of crafting words to his advantage – but I can't explain it, something about the image of him romancing Melina makes me feel nauseous. It's more than just wanting to be with her myself. Even if I wasn't in the picture, I would think they were a mismatch.

But that isn't my decision to make.

I sigh, then head across the auditorium. Most of my coworkers are there, clustered in a circle as they analyze the debate. I have zero desire to join in the conversation. At the moment, I don't care whether Madelyn came off as graceful and dignified or guarded and aloof. The candidates' traction on social media matters even less to me. The whole thing seems pointless. We work day in and day out, trying to convince people why and how they should vote. For what? We can have all the right people in office, and the changes they make won't resonate half as much if we have no one to share our lives with, no one to make them better in other ways.

"Whoa," Hannah says, as I reach the group. Kristi's talking, something about Madelyn not doing enough to win the debate, and Hannah lowers her voice so as not to compete with her. "What the heck happened to you? No offense, but you look like somebody stole your best friend."

I think of Lucas, back in Georgia. We haven't talked much lately – I've been busy with work and he's been busy with his girlfriend – but I know he would be there for me in a second if I needed him. I should give him a call. See if he has any advice now that he's in such a great relationship. Because Hannah's right: in a way, somebody *did* steal my best friend. Not Lucas, but Melina.

"You're not too far off base," I say.

Hannah frowns. "I was being facetious. Or, at least, I thought I was. What happened?"

"Long story."

"Wanna talk about it? I've had enough of this election stuff for tonight. My brain needs a break from it." As she smiles, Melina's earlier comment comes to mind. She really thought she was doing me a favor by telling me to date Hannah. Maybe I can do *her* a favor now. A burst of energy ignites inside me. I have an idea.

"Agreed," I say. "And yeah, sure. Feel like grabbing a drink?"

"Now that we managed to get through the first debate without a major disaster?" She nods. "A drink sounds good." We say our goodbyes to the others and walk outside. "So what's up?" Hannah asks, as a blast of chilly air hits our faces. It's that point in September when the days are still warm, but the nights are starting to cool off.

"Melina," I say. The breeze sneaks by the lapel of my suit jacket and creeps beneath my collar.

"Who's that?"

"The woman I was seeing, the one who works for Nathan. She's ... "

I pause to glance in the front window of the wood-paneled tavern next door. Come on, fate. Do your thing. I've never been one to believe in that stuff, the thought of the universe determining our destiny, but if there was ever a time when I needed it to exist, it's now. Please, please let this be the place where Cole took Melina. There are a lot of people inside. People at tables, talking as they eat a late dinner. People at the bar, watching football. People by the old-fashioned jukebox and people by the pool table. I don't actually see

Melina or Cole, but it's pretty dimly lit inside and it isn't like I have a view of the entire place from out here on the sidewalk.

I guess it's worth a try.

"She's ... what?" Hannah prompts.

"She's on a date," I say. "With Cole."

"Cole? As in, Nathan's speechwriter?"

"The one and only."

A light bulb must go off in Hannah's head. "Aha," she says. "So that's why we're actually here. You're hoping to crash their date."

Heat seeps into my cheeks. "I know, it's petty and immature and unfair."

She grins. "I was going to say it's brilliant. Come on. Let's do it."

It's loud inside, with an undercurrent of music running below the conversation, and as a hostess leads us to a table toward the back, I do my best to scan the area. Is that them in the booth next to the dart board? No. The table by the framed sports memorabilia? No. Each time I think I see them, it turns out to be somebody else. They must have gone to a different place.

"I'm sorry," Hannah says, as we sit down. "No sign of them, huh?"

I run my finger along the edge of the table. "None," I say.

"Do you just want to leave?"

I'm about to say yes when I hear it. Melina's unmistakable laugh. Immediately, I snap my head up to follow its trail. There. Across the tavern, four tables up, partially blocked by a low divider wall. Melina is facing away from me, her elbow resting on the tabletop and her chin in her hand, and Cole is leaning forward, gesturing animatedly as he talks. It makes my heart wrench. I'm not sure what I was expecting, but it wasn't this. They look comfortable. Relaxed. Happy.

I think I'm going to be sick. "This was a mistake," I mutter. "Let's go."

Hannah follows my gaze toward them. "That's it?" she asks. "You're giving up?"

"Just look at them."

She observes for a few moments. "I'm not convinced," she says. "I think we should hang out for awhile and see what happens next." She slides a menu across the table at me. "Things were so nuts with the debate that I never got to eat dinner, and I doubt you did, either. You've got to be hungry."

I exhale heavily. "Fine," I say. "But then we're out of here."

"Deal."

Once I get my food, though, I can barely touch it. Every time I take a bite, my stomach coils into knots. Usually I love a good burger and fries, but everything I eat tonight tastes like sawdust. "Ugh," I mutter, pushing the plate away. "I can't."

"I'm sorry," Hannah apologizes. "I shouldn't have suggested we stay. I really thought the whole thing was an act, and that the longer we sat here, the clearer it'd become."

"An act? You mean, for my benefit? But they don't even know we're here."

"No. For Melina's benefit." I guess I must look puzzled, because Hannah launches into a more detailed explanation. "Before I met my husband," she says, "I was dating this guy I met at a concert. He was nice, and funny, and we were good together. He never wanted to commit, though. If I even so much as mentioned that one of my friends was engaged, he'd get all clammy. You'd think I would have taken that as a sign to get out, but I didn't. I stayed for three years, knowing full well that the relationship was at a dead end. The point is," she says, shaking her head a little, "I did a great job of convincing myself that it was okay. I think we can pull the wool over our own eyes sometimes, and it's even more dangerous than when another person is deceiving us."

"And you figure that's what Melina's doing? Fooling herself?"

"I did." She peeks over at Melina and Cole, who are still ensconced in conversation. "I assumed it was her attempt to force herself into getting over you. She just seemed a little *too* into the date. I don't know, though." As Cole says something that makes Melina throw her head back and laugh out loud again, Hannah sighs.

"I hate to say it, but their interaction doesn't seem contrived."

No, it doesn't.

I take out my wallet and yank a few bills from its pocket. "I've got to leave," I tell Hannah. "This is too hard to watch." She nods, finishes off her last onion ring, and grabs her purse. Then we make our way through the tavern and back out to the street. I don't stop by Melina's table. I don't crash her date, despite my brain nagging me to do just that. All I want for Melina is happiness. If Cole can give her that, who am I to interfere? I knew the possibility of us getting back together was slim, but I had to try. She makes me want to take chances. To live my life outside of its boundaries.

But some boundaries can't be crossed.

Realizing that hurts. It hurts a heck of a lot.

The pain feels bigger than anything I've experienced before. It's even worse than when Melina broke up with me, because at least then I had nobody to blame but myself. This time, though ... she isn't running from my lies, or my secrets, or my life. She's running from our love. It's like somebody has punched me right in the gut.

I try to distract myself once I get home. I call Cameron, but he's in the middle of reading a book to Lissie as he attempts to soothe her back to sleep after a bad dream. I try Lucas next. It rings once and then Caroline, his girlfriend, picks up.

"Hi, Bradley," she says. There's a smile in her voice. "Lucas is on the other line with a patient's mom. He's on call tonight."

"Ah, a life in medicine," I say. "Always ready to jump into action."

"And a life in politics," she says. "From what Lucas tells me, you're always doing the same."

"It's exhausting," I admit.

"I'd certainly imagine so," she says. "Well, if things ever settle down and you get an opportunity to break away and visit, I'd love to meet you. Lucas is always telling me stories about when you two were kids. It sounds like you had some great times."

"We did. I miss them," I tell her, and it hits me at full force, just how much I really *do* miss those days. Everything was much easier back then. Now my life has become a jumbled mess. I spend the majority of my time working for a woman who may or may not be rigging the election, then I come home to an empty house with nothing but the TV and a pile of cookbooks to keep me company. It's lonely. I can't even adopt a pet, for God's sake, since I'm on the road so often. That English Spot is still on our rescue's website. I haven't been to Callie's since she took it in. I don't know if I'd be able to resist those big brown eyes in person.

I shouldn't have to. I shouldn't have to resist and regret.

"I'd really like to meet you, too," I tell Caroline. "Things will be insane until November, but after that, I'll definitely plan a trip back to Georgia. Hey, and thank you," I add. "For making Lucas happy. I'm so glad you found each other."

"Me, too," she says. "Sometimes happily-ever-after does exist."

I don't think so.

Now that I've lost Melina, I'm actually pretty sure it *doesn't* exist.

But I don't tell Caroline that. I just ask her to tell Lucas that I called. When my phone rings a few minutes later, I assume it's him calling back and pick up without checking to see who it is. "Hello?" I say.

"Bradley!" Mom's voice blasts through the line. "Hi. How are you? Do you have time to talk?" She doesn't bother waiting for an answer. "Did you know Jake and Gwyn set a wedding date? April fourth of next year. Oh, and Eric got a promotion at work. He's tenured now."

Same story, different day.

"That's excellent," I say. "I'm really happy for them."

"Me too," she agrees. "And how about yourself? What's new and interesting in your life?"

I don't know how to answer that.

If I tell her about the investigation into Madelyn, she'll just start in on me about the importance of loyalty in politics. She and Dad are all about staying the course. It's how they forged their places in the political world. They paid their dues. Got to work before the sun rose and didn't leave until it had set. One day at a time, they started off small and grew into a big presence at the Georgia state house. If there's one thing my parents believe in, it's the power of allegiance – to our country, to its people, and to their family. It's why Mom is so insistent on planning the reunion every September. That reunion is her baby, and for me, it's also a perfect diversion.

"Nothing much is new," I tell her. "Working hard. The usual. But enough about me. How goes the reunion planning?"

As she launches into a story about the invitations she sent out, something shifts in me. I think of the election. Of the debates, the rallies, and the many hours meeting voters. I think of Madelyn and the charges against her. I figured that'd be national news, but Mom hasn't mentioned it. I wonder why. But mostly, I think of Melina. I have to get away from her. Staying here and plotting with her to expose the corruption in this election isn't going to work. If she wants to gallivant with Cole, that is her prerogative. I can't have a front row seat for it, though. My heart won't survive that.

I need a break from it.

I need a break from it all.

"You know what?" I say to Mom. "I know I said I wouldn't be able to make it to the reunion this year because of work, but I just changed my mind. I'll be there."

When I walk out of the airport a week and a half later, it's a breath of fresh air. I was so eager to move away from Georgia. I couldn't wait to leave my family's footprints behind and create my own imprint instead. But today it feels comforting. This may not be where I live anymore, but it'll always be special to me. Part of my heart will always linger here, strung up in the peach trees and sitting on the gazebo steps at Glover Park. I used to escape there during my high school years, so desperate to distance myself from the expectations at home. I'd sit in the gazebo or at the fountain nearby, and brainstorm ideas for the school newspaper. Sometimes I'd read or do my homework. That park was my place. My brothers were always too busy to go. They used to tell me I was missing out, wasting valuable time when I could've been doing something more productive, but I think they are the ones who missed out.

Or maybe not.

Because Jake is getting married in just over six months.

Eric has made a name, and a life, for himself in Connecticut.

When they arrive for the reunion, they'll bring with them joy and excitement and success.

And then there's me.

What do I bring?

What do I add?

I really don't know anymore.

31

Melina

"What do you think?" Cole asks, handing over a take-out menu. Its paper is wrinkled, like it was left out in the rain and then air-dried. "Extra cheese? Black olives? Spinach, tomato, and broccoli? What are your favorite pizza toppings?" He throws a grin my way. "I've always thought you can tell a lot about people by how they like their pizza, you know. Since it's our third date, I figured I should see how your preferences stack up."

I smile. "I guess I'd better choose wisely, then."

"Don't worry," he says. "I'm enjoying your company so much that you could go for a pineapple pizza and it wouldn't make a difference." He chuckles, and looks at me expectantly, like he's waiting for me to do the same, but I can't seem to manage it. Of all the possible toppings, I can't believe he had to single out that one. Instantly, it reminds me of Bradley. That night back in May, when I was out for dinner and that guy wouldn't leave me alone, Bradley joked about pineapple pizza when he helped me out of that tough spot. The memory of it floats to the surface of my mind. Now isn't the time to be dwelling on Bradley, though, so I shove the thought aside.

"Extra cheese," I say. "So ... what does that tell you about me?"

"It tells me you have good taste," he says. "That just so happens to be my favorite topping, too. See, I knew I liked you." The words roll off his tongue easily, naturally, and I wait for them to inspire something in me – a flush of the cheeks, a skip of the heart, a prickle of the skin.

There's nothing, though. Damn it.

Maybe I'm not trying hard enough.

Or maybe, I have to allow, I was just trying *too* hard on our first two dates. It was easy when we went to that tavern after the debate. I was flying high on Nathan's excellent performance. Combine that with how desperate I was to erase Bradley from my thoughts, and no wonder I had a good time. I remember feeling an overwhelming sense of relief, like maybe I could do it for real. Maybe I could get over Bradley, or at least manage to tuck him away in a closed crevice of my heart. Then, when my second date with Cole also went fairly well, I let a tiny ribbon of hope twirl free. My plan would work, I just knew it.

So why can't I stop thinking about Bradley tonight?

It's not only the pineapple pizza. When dinner arrives and Cole tosses a handful of paper plates onto his kitchen table, I remember how Bradley would use his good dishes when he cooked for me. When Cole rummages around in his pantry to find dessert and can only come up with a box of candy that's half stale, I remember the way Bradley taught me to make cream puffs. And when Cole leans over, winding his arm around my shoulders as we sit on the sofa, watching a movie, I remember the dream I had about Bradley. I'd have given anything to turn it into a reality, to share myself with him completely. But I didn't, and now I won't. I can't. Bradley is better off without me, and I am better off without him. Once I can get myself to remember *that*, I'll be golden.

I just have to try harder. I let my body relax and lean in to Cole.

"I love this movie," he says. It's an action film with a lot of running and chasing and fighting, and I force myself to concentrate on it.

"Remind me again," I say. "What's it about?"

He wiggles his eyebrows. "You mean you haven't been paying attention?"

"Would you be angry if I said no?"

"Angry at you?" His hand shifts on my shoulder, resting flat and laying heavy. "Never. Not over a movie, anyhow. Now, if you said you were abandoning Nathan to cross over to the dark side and join Madelyn's team ... " He trails off, and something seizes at me. Why would he say that? I don't like the implication of his words.

I pull back. "Excuse me? Care to elaborate?"

He looks affronted. "Geez, I was kidding."

"Were you?"

"Yes." He sighs in exasperation. "Sorry, I guess it was in poor taste. It's just that we don't have a lot in common, so I was trying to find something we share. That's Nathan. He's what we share. I promise," he says, inching closer again until our legs are almost touching, "it was only a lousy joke. I don't question your loyalty. Nobody does."

"Good."

Cole puts his arm around me again, and we go back to watching the movie, but now it holds my attention even less. My brain is working overtime, trying to figure out if he could have seen Kira and me snooping around. We never found anything to suggest that Nathan was behind the sudden shift in the election tides, and I think we were pretty inconspicuous about it. There's no way Cole knows. It was just a dumb remark.

It all feels wrong now, though.

We sit in silence until the credits roll, and even after Cole grabs the remote and the TV flicks into darkness, there still isn't much to say. I should leave, but instead, I give it one more shot. "So I take it you aren't a fan of happy endings," I say, making my tone light, airy. "The whole movie, that poor couple was literally racing across the world and battling all their enemies to be with each other, and then one explosion ruins it all."

"Uplifting, right?" He laughs. "I suppose it's not the ending that matters to me. It's the journey. Think about how much they loved each other. They were willing to fight everything and everyone to be together."

"Still, you have to admit, it would've been nice if they got a happily-ever-after."

"It's funny," he says. "I wouldn't have ever pegged you for the mushy-gushy type. You're a total force to be reckoned with at work. A badass, if you will. Nathan could learn an awful lot from you." He moves his hand from my shoulder, letting his fingers graze the side of my jaw. I know where this is going, or where he wants it to go, and a knot forms in my stomach. I don't want him to kiss me. I don't want his mouth on mine.

And what does he mean, Nathan could learn an awful lot from me?

He's getting closer, closer, closer.

I can smell his cologne, this combination of musk and bourbon, and it's too strong. Too wrong. There's a reason my efforts to throw myself into this date haven't been working. Cole isn't right for me. He's not going to be the one who helps me to forget about Bradley. I've been deluding myself, but not anymore.

I duck out of his grasp and jump up from the sofa. "I'm sorry," I say. "I can't do it."

He narrows his eyes. "What do you mean?"

"You, me, *this*," I say, gesturing at the empty space between us. "It's not working."

"It isn't?" He stands up, too. "I thought we were having a good time. Was it something I said? Something I did? Is there any way I can change your mind?"

I don't even know how to answer him. It *was* sort of something he said and did, but also, it was a thousand things he didn't say or do. "No," I tell him. "I'm afraid not. I wanted this to go well, and I tried, I really did, but I think we're better as colleagues. I just don't have feelings for you. I thought I could make myself – "

"You thought you could *make* yourself? Gee, thanks. That's flattering." Annoyance crashes into his eyes.

"I'm sorry," I repeat. "I wanted to like you, I wanted that more than you know, but there isn't a spark between us. There's no attraction."

"And you'd know that how?" he snaps. "You didn't even let me kiss you. You're acting as judge and jury without giving me a chance to plead my case." He crosses his arms. "Maybe you should go, Melina."

I nod. "I think that'd be best."

The walk over to his door feels interminable. His gaze is on me every step of the way, and when I turn back around to face him, the intensity of his expression makes me uneasy. What happened to the fun-loving man who has a grin big enough to fill a room? Or the savvy speechwriter who knows exactly what to say? I don't see any of that reflected in the man scowling at me. This version of him is unrecognizable.

"One more thing," I say. "What did you mean before, about Nathan learning a lot from me?"

"Nothing." His nose flares. "Evidently I was wrong about you."

Evidently I was wrong about him, too.

He doesn't open the door for me. He doesn't say goodbye. He doesn't even flinch as I walk out of his house. Talk about misjudging a person. If he gets this upset after only three dates, I'd hate to see what happens when a long term relationship fizzles. I pity the woman who has to deal with that ... though, as I drive off, it occurs to me that I'm going to have to deal with it, too. There's no getting around the fact that we'll have to collaborate at work, especially with the election just over a month away.

Ugh.

Never again will I go out with a colleague, not when there are so many variables at play.

I'd rather focus on the things I can control, like my work. It's late already by the time I get back to my apartment, but instead of crawling beneath the covers, I turn on my laptop. Nathan promised he'd highlight my program in the second debate, and with just four days left to go, I need to prepare some bullet points. I open a blank Word document and start typing. I'm in the middle of the second paragraph when I have a light bulb moment. It's like my brain starts buzzing with excitement. I stop what I'm doing and go to my email inbox, scrolling until I find the message I'm looking for, from the director at Helping Hands. Apparently she loved my camera idea so much that she decided to keep up with it. She sent me an email last week with some of the new pictures, and I'm thinking ... how cool would it be to use them on the debate night? Candidates aren't allowed any visual aids for the actual debate, but I wonder if there's a rule preventing us from setting up some sort of display in the lobby. At the very least, could we hand out pamphlets? I think back to the last debate. Did Perry's team do anything like that? Madelyn's? I feel like they might have, but I was so focused on Nathan that I can't be a hundred percent positive. I know these photos would go a long way in driving home his position, but it'd be silly to plan for it unless I'm sure it's allowed. It's too late at night to call Kira and ask. Bradley, though, he might be awake.

My gaze drifts to my phone.

Calling wouldn't mean I'm betraying my decision to distance myself from him. It's not like I'd be doing it only to hear his voice; there's a real, legitimate reason to be in touch. I run my fingers over the screen of my phone, tracing its outline as I admit to myself that I don't actually need to call him, I *want* to. Damn it. Maybe I should email instead. It's less intrusive, which will be better for both of us.

My note is all business:

B –

Do you know if there's a rule against using visuals before and after the debate? Did Madelyn do that last time?

– M

P.S. I think perhaps I should fly solo on the plan for getting the truth out of Nathan and Madelyn. Given the recent circumstances, it'd probably be best. I thought I could just sneak someone into the audience, but it's going to be all undecided voters, selected by an outside organization. I guess I'll try to get one of them to ask the question instead.

P.P.S. Hope you're doing well.

I click the 'send' button before I can second guess anything.

Then, so tired my eyelids won't stay open a minute longer, I drag myself to the bedroom and fall asleep immediately. It is a deep, sound sleep, free of any sort of dream or nightmare or interruption … until my phone starts blaring at me. Its pitch gets higher and higher, the ring urging me to pick up, and I crack open my eyes. What time is it? Clearly it's morning, because sunlight is pouring into my room, warming me like a blanket. I yawn as I reach for my cell. Amie's name is on the screen, but it isn't her calling. It's her husband, to tell me that she had the baby overnight.

"Rosalie Elaine Wellington," he says proudly. "She's so beautiful. Looks just like her mama." He rambles on excitedly, barely letting me get a word in, and by the time we hang up, I'm wide awake and determined to get myself to New Jersey. Forget about using the weekend to work. Somebody who used to be very important to me, who still *is* very important to me in many ways, just brought a new life into the world. So what if we aren't as close now as when we were kids? Things will never go back to the way they used to be unless we continue making an effort. Being there for Amie now, at this joyous time in her life, feels like the perfect opportunity.

Within an hour, I am on the road, and when I walk into her hospital room, Amie's face lights up. She smiles at me, glowing in a way that seems almost supernatural. Maybe it is. Maybe a mother's love is out of this world.

"Melina," she says. "You didn't tell me you were coming."

"You had a baby today," I reply. "Where else would I be?"

I can't take my eyes off the little bundle in her arms. She's swaddled in a blanket, and her face is like a doll's – sweet and delicate, with heart-shaped lips and pudgy cheeks. She's lovely.

"Come and meet her," Amie invites. I walk over and lean down by the bed, brushing a finger to Rosalie's cheek. Her skin is so soft, so silky. "Do you want to hold her?" Amie asks.

"Sure."

Amie gazes down at her daughter. "This is Melina," she tells her. "She was your mommy's best friend when we were younger. Actually, she was more of a sister. I hope you will have that one day, honey. Everyone deserves a friendship like Melina and I had. It was the best."

Something tugs at my heart.

It *was* the best.

I want it to *be* the best.

"Maybe it still can be," I say softly, and stretch out my arms.

It's unlike anything I have experienced. Holding Rosalie in my arms and looking into her big blue eyes, shifts something in me. I can't get over how incredible it is. This sweet little newborn has her whole life ahead of her. She can do anything, be anything. Maybe she'll follow in Amie's footsteps and be a teacher, maybe she'll follow in Tom's and be an architect, or maybe she will blaze her own path. That's the beauty of it: the world is now hers for the taking. It's lives like Rosalie's that I want to fight for. I want to make certain each baby has a chance. All of them deserve it. And, it occurs to me, as I kiss the newborn's forehead and inhale her perfect baby scent, that maybe I deserve it, too. Maybe I even want it, somewhere down the line: a home, a family, a love like Amie and Tom's – one that makes you feel like you're walking on air, even as it grounds you right here on earth.

I already have that part of it. It's waiting for me, if I can only reach out and take it.

I let myself think of Bradley, let myself drink in the image, the memories, and the emotions.

Perhaps our love won't be enough. Perhaps we'll fail, like my parents did, but perhaps, also, we won't. I'll never know unless I try, unless I open myself up again. Inviting in the possibility of failure might not be the worst thing. Shutting the door on it could be even worse. I've spent so long letting the past dictate my present and my future, but not anymore.

The first thing I do after leaving Amie's hospital room is to pull out my phone and dial Bradley's number. I've wasted so much time already. I don't want to squander even one more minute.

32

BRADLEY

Temperatures in the low eighties. A cloudless sky that's robin's egg blue. Freshly cut grass that brings with it the sweet scent of summer, even though it's technically fall. Cold drinks on one table and bowls of salad on another. Hamburgers and hot dogs on a massive grill. Kayaks lined up by the water. Music blaring over a speaker. Adults and children talking and playing. It's the kind of scene that makes me feel like I'm inside a postcard – or maybe like I'm outside of it, holding it in my hands and observing all the little details that make it unique.

Looking in. Watching from a distance.

I never used to feel this way at all our family reunions. When my grandparents organized them, I loved to go. They'd rent out a banquet room at one of the local country clubs, and it'd be an entire day of swimming, playing tennis, and riding in golf carts. My brothers and I would hang out with our cousins, throwing horseshoes and eating ice cream. Everybody would go home exhausted, tanned, and happy. That all changed when Mom took over the planning. She decided it'd be fun to choose a new place every year, to, as she put it, "create different sets of memories." I enjoyed it at first, but now, as I sit under an oak tree, its leaves casting ever-changing shadows as they rustle high up in the air, I can't help wishing for that old country club. Things were much simpler then. Or maybe it's not necessarily the place that made those reunions special. Maybe it was the people. Maybe it was just being a child.

I shift my gaze to the left, where a big group of kids is playing

Frisbee. The youngest, my cousin Rebekah's son, is four. The oldest, my cousin Beth's daughter, is seventeen. But they're all getting along well. The teenagers aren't glued to their phones, and the younger children aren't sitting with their parents. They're out there, together, having a good time. I'm tempted to join them. I used to love that, when my relatives would play with me at reunions. I'm ignoring my phone, too – I turned it off when my plane landed and am determined to keep it off until I leave tomorrow so I can have a true break from everything in Pennsylvania – and so hanging out with all the kids seems like a good distraction.

Before I can get up, though, Eric drops down beside me. "Hey," he says, handing me a bottle of chilled sweet tea. "You've gotta try this. It's almost as good as Grandma's."

I twist open the cap and take a sip. "You're right," I agree.

A glint appears in his eyes. "What was that? I'm ... what?"

"You're right," I repeat. "Like always."

"Not always." He gives a half-smile. "Just ninety-nine percent of the time."

He's kidding and I know it, but something about it still rubs me the wrong way. "Must be nice," I say. "I sort of feel like I'm *wrong* ninety-nine percent of the time."

The glint fades from Eric's eyes. "Why would you think that?" he asks.

"Oh, there are lots of reasons." I set the bottle down on the grass and begin ticking the reasons off on my fingers. "I'm in love with a woman who loves me, too, but refuses to actually be with me. I'm working for a politician who could very well be corrupt. I'm on the road constantly, now that the election's so close, and all I can think of when I check into yet another hotel is how I'd rather eat my own food and sleep in my own bed." I reach down, plucking a few blades of grass and letting them fall back onto their green blanket. "Do you ever wonder what life would have been like if Mom and Dad didn't work in politics?" I ask. "Suppose they had been doctors, or accountants, or lawyers. Do you think you'd still have fallen into the political life? I don't think I would have." I can't believe I'm telling him this. It's been so long since we've had any sort of deep discussion.

I guess I just feel like I don't have anything to lose at this point. It's why I asked Madelyn for the weekend off to come here, even though it's unheard of to take vacation days this late in a campaign. Most candidates would've shot down my request, but Madelyn must have heard the desperation in my voice, because she agreed. Criminal or not, she treats her staff well.

I just don't think I want to *be* part of her staff for much longer.

"What would you have chosen?" Eric asks. "If you didn't go into politics?"

"Journalism."

"Really?" He cocks his head at me. "Is that why you became editor-in-chief of the high school's paper? I always thought you were trying to show Jake and me up. You know, since that was one of the only extracurriculars we didn't join."

I smile wryly. "Okay, that might have been part of it at first. The thing about being the youngest brother is that you're always sprinting to keep up, while at the same time needing to find your own race to run. It was odd. I used to idolize you and Jake, but I also felt like you were taking everything from me. There was nothing I could call my own, because you both had done it already and done it better. Until I signed up for the newspaper. That was my thing."

Eric's eyes look like they're about to bug out of his head. "Why didn't you tell me this before?" he asks.

I shrug. "It sounds stupid and trivial."

"No it doesn't." He leans back and rests his palms on the grass. "I used to feel the same about Jake. Every time a teacher would ask if he was my brother, every time I'd sign up for an activity and be reminded of how well he'd done it three years earlier ... not going to lie, I sort of hated him for it. But it wasn't Jake's fault. He wasn't responsible for my life, and it wasn't fair to ask him to get out of the way."

"I know." I glance up for a moment, seeking out our parents. They're sitting by the water, Mom with a big floppy sunhat and Dad with a beer in one hand and a camera in the other. It's rare to see them relaxed like this, with the dial turned down low. "I think it was that sense of responsibility that stopped me from pursuing journalism," I explain. "I felt an obligation to measure up. Mom and Dad were always so proud of you both, and I wanted them to be proud of me, too."

"You didn't think they would've been proud if you became some hotshot news reporter?"

And there it is.

"See, that's exactly it," I explain. "I don't want to be a hotshot anything. That's so far from who I am."

He looks at me. For the first time in a long time, maybe even since I was his kid brother, tagging along to play with him at the park, he really looks at me. He's quiet for what feels like forever. The kids are screaming, something about the wind carrying the Frisbee too far off, and at a nearby picnic table, I hear Grandfather telling a story about his war days. But Eric says nothing. He only motions for me not to move, then stands up and strides off. When he returns a couple minutes later, Jake is with him.

"What's going on?" he asks. "Eric said you need to talk to me."

"He did?"

"Yes." They both sit down. It reminds me of the days when we would play pick-up-sticks in the backyard of our grandparents' house. Jake and Eric used to let me win. I didn't realize it for awhile, since I was only five. Then one day, I overheard them talking about it. It's the first time I remember feeling like a fool. There I was, trying to play fair, and they'd been throwing the games. I confronted them, stomping my Teenage Mutant Ninja Turtle sneakers and declaring how unfair it was for them to 'treat me like a baby.' All this time later, it still feels like they do that sometimes.

Not today, though.

"Go on," Eric says. "Tell him what you told me. He should hear it, too."

So I do. I tell him the whole thing and even go a step further. "I wouldn't pick journalism now," I say. "I'd go for something completely different. Culinary school. I mean, I enjoy writing

Madelyn's speeches, and I do still get excited when something breathes new life into the campaign. Maybe I'd miss that if I gave it up, but right now I just want to slow down. I want to be home more than I'm on the road. I want to have more time to cook and maybe even create my own original recipes. I want to try something different."

"Then you should," Jake says.

This surprises me. He's always been a champion for following in our parents' footsteps.

"Really?" I ask. "You think so?"

"Sure. If you aren't satisfied with your life, you should change it. Don't stick with something to make other people happy, especially if it's making you miserable."

"Every semester, I start my classes with the same question," Eric chimes in. "I ask the students what they'd do if they knew they couldn't fail. Sometimes their answers are what you'd expect from poli-sci majors and sometimes they aren't. But I always tell them to go for it, that no passion is too big or too small." He smiles. "To answer what you asked before, I would've gone into politics even without Mom and Dad's influence. Education, too. I love it. Each day, I wake up excited. If cooking is what does that for you, then you should go for it."

"And don't look back," Jake adds. "Don't question your intuition."

It's good, solid advice. The kind I've always craved from my brothers, but never asked for.

"You know what?" I say. "I think you're both right."

"Ninety-nine percent of the time," Eric says, and this time I laugh with him.

* * *

The sun is starting to sink lower in the sky by the time I go off in search of my grandparents. It's hard to pull them aside at these reunions. Grandfather can almost always be found with a child on his lap and Grandma with a plate of food in her hand as she serves a meal to someone. They are the stars of the show, the pillars of support that build the foundation of the family. Sitting in a couple of Adirondack chairs now, they're holding hands. It makes my heart swell. All this time later, and their love is the strongest it's ever been. We should all be so lucky.

I used to think I was. I thought Melina would be the woman who would stand beside me in this life so we could experience it together. All the beauty and turmoil and fury and joy. I wanted to feel all of that with her, like my grandparents do with each other. When I look at them, I don't only see the wisdom in their eyes and the wrinkles which create roadmaps over their skin. I see their spark. I see the soldier who saved a terrified eighteen-year-old. I see the couple who pledged their hearts to each other on their wedding day and again on every tenth anniversary when they renew their vows. I see the proud parents who raised my dad and his sisters, and the proud grandparents who look on with beaming smiles as their legacy grows before their eyes.

Legacy.

What will mine be?

What do I *want* it to be?

I ponder that as I pull a chair over to join my grandparents.

"How are you, my boy?" Grandfather asks. "Enjoying yourself?"

I let my gaze do a wide sweep of the park Mom decided on for this year's reunion. One group of people is playing volleyball, another is gathered by a tetherball court, and a third is getting ready to toast marshmallows. The air smells earthy. Smoke and grass, dirt and water. Perfect. "Yes," I say, and am pleasantly surprised to realize I mean it. "I am. How about you guys?"

A smile writes itself across Grandma's face. "It is always my favorite weekend of the year," she says. "All these outdoor activities on Saturday and brunch on Sunday. You are coming to that, too, right? Or do you have to leave early tomorrow?"

"I'll be there," I promise. "My flight isn't until the evening. I couldn't possibly come all the way here and not eat a meal prepared by my favorite chef."

Her cheeks flush a happy pink at the compliment. "Maybe you could help me," she offers. "I'm not as quick in the kitchen as I once was. These old hands could use an assistant."

"They're not old," I tell her. "But yes, of course. I'd be honored to share the kitchen with you."

This is it. This is the perfect opening to tell her, to tell them both.

I clear my throat. Clasp my hands. Unclasp them. Lean forward in my chair. "Actually, it will be good practice," I say. "Nobody knows this yet other than Jake and Eric, but I'm applying to culinary school." Saying it out loud is like a breath of fresh air. It fills me up, gives me sustenance.

So does their response.

"Culinary school!" Grandfather exclaims. "Well, I'll be a monkey's uncle! That's great! I will be visiting to do some taste-testing." He laughs, a hearty, deep laugh that resounds through his chest. "Not that you'll need it. You've always had a talent for cooking."

"Ever since you were little," Grandma says, a twinkle in her green eyes. "I could always feel the joy when you helped me in the kitchen. That's a blessing, Bradley. Not everybody finds something that brings them happiness."

"You're really okay with it?" I ask them. "Even though it might mean giving up politics? I know you're both so big on patriotism, and – "

"And nothing." Grandfather cuts me off, slicing his hand through the air. "We will always be so proud to live in this incredible country. It's done a lot for us, and I'll keep trying to repay that favor until the day I die. But that doesn't mean I expect you to stay in a career that doesn't fulfill you. My favorite thing about America," he says, "is that it is a land of infinite opportunities. There are many ways to give back. Politics is one way, sure, but cooking is another."

"Cooking?" someone asks.

The gruff voice comes from behind me, and my palms instantly go sweaty.

It's Dad.

Well ... this was not how I planned on him finding out, but I guess there's no choice now. When I swivel around to face him, I notice that Mom is at his side. They must've been taking a walk and just happened to be behind us at exactly the wrong time. Or perhaps it was the right time, I can't quite tell. Whatever the case, there's no getting out of this.

"Why don't you both sit down?" I suggest, motioning to the empty chairs nearby. Once they've joined our little circle, I take a minute to look at them. It has been nine months since the last time I was back here, to celebrate Christmas and Hanukkah with everyone, but to see them, you wouldn't know it. Nothing has changed.

Nothing about them ever changes.

"So," my dad prods. "Cooking? Who's cooking? Are you talking about brunch tomorrow? I told you," he says to my grandma, "that everyone would be fine with going out to eat this year, if it's too much for you. We can still do that."

"No, no," she says waving a hand. "It isn't that. Bradley's going to help me with it, actually, and that's fitting, because he has some news."

There she goes, laying down a cushion for my words, making them easier to speak. She's done it since I was a child, always smoothing the way between my parents and me. Never have I been quite so grateful, though, as today. "Yes," I say, and this time I don't have to clear my throat. My voice is already steady on its own. "I'm applying to culinary school. You know how I love to cook, right? Or maybe you don't, since you've always only seen me the way you want to."

It's a bold accusation.

Brazen.

And true.

Dad's eyes narrow and his eyebrows push together until they look like a single line. But he does nothing to refute my claim. "So what you are telling me," he says evenly, "is that you're abandoning your career. You are going to let down all those people who need you, just so you can mess around in the kitchen? For what purpose? What's the end goal?"

"I truly thought we taught you better than this," Mom adds. "We raised you to serve the people around you."

I shrink back a little, into my chair. "Yes," I say quietly. "You did, and I do. But don't you get it? We can all serve people in our own way." I force myself to sit up tall. "Look, there are times when I really enjoy politics. It keeps me on my toes and makes me more aware. But it doesn't give me the same sense of purpose it does for you. I want something more."

"So that's it?" Dad asks. "You're just giving up? The Williams family isn't made of quitters."

"Stop it!" Grandma snaps at him. "Stop it right this instant."

It is the first time I have ever heard her be short with someone. Apparently the same is true for Dad, because his mouth drops slightly. "I'm only pointing out that it would be in his best interest – " he starts to say.

She doesn't let him finish. "It'd be in Bradley's best interest," she says, "to follow his heart. You should know that, because it's what your father and I tried to teach *you*. As parents, we should aim to broaden our children's horizons, not narrow them."

I should have known she and Grandfather would be there for me unconditionally. They always have been. "I think you should both take a good, long look at yourselves," Grandfather says to Mom and Dad. "And then you should take an equally good, long look at your sons. You can, and you will, do right by them. I have faith."

I don't.

As I watch my parents walk off, and later, too – as I play baseball with the kids, as I go to Lucas' house to hang out with him and meet Caroline, and even the next day, as I tie one of my grandma's floral aprons around my waist and act as her sous chef – I realize that it may be too late. Too late for my parents to see me as anything other than the black sheep who destroyed their family portrait.

I care. I'd be lying if I said I didn't.

But for the first time ever, I'm not going to let it stop me.

I'm not going to follow along, placing my footsteps neatly in the ones they've left in the sand.

I'm going to test new waters.

Maybe culinary school is the answer and maybe it's not.

Maybe I'll keep working for Madelyn at the same time and maybe I won't.

All I can do is try. All I can do is keep believing that there *are* so many ways to make a difference in the world.

As I pass through airport security later in the day and settle myself in one of those not-so-comfy chairs by the gate, my head feels lighter. My heart feels lighter. Everything feels lighter.

Then I turn on my phone.

33

Melina

Maybe I was too late.

The whole remainder of the weekend, I am glued to my phone, hoping and waiting and praying for Bradley to return my call. My heart lifts a little every time it rings, but then it drops back down in rapid succession when I see that it's someone else – Kira, to ask if I've read the newest poll numbers for the gubernatorial race; Serena Spencer's manager, to confirm that she'll indeed be performing at Nathan's final rally this November; and Gabrielle, to see if I can pick her up at the train station. Dad has asked us all to meet him at the park across the road from our old house so we can have a family discussion. I'd be grateful for that any day, the chance to finally ask all the questions I've had since he confided about his gambling, but I feel especially thankful today. It will be a perfect way to keep myself from dwelling on the fact that Bradley isn't calling back.

I honestly thought he would.

I mean, it's not like he knows what I wanted – after all we've been through, it didn't feel right to leave something like that in a voicemail – but I assumed he'd hear my message about needing to talk to him and at least be curious. Maybe that isn't enough, though. I know I hurt him, making such a grand show of leaving with Cole after the debate. I thought I was doing a good thing, that seeing me with another man would give him the closure he needed to move on. Suppose I succeeded? I don't think I could forgive myself if I pushed him into the arms of someone else. Bradley has my heart. It is right there in the palm of his hand, exposed to all the elements and unprotected from everything that could hurt it. I am putting myself out there in the most frightening way imaginable. It's exactly what Bradley wanted me to do, and now I am. I'm walking that tightrope with no safety net in sight, and he isn't there anymore to catch me.

I had my chance, I had many chances, and I blew them all.

If Bradley's finished with me, I have no one to blame but myself.

It is an exhausting realization, one that zaps all the energy out of me. Ever since I was a kid, I've tried so hard to do right by others. I've worked to give people a good life, a happy and fruitful one. In the end, though, maybe I was so focused on them that I forgot to look at myself. I love what I do. It's much more than just a job, but that doesn't mean it's okay to use it as an excuse. It isn't right to hide behind my work, or even my family. Yes, my parents fought. Yes, they're proof that sometimes good things, truly good things, can fall apart. That doesn't discount what they once were, though. It doesn't mean I should live my own life in fear of crashing and burning. If I do, then I'll extinguish the flame all on my own.

I want to tell Bradley these things. I want him to know that I choose him. I choose us.

If only he'd call back.

I check my phone again as I sit at the train station, waiting for Gabrielle to arrive from New York. There is nothing – no missed call from Bradley, no text, not even a response to the email I sent. It's been over twenty-four hours now, and he's the kind of person who always has his phone nearby, so I guess it's time to acknowledge the painful truth: he isn't going to stretch out his hand to link it with mine again.

"Let it go," I say aloud, hoping that if I actually hear the words, I'll be able to follow the advice.

No such luck.

"What's wrong?" Gabrielle asks, the instant she slides into my car.

"Nothing." I put on my brightest smile. "How are you? How was the ride?"

She gives me a sidelong glance. "Good," she says, tucking a

stray blonde curl behind her ear. "It was a pretty quiet train car. That isn't going to work on me, you know," she adds, as I pull out of my parking space. "Changing the subject. I know when you're avoiding a question, so let me ask again: what's wrong?"

That's it. As soon as she flips the latch on the floodgates, it all comes pouring out.

"I ruined everything," I say, and something pinches my heartstrings, yanks them tight. "It's like you said before: my heart wasn't ready to give up on Bradley yet. I should have listened to that. For once in my life, I shouldn't have let the fear win out."

"It sounds like you didn't." She offers me a smile. "At least, not now. That counts, Sis. It counts for a lot."

"Even if it's too late to salvage things with him?"

"It's never too late."

When we meet up with the rest of the family at the park, I learn just how true that is. Mom and Dad are sitting across from each other at the picnic table where we used to have dinner sometimes, the one beneath the towering magnolia tree. As Gabrielle and I join them, I can still smell the sweet scent of the petals, even though they're no longer in full bloom. I can hear the buzz of the bees that used to dive-bomb near us while we ate, I can taste the juicy watermelon that Mom cut up for us as kids, and I can feel the breeze kiss my cheeks and ruffle my hair. I can touch all the memories of the past.

"Thanks for coming," Dad says, once Lara and Dylan have arrived. He folds his hands and looks at us, eyes brimming with regret. "Now that I've told you all the truth, I owe you an apology. I was wrong to gamble away so much all those years ago and I was even more wrong to hide it from you. I thought … " He gazes across the street at the two-story brick house that used to be ours. "I thought this was a good place to get everyone together. To make amends. And maybe to say goodbye once and for all, since we didn't do that before."

He's talking, I know, about our home. We never got to give it a proper farewell.

This evening, we do.

We sit there at the picnic table, a family of six for the first time in so many years, and talk it out. Our words are messy, the kind that topple and jump all over each other, but they are also cathartic. I learn that the money to pay Dad's first round of debts came from the last of our savings – that it's why, essentially, we lost the house. I learn that it was the divorce that finally made him go to rehab for his addiction, and that no, he has never relapsed since. I also learn, as Mom sits quietly, listening as Dad pours out his soul, that every now and then, time really can heal the pain. There is no anger in her eyes when she looks at him now, only a warm affection that comes from having been through the worst with someone and resurfacing on the other side.

Mom and Dad will never be together again.

Our lives can never go back to what they once were.

And yet, we're all okay. We're all sitting here as a group, scars on display.

I learn something else, too: that maybe scars can actually be a good thing. They show that we're survivors, after all. As I walk across the street with my family, as we stand in front of that house and take the time to really, truly, put it behind us, I realize that I have to own those scars. I have to show them to the world and show the world to them.

Maybe Gabrielle was right. Maybe it's not too late.

Before I get into bed that night, I send Bradley another message – a text this time.

Please, I write. *Just hear me out. It's important.*

A loud clap of thunder booms outside, then another and another. The sky is mad tonight. I am, too. I'm *so* mad at myself.

But when I wake up the next morning, there is, finally, a message from him. My heart leaps into my throat when I see his name, and I grip onto the phone so tightly that pools of white stretch over my knuckles. Then I start to read.

Hey, sorry for the delayed response. I was down South for my family reunion this weekend and I turned off my phone while I was away. Life's been a little tough to handle lately, and I really needed a break. Anyway, I didn't get your message until yesterday evening, when I was at the airport. I was in the middle of texting to tell you I'd call after I got home, but the plane started to board so I had to stop. Then there was a problem with the flight crew hitting their maximum amount of hours and we were stuck on the tarmac forever. Between that and the storms up here, I didn't get home until the middle of the night. Now I have to be at work early and won't leave until late. Things are nuts with the debate tomorrow. I'd like to talk, though. Unless this is about your email? I can answer it now: Madelyn didn't bring any visuals to the last debate venue. Not sure about Perry. Maybe Cole would remember. Hope things are going well with you two.

It is a long block of text. Below it is a much smaller one.

Actually, that's a lie. I want you to be happy, Melina, but I really don't think Cole is the person to make that happen.

A smile spreads across my face.

Hope is a funny thing. Right when you lose it, it reminds you it's never truly gone.

Fast as my fingers can type, I write back.

Cole and I are already finished. It's a long story that I'll tell you when we talk. Call whenever you can.

I hop out of bed and pull back the curtains. Gone are the storm clouds from last night.

Today, there is sun.

* * *

"Five minutes until air," a voice blares over the speakers. "Audience members, please take your seats."

All around me, people start scuttling to the chairs lining the television studio where Nathan and his opponents will have the second debate. We're in Pittsburgh this time, and as I hurry over to join the rest of Nathan's team at the side of the studio, I can feel the energy in the place. It's edgier now than in Harrisburg. The election is closer, the polls are showing a race that's tighter than we thought it would be after Madelyn's bad press, and with an audience comprised of undecided voters, there's a sense that anything could happen.

I look across the room at Bradley.

Anything.

Maybe even everything.

We didn't get to talk yesterday – I was on the campaign trail with Nathan until nine at night and Bradley was up even later, rewriting Madelyn's speeches for today. Our discussion will have to wait until after the debate. As excited as I am for Nathan to dazzle these voters and show them why he's the best candidate, I'm even more excited to tell Bradley that I've changed my mind. That I'm ready to let our love stand on its own. That I want to plant roots and see where, and how, they grow.

First, though, the town hall meeting.

Just like with the previous debate, a moderator introduces the candidates and they shake hands. It seems more tense this time. Perry grips Nathan's hand for a few seconds too long and Madelyn's smile is tight-lipped. Is the pressure getting to them, or is it the prospect of answering questions off the cuff? A town hall meeting in a setting like this is markedly different from what all the candidates have been doing on their own. Here, they'll have to contend with people who are still searching for the inspiration that a candidate is supposed to stir up.

They'll also have to contend with the woman I talked to earlier. I let my gaze travel over to the middle of the room, where she's seated. She has curly hair and glasses, and she's the kind of person who just looks like a professional. It's what drew me to her as I eased into the crowd and started to search for somebody who could carry out my plan. Part of me felt guilty, like I was tampering with a pristine process. I know a lot of people are cynical when it comes to politics, and they don't believe in the sanctity of it anymore. I do. That made it tough to pull this woman aside and ask if she would be willing to tack on an addendum to the question she'd already prepared and submitted. It was a necessary transgression, though. With the election just a month away, it's imperative that we finally separate the truth from the lies.

Twenty minutes into the debate, the time comes.

I hold my breath as the woman stands up to ask her question. "This is for all three candidates," she says. "If you're elected, what would be the first legislation you'd try to pass as governor? Also, and this part is only for Nathan and Madelyn, since your ethics haven't been disputed, Perry – would you ever submit to a lie detector test in order to help prove your innocence in the allegations being thrown your way?"

The studio, which had already been quiet, drops into a stark silence. Madelyn's mouth twitches, Nathan starts tapping his foot against the floor, and Perry side-eyes them both with the faintest hint of a smirk. Nobody talks until the moderator finds his voice. "Ms. Morgan," he says, "Mr. Ford. Do either of you want to take the lead on this question?"

Nathan nods. "I'd be glad to," he says. "First, thank you for coming," he tells the woman. "It's so appreciated. To answer your original question, my initial focus would be to help those who need a hand to steady them. I would like to open ten new homeless shelters across the state, along with increasing funding for those that are already established." Here, he smiles at me from the stage. "I have a fantastic policy director who has made it a mission to get as many people as possible back on their feet and into these safe havens, where they can work toward the next chapter in their lives. It is my hope that we can grant everyone in Pennsylvania a chance to turn their dreams into reality. I want to bring a sense of promise and optimism back to this office." He clears his throat. "And as for the second question, yes, of course I am willing to undertake any measure to reassure voters of my sincere desire to serve them. I care deeply about the people of Pennsylvania, and from day one, I've maintained that the newspaper article was full of inaccuracies. If a lie detector test is what it takes to prove that, fine. Sign me up."

"Me, too," Madelyn says. "We've all experienced political campaigns that play dirty. I am sure most of you have turned off your televisions upon seeing an attack ad, or hung up your phones upon receiving one of those automated calls. My theory is this: there is already too much negativity in the world. My campaign has always been about the positive changes I want to bring about in this state. I did not ... did *not*," she repeats with an added emphasis, "embezzle funds. It'd actually be a delight to take the test so everyone will see that I have nothing to hide."

Madelyn's answer is good, but that's not what grabs my attention.

It's Perry's expression.

That tiny lopsided smirk is gone now.

His mouth is set in a straight line, his gaze steely and his hand curled into a fist, like he's trying to constrain his annoyance and box it up. It's like he's struggling to keep up with a facade.

Oh my God.

It was him. It *has* to be him. Why didn't I figure it out before?

All along, the underdog has been scheming to take down the frontrunners.

Perry's trailing so far behind in the polls, and Pennsylvania has never had an independent in the governor's mansion before. It was easy to discount him – and that's precisely what he was counting on. He knew exactly how his manipulation would play out. Nathan would accuse Madelyn, Madelyn would accuse Nathan, and they'd both look petty and crooked. Meanwhile, he has been portraying himself as a breath of fresh air, the "candidate who's just a regular person, like all of you." It was an ingenious plan. Disgraceful and desperate, but ingenious.

A vein throbs in my temple.

How dare he. How *dare* he.

I want to stand up and shout the truth for everyone to hear.

First, though, I need proof.

I can't wait to tell Bradley. I want to hurry over to him the instant the debate is over, but he's in the middle of a briefing with Madelyn and I have to do the same with my own team. Usually I enjoy these meetings. It makes adrenaline zip through me, getting to examine how things went and what we can do better the next time. Tonight, it's all I can do to pay attention. My mind is racing ahead, thinking of all the revelations and ramifications.

How do we pull back Perry's mask before it's too late?

How do we save the election?

They are important, life-altering questions.

But when, an hour later, I meet up with Bradley at the hotel across the street from the television station, they aren't the questions clamoring to make themselves known. For the first time in longer than I can remember, work isn't my priority. It is an odd, terrifying feeling, but also an empowering one. I can do this. I can jump into my own life with reckless abandon, even if there's no guarantee I'll land on both feet.

Maybe that's what makes the journey worth it.

Maybe it's only when we launch ourselves into a free-fall that we find out how far we can fly.

"Hey," I say, settling myself into the chair across from Bradley's in the hotel lounge.

"Hey." He smiles tentatively. "How are you? What's up?"

I move my feet to the edge. One, two, three. I take the leap.

"I was wrong," I say, "about so much. I was wrong to think our politics would come between us. I was wrong to push you away. I was wrong to take your love for granted." I lock my eyes with his, and I swear, they tell a story all their own. Bradley and I, we can have such a beautiful conversation without saying a word. I want to say the words, though. I want to put them out there, and I want to finally speak my soul. "Love scares me," I confess. "More than just about anything. I've seen how it takes lives and turns them into a shadow of what they used to be before. For so long, too long, I've run from it. I don't want to do that anymore." I reach my arms out and flip them over so my palms are face-up.

Slowly, carefully, like he isn't sure if this is real or fantasy, Bradley rests his hands atop mine.

The creases in his palms travel alongside the lines in my own.

"What, exactly, are you saying?" he asks.

"I'm saying that I want to be with you. I want to give myself to this fully and see where it goes. I want to let myself love, and let myself live, and who knows? Maybe it won't work out. Maybe we'll just be a chapter in the story of each other's lives. Or maybe we'll be *the* story." I feel a tear prick at my left eye, then my right. "The one that defines our lives. Maybe, in fifty years, we'll be sitting on a porch in matching rocking chairs, telling our grandkids about the night I finally came to my senses. That is," I say, "if you'll still have me."

He is quiet for a long time, and my heart beats quicker and quicker. This moment, I realize, will change the course of my existence from here on out – just like my parents' divorce did, just like the shelter did, and just like my dad's gambling did. I understand now, though, that sometimes the mile markers along the roads we travel are there to point out the blessings, not the hardships. I hope my epiphany isn't too late.

"Well?" I breathe.

He squeezes my hands tenderly. "There's so much I could tell you. But I don't have to," he says. "Not right now, anyway. We have plenty of time for that ... because yes, of course, I still want to be with you."

I laugh. I cry. I think I even squeal a little bit.

Then I take his hand and lead him out of the lounge. We are both staying at the hotel tonight – most of the campaign staffers are, since it's too far of a drive back home – and all I want is to make love to him. I want to feel his lips on mine again, his arms encircling me. I want to explore each inch of him, to let him discover new things about me, to take this relationship and ignite its sparks into a sky full of fireworks.

And we do.

From the moment he clasps his hand around mine, helping me with the key card to my room as I manage to drop it in my anticipation of getting inside, to the moment he teases me with the zipper on my dress, releasing it inch by inch, to the moment I trace figure-eights along his chest, it is, truly, perfect. It's a wish fulfilled, an experience shared, a treasure to have and hold. The way he blankets my body, his fingers intertwined with mine, makes me weak. But in this case, weak is also strong.

Maybe love doesn't always break us. Maybe, also, it can make us.

Our bodies fit together like puzzle pieces, as if they were always supposed to be complimentary halves. That doesn't mean we're not whole on our own. We are. I don't believe any person needs another soul to complete theirs – but when we find our soulmate, when we find the one who makes us feel like life is bursting with magic, I understand now that it's alright to want that. It doesn't make us any less. It makes us more.

"I love you," I whisper, and Bradley pulls back a bit, brushing the hair from my face. His thumb is hot against my skin, and it sets off a million little electrical currents beneath the surface. This man is like my air. I breathe him in, drink him in.

"I love you too," he whispers back. I wrap my arms around him again, bringing him close, letting his heart beat in time with mine. There's so much to tell him – about Perry, about how it took a new baby to teach me the most important lessons of all, about where we go from here. But like Bradley said, we have plenty of time for that. Tonight is for us. It's for the kisses he rains down on my neck, the ones I trail along his back, and the ones that explode every time our lips touch. It's for the way I fall asleep in his arms to the rhythm of his heart tapping against my back.

It's for love.

34

BRADLEY

*I*s this a dream?

It sure feels like one when I wake up. Melina's fast asleep beside me, her hair splayed across the pillow and the white hotel sheet tucked under her arms. She looks like an angel, or maybe Sleeping Beauty. I can smell her perfume, traces of it still lingering from last night, and as I shift slowly, trying to stretch my muscles without disturbing her, she stirs a little and smiles in her sleep. That's all the answer I need. Yes, I am dreaming, but with my eyes wide open. I could stay like this forever. Here with Melina is where I'm supposed to be. It's funny, the way life plays out. Right when I had finally accepted the fact that Melina and I were over, she gifted us the opportunity to begin again. I guess sometimes we have to give up on things in order to see that they're not ready to give up on us quite yet.

Melina's eyes flutter open, and I lean over to kiss her. "Mmm," she murmurs. "A girl could get used to starting her day like this." She looks at me, squinting against the sun's rays slanting through the hotel blinds and making the bed look like it's half striped in light, half in shadows. "So," she says, "was last night everything you thought it'd be?"

"More."

She smiles again. "Same here."

I dance my fingertips over her shoulder. "Wouldn't it be nice if we could skip out on work today and spend the day with each other instead?"

"That would be marvelous," she agrees. "If only we could put the election on hold." She sits up, the sheet still enveloping her, and leans against the headboard. "Speaking of which, I've got a lot to fill you in on. How much time is there before you have to leave?"

I glance at the clock. "Maybe an hour and a half? You?"

"Ditto."

"How about I order some breakfast?" I ask, reaching for the room service menu. "You can bring me up to speed over – " I scan the choices. "Pancakes? Eggs and potatoes? Cereal and fruit?"

"Eggs and potatoes," she decides. "Although I'm certain they won't come close to the ones you would make."

That reminds me: I have a lot to fill her in on, too.

I think I would rather show her than tell her, though. My news can wait. But she dives into hers, after we've showered and are sitting at the table with our breakfast. "I'm pretty sure I know who's framing Madelyn," she says. "Nathan, too. I'd wager money that it's Perry. Did you see his reaction yesterday when they both said they'd gladly take the lie detector test?"

I stop buttering my toast mid-swipe. Perry's reaction. I was mostly focused on Madelyn and the awesome answer she gave. "I know he didn't seem pleased," I say, calling up a memory of his pouty expression. That's right. He reminded me of Lissie when she doesn't get her way. "Kind of like a kid about to throw a tantrum," I suggest, and Melina nods.

"Exactly – or like an adult whose plan is falling apart."

"I don't know," I say. "Even if he was the mastermind behind it, would he have been able to pull it off? How would he have had access to Madelyn's financial records and Nathan's camera?" Then it hits me. It slaps me in the face, and I realize it's been there all along, waiting for us to uncover it. "Unless," I add, "he had help on the inside."

The fork Melina's holding slides out of her grasp and clatters onto her plate. "That's it," she says triumphantly. "That *must* be it. Perry's embedded his own people onto our teams. Now we have to figure out who the traitors are. Has anyone been acting suspicious lately? Have there been any new hires who might be plants for Perry?"

"Madelyn did bring a few people on board recently," I tell her. "I think she realized Nathan was going to be a tough opponent to beat and wanted to expand her circle." A bolt of energy strikes me as I reach for the hotel's complimentary notepad and pen. I may not want to work for Madelyn very much longer, but I can't wait to expose the person – or people – who did this. As I jot down names of potential suspects, Melina jumps up to get her phone and then scrolls through it, biting her lip in concentration. I pause for a moment to watch her, and almost feel the need to pinch myself. I can't believe we're here. I went from thinking I would never see her again to sitting at the table with her, sharing breakfast after what was the single most amazing night of my life.

I am a lucky, lucky man.

Melina glances up. "Why are you staring at me?" she asks.

"I'm just thinking about how happy I am."

Her smile is instantaneous, almost involuntary. "I am, too. Deliriously happy, the kind of happy I used to scoff at, because I was positive it didn't exist. My other relationships were never like this. I think that's why I couldn't stay with Cole. You were always in the back of my mind, no matter what he said or did." Suddenly, her eyes go wide as saucers. "Oh, my God."

"What?" I ask. "What is it?"

"I know who the plant is on Nathan's side," she says. "It's Cole."

"Cole?" I ask. I don't want it to seem like I'm questioning her, but he seems like a weird choice. He's been with Nathan since the beginning and is one of the primary people responsible for making him look good. "Are you certain?" I ask. "If he's really working for Perry, why would he do such an outstanding job with Nathan's speeches?"

"To deflect suspicion. Think about it," she says. "Would Nathan ever doubt him?"

She does make a good point.

"But it's more than that," she pushes on. "My last date with him ... he said a couple things that really rubbed me the wrong way. He mentioned he'd be angry if I ever – and this is a direct quote – abandoned Nathan to cross over to the dark side and join Madelyn's team."

"Another chance to disguise his disloyalty," I muse. "Kind of like he was hiding in plain sight."

"*Exactly* like that. There was more, too. He also called me a badass and said Nathan could learn a lot from me. When I pressed him on it, he refused to elaborate. Maybe it was a slip of the tongue. Maybe," she says, leveling her voice, "he's been masquerading as Nathan's ally and plotting to bring him down the whole time." Her cheeks are going red now, hot with fury. "What about on your end of things?" she asks. "Is there anyone who could be a traitor?"

I glance at my list. Then I think of that day in Madelyn's office. The woman who snuck in wasn't working with her, after all. She was working against her. Dark hair. Tall. Ankle tattoo. One by one, I go over the list, searching for somebody who fits the description.

Kristi.

Kristi, who has brown hair. Kristi, who pushed for Perry to join in the debates. Kristi, who books our travel using Madelyn's credit cards and the campaign funds. Kristi, who frequently wears pants instead of a skirt, so I wouldn't have recognized that tattoo. Kristi, whose family was tight on cash. I remember her saying once that she had no choice but to give up her days as a stay-at-home mother and go back to work.

Bingo.

"I think I know who it is," I tell Melina. "Kristi Walton. She's Madelyn's travel coordinator. I bet she's the one I saw in her office. The timing works. It wasn't long afterward that Madelyn headlined the news for her supposed embezzlement. Kristi must've taken the credit card statements from her desk and somehow used them to her advantage."

I stare at Melina.

She stares at me.

"I think we did it," she says. "We solved the mystery."

"But we need proof," I say. "And we need it fast. Any ideas?"

"No," she admits. "We'll figure something out together, though."

Together.

I like the sound of that.

I also like it when, as we leave her room and head toward the elevator, she slides her hand into my own. It's a small thing, but also *everything*, especially when we emerge into a hotel lobby that's filled with our colleagues and she still doesn't let go. "It's okay," I tell her, "if you aren't comfortable with our relationship being public knowledge. It won't insult me."

She shakes her head. "I don't care who knows," she says firmly. "Let them think whatever they want. Let them judge us and talk about us and question us. It's their prerogative, and this is mine." As we reach the end of the line to check out, she presses a kiss to my mouth. It's difficult to believe this is the same woman who said it could never work out for us, that our politics were on a collision course that'd set us both up for a nasty crash.

But we are not the candidates we represent. We're our own people, with our own lives and our own priorities.

Will we disagree on some things? Sure. When it comes to politics, we'll probably disagree on a lot of things. I think that's okay, though. Melina and I will challenge each other, but that's not bad. It's good. It means we'll help one another to see the world in new ways.

My politics are part of me, but they're not all of me. They're not the priority anymore.

It's time to concentrate on what is.

"Where are you headed after you leave here?" I ask Melina, as we inch forward in line.

"Back to Hershey," she says. "With a bunch of stops along the way to meet voters in the towns in between." She peers at me through her eyelashes. "It's going to be a long day, and I'll be pretty tired by the end of it. I'd hate to have to drive back to Philly with my eyes half-closed. That could be dangerous."

"Well, we can't have that. Good thing I know someone who lives nearby and would be happy to have you stay overnight at his house." I lean closer to her and drop my voice to a whisper. "And in his bed."

Her dimple emerges, smiling at me from her cheek. "I'm already counting down the hours."

All day long, I do the same.

Madelyn has five events scheduled, and I try to keep my attention on them, but it's difficult. My thoughts ping-pong back and forth. Melina. Perry, Cole and Kristi. The culinary school application. That's why I asked what Melina's plans were. I was hoping she'd be in the area so I could invite her over. I don't want to just tell her about my decision. I want to show her. During that first meal we shared together, when she sat at my dining room table and asked if I had considered diving into the culinary world instead of the political one, I told her no. And it was true at the time. For as often as I'd studied those applications online, I had never really thought about doing anything with them. It was her comment that started the gears turning. In the past, I always exited out of the applications. I always closed them down. Closed myself down.

Until Melina.

When she rings my doorbell that evening, I'm reminded again of the first time she was here. So much has changed since then. She doesn't linger on my front step today. She bounds inside, resting her hand on the back of my neck as she pulls me into a long kiss. "I missed you," she says, and it's so casual, so comfortable and right, as though she's been saying it forever.

I hope she will.

I hope tonight is only the beginning of us coming home to each other for the rest of our lives.

"I missed you, too," I tell her. "How did it go with Nathan?"

"Good," she says. "I was going to tell him our suspicions, but I couldn't get him alone all day and I figured it was best not to broadcast it. If Cole and Kristi realize we're onto them ... "

"They'll destroy all the evidence." I nod my agreement. "I think it's best to keep it to ourselves for now." I motion for her to follow me into the dining room. I didn't have time to prepare anything fancy, but I did throw together a homemade pizza. It's waiting in the oven, and as I maneuver it out, Melina tiptoes up behind me in the kitchen and wraps her arms around my waist.

"That smells delicious," she says, resting her chin on my shoulder. "If it tastes even half – " She breaks off as she looks at my creation, then bursts into laughter. It just might be the most beautiful sound in the world. "You didn't!" she exclaims.

I turn around, pizza in hand. It's mostly plain, with extra cheese since she mentioned once that that's her favorite, but there are a few pineapple slices, too. "It *is* the best topping, after all," I say. I give her a little wink, and her eyes glitter.

"I'll eat it if you will," she says.

"Is that a dare?"

"Damn straight." She picks up the pitcher of lemonade I have out on the counter and pours two glasses. "Come on, hotshot. Let's see you eat your words, literally."

"You're on."

As it turns out, the combination isn't half bad. We both finish our slices. "This," Melina says, "is how you know you are a cooking connoisseur. If you can make pineapple pizza taste good, you can do anything."

This makes me smile. I'm finally getting to the point where I no longer need anyone's approval, but I have to admit, Melina's opinion means the world.

"Thanks," I say. "I'm hoping the admissions department feels the same way."

She shoots me a quizzical look. "What admissions department?"

"The one at the culinary school I'm applying to," I say.

"Really?" she asks. Her smile is dazzling. "You're actually doing it?"

"I actually am," I confirm. "Thanks to you."

Immediately, she shakes her head. "I didn't have anything to do with it."

"Oh, but you did." I stand up. "Come with me."

Once we're in the study, I open the desk drawer and pull out the application. "I used to wonder what it'd be like to create my own recipes and work at a restaurant," I say. "Perhaps even own one someday. But that wasn't what my family did. It's not what they do. So it was never anything more than a fantasy. That night you asked about it, though, things changed. I barely knew you, but from the start, you were able to see right through me. I guess it made me look inside, too."

She perches on the edge of my desk. "And what did you find?"

I sit down in Grandfather's leather chair and pick up a pen. "I found someone who likes politics, but maybe doesn't want to live them anymore. Someone who'd much rather spend his days mixing ingredients instead of writing speeches. I'll stick with Madelyn until the election," I say, "but even if she wins, it'll be the end of that road for me. I'm ready to travel another one." As Melina watches, I begin to fill out the application.

"I'm proud of you," she says.

"Even though it's a risk? I may not even get in. Then I'll have resigned from my job for nothing."

"No. Not nothing. You're taking a chance on your dreams. That's everything. I think we've got to take risks like that sometimes. It's how we find out who we are. For the record," she says, taking my hand and giving it a squeeze, "I think you're someone amazing. I bet your family will, too, when you tell them."

"I already did," I say. "At the reunion."

"And?"

"And you're half right. My grandparents are happy for me, and surprisingly, so are my brothers. My parents ... not so much."

She wrinkles her nose. "What did they say?"

"Exactly what I expected – that I'm betraying the family name and letting down everybody who was counting on me. They essentially called me selfish." I look up at her, searching her eyes. "What do you think? Is it unfair to pursue this if it means stepping away from public service?"

"Bradley Williams," she says, "you are one of the most selfless people I know. You're kind, and caring, and giving. You're always looking for ways to help people, and your volunteering has literally saved the lives of countless rabbits. If your parents can't see how wonderful you are, it's their loss. Following your heart doesn't make you selfish. It makes you brave. I'm starting to learn that letting ourselves be happy is one of the most important things we can do. It helps us to spread that joy to others." She shifts down onto my lap. "You are a good man. Don't you dare let anybody make you question that. Just promise me one thing."

"What's that?"

"That when you have your own restaurant one day, you'll name a drink after me."

I laugh out loud. "You've got it."

"And you've got me."

I think of the night I met her, when I sat here in this same study and hated myself for what I was about to set in motion by passing along that recording of Nathan's staff meeting to Madelyn. I couldn't look in the mirror. I was too afraid of seeing what I had become. Even if this decision of mine fails drastically, even if it's a path riddled with uncertainty and challenges, I won't have that problem anymore. When I look at myself now, I like who I see reflected back. Melina's right. Sometimes we have to take chances. It might not be the only way to live, but it is, for sure, the best way.

35

Melina

I get to work bright and early the next morning, but instead of going inside, I stay in my car. It is part of the plan Bradley and I concocted over breakfast, a stake-out of sorts to catch Cole in the act. Bradley's going to do the same thing with Kristi, in the hope that one – or both – of them will slip up and give us the evidence we need.

Unfortunately, they don't make it easy.

There are no phone calls when Cole pulls up, and no clandestine meetings with Perry or Kristi. I wasn't expecting there to be – he's too smart for that – but I was still hopeful. Even stealthy people have to mess up at some point. They get overly confident in the deceit and make a careless mistake. At least, that's what happens on television shows and in novels. Life isn't a novel, though. It's not a detective drama where the case gets solved within the hour. Life is a work in progress. It's a to-be-continued.

So we keep going.

Day after day, Bradley and I keep tabs on our colleagues. I learn a lot about Cole, including what gym he works out at and what his favorite restaurant is, but by the morning of the third debate, I'm no closer to proving that he's really working for Perry than I am to winning the lottery. I know he is guilty, I feel it in my bones, but he's so good at hiding his real motive that no one's going to believe me unless I show them the evidence in black and white. Otherwise it will just stir up a pot that's got nothing inside. Cole and Kristi will deny the accusations, so it's best not to cause an uproar until we can back it up. At least, I figured it'd be best that way. As I stand in front of

Nathan's wall of letters, pretending to read the new additions to the nearly full display but actually eavesdropping on Cole as he talks on the phone, I start to question that. Maybe Bradley and I should've handled it differently. Maybe, rather than saving the election, we're handing it to Perry on a silver platter. The idea of him winning, of earning voters' trust by playing them for fools, makes me sick.

I can't let him do it. I won't.

I strain to make out what Cole is saying. Something about press coverage, I think?

Then another voice rings out, this one much closer. "Pretty amazing, huh?"

I jump, startled. "What?" I blurt.

It's Kira. She's been away from work for the last week, taking care of her little girl who caught a bad virus and ended up in the hospital, her fever was so high. Today's her first day back. "The wall," she says, gesturing at it. "You know ... what you're looking at? Nathan wanted to have it covered by the election, and it looks like he will." She peers at me. "Are you okay? You seem kind of jittery. Is it Bradley?" She keeps on talking, something about love conquering all, and I want to tell her I can't hear Cole at the same time I'm listening to her, but that isn't possible, obviously. If I'm close enough to eavesdrop on him, he'd just as easily be able to hear me.

"No," I say. "We're good. We're great, actually."

"So would this be an appropriate time to say I told you so?"

I steal a look at Cole, who is back to work on his computer now. Then I motion for Kira to follow me outside. "Yes," I say, as we walk. "I wish I'd listened to you sooner." But then I realize that's not true. Maybe Bradley and I were supposed to come together this way. Maybe we needed to smudge the boundaries of our relationship before we could draw new ones.

"I'm glad you guys are finally together," Kira says. "I know you don't believe in all the meant-to-be stuff, but I swear, I saw it from the start – you and Bradley fit. You remind me of my friend Remi. She was the same as you, bound and determined to drop-kick Cupid to the curb. Then she met the love of her life." She smiles. "They're getting married next spring."

"Okay, so it really does work out sometimes," I say.

"It really does." She tilts her head toward me. "But something tells me you didn't bring me out here to talk about Bradley. What's going on?"

"Cole. He's the one who stole the camera."

"What?" Her voice rises like it always does when she's confused.

"I was going to tell you as soon as I figured it out, but then Gemma got sick and I didn't want to bother you. It was him, though. I'm sure of it. I don't know if he actually doctored the photos or if it was someone else, but he was definitely in on it. He must've slipped the camera out of my pocket when he hugged me goodbye that night." Quickly, I bring her up to speed on all Bradley and I have pieced together.

"That snake," she mutters. "I can't believe he'd do that to Nathan."

"See, that's the problem," I say. "Nobody will believe it. It'll seem like an eleventh hour ploy to clear Nathan's name. That's why Bradley and I have been so tight-lipped about it. We didn't want it to come out until the right time."

"Which is ... when?"

"We were hoping for tonight's debate. There is no way Perry could dodge the accusations if he was faced with them on live television." I sigh. "We haven't had any luck, though. Bradley was able to confirm that Kristi's the one he saw in Madelyn's office that day, thanks to her tattoo, but beyond that, we have nothing."

As the day goes on, and we make the drive to Philadelphia for the debate, it becomes more and more obvious that the plan isn't going to work. Perry will take his place on stage and continue lying. I'm so livid. I slam my car door after stepping out into the parking lot, and the sound reverberates in the cool October air. "Whoa there," Cole says, from the parking space next to me. "Who pissed you off? Let me guess: somebody you actually have real feelings for, instead of having to – how did you put it? – force yourself." He half-frowns at me, half-smirks, and it takes all of my self-restraint not to slap his smarmy face. He's so sure of himself, so sure he has the upper hand over me and everyone else.

I refuse to give him the reaction he wants. Instead, I shoot him a withering glare and storm off. Maybe that'll let a little air out of his overinflated ego.

I yank open the door of the auditorium where the debate is being held and quickly make my way backstage. Nathan is standing alone in a corner, reviewing a stack of notecards, and I'm about to go over and tell him the truth – because, at this point, I don't think there's anything more we can do – when I realize that I left my purse in the car. Things like that tend to happen when I'm mad. It's like my brain zeroes in on the area of concern and takes a vacation from the rest.

I turn around and march myself back outside.

That's when I hear Cole.

"I think she's on to us ... or to me, anyhow. There was something about the way she just looked at me." He's standing a couple feet away, his back to me, so absorbed in his phone call that he has no idea he isn't alone. Slowly, quietly, I inch the door open again and hide behind it so I can keep on listening without worrying about him turning around and seeing me. "No," he says, voice dripping in annoyance. "I can't be entirely certain." Then, "Yes, of course I understand that I would be given a position of power within the cabinet."

He must be talking to Perry.

I need a phone so I can record this, but mine is in the car.

I turn around, searching the auditorium for Bradley or Kira. There are dozens of people around: campaign staffers, reporters, the tech and lighting crew. Try as I might, though, I can't find either of the two people I so desperately need. This is awful. I actually have Cole right where I want him and there's nothing I can do about it ... until *finally* I catch sight of Bradley across the room. I wave wildly at him, making my arm motions big and sweeping, and he comes running. I hold a finger to my lips when he gets close, then gesture at his phone, which he gives me without even asking why. Fast as lightning, I open the voice recorder and inch the phone around the door.

Cole is still talking. He's yelling, actually, and it makes me grin, because in the end, it's going to be his own big mouth that brings him and Perry down. What's that saying? Loose lips sink ships. It will be a pleasure, watching this boat go under.

The conversation I'm recording may not be enough to toss Perry in jail, but when it comes to the court of public opinion, it should be sufficient in casting reasonable doubt. Once the voters hear it, they'll hopefully realize that Nathan and Madelyn were set up.

"Come on," I say to Bradley, after I've gently closed the door again. "We have to share this with Madelyn and Nathan."

"What's going on?" Nathan asks, once we've gathered them together into a corner.

I don't answer.

I just play the recording.

It's almost comical, watching their expressions. Nathan's eyes get wider and wider, until they're practically popping out of his head, and Madelyn's jaw drops down so far that she looks like a baby bird waiting to be fed by its mother. "Perry?" she sputters. "My God. How could he?"

"And Cole." Nathan takes the phone from me and plays the recording again.

"And Kristi," Madelyn adds. She's gone white in the face. "I trusted her with so much."

"I'm sorry," Bradley says. "You deserve better."

"You both do," I chime in.

Nathan looks at Madelyn and she looks at him. "Now the question is," she says, "how should we handle this?"

He holds up the phone. "It'd be a real shame for Perry if this all came to light during the debate, don't you think?"

Madelyn smiles. "Yes," she says. "A terrible shame. A complete travesty."

"Do you want to do the honors, or should I?"

Madelyn turns to look at Bradley and me. Her gaze swivels back and forth, and I see her piecing it together – why I had Bradley's phone, why he's standing so close to me, what we were doing with each other in the first place. "I think we should take a page out of our staffers' book," she says, "and join forces. Wouldn't that be fun for Perry, knowing we put all of our differences aside and worked together to expose him?"

"Count me in," Nathan says, then he looks at Bradley and me. "Thank you so much for what you did. There are no words to express my gratitude."

"None are needed," I say. "Seeing you turn the tables on Perry will be all the thanks we need."

And it is.

My heart starts racing the moment the debate begins. I don't know when they're going to drop the bomb. Each time the moderator asks a question, I prepare for the detonation. It happens about halfway though, right after Perry's spent his allotted time for a question going on and on about the importance of having a governor with a clean slate.

"The thing is, Perry," Nathan says, "you aren't that candidate. You could have been, if only you had decided to run a fair campaign instead of playing dirty."

Madelyn looks directly at the moderator. "Why don't you ask Mr. Talmudge about the extent of his involvement in the smear campaigns launched against Nathan and me?"

Nathan reaches under his podium. "Or if you'd prefer," he says, "I can clear that up right now." He holds the phone up to his microphone and pushes the 'play' button. Cole's voice blares through the auditorium.

I filled Kira in on what was going to happen, but she still gasps. Behind us, so does the audience. I sneak a glance at Cole, who's sitting a few seats away from me, and watch as the color drains from his cheeks. His eyes shoot first to Perry, then to me.

Oh man, if looks could kill.

Perry's expression is even more venomous. I was expecting him to battle back and to deny any involvement with Cole and Kristi, but instead, he shoots a look of disgust at his fellow candidates. "I feel sorry for the people of Pennsylvania," he says, "because now they're stuck with you. Consider me off the ballot. I'm finished."

Then, his face bright crimson red, he storms off the stage and cuts the candidate pool down to two.

* * *

The fallout from the scandal is swift and sensational. By the end of the night, the news has been plastered everywhere, from television reports to social media to online newspaper columns. It is an explosion of information, and I'm not surprised – this is the sort of story journalists live for, one that takes everything the public thought it knew and flips it upside-down. And the best part? It also gets people discussing Nathan and Madelyn again. Their plans and policies are back on the front burner, rather than falling victim to all of Perry's trumped up charges. In the last couple of weeks leading up to Election Day, the race goes back to what it should have been all along, one where the candidates are judged solely on their merits. Their poll numbers bounce up and down. Some days Nathan has the edge and others Madelyn inches ahead. It's going to be a close one.

I do everything I can to ensure that Nathan comes out on top. I draft new proposals, meet with more voters, and even help Kira write a few of Nathan's speeches, now that Cole is gone and it's too late in the game to bring in somebody new. Then there's the final rally. It's being held the evening before the polls open, and the entire staff joins together to ensure it's the biggest and best one yet. Hundreds of people attend – including Amie, who's traveled all the way from New Jersey to support me. There are balloons, an American flag backdrop, and an impressive line-up of politicians who all stand together with Nathan and sing his praises. The best part, though, is the performance. When Serena takes the stage and sings "Watercolors," it makes goosebumps rise straight to the surface of my skin.

"A ripple in the water, spreading circles wide," she sings. "We can change the world, if only we try. We get what we give, so let's paint this world bright. Fight for each dream, celebrate each life."

Hearing this song on the radio gave me pause. Experiencing it in person gives me chills. That is the awesome thing about art. No matter what it is – a book that takes you on a journey along with its characters, a song that stirs up an indescribable emotion inside your heart, a painting that evokes another time and place – there's a transcendent sort of power to it. Art speaks to the soul. It moves us, touches us, inspires us. That's why I'm working on a special series of paintings for Helping Hands and why I want to create one for Bradley, too. Tonight, though, is about music. I couldn't imagine a better way to celebrate Nathan's campaign and all it stands for.

"That was wonderful," I tell Serena after she's finished. "Your song is so special."

She smiles. "Thanks," she says. "But really, my best friend Eden deserves the credit. She's the one who wrote it." She gestures to a woman standing nearby, who's holding a curly-haired little girl and chatting with a man whose wedding band matches hers. "Eden gave this song life. I'm just the one who gets to share it."

"Then I owe you both my thanks," I say, as Eden joins us. "For the song itself and also for flying here and lending your voices to Nathan's campaign. We appreciate it so very much. I ... " I stop for a second, but this time it isn't because I'm afraid of the words, it's because I'm empowered by them. "I used to live in a homeless shelter, too, so 'Watercolors' truly speaks to me. It does an amazing job of showing what that experience can be like – what any experience can be like, honestly – if only we don't shut ourselves off from it."

It strikes me then, how that actually describes my whole life.

I used to be shut off, trapped inside the walls I'd tossed up to my protect myself. Now I can see that the walls we build don't just keep others out. They also lock us in. I don't want that anymore – not when I've found my key.

Not when I've found Bradley.

When I go to sleep that night, it's in his bed, and when I wake up the next morning, Election Day, it's in his embrace. "You know," I tease, "we're literally sleeping with the enemy here. What do you think Nathan and Madelyn would say?"

His laughter is warm and all-encompassing. It sounds like a hug feels. "I am pretty sure they've figured out that we're seeing each other," he says. "Or Madelyn has, anyway. I talked to her about my resignation yesterday and she said I should take some time off and center all my energy on you. I think she really regrets not having had a chance to do that with the man she cared about. But she might have an opportunity with her daughters," he adds with a smile. "She told me they've reached out and want to get to know her."

I prop myself up on an elbow. "That's great."

"It is," he agrees. "And you should also know, I told her the sky's the limit with you. Maybe that sounds corny."

"No." I shake my head, grazing my thumb on the stubble on his jaw. "It actually sounds lovely." I lean over to kiss him, then force myself to get up. "But the sky will have to wait a little while. Right now, we both have to hit the ground running."

It's more like sprinting, really.

It is, quite possibly, the longest day of my life. It starts with a drive back to Philadelphia, where I cast my own vote and then park myself outside of polling locations, passing out flyers about Nathan. Some people ignore me. Some refuse the material. Some ask me about Nathan's views, confessing that they still haven't chosen whom they're voting for, and others say he is already their candidate. It's such a mix, and it does nothing to give me any kind of idea about who's going to win the election come tonight. By the time I'm back in Hershey, where Nathan's hoping to have his victory rally later, nerves are churning in my stomach. We have worked so hard on this campaign, and for so long. It's been an honor, a joy, a privilege. I know it's the journey that's most important, that we're supposed to learn more from how we get to a place than the destination itself, but still ... I want him to win. I want him to win so very badly.

"What do you think?" I ask Kira, as we sit at a table and try to have some dinner. My stomach's too topsy-turvy to eat much, but it was nice of Nathan to have the meal catered for his staff and I'm doing my best to take part.

"I honestly don't know," Kira says. "It's a pretty split electorate." She nods at my phone, which is sitting on the table. "Check online. See if there are any updates on the exit polls."

"I've already checked five times."

I do it again anyway.

For the next several hours, as the polls close across the state and the votes start to be tabulated, I am glued to my phone. We all are. Everyone's watching, wondering, waiting. But when my phone buzzes with a text at ten o'clock, it isn't a news alert or a message from anyone involved in Nathan's campaign.

It's from Bradley.

Can you break away for a minute? I'm outside. There's someone I want you to meet.

I stare at my phone, confused.

He's outside? Here? I mean, I know he's leaving politics behind after tonight, but he never said a word about not staying with Madelyn until the final vote had been counted and the new governor announced. So why isn't he at her campaign headquarters? And what does he mean about wanting me to meet someone? What is he talking about?

"Be right back," I tell Kira, then hurry through the room and outside into the chilly evening air. It is a clear night, and the sky is a canvas of stars, like a magician waved his wand and trailed sparkling stardust across the celestial blanket. Bradley's sitting on the bench by the building, a pet carrier next to him. He opens it slightly as I approach, and even before I see the whisper-soft whiskers and big ears, I know what's inside. It's the rabbit he has been telling me about, the sweet English Spot whose picture he showed me on the rescue's website.

"I'd like you to meet Jellybean," he says with a grin, as I sit down beside him. "I just signed the paperwork to adopt him."

The rabbit pokes his head out of the carrier, his nose twitching. "Hey there," I say, leaning over to pet his forehead. Instantly, he nuzzles his nose into my hand. "Look," I tell Bradley. "He likes me already."

"That's because he's smart."

I smile, then pet the bunny again.

I really shouldn't. I should congratulate Bradley on the new addition and go back inside. With a good portion of the votes already counted, the winner will be announced soon. It'd be wrong to be out here when that occurs. But it also feels right – because, no matter who takes the oath of office on Inauguration Day, Bradley and I are the real winners. This election gave us each other, and that's the best result of all. The best gift of all.

"It's okay," Bradley says. "I know you can't stay. I don't want to take you away from anything, and I should really get back to Madelyn's headquarters. I just took a break to pick this guy up, and I thought you should be the first person to meet him, since you'll hopefully be spending a lot of time together."

"Oh, we will be," I say. Already, this rabbit has stolen my heart, just like his owner did. Bradley is always saying a bunny's love is special, and I'm looking forward to experiencing it. With Bradley, I am looking forward to experiencing a lot of things. He looks so happy, now that he's on the way to creating his own path. I'm happy *for* him. I'm happy for us. "I'm glad you stopped by," I say. "This is the best part of my day."

Just then, my phone vibrates and Bradley's rings, almost simultaneously.

The election results must be in.

We stare at one another for a long moment, knowing that this will change everything ... but also change nothing. No matter who's won tonight, we'll still wake up tomorrow morning as Melina and Bradley. I'll still fight for the future in politics and Bradley will still mail off his application to culinary school. Who knows what's in store for us? Maybe I'll run for office one day. Maybe Bradley will be a famous chef. Maybe we'll live a big life, or maybe we'll live a quiet one, just the two of us. I smile at Jellybean. Make that the three of us.

Or maybe more. Maybe we'll start a family of our own someday.

I think I'd like that. I think I'd like it a lot.

I reach for Bradley's hand as I check my phone.

Nathan. Nathan won.

A flood of emotion pours over me. I knew he could do it, I knew in my heart that we had it in us to make a real difference, and yet that knowledge did nothing to prepare me for this moment. It's a dream come true, a prayer answered, a wish granted. Even with all that, though, my mind still goes to one very specific thing: my apartment.

I'll be working in Harrisburg from now on, and although I could technically keep commuting, I'm ready to throw caution to the wind. I'm ready to embrace the uncertainty, because with uncertainty comes possibility. And besides, it really doesn't matter too much where I live anymore.

I lean close to Bradley, who winds his free arm around my shoulder and kisses me on the top of my head.

"Congratulations," he says, and I know he means it.

"Thank you. Madelyn was truly a worthy opponent. She did – "

"Stop," he says. "It's okay to just be happy. You don't have to justify it."

This is why it doesn't matter where I live – because, sitting here with Bradley under a sky full of stars, I understand, maybe for the first time, that it isn't the four walls of a house that make a home. It's the four walls of a heart. This is what I know: that it's the people who matter, the love that lights and shimmers and sweeps us off our feet. We can find that in the most unlikely of places and in the most unlikely of ways, and it's up to us to hold on to it. It's up to us to hold on tight.

"I love you," I tell Bradley.

"I love you, too," he says.

The four walls of a heart.

Indeed.

Finally, I am home.

Shari Cylinder believes in the importance of dreaming big, working hard, and embracing our own stories. She is a graduate of Arcadia University and lives in the suburbs of Philadelphia, where she spends her time as a writer, transcriptionist, and a member of the Board of Directors for Luv-N-Bunns Rabbit Rescue – and, thanks to her own rabbits, also a makeshift sprinter and gymnast who tries very hard to keep up with bunnies that run much faster than she does. Sometimes she's even successful.